Molly Malone and the San Patricios

Molly Malone and the San Patricios

Michael Hogan

FONDO EDITORIAL
UNIVERSITARIO

Portions of this novel were first published in a serialized version in the March and April, 1997 issues of *El Ojo del Lago*. Permission to reprint is gratefully acknowledged.

First printing

ISBN 968-7846-08-9

FONDO EDITORIAL UNIVERISTARIO
Madero 687
44100 Guadalajara, Jal.
Mexico
fax 52 (3) 827-1026
e-mail: noche@compuserve.com

Cover: Rosana Sánchez

U.S. Distributor:
Q Trips
688 Atherton Place
Hayward, CA 94541
Fax (510) 583-7710
email: lqqkame@pacbell.net

Contents

For Sheila and Bob Barlow
With love and gratitude

Preface

Even casual visitors to Mexico will observe an occasional freckled-face child with green eyes speaking fluent Spanish. The more curious might note as well the large number of Irish names found in the phone book: Pedro McGinnis, Miguel O'Hanlon, Gonzalo Lynch, Francisco O'Connor. Such names are found even among the more prominent and wealthy families in Mexico City, Monterrey and Guadalajara. There are the O'Farrells, for example, who publish the popular *Mexico City News*, and the O'Rourkes who manage the prestigious Lloyd's investment house. In addition, the visitor will observe some place names that apparently have Irish origins such as the town of San Patricio (St. Patrick), the village of Melaque (malarky) and the street of Mártires Irlandeses (Irish Martyrs).

Few people realize that there was an Irish battalion which fought on the Mexican side during the U.S. invasion of 1846-48, sometimes referred to as the Mexican War. This war, an ugly episode in the U.S. expansionist era, is little noted in American history. Most American students learn only of the "Manifest Destiny" of the U.S. to encompass the whole continent and the wealth of California, as well as the concern that Texas, if admitted as a slave state, be balanced by a non-slave state.

More serious students might go on to learn that the Mexican War was begun on a pretext by a expansionist administration. Unpopular with many citizens, it was called "Polk's War," after James K. Polk, a little man with big ideas who, taking advantage of a minor border clash and political instability in Mexico, ordered an all-out invasion with the clear intent of territorial expansion. His actions were deplored by many U.S. citizens, among them the New England philosopher Henry David Thoreau who was jailed for refusing to pay taxes that he felt would support this unjust war. His "Civil Disobedience" written during this time, has become a classic of passive resistance to wrongful exercise of power.

Against superior force of arms, however, resistance was to prove futile. Mexico was divided by political factions, its financial base was negligible, its army was poorly equipped, and led by a blundering commander-in-chief. Despite valiant resistance by the Mexicans at several battles, General Winfield Scott was able to occupy the Mexican capital on September 14, 1847. The Treaty of Guadalupe-Hidalgo which ended the war on February 2, 1848, and the subsequent "agreements" which followed, secured vast new territories for the United States out of which would be carved the states of Arizona, California, New Mexico, Nevada, Wyoming, Utah and parts of Kansas and Colorado. The war and the treaties which followed deprived Mexico of two-fifths of its national territory, and enlarged that of the invaders by a third, admitting the United States to the ranks of the imperialist nations. In a revisionist effort to avoid this judgment by future generations, textbook publishers in the U.S. have relegated the chapter covering 1846-48 in standard U.S. histories to mere anecdote and self-serving generalities. As a result few U.S. citizens know much about the Mexican War; fewer still could name a single important battle. Almost none are aware that there were Irish immigrants who fought on the Mexican side, and who are considered national heroes.

The story which follows is based upon little-known historical fact and traces one company of the Irish battalion, Los San Patricios ("Those of St. Patrick"). Although historians differ on the motivation and the values of these soldiers (depending on which side the history is being written from), they agree that the battalion served with distinction at the bloody Battle of Churubusco. A bronze plaque at the

Ex-Convento of San Mateo in a suburb of Mexico City commemorates their steadfastness and courage. Many were killed at that battle, many more were hanged when the American army took the Castle of Chapultepec and effectively ended the war. But others survived, continued to serve honorably in the Mexican Army after the war; they defended Mexico's new borders, fought against the French invaders in the 1860's, and raised families in Mexico. Their descendants are Mexican citizens today in all walks of life.

The battles, the places, the dates, the names of the officers listed here are factual. The hangings and other depredations inflicted on the members of the battalion who were captured are drawn from official records. I have occasionally imagined the feelings of these men and invented some of the dialogue. In most cases, however, remarks of the officers and enlisted men, songs, field orders, letters and dying statements have been drawn from actual documents.

This is one story among many of the San Patricio Battalion, their desertion from an invading army, and their gallant but doomed fight on the losing side. Fighting a losing battle was a role the Irish were used to, and it is a role they would re-enact in their own country in 1916. But history is not always written by the victors of the moment. Sometimes it is written by those who merely survived. And, just as the Irish Revolution would send the Wild Geese storming across the sea, so too would the gringo invasion be countered by an unprecedented Mexican migration northward which today has all but re-populated the lands lost by their ancestors.

This is the story of the meeting of the Irish and the Mexicans and how they came to fight together, work together, and create a new generation distinguished by a natural grace, a pervasive Catholicism, and a love of a newly-awakened land which has become a dominant cultural force in this hemisphere.

Michael Hogan
Guadalajara, Jalisco

CHAPTER 1

This is Good Old Boston

When Kevin Dillon walked up Skully Square it had been raining for most of the week. Although it was still August in Boston, the air was damp and cold. The unrelenting breeze from the harbor chilled him and he pulled up the collar of his worn cotton jacket. He had a bit of money in his pocket. Enough certainly for a drink and a meal. He had unloaded eight wagons down by Faneuil Hall in the market district. Though he had begun at daybreak, it had taken him well past noon since he had stayed to set up the stalls and help the vegetable vendors. Now he wanted a stiff drink and maybe one of those free lunches that the pubs in Boston were famous for.

He walked into the Boar's Head Tavern and crossed the sawdust floor breathing in the rich odors of draught beer, pickled eggs and herring, cured ham, and whiskey. If he had been more alert he would have noticed the heads turned to look at him, the conversations stopped in mid-sentence, but he was tired and hungry and his customary cat-like alertness had forsaken him. The bartender was serving a customer at the far end so Kevin reached over to the pickled egg jar, grabbed two and swallowed them as if they were lozenges.

"A whiskey, my friend," he said when the bartender finally arrived. He had by that time secured a large roll and two thick slices of marbled ham.

"You're no friend of mine, Paddy," the bartender growled, his fat cheeks puffed out in disgust. "Put the bread and meat back and get the hell out."

"What? I'm orderin' a whiskey," Kevin said. "Here's my money, sure and it's as good as any man's. Hard earned it was, too, for all I worked..."

The bartender, a balding and red-faced Tory of the second generation drew back his lip in contempt. "I don't want your damn pence, ye dumb Mick. Din' ye see the sign on the front winder?"

The bartender walked over to the window at the end of the bar. All conversation now had ceased and even the men furthest away were watching quietly as the bartender flourished the hand-lettered sign in Kevin's face.

NO DOGS
NO NIGGERS
NO IRISH
ALLOWED

"Would ye like me to read it, mackerel snapper, or did one o' yer Papist friends learn ye English?"

Kevin was tired. It was only his second day in America. The first he had spent walking up and down the docks, offering to unload the ships, carry baggage, clean out the holds. Twice he had been run off by longshoremen and once by a policeman. He had made a few pence that day, bought a loaf of bread and some cheese, and slept that night under a loading dock. In the morning when he awoke, he had several rat bites on his legs. He felt feverish, flashes of hot and cold, and his thin body shivered in the early morning fog.

He had woken up to the sound of produce wagons coming by on their way to the market. When he crawled out reluctantly from his hiding place, one of the wagoneers shouted to him.

"Hey, Mick! You're certainly a blight upon the morning! Are ye looking for work?"

"That I am," said Kevin making a futile attempt to draw his lanky sixteen-year-old frame into some semblance of manhood.

"If ye can do a half-day's work, ye'll get a half-day's pay unloading wagons the likes of these at the market. But ye look a mite feeble to me, lad. Are ye ill?"

The year was 1845, and Boston was one of the most civilized and cultured cities in America. The Revolution, begun seventy years ago, had brought a spirit of freedom and ambition to the new nation. America was growing, expanding. New territories in the west had opened up, commerce had increased the wealth of the nation, and continental expansion was in the air. "Manifest Destiny!" was the new rallying cry. America was to be a nation as mighty as any empire that had ever existed in history. No longer was America a small enclave of thirteen colonies, a fledgling quacking in fear of the English and French. Now it was a robust nation, bursting at the seams with lusty, heady young men willing to risk their lives for land and for the freedom to own it and work it for themselves and their children. It was a freedom denied them in their native land. So they had no qualms of abandoning their loyalty to a country which denied them opportunity, made them landless serfs, and treated them as less than human.

The English had prospered here in this new land, as well the Scots, the Welsh. Their loyalty was not to an sterile concept of a nation state with its codes of honor and loyalty. It was instead to freedom, to the dignity of the human being, to self-sufficiency and self-determination. They had prospered in this new land, and formed what De Toqueville had envisioned as the uniquely American character.

But these Irish were another thing entirely. First of all they were Catholics—believers in a religion which the Puritan fathers of the nation had come to hate as decadent idol worship. Second, they were peasants, the dregs of an agrarian nation that could not feed itself and was forever fomenting revolt. They were quick-tempered, emotional, and spoke in a strange accent.

Thomas Browning looked down from his wagon at the boy. He would have had a son that age if Robert had not died of the influenza. He shook his head. The problem with the Irish was that there were so damn many of them every day. He was not prejudiced. Having a farm across the Charles River in Cambridge he did not have to deal with them on a day to day basis. If he lived in the city it might be different. It would be hard not to be prejudiced. Here in Boston there were thousands, tens of thousands, with more arriving each day. They lived crammed together in slums that no Christian would tolerate. There, unemployed and under-employed, they fought with one another, turned to drink, lived their short violent lives in filth and disease, and died. Longshoremen told of fishing them out of the Bay where, where beaten by sailors or overcome by the bad booze, they had fallen in and drowned. He had heard stories of Irish babies dead at birth and cast away to clog the sewers in Dorchester and cause flooding during the summer rains. There was no hope for these people and yet more arrived each day.

"I said, Are ye ailing, boy? Speak up!"

Kevin Dillon was ill. He had a high fever; he was suffering from severe malnutrition and pleural pneumonia. He was thirty pounds underweight. Only his youth and a grim determination inherited from his mother was keeping him upright. His worn brogans had slits on the side, and the soles flapped like the tongues of two dogs worn out after chasing a hare.

"No, I'm not sick at all," Kevin said. "Just feeling the chill of the morning is all. I have half of loaf of bread and a bit of cheese here and, as soon as I get it into me gullet, I'll be well."

Thomas Browning sighed. He was a decent man who had worked hard all of his thirty-eight years to build a good life on his small farm. His body, brown and heavily-muscled, mirrored his life of labor. His kindly but sorrowing eyes bespoke his losses: his older brother killed in a sea battle in

1812, his first children, twins, dead of fever in 1828, his wife gone giving birth in 1832, his first son dead of influenza in 1843. Not a decade without a tragedy. He had come to rely on his faith as the years passed. A simple faith, based on the Bible and the teachings of Jesus; it strengthened him and deepened his natural goodness.

Although he did not wish to encourage these people who bred like rabbits and worshiped plaster virgins, he was a Christian. He believed in helping a fellow human if he could. The boy's eyes, so strange and light-colored, had riveted the farmer, and he made his offer for half a day's work. But now, as the wind stirred and he saw the boy shiver, he had second thoughts. The boy's face was red and feverish. His shirt soaked through with the morning's damp mist.

"Are ye sure that you're up to a hard mornin's work, lad?" he asked kindly.

"I'm am that!" Kevin exclaimed, his green eyes darkening in his pale face.

"Let's get to it then," said Thomas smiling in spite of himself as he gave the boy a hand up on the wagon.

Now in the Boar's Head Tavern Kevin's green eyes darkened again. The tavern owner could not have seen them in the dim light. Nor would he have suspected that this skinny boy would dare raise his hand against a grown man twice his size. So it was surprise, more than the force of the left hook which flashed across the bar, that sent the bartender crashing against his own front windows dragging the offending NO IRISH NO NIGGERS sign onto the muddy sawdust of the floor.

But when the fight was over (if you can call four grown men kicking a young boy's ribs in, a fight), it was Kevin who lay bleeding and unconscious in an muddy alley to the side of the tavern. His lungs, filling with liquid and blood, were close to collapse. The rasp of his breath, the fleeting pulse, slackened as the hours passed.

CHAPTER 2

Yankee Doodle Dandy

Mrs. Garrison's Chowder House was a friendly place. The warm odors of rich soup, the steamed clams, crab and lobster, the fresh smell of bread, and the good conversation made it Thomas Browning's favorite stop during his weekly visits to Boston. Here he would find out what the news was in other parts of the country, what new books were being talked about, and what masterful sermons had been preached in the South Meeting Hall or the Old North Church. Since his wife's death, he lingered on market days in this pleasant inn for hours after his produce was sold.

This afternoon a group of merchants were engaged in a close discussion. Two were dressed nattily in tailored tweeds with brocaded waistcoats. The other two wore black broadcloth suits such as had gone out of fashion in most parts of New England, except Boston, where simple and conservative was still considered proper. Despite the plainness of their dress, however, each had a heavy gold watch chain which hung from a pocket in the waistcoat. The oldest of the two occasionally and indiscreetly pulled his watch out to check the time as if he had urgent business elsewhere.

The topic, which even the least determined eavesdropper could not help overhear, was investments in the West.

"It's hard to convince people here," said the youngest and most intense of the nattily-dressed men. "They have no idea of just how much money is to be made. Literally thousands, Mr. Trumbull, thousands!"

"Well," said his companion, a pocked-faced man with a broad nose and a narrow face. "Not all of 'em have seen what you've seen, Mr. Peale."

"But, by damn, they can read can't they? Why, the Louisiana Purchase alone gave us 820,000 square miles and thirteen more states. Plus, it got France off the damn continent entirely. New England is a very small piece of the pie these days, a very small piece."

"Yet, it's the piece you need if you are to have a pail to pick your blueberries, Mr. Peale." The author of this remark was one dressed in black broadcloth. A closer look showed however that his suit was carefully tailored and that his calm handsome face betrayed an aloof amusement. The man next to him, a slightly older version of the same elegant features, nodded slightly.

"Well, put; well put. You have a fine way with words, Mr. Shaw."

"And you and your father..." Here Mr. Peale nodded respectfully toward the elder Mr. Shaw. "You have both done well here in New England. There is no doubt on that score."

"We've done well in other places, too, dear sir. Need I point out our success in the China trade, our six whalers out of New Bedford, our large number of railroad shares on the Baltimore and Ohio."

"And yet", Mr. Peale said, "you seem to have no idea whatsoever of what is going on in Texas, in California. The possibilities..."

"The possibilities are endless, I'll agree," interrupted the younger Shaw. "However, the political instability of these regions, the difficulties of making treaties with Mexico, the riffraff who have settled in these areas, all make any investment highly risky."

"People considered Old Hickory riffraff, too, my good sir, and Robert Fulton a fool. But the first won a war and the

Presidency, and the latter opened the rivers of the world. It may be that you'll find Sam Houston and Samuel Colt similarly underrated."

"That may be, sir. If Mr. Polk doesn't have Houston hanged first, or the Mexicans don't. Understandably in either case."

"What! Are you an apologist for the Mexicans, sir?"

"I have no love for Mexicans. Nor trust for Catholics. However, I have even less for those who swear that they are Catholic and loyal to Mexico in order to get a settler's land grant and then renege on their vow, revolt against new nation, and then have the arrogance to declare themselves independent."

"But Texans are Americans!"

"Are they? I haven't heard that Texas statehood been approved, sir. And as far as the Massachusetts Legislature is concerned, we'll vote against ratification. We want no more slave states in this country, sir, I assure you."

Thomas Browning ordered a large bowl of chowder and biscuits. He took out a cigar and looked at it thoughtfully for a moment. It was hard to tell what he was thinking, if anything. Then, apparently having second thoughts, he put the cigar back into his coat pocket.

The mistress of the inn left his table and began helping a serving boy clear off the businessmen's table.

"How about some mulled wine for a cool day like this," offered Mr. Peale.

The elder Mr. Shaw demurred. "No thank you, I do not imbibe. No offense to those that do."

"None taken," said Mr. Peale.

"But I've found no need to dull the senses," the old man continued as if Peale had not spoken. "The country itself is in such a muddle that we need clear minds and quick wits if we are to get ahead. Let's be gone, Oliver. Good day to you, Mr. Peale," he said rising and placing a silver coin on the table. "And to you, sir," he said nodding brusquely to Peale's companion.

Thomas Browning had no strong opinion on the discussion that had gone on at the table. Eating his chowder and buttered biscuits he felt that most of the issues were too remote to be of interest. At thirty-eight he was conservative enough to side with the Shaws of the world. Yet, there was something in the young man's tone that interested him. There was an energy, a spirit that he had felt once himself. The feeling that there was more to this country than just Massachusetts or even New England. A vision of a nation that swept from ocean to ocean. A vision he was not willing to say, even now, was entirely absurd.

He finished his chowder and wiped his mouth. Getting the better of his natural reticence he turned to the table where the two gentleman drank their after-dinner wine.

"Excuse me," he said. "Are ye gentlemen new to these parts?"

"We are," replied Mr. Peale graciously. "I'm Amos Peale and this is my associate Lester Trumbull. Originally we hail from Ohio, but these days we're working mainly out of New Orleans. And your name, sir?"

"Thomas Browning. I own a small farm in Cambridge, across the river. Would ye care to join me? Even a modest repast tastes better when seasoned by good company."

Thomas ordered steamed clams and another round of mulled wine and they spent the next hour exchanging views on the world of Boston and the larger world to the south and west. Thomas learned of the enterprising Sam Houston and the growing power of Texas. Despite Mr. Shaw's negativity, it seemed, as the newcomers explained it to Thomas, that Texas would be admitted to the Union. He learned about the wealth in California both real and speculative, about the attempt to buy it from the Mexicans and after this failed, the mood in Washington to simply wrest it from them in a war.

"Would we invade do ye think?" asked Thomas, finally giving voice to what to him and most people in Massachusetts seemed unthinkable.

"We might not have to. When Texas becomes a state, the federal army will be obliged to defend its citizens. That means sending patrols to Río Grande Del Norte. We consider that river the southern boundary of our new state. The Mexicans mark it further north, up around Rio Nueces. It's only a matter of time before there's a clash and thus an all out war.

"It will be, moreover, a war the Mexicans cannot win. They've got too many chiefs who can't get along. And the Indians (excuse the pun)—real Indians in this case, down in the Yucatan—are on the verge of revolt."

Thomas Browning lit up his cigar to conceal his astonishment at this man's assessment. The amoral matter-of-factness with which Peale revealed the nation's strategy shocked his sense of propriety. Even more, it shook the very foundations of what he believed about his country. The young man, meanwhile, leaned back in his seat, with an air of self-satisfaction. He felt that he had explained things very well to this simple farmer and was pleased to see him suitably impressed. Thomas, disturbed to his very core, nevertheless decided to press for more.

"And what would be the outcome of all of this... war... assuming, of course, that things fall out as ye say?" Thomas asked.

"The outcome," Mr. Peale said, with careful deliberation, "will be the greatest territorial expansion in the world. Comparable only to Alexander the Great's conquest of Asia or Caesar's of Europe and Africa. America will be the greatest power in the world, with hundreds of thousands of miles of new territory, room enough to embrace the new immigrants, and riches which are beyond imagining."

"Your two companions earlier did not seem to think much of your ideas," noted Thomas, puffing thoughtfully on his cigar.

"Don't let them fool you, those proper Bostonians!" interjected Trumbull. "He's a hard one, old man Shaw. But he stands to make large profits whether he goes in with us or not. He owns half the garment mills in Fall River and will likely get most of the army contracts for uniforms when the war comes. We were only hoping for a small loan to get a munitions plant operating so that we could furnish weapons to the California army."

"What? The California army!"

"Ah, yes," said Peale smoothly, sipping on his wine. "While our federal troops are busy with the Mexicans, down south, you see, a private expeditionary force will head to California. Not exactly with official approval... but you know, a wink is as good as a nod, as they say in Washington, and President James K. Polk knows the score."

After four cups of wine and more of this kind of conversation, Thomas's head was spinning. Things were moving far too fast and his concept of America had become badly bruised talking to these men. Where would all this greed and lust for territory lead? he asked himself. And what happens to the moral foundation of a nation when it deliberately turns away from its ideals and engages in the kind of Machiavellian tactics which corrupted European statecraft and plunged mankind endless warfare? He entertained some hope that what they said was not true. Yet, the confidence of the young men, recent reports in the news, and the fact that the Shaws did in fact meet with them, indicated there was some substance to their remarks.

He paid his bill and took his leave of the transplanted Ohioans. They were people without roots really. In Ohio yesterday, New Orleans today, Texas tomorrow. Men without roots were men without loyalty, he believed, and thus not to be trusted. Yet, it was precisely those kind of men who were settling the frontier and making America the nation she was. A troubling thought for a concerned land owner and voting citizen like himself. And yet, he had the feeling, that things were already moving beyond the control of men like himself. The government, which Thomas Jefferson so strongly wanted limited for reasons which were indisputable, had in less than seventy years so overstepped those limits as to be unrecognizable. A sacred trust was now being administered by skallywags. And there was little for the ordinary citizen to do but go back to his farm.

It was still an hour at least until nightfall and, unwilling to drive the wagon across the river with the effect of the wine still heavy on him, Thomas checked the harness on the wagon, gave the horse a pat and a couple of kind words, then set off on a brisk walk down the cobblestone street. He thought to make a wide circuit of four blocks and then return, refreshed and ready for the trip back across the Charles. In real life, as in fiction, such whimsical decisions often have unlooked-for results which extend far beyond the life of those who make them. So, it would be with Thomas, troubled by the comments of his new acquaintances as he walked away from his wagon, followed only by the questioning eyes of his horse anxious to return home to the barn.

CHAPTER 3

My Dark Rosaleen

Kevin Dillon had been lying in the muddy alleyway for almost three hours. He was more dead than alive. An inventory of his external injuries would have been extensive but not fatal: broken nose, two cracked ribs, dislocated shoulder. But it was his lungs now which, on the verge of collapse from the pleural infection, presented the thinnest of membranes between life and death. Several people had passed him by in the hours that he lay there, but none was willing to stop. An inventory of the Pharisees who cast a brief looks and then went on might remind the reader of another story from another age. But there is no time for such romantic speculations. This was the real world. A cold, indifferent world. It was 1845 in Boston and a young Irish lad would surely die before the sun came up tomorrow.

Thomas Browning walked along, downcast and worrying to himself about the impending war, the callousness of men, the changes in the world since the days when his father fought at Tarrytown. Why he turned right when he could have turned left, cannot be explained. But this last twist in his aimless ambling brought him past the alley where young Dillon lay dying. Thomas continued on a few feet and then stopped. Something he saw in the periphery of his vision perhaps? Some cast away clothes?

A dead animal? He retraced his steps. Something familiar about the bundle next to the barrel? No nothing. He started off again, and then... he saw. One of the split brogans; the sole like the lolling tongue of a dog. Dillon!

He sobered up instantly and rushed over to the boy. He chafed the boy's hands, listened to the heart, faint, faint, then thumped the chest. Alive, at least. Though barely. He picked him up easily, and carried him down the street to his wagon. He wrapped him in blankets and set off across the Charles River to Cambridge.

"Besides having got the hell beat out of him, which I can fix up, the boy's also got lung fever, Tom," Dr. Broderick told him when he reached the office. "And lung fever I can't fix up. I'm afraid there's not much hope, given his condition."

"Is there no medicine ye can give him, Matt? The money's no problem, ye know that."

"It's not a question of money, Tom. Pneumonia is an incurable disease. We're not sure exactly how it works even, but most likely a bacterium coupled with fluid gets into the lungs. Some people recover, if they're strong, with scarred lungs and trouble most of their lives. But most don't recover at all.

"There's not a whole lot that can be can done. Keep him warm, get him to discharge whatever phlegm comes up from the lungs. Get him to take broth and build up strength. Hell, Mrs. Crump and your daughters can handle that. You don't need a doctor."

"Will ye come by and look in on him, Matt?"

"Sure, Tom, I'll come by. But it might simply be to sign a death certificate. The boy's skinny as a picket fence. Doesn't look like he's had a decent meal in weeks. And I've seen grown men with meat on their bones not pull through after the fever gets them."

The wagon rocked young Kevin Dillon so gently he dreamed himself in the donkey cart as his father drove over the County Kerry road from Waterville to the small village of Baleen. Everything was green: the trees, the moss on the road, the fields of grain, the peat, the ivy on the stone walls. He was in a green world as he lay back in the wagon listening to his father's soothing voice.

"Sure and we got a good deal from Kitty O'Reardon. She wouldn't have sold the horse if her old man had not passed away."

His father was a tall man, over six feet, and he dressed in a heavy tweed suit over a boiled white shirt with a high starched collar even on the warmest of days. His voice was sure and knowledgeable and he sat erect and stiff on the seat of the cart, like a brigadier.

"McGuillicuddy was saying to me the other day, how Cahirsiveen was a one horse town. Sure, they're mostly one horse towns in Kerry. And the man who owns a horse can rent it out at harvest time and make a pile o' money."

"Now don't be thinking greedy, Francis Xavier Dillon!" his wife said. "You're a fine broth of a man and I admire your ambition. But don't get a swelled head. What we have, we owe to the grace of God. Them that can pay, will pay. But them that can't, iffen they be neighbors, we'll help as well."

Francis Dillon smiled at his rosy-cheeked wife, her open peasant face serious beneath her stiff felt hat.

"Sure, you're an angel, Mary." He leaned over and kissed her on the cheek. "The Lord knew I could not make do with an ordinary woman and He sent me an angel."

Behind the cart trotted the horse, a white mare with muscular haunches, a steady gait and intelligent eyes. They called her simply "Colleen", the diminutive in Gaelic for "girl," an endearment really, and from that day Kevin loved the horse. He fed her, he groomed her, he took her down the road in the early morning to hitch her up to a neighbor's plow, and led her back to their farm at night. Kevin was fourteen and the world had never seemed more precious, more filled with possibilities. Each day was a new adventure in a green and magical kingdom and it seemed like it would go on forever.

Thomas looked back at his patient in the back of the wagon. Kevin's pale face shone in the moonlight and

Thomas thought he could detect the trace of a smile. Perhaps, he thought to himself, things are not so bad as the doctor fears. The lad looks peaceful enough.

Kevin's older brother Seamus helped his father run the farm in Ireland. Seamus would take over the farm, as well, when he came of age and took a wife. It was the law of primogeniture. The first son would inherit all the land; there would be no sharing with sisters or brothers. It was a law mandated by necessity, to keep the family parcels that did exist in one piece. Divided among several children the land would not be able to support even one family. Kevin knew this. He also knew that his possibilities in life were limited. He could become a priest if he had the vocation and the Latin. But he had neither, and his father could not afford to send him to Waterford to study.

He could join the British army. Each winter, when the stores of the bleak harvest dwindled and one less mouth to feed was a blessing, an army recruiter would come to the village. To sign on meant regular rations, money to send home to the family, and at least a chance at life. But he had been taught to hate the British, the Protestant landlord who had seized his grandfather's estate, the Crown tax collector who even now robbed his father of produce from the small parcel of land which remained. He was told often enough, too, by his grandfather, of the redcoats who enforced the terrible Penal Laws which made it a crime to practice the Catholic religion, which sent priests into hiding, and hanged many innocent men.

When he turned fifteen, these thoughts weighed heavy on him. But it was a golden summer, working in the fields, feeling his muscles harden with the labor, eating fresh cheese and homemade bread at noon, then talking to his horse on the long walks home at the end of the day down the shady lane leading to his family's small farm. It was a perfect summer; the kind that every Irish child knows can never last. Nothing good ever lasted long; one learned that at an early age without parental advice or the sermons of the priest. Life itself taught you that.

It was after the harvest of '44 when the tax collectors came and asked for their tithe.

"I haven't the wherewithal to feed my own for the winter. How am I to be giving the Crown any of it?"

"Ye'll be givin' the Crown all of it, Frank Dillon, if ye don't pay the tax," the collector told him. "They'll send soldiers in and take the land for what ye owe and throw ye and the wife and family out in the lane."

It was then that his father decided to sell Colleen, the beautiful white horse and companion of the past two summers. A Cork horse trader had been anxious to buy her for months and had offered a good price. The money from the horse could, his father said, both pay the tax man and cover a fourth class passage on the boat to America.

The boy in the wagon moaned as Thomas turned into the lane leading to his farm. Careful as Thomas was, the wagon still swung and bounced over the ruts in the road.

Kevin's fourth class ticket bought him a narrow space in the dark hold of a converted slave ship. He was seasick the very first day, and the brackish water, and mouldy biscuit that was his only food during the weeks of the crossing, kept him vomiting convulsively each morning, and sleeping fitfully each afternoon. Seven people died in the hold during the journey. He himself slept next to a dead body for two days before the odor of rotting flesh (one foul smell among so many other was barely noticeable) finally alerted him.

They sang songs in the hold of the rank-smelling ship. It was the music and the black humor of some of the older men which sustained him. They sang of Ireland. Some of their songs were in the mournful tones that had characterized the Negro songs, sorrowful music which echoed in holds just like this one; songs of another race who had left their homeland forever and come to a new world, to a new life beyond all imagining.

Ireland was a troubled country, there was no doubt. Famine, under-productive land with the best of it seized by England absentee landlords, deadening poverty and hopelessness. Occasionally an attempt at revolt, a hope of freedom soon dashed by superior force or lack of organization.

And yet Ireland was more than a country, more than the land itself. It was a feeling felt in the blood and which vibrated in the hearts of each of these men. It was a land of poetry and song, a land of faith and fierce hope, and it was this other Ireland which would sustain these men long after they left her shores.

Other songs reflected this feeling. They were not mournful but defiant. They spoke of Ireland as a woman. A woman of transcendent beauty and dignity whom they would love forever. These songs were accompanied by hand clapping, or by beating on the sides of the hold as if sounding out a slow, undefeated battle drum.

There was one he would never forget. It was written by the great chieftain, Hugh O'Donnel at the end of the 16th Century. And Ireland in this song, was a woman, the beautiful, dark Rosaleen.

> Oh the Eiren shall run red with redundance of blood
> The earth shall rot beneath our tread and flames wrap hill & wood
> And gun peal and slogan cry wake many a glen serene
> Ere you shall fade, ere you shall die, my dark Rosaleen.

His fist beat against the side of the wagon now as it pulled up in from of the Browning house. Mrs. Crump, the housekeeper, her face red from the oven and anxious concern, came out to meet the wagon with a oil lamp in her hand.

A cheerful woman in her fifties with her gray hair pinned up in a serviceable bun, Mrs. Crump's clear blue eyes were curious.

"Welcome home, sir! I was a mite concerned when ye didn't come by before sundown. And then it got later still. I hope ye had no accident or troubles."

"There's a surprise of sorts in the back," Thomas said grimly pointing to the bundle covered by blankets.

Mrs. Crump leaned over the back of the wagon. She gingerly pulled back the edge of the blanket and looked down at the young Irish boy.

"He's very sick, Mrs. Crump, and likely to die," Thomas said before she could comment on his guest. "We'll just have to do what we can. Dr. Broderick has already looked at him and offers little hope."

Mrs. Crump lowered the lantern so she could see the boy's face. Twisted in defiance, the jaw set firmly, it was the face of someone ready for a fight. His fist pounded weakly but steadily, as if in a drum beat, on the floor of the wagon.

> Oh, my own Rosaleen.
> The judgment hour must first be nigh
> ere you can fade ere you can die
> My dark Rosaleen. O my dark Rooo-saa-leen.

"He's in bad shape, all right," said Mrs. Crump. "But there's something tells me, he's going to make it."

She reached down and picked him up, blankets and all, as easily as if he were a baby. She brought him into the warm farmhouse and set him down close to the fire.

CHAPTER 4

Share my Harvest and my Home

The Browning house was a substantial two-story affair, set back from the road on a smooth, built-up terrace. It was unlike any other house in Cambridge, and certainly not what one would expect of a New England farmhouse. The lower half was of Vermont granite, carefully chosen for its reds and golds. The upper portion was of wood frame, painted not whitewashed, with a thick oil-based coat to protect it from the weather. There were low French windows overlooking the flower gardens in front, a "widow's walk" or balustrade around the roof with bronze eagles from Revere's shop mounted at each corner. Classical white pillars stood sentinel at the front entrance and a covered transom stretched between them.

His wife's bedroom upstairs stayed as it was the day she was taken to the churchyard to be buried. A large wedding quilt of rose and silver satin squares bound in rope pattern of blue and silver cotton. Each of the rose blocks had an embroidered "B" in the center and in the bottom corner of the quilt sewn in silver thread: "Katherine Anne and Thomas Scott, June 14, 1827." At the foot of the bed was a large cedar chest, covered with a sampler which read: "Wear Life Like A Loose Garment."

Thomas slept in the other front bedroom overlooking the garden. His two girls, Samantha, age 13 and Tabitha, age 11, slept together in the back. Each bedroom had its own fireplace; four small chimneys and two larger ones of red brick stood regally in the August night. It was a house made with care and, if to some neighbors it seemed a bit overdone, they also understood the love that went into it and that even now reflected the romantic notions of Katherine Browning who was determined to have a bit of the elegant old world mixed with the new.

Kevin slept fitfully by the large fireplace in the dining room, while Mr. Browning sat at the dining room table. Although she had a perfectly serviceable wood stove in the kitchen, Mrs.Crump always kept a fire in the dining room as well where a pot of brown beans sat bubbling for those nights when the master came home late. She served him a plate of the dark beans in a molasses syrup with some warm brown bread, and then tended to the boy.

"What was that Matt Broderick thinking of? He's got the boy's ribs all gummed up here. That 'un will never be the doctor his father was. I remember when I changed the bum napkins on that un. He was a rascal then, and he's a rascal now. If ye ask me..."

"I don't recall asking, you, dear Mrs. Crump," Thomas said wryly. "But Doctor Broderick taped his ribs because a couple were cracked when the lad was beat up. Ye'll note the bruises as well. I found him in the alley next to the Green Dragon. He'd obviously been beaten bad. When I took him to Matt... uh, Doctor Broderick, he said that it looked like he had the lung fever as well. He taped the ribs lightly, he said, so as not to interfere with the breathing."

"Humph! I'm not impressed by titles, Doctor this, Master that. I think the Quakers have the best of us with their 'thee' and 'thou' and 'friend'. We Congregationalists claim democracy but give false honors all the same. I'll prepare a poultice for his chest, Squire Browning. It'll drain some of the poison from the lungs. He'd best be kept here by the fire tonight and we'll see if he can get through the worst of the fever. It'd be dangerous to move him any more."

Mr. Browning, gave an exasperated grunt and turned back to his beans and brown bread. He was relieved that Mrs. Crump had taken over and could feel the knot in his stomach ease with the warm food and the release of tension. She had her ways, but she was competent, and he trusted her, if truth be told, as much as any doctor.

He had taken no more than two spoons of beans when, from the top of the stairs came a bright female voice. "Father! Is it you?" And then the light, almost dancing tread of a slippered girl descending the stairs.

Samantha Browning was a bright eyed slip of a girl in that tender and troubling age that presages womanhood. Her long blond hair, braided for bed, hung charmingly beneath a ruffled cap. Her nightgown of gray flannel trimmed with yellow lace, reached all the way to her delicate ankles. Irrepressible and smiling with delight, she did a dance step and a pirouette at the bottom of the stairs and then ran to her father and threw his arms around him

"Papa, Papa, it's you! It's you! I could not sleep until I knew you were safe at home. Tabitha tucks her head in like a bird and falls fast asleep. But me, I brood and worry so. What if the wagon broke a wheel? I think to myself. What if you were set upon by Irish ruffians?"

She kissed him prettily on the cheek and then snuggled up against him, accidentally dragging the table cloth with her foot.

"Here, here," said Mrs. Crump in mock anger, reaching to set the table cloth back. "Would ye upset the whole table and send the beans aflying? Get back up stairs with ye, and get a warm robe on! There's work to be done. Yer Pa has brought home a young lad sorely ill and wounded and I need yer help to care for him."

Samantha looked over to where Kevin Dillon lay by the fire. His legs were pulled up against his chest, his hair matted by blood, His breathing rasping and weak.

"Oh, father, who is it?" Samantha asked tugging her nightgown protectively against her breasts. "What in the world happened to him?"

"He's a lad who did a bit of work for me earlier today and then was set upon by thugs. I should guess that he's got a bit of the lung fever as well. He very much needs our help, Samantha."

"Off with you, then," cried Mrs. Crump. "He'll be deader than Oliver Cromwell by the time ye get a robe on."

"Oh no, he won't, sweet Mrs. Crump, my dear Mrs. Crump. No, he won't. Please don't say that. We shall save him, won't we, Papa? Won't we, please, my dear Mrs. Crump?"

At this tears came to her eyes. "Say we shall save him, Father! Please, say we shall save him."

"If it is God's will, lass. Now, do what you're told. Hurry up and get a decent robe on, then ye can come back and be a nurse for a bit."

"Oh, I shall, Papa. I shall be the best, most careful, most solicitous nurse you have ever seen," she said solemnly.

And in her eyes, Thomas Browning suddenly detected a compassion that quite overwhelmed him. She gets that from her mother, he thought. And the determined set of the jaw, as well.

When Samantha returned, Mrs. Crump was in the kitchen stirring up a vile mixture of garlic, mustard, pennyroyal and camphor.

"Yecch! What is that stuff?" Samantha asked.

"It's what will make our guest well, Miss Samantha.

"And asphyxiate us all in the process."

"Ah, its not so bad as all that," said Mrs. Crump. "Here. You stir this for a bit and I'll get some cool cloths to put on his head. We'll see if we can lower the fever a mite."

"Oh please, kind Mrs. Crump. Could I do that, while you stir this evil brew?"

Between the two of them they managed to get the blood and dirt cleaned from Kevin's face and upper body. Fresh, cool cloths were wrapped about his head, and a strong-smelling poultice put on his chest. He went into paroxysms of coughing after the poultice was applied, and he coughed up a bitter yellow phlegm. His coughing became more frequent and violent each time a new poultice was applied. For over two hours Mrs. Crump and Samantha took turns holding his head so that he would not choke as he struggled to expel the fluid from his lungs and to breathe.

It was midnight when his features finally smoothed over and he fell into a shallow fitful sleep. Mrs. Crump felt his head.

"The fever has subsided a bit, Samantha. Perhaps you should go up to bed now."

"No," Samantha said. "You go to bed, Mrs. Crump. You have to get up at dawn to make breakfast for Father and Hezekiah. I can sleep in. Besides, I want to pray for him, Mrs. Crump, and I wouldn't feel right doing that in a comfortable bed."

Mrs. Crump stroked the girl's hair, golden and flame colored in the light of the fire. Such a dear child. So like her mother in tenderness and faith. Although, God forgive me, where were You, Jesus, when she lay dying? Mrs. Crump had prayed little since the death of her mistress. She doubted the efficacy of prayer. But Samantha still believed, and Mrs. Crump deferred to that belief instinctually.

Mrs. Crump could hear the girl's voice as she ascended the stairs. "Thy kingdom come, Thy will be done on earth..."

Throughout the night Samantha said the Lord's Prayer over and over again, holding on to the boy's hand with both of hers. She pictured him in her mind as already heathy, already cured. She did not ask that God cure him. She simply asked that God's will be done, whatever that might be. Unlike Mrs. Crump, Samantha believed that there was no such thing as an unanswered prayer. She felt that people simply did not know what to pray for. The boy's death now might spare him a lifetime of sin, or a more horrible death at a later time. So, she did not pray that his life be spared. She only prayed that God would look down on him now, forgive him his sins, and restore him to wholeness either in this life or the next.

Six days later Kevin Dillon awoke and felt the breeze on his skin from the open French windows which let in the autumn redolence of the countryside: the rich odors of the hay and oats, the pungent droppings of horses and cattle. He could hear the sound of running creeks, the rustling of tree branches and the chickens scratching and clucking in the back yard. Outside the window he could see the gold-red of the maple and the yellowing oak. The air was cool and sweet, the last breeze of Indian summer chased by the ghost of fall.

Dust hung in the air like golden motes, fireflies sparkling in the sun. He thought of golden hair, and a soft voice holding his hand in prayer. A prayer he could not believe at the time, lost as he was in fever, but he hung on to the faith of the other. He had hung on through the long nights of fever and coughing, and sweat-filled nightmare sleep.

"Hello!" Samantha said, opening the bedroom door.

"Hello, yourself," Kevin said pulling the bed quilt chastely up over his shoulders.

"You needn't be so shy. I've put poultices on your chest you know, and quite seen my fill.

"I thought I dreamt you, little girl," Kevin said still wonder-struck.

"Let me hasten to inform you," Samantha said indignantly, "that I am not a little girl. I am Miss Samantha Browning, currently mistress of this house. But you're an Irish, aren't you?" she said wriggling her nose. "So I guess that's to be expected."

Kevin ignored the last bit, and the tone in which it was said. He decided gratitude and charm were called for here, not offense. "Yes, I'm Irish," he said smiling. "I'm from County Kerry, the loveliest place on earth I thought until now. Did you know you look just like an angel?"

Samantha smiled. "Well, that's a bit better. Do you believe in angels?"

"I do now. I saw one, you know, at night when I was sick and out of my mind and thought that I was dying. I heard it pray, and I felt it hold my hand in the heat and the darkness and the terror of the night. I knew if it ever let me go, I should die."

Samantha blushed and turned her eyes away. "I'll have Mrs. Crump bring you some beef broth. You need to begin getting your strength back."

"How long have I been here?" Kevin asked.

"Six days," Samantha said. "And Mr. Browning said that you'd better be getting well so that you can turn your hand to some honest labor around here and earn your keep." The sternness of her voice was belied by a trace of a smile. But Kevin did not notice. He seized upon the name of his benefactor.

"Mr. Thomas Browning?" asked Kevin.

"The same. And I'm his eldest, Samantha." She did a mock curtsey and then went off in search of Mrs. Crump and the broth.

Going down the stairs she suddenly felt warm and a bit light-headed. She had not noticed before just how green his eyes were, or how they brightened when he smiled. Why, there was something about him, she thought, lean and hungry as he was, that might even be termed handsome. She decided that she would not bother Mrs. Crump. The poor woman was busy with her own work. She would bring Kevin up the broth herself. She would watch how his smile lit up his eyes. She would listen to the lilt of his voice so unlike that of the Cambridge farm boys, and she would wipe his lean face with the napkin when he was done.

CHAPTER 5

Season of Mists

Hezekiah Akley was not a pleasant young man, either in appearance or personality. His face was heavily pockmarked from the ravages of childhood smallpox, and his thin lips were set in a perpetual smirk. His gray eyes, set a bit too narrowly together, gave him a furtive look. Known simply as Heck to the Brownings and Mrs. Crump, he was tolerated rather than liked. His arms were well-muscled and tanned from working in the sun but they hung down, simian-like, almost to his knees.

Thomas Browning had hired him after Heck's parents died in 1842, the same year that Thomas' own son had died of fever. Mrs. and Mrs. Akley and two daughters died in a mysterious house fire and, although Heck himself was spared, he never seemed quite right after that. A quiet child, he had grown into a sullen and recalcitrant young man with a defensive look about him as if he was getting ready to deny whatever anyone thought to accuse him of.

Although of indeterminate age, Heck had been out of school and farming with his father for five years when the tragedy occurred. He looked to be about sixteen when the Congregational minister, accompanied by two well-meaning church ladies, brought him to Thomas' door. Thomas, who had in fact needed an extra hand since the death of his own son, took him on. That was three and a half years ago.

Today Hezekiah and Kevin were raking and sheaving hay in the north field. They had been cutting hay for the past five days. Both boys were strong workers and steady with the scythe. Now it was time to rake, and this work—though perhaps equally hard—used a different set of muscles and gave their forearms and biceps a break. They talked little and seemed intent on their task.

Thomas watched them from the shade of the woodlot where he had just parked the wagon. The Irish lad had recovered just fine, he thought, watching Kevin drop the rake and gather the sheaves together. His arms, too, were becoming muscled and his face without the pinched famine look, was handsome.

Once they're done with that, he thought, we'll take a couple more days getting the sheaves of hay to the barn. Then pick the last of the late corn, except for the cow corn, gather the husks, and plow under the rest. Then there were repairs to the barn, cleaning and patching in the tack room if the rain came, re-shingling the main house for winter, fixing the old cistern pump, slaughtering a couple of hogs. Yes, he had work enough to keep both boys busy. Enough to leave them weary at the end of the day and grateful for a cozy bed in the barn.

Hezekiah, he knew, did not expect much more out of life. The daily chores of the farm, the simple but decent food, a clean place to sleep. He had no education beyond learning to sign his name, and the scripture readings of Mrs. Crump each Sunday afternoon. But the Irish lad seemed more restless and more intellectually curious. He had borrowed a copy of *The North American Review* that he had seen Thomas reading, and he had commented to Mrs. Crump last Sunday on the sermons of John Donne, a book he said his father owned back home. For such a lad, this life would likely prove too narrow eventually. Or, he'd begin to think that he deserved a higher position than that of a hired hand.

Samantha was young now, of course, only thirteen. But in a year or two she'd be making eyes. And what if they fell on this Irish lad? Proximity has more to do with romantic love than most folks think. And she sees the lad each day, coming and going from the fields. It would just be a matter of time before she would come to appreciate his clean good looks, his polite way with words, his native intelligence. Wouldn't that be a fine thing! A Papist son-in-law trotting poor pregnant Samantha and twelve children off to morning Mass in Charlestown. A match made in hell! Why, he'd be damned if...

"Papa! What are you thinking about!"

Thomas turned around in his seat quickly, jerking the reins as he did so. The horse cut by the bit, tossed its head and reared up.

"Whoa, girl. Whoa, Nellie! Watch it, girl! What in blue blazes do you mean coming up on me like that, Samantha? Didn't anyone ever tell you not to sneak up on a man, you little ninny!"

"Oh, now I'm a ninny, am I, dear Father?" she smiled delightedly. "A ninny!" she laughed at the sound of the word as much as the foolish insult which she knew her father did not mean.

She was in a light calico dress with long sleeves and a high ruffled collar. Her blond curls were only partially restrained by a blue sunbonnet which tucked under her chin with a white velvet ribbon.

"No," Thomas smiled back. "Never, a ninny! Of course not, dear child. No, no. Excuse the rash word. I just feared, when the horse jumped, that ye might be hurt. And ye did come up on me sudden like."

"I called to you three times on my way, Father. You must have been in a reverie. I know how that could be since I spent two hours this morning chasing an orange and gold butterfly and quite imagined a jungle world he came from down in Mexico... But... what could you have been thinking about, dear father, that took you to such a deep and distant place you could not hear me?

"What indeed?" said Thomas. And he blushed to remember his thoughts. Why, here was no grown woman about to put herself in anyone's arms overnight. She was only a simple child, gathering wildflowers to make a bouquet for her pony one minute, and chasing butterflies in the field the next. She had no more notion of men than the willow tree by the river bending this way and that in the whimsical breezes of the hour.

"I've brought a stone jar of cold lemonade, a fresh pan of corn bread that Mrs. Crump made, as well as some scrod that you carried home from the market. I thought I'd take it to the boys for their midday meal, and then you and I could see what Mrs. Crump has for us up at the house."

"Hop up here then, and I'll ride you down. We treat these boys so well they'll start thinking they're hotel guests, not workers. Fresh bread, scrod and lemonade! We'll be lucky if we get any labor at all out of them this afternoon."

As he drove the wagon down to the fields, the boys looked up briefly and then went back to their work.

"Here she comes," Hezekiah sneered, wielding the rake with fury. "The lady of the manor. I'd like to have her alone for a few minutes; we'd see then what unladylike squeals she'd let loose."

"Watch yer tongue!" Kevin snapped. "If I hear you talk that way again about Miss Samantha, I'll thrash yah."

"Oh, and I suppose the thought never entered your mind, Irish? Don't be fooled by her ways. She thinks yer trash, too. I'm an orphan and yer a Mick. Yer just newer trash around here, so she's curious, nothin' more. And if ye think you can give me a thrashing, well..."

"Jabbering away, are ye lads?" Thomas shouted as he drove up. "Talkin' won't get the hay in before the rains, ye know. If ye've got that much extra breath, use it to rake faster."

"Good day, sir," replied Hezekiah, doffing his cap. "And good day to ye, Miss Samantha."

"Good day, Heck," replied Mr. Browning. Samantha favored him with a curt nod, and then smiled down at Kevin.

"A grand day, Miss!" Kevin smiled looking up shyly, his cloth cap held tightly in both hands.

"It is, Mr. Dillon. Good day to you! We have a bit of noon dinner for you both. Some delicious scrod, my father brought back from Clarke's Wharf in Boston."

"I know that place well, Miss," Kevin blurted out.

"You do?"

"Aye, Miss. It was my introduction to this fine land," said Kevin with a trace of bitterness. "Where I first landed on an old slaver. Down in the hold with kegs of molasses from the Indies. Not a pleasant memory, I assure you."

Samantha frowned, and for a moment was at a loss for a reply.

Kevin could have bit his tongue. Anxious to make a good impression, or to just say anything at all, he always seemed to blurt out some inappropriate remark.

"Well, that's behind you now, Mister Dillon," Samantha said.

"It is that," replied Kevin. "Excuse me for mentioning it, Miss."

"Thank you both for the fine lunch" Hezekiah said ingratiatingly. "I appreciate you both driving all the way down here to give it to us. I'm sure the scrod will be fine, and... mmm... Mrs. Crump's fresh bread as well."

"Don't mention it, Heck," Mr. Browning said, as Hezekiah unloaded the food basket and Kevin took the jug of lemonade. "Eat up and then get back to work. Let's get this field done by sundown."

Samantha gave her father a nudge and Thomas clucked at the horse and snapped the reins. They drove away leaving Kevin feeling several kinds of fool. A fact that Hezekiah Akley did not overlook.

"Excuse me for mentioning it, Miss Samantha," he mimicked. "You dumb Mick! I see I've got no competition from you in the ladies department. Why you'd scare off a female cur in heat with that dark cloud hanging on your lip."

"Aggh, eat yer dinner then, and leave me be," Kevin growled.

"We Irish have had such a difficult life, Miss. Won't ye have a little pity?" said Akley in a whining, sissy tone of voice.

"Leave me in peace, can't ye?" Kevin snapped.

"If it's peace ye want," Hezekiah said, "Ye've come to the wrong country. Now why don't ye get yer dukes up and show me if ye've got any man in ye at all."

Kevin dove at Akley's legs and dropped him like a stone. But Akley recovered quickly and hit Kevin a solid blow behind the ear. Akley was stronger and in much better shape. He had not been on his back for six grueling days with lung fever. In addition, he had plenty of practice rough housing and dirty fighting among the farm boys of the area. Kevin got in a solid blow or two but Heck's weight finally subdued him and he ended up flat on his back with the older boy punching him at will. When Akley finally let him up, Kevin's right eye was half-closed, his ribs (only half healed from his earlier beating) were throbbing painfully, and a front tooth had been loosened.

Next time, he thought to himself, I won't be that stupid. Nor that weak.

"Next time," Heck said, as if he could read Kevin's thoughts, "I won't be that easy on ye. I'll kick yer sorry Irish head in until it's pumpkin mush."

Kevin's mouth was sore and he could eat little of the rich corn bread or fresh scrod. He forced himself to take a few bites so that he would have strength for the afternoon labor. Finally, taking a long draught of the cold lemonade, he picked up the heavy hay rake.

"Not hungry, my dear Mick?" Akley asked mockingly. "Oh, well, that's more for me then, ain't it."

The afternoon dragged by. The heavy wool of his shirt itched with sweat and bits of hay, and the bites of ticks and gnats. He would have loved to pull off the shirt and feel the cool breeze on his chest but that was not allowed. In New England it was considered improper for a man to show his chest. For a laborer on a farm where there were women folk about it was scandalous. Laborers had been sent away from the farms and black-listed by local squires for taking such liberties.

So he worked through the long afternoon keeping pace with the steady rhythm of Hezekiah Akley, breathing through his nose so that his mouth would not be full of hay dust and mites. The afternoon dragged on interminably. The boys did not speak to each other as the sun moved slowly behind the trees, and the goldenrod bowed like blond acolytes on the side of the field. Then the welcome purple gathering of the twilight, and the maples and oaks of the woodlot cast long shadows, and the crows clustered in their branches calling: *That's all, that's all*, as the wind freshened, drying the sweat on their necks, and sending a cool reminder of the season up their spines.

The boys shouldered their rakes and began walking back to the barn.

There they would wash themselves with cold water at the horse trough, shake out the dust and hay from their clothes, and then begin their evening chores. First the cattle needed to be fed, then the horses, both oats and hay. Then the sheep, the hogs and the chickens. When they had finished all that, they needed to scrape off their boots and then go up to the back door of the farmhouse. If supper was ready, Mrs. Crump would tell them to scrape their boots again, "Real good now, hear? I'll be having no muck on my scrubbed floors!" and let them in to the kitchen.

The family would have already finished their dinner and the boys would eat whatever leftovers remained. This was not as meager as it sounds, however. Mrs. Crump always cooked large dinners and made extras of everything so the boys always ate their full.

Tonight there was roast pork, with red potatoes and gravy. There were homemade biscuits, corn on the cob with fresh butter, snap beans and lima's mixed together, and pitchers of fresh milk and lemonade. For dessert there was peach cobbler.

The boys ate without looking up from their food and without conversation. They ate with a speed and single-mindedness that quite astounded Mrs. Crump.

"It's no wonder hired boys eat in the kitchen," she remarked aloud without turning from the sink where she was washing a greasy pan. "Why, look at you both. Like pigs!

Not a drop of talk about the day, nor news, nor weather. Not a pause for a breath."

Now she turned around to face them. "Not a pause for a breath, I say! Just the steady IN-HALE-AY-SHUN of food as if it was corn meal MUSH ye was snuffin' down yer SNOUTS like fattenin' hogs.

"Course, poor Heck here ain't had no raisin' proper, with his folks dead and all. But you, boy," she said shaking her head sadly at Kevin. "Ye ought to know better."

"He ain't no better n' me," Heck said pausing briefly in his all-out attack on a ear of corn.

"No one said he was, Heck. Don't be defending yerself when no one attacks. And if this one keeps getting his mug punched in," she said, looking narrowly at them both, "I won't be able to tell the two of ye apart."

Kevin wiped his face with his napkin and set it beside his plate.

"Thank you, Mrs. Crump. It was a delicious meal. I'm sorry about my manners but I was about starved. I didn't much feel like lunch because..."

He stopped himself. He was about to launch into another self-pitying remark about his mouth being sore. Just like the sissy that Akley accused him of being.

"Yeah. Ye see Kevin don't like scrod very much, Missus," said Hezekiah. "It reminds him of the evil times from the old country."

"An Irishman that doesn't like fish! Now I've heard everything!" exclaimed Mrs. Crump.

Kevin got hastily to his feet, mumbled a thank you, and headed out the door.

"Ye'll taste a bit o' my peach cobbler, won't ye?" she called after him. But Kevin was already half way to the barn before the back door swung closed.

"Well, I'll be. What got into that boy?" asked Mrs. Crump.

"He don't appreciate nothin'," said Hezekiah. "I'll have a big piece of that delicious peach cobbler, Mrs. Crump. Why, never mind what that dumb Mick says. I think you're about the best cook in New England."

Mrs. Crump frowned, and then checked herself. Heck's compliments were seldom what they seemed, she thought. But that was not a Christian thought, she knew, so she said simply, "Help yourself, Heck. There's plenty more."

Kevin stood outside the barn looking up at the clear September sky. The moon was gibbous; day after tomorrow it would be full. But even with the moonlight the stars shone brightly in the sky. Their clarity reminded him of his murky existence. He was making a mess of his new life in this country. He knew that. He was acting like an ungrateful child in front of the housekeeper, a sissy in front of the hired hand, and a fool in front of young Miss Samantha. Mr. Browning had lent him the *North American Review* with a tight smile as if he thought Kevin was uppidy. So he had not made an impression there either.

He should be grateful; he had survived a fever that Dr. Broderick said should have killed him. He was getting stronger each day, eating well, and living in a fine place.

But it was not his place. He did not feel at home among these people, or this country. Beneath even the kindest of them, like Mr. Browning, there was this edge of contempt for his race and his religion. Plus, this part of the country was all built up, set out in parcels, and claimed for two or three generations already. The Revolution was over. Those who came to New England now would be foreigners, outsiders, mere peasants on the land. He had heard of land further west in Louisiana Territory, and folks said if that was too crowded there was even more and in Oregon country.

It looked like Mr. Polk would get elected this year, according to Mr. Browning. If he did the country would be expanding its frontiers. Texas, already independent for ten years, might well become a state before Christmas if the Senate finally approved it. Some folks were even talking about the Congress buying California from the Mexicans. There were plenty of places a man could go and start a new life away from the prejudices and narrow restrictions of New England.

Kevin just didn't quite know how he would go about getting to any of these places. He had no money, no horse, and no friends in this country. But he felt deep within himself a reservoir of strength and belief.

The oak trees rubbed against each other in the evening breeze. Somewhere in the woods an owl sounded. Grateful now for the warm cotton shirt, Kevin pulled his collar up around his neck, and shivered. It would be a cold winter, he thought, looking up at Venus blazing in the western sky, but I will be steadfast. Somewhere in this new world is a place for me, a place where I will be respected and honored. I do not know where that place is yet, but I will find it, and when I do, I will cling to it tenaciously and fight for it against every other power on earth.

CHAPTER 6

October Moon

What Kevin tried not to think about, especially after the dirty remarks of Akley, was Samantha. She was lovely; he was aware of that. And if he had once felt stirrings in his loins as any young man might, he repressed them with hard work, and the reminder that she was the same age as his sister Kathleen. Much too young for him to have such thoughts about.

It was a rainy day in mid-October and he was repairing a saddle hitch in the tack room. He had already finished his most irksome chore, that of cleaning out the chicken coops. Akley was still dawdling in the cow barn where he was supposed to be shoveling out muck. He, too, would repair tack before the day was over but right now he was lying back in the straw indulging an adolescent fantasy. His imagination was not subject to the same restraints as Kevin's.

Kevin had just reached up for a length of rawhide when he heard the door opening. Thinking it was Akley, he said, "It's about time," and turned back to his work.

"I know," said Samantha, throwing off her wet shawl and shaking out her blond curls. "It certainly is about time, dear Mr. Dillon."

"Uh, Miss. Sorry, I..." Kevin muttered embarrassed and ill-at-ease.

"It's okay, Kevin," Samantha smiled, putting her hand on his shoulder. "Don't get up. I'm just her visiting dear Nelly, and my pony, Penelope. They both get frightened in storms, you know. Such dears. But did you know Papa went to Charlestown today? And do you know what for? Well, to buy me my own riding horse. It's a beautiful bay gelding that I admired several months ago, and now, if Mrs. Crump is to be believed, he has gone to get it for my birthday.

"About time, too. Although Nellie is a darling, she's still a farm horse, isn't she? And Penelope? Well, she's a pony, and a pony is for a child."

Kevin smiled. "And you're not a child."

"Indeed not, my dear fellow! I am fourteen years old today. And how old are you, may I ask?" she added when she saw Kevin's condescending smile.

"I'll be seventeen in July."

"Oh, July is it? Well, I'll be almost fifteen by then. So there, Mister Older Than Thou."

Kevin laughed in spite of himself. He supposed he did come off as sounding superior. "I apologize, my good lady. And may I be among the first to wish you the warmest returns of the day."

"Thank you, kind sir. And what did you have in mind to give me as a present for my birthday?"

Kevin paused for a embarrassing length of time. "Well," he said finally. "How would it be if I braided you a smart new riding crop for your mount."

"Excellent. Quick thinking, my dear Kevin. But you certainly won't finish that in one day. Why, that will take you at least a couple of nights after work. Which I shall enjoy, thinking of you thinking of me, as you braid."

With this she stood over him, and twisted a lock of his hair in her fingers.

He looked up at her. The curls like tendrils against her fresh skin. Her blue eyes deep and mocking. Yet, he thought, he detected a tenderness there as well.

"Well?" she said, moving herself closer so that the front of her dress rustled against his thigh.

"Well, what?" Kevin said.

"What will you give me today? Today is my birthday. Not two days from now."

"I have nothing to give," Kevin said breathing deeply. She was so close now he could smell the warm milk of breakfast on her breath. He could feel the heat of her leg through the soft cotton of her dress as she moved even closer to him. The air in the tack room seemed close, but also sensual and musky with the odors of horses and leather and hay.

"Nothing to give, hmm," she said coquetishly. "Well then, I shall just take what I want!"

With this she leaned close to him and put her soft lips firmly against his. She lingered with her body against him. And in the stillness of the barn Kevin felt his stomach go empty and his legs weak. A rush of blood flowed through him. He felt dizzy, and then scared, and then, whatever had been sleeping in him arose, and he returned the kiss.

Samantha stiffened for a moment with surprise at his passion, and then wrapped her arms around him. "Oh, Kevin," she whispered. "That was the best birthday present ever."

They held hands and looked deep into each others eyes. "You are so beautiful, Samantha," Kevin said. "Your eyes are deep as the River Boyne and as sparkling as the sun. If I looked into them too long, I'm afraid I'd go blind, or drown myself entirely."

"There are worse ways to die," Samantha whispered.

They kissed again. This time it was a prolonged, breathless kiss in which their bodies pushed full length upon each other. They each felt the heat and the passion of the other's blood. And the moment extended, spun in and out and away, until it seemed they had transcended time. When they parted, breathing deeply, it was with new knowledge of themselves and of their natures.

Hezekiah Akley had finally finished cleaning the muck from the cow barn. He was in a foul mood. The Irish bastard had been up to his old tricks again, borrowing books from the master, trying to impress Mrs. Crump with his new-found manners. Something told him he should look through the window of the tack room before opening the door. Who knows what that Mick might be up to. Especially if he doesn't know he's being watched. Might be stealing tack to sell on the side, or doing one of his secret Catholic rites with the animals.

What he saw when he looked through the window far exceeded his expectations. Well, the little rat, he said to himself. The evil conniving rat.

He crept slowly into the stables and listened as the two lovers exchanged their breathless embrace. He licked his thin lips, and rubbed his hands together. *Ah, would ye, my fine little lady? Would ye? Well, here's a real man ready for ye. Here's a real man, little lady.*

Outside, the fury of the storm diminished, and muffled thunder rumbled in the distance as the storm moved slowly out to sea. But it was not the last of the autumnal storms which would crash against the coast, nor was winter far behind.

CHAPTER 7

We'll Bid Farewell to Cadet Gray

Kevin heard the rhythmical hoofbeats before the doctor's horses actually came into view prancing down the lane. The doctor guided the handsome pair of grays into the drive and pulled under the portico of the house. Bundled against the cold in a black greatcoat with a patchwork quilt covering his legs and feet, the doctor looked almost too snug to get down from his two-in-hand. It was late afternoon in November and the leaves had swirled into corners by the front steps. No longer the bright reds and grays which decorate the Massachusetts autumn, they were faded, mudcolored, yellowing in the cold damp.

A pair of seagulls wheeled past, screeching their dismay at the loss of good pickings. They, too, seemed unkempt and faded, the white and grays of their plumage had bled together into the color of damp clay. Angry, raucous scavenger birds whose stores of food were dwindling daily, they cried bleakly in the November sky.

Kevin was raking the gravel drive in front of the house. Hezekiah, on a rickety ladder of his own construction, was cleaning the roof spouts and the drains of leaves and branches.

Dr. Broderick folded the quilt and put it to the side. Slowly, as one awakening from a dream, he got down from his buggy. He was a big man with a handsome shock of gray hair which he brushed back from his heavy-lidded eyes. He looked around and blinked up at the gray sky.

Kevin walked over and took hold of the bridles. He clicked his tongue appreciatively at the horses, and patted the outside gray on his neck.

"Good day, Dr. Broderick," he said. "I'll curry these two and get them warm in the barn. Feed them and water them for you, too, later on, if you intend staying a while."

"Just a minute, young man," Dr. Broderick said, taking Kevin gently by the arm. "Let us speak for a moment. How is your health these days?"

"Fine, sir," Kevin said quickly. "No problems. Thanks to your help."

"Thanks to a Greater Physician than any in Cambridge, my son. And no doubt the nursing of Mrs. Crump demands a share of the credit. But none for me. I'd already given you up for lost the night Mr. Browning found you.

"Come closer," he said in a quieter voice, taking Kevin by the shoulder and laying his ear to his chest. "Let me give a listen to those pulmonary sounds."

Kevin looked up and saw Heck watching from his perch on the ladder. A cynical smile was on his face. Kevin felt his own face redden in embarrassment as the doctor leaned his leonine head against his chest.

"Breathe in. Deep breath, please! There we go, that's it! Deep breath in. Hold it! Now, out. Good! Once more: in... now out.

"Hmm," the doctor seemed lost in thought. "Hmm," he said again.

"What is it?" Kevin asked distractedly.

"Hmm? Ah, rales, I should say. Tell me: do you feel any pain when you breathe?"

Kevin, feeling the contemptuous eyes of Hezekiah on him, was distracted and self-conscious.

"What?" Kevin asked.

"Pay attention, boy," said the doctor not unkindly. "Do you feel any pain, I say. You see the sound you make, rales we call it, indicates some residual problem. There would have to be some scarring of the lung tissue as well."

"Well, sometimes, if I'm breathing hard like after cutting a cord of wood. You know, if I breath deeply."

"Just so, just so. Well, that will pass," said the doctor, quickly losing interest in the subject now that his diagnosis had been confirmed. "Tell me, what will you do with yourself now that you've recovered?"

"I don't know, said Kevin.

"Well, you're probably here for the winter, I suppose. And I imagine you're earning your keep these days. But you best be thinking about your future. The army is a fine opportunity for one such as yourself. A chance to give your life some substance, some... ah... stature, you know."

"But I'm not a citizen of this country, sir," Kevin replied.

"That's of no account. A citizen! Indeed! I should think not. You need to take on some responsibilities before you can reap the rewards of citizenship, my young buck. Why, how many citizens do you think fought at Valley Forge?"

"I don't know, sir."

"Of course, you don't. Of course you don't, so I'll tell you. None, sir. That's how many. They were all British subjects and would have been hanged for their valor as traitors. But they won, you see. There's the point. They won!

"And my father," the doctor continued scarcely drawing a breath, "fought at Ticonderoga and earned the privilege of citizenship for me, as you shall for your children. And, if you serve honorably and well—who knows—you may even have a son at the Point one day. As I do, sir," he added proudly. "As I do."

"The Point?" Kevin asked.

"West Point! It's where the army trains young men to be officers, you see. I spoke there myself at last year's commencement. I served, you know, in the last of the sea battles with Farrugut. Ship's surgeon, I was, though I helped load cannon, too—who didn't in those days?—and I've used a grappling hook as well. You can believe that!

"Well that's enough about history, my boy. You'll learn it on your own in time, I expect. Off with you now before the horses catch chill, standing in a froth out here in the frosty air, while you badger me with questions about the wars."

As Kevin turned toward the stables with the horses, Samantha and Mr. Browning appeared at the door.

"Welcome! And come in out of the damp, Matt!" Mr. Browning called to his friend.

"Hello, Doctor!" greeted Samantha running down the steps and throwing her arms around him. "It's so good to see you. You visit so seldom for a neighbor. And what do you hear from Brad?"

"He's well, lass, and thinks of you between his drilling and sweating away at the books. And you, let me look at you," he added, stepping back and holding her at arm's length. "If you're not enough to break a young man's heart! And an old one's as well."

Coquettishly, Samantha took Dr. Broderick by the arm and led him up the steps. He stopped at the head of the stairs and shook hands firmly with Mr. Browning. The other gave the doctor a brotherly pat on the shoulder.

"Good day, Thom, my good friend," Dr. Browning said warmly. Then he turned to look as Kevin led the horses away. "Well, my Good Samaritan to the local Irish population, it looks like you've saved another one for the hangman's noose."

"What a terrible thing to say!" Samantha protested.

"Just joking, my dear. Just joking. The boy seems to be doing well. Let's hope he'll get on with his life now that he's healed."

"Come in out of the damp, Matt," said Mr. Browning. "I'll have Mrs. Crump make us a nice pot of tea."

"Tea! For an old salt?" The doctor raised one of his bushy eyebrows comically. "Surely, a jest." Then turning to Samantha, "Tell me, darling, what is it an old seafaring doctor needs after a long, damp drive?"

"A good rum toddy!" cried Samantha.

"There's my girl," the doctor replied with a cheerful salute which Samantha smartly returned. "Off with you then! And when you return, I have a bit of a gift for you."

Mr. Browning sat down on a comfortable stuffed chair, covered in brocaded fabric and lace antimacassars. He nodded toward a similar one for his friend. "Take a load off your feet, Matt, and tell me all the news.

"President Polk is in, of course. I know that much. What's he got on the agenda? As if I couldn't guess."

"Expansion, my friend!" Dr. Broderick replied enthusiastically. "Expansion and growth! From sea to wind-tossed sea, and down to the sunny Gulf. Continental expansion is the agenda of the new regime

"I can't say I like it," Browning replied. "If the Senate approves Texas statehood, that'll be another state to which the slaveholders of the South will bring their people. A plague on the country, that despicable institution of one race in bondage to another!"

"I agree, Thom. I couldn't agree more. It is a damn shame, all right. And yet, they'll be new states to balance out Texas after the war with Mexico."

"War? What war?"

"It's in the wind. Surely Bustamante and Santa Anna won't stand for a new American state on their border. And if they do, we'll push our advantage. California will be next, my good man. And I suspect the Mexicans will stand their ground sooner or later. A matter of honor.

"Yes, they'll be a fight all right," continued the doctor. "A glorious one, I believe. Although I don't think we'll take too much of a blooding."

"Houston and Fremont and the rest won't settle for anything less, you mean," Thomas countered. "As if those men represented the nation."

"This country won't settle for less, Thom. What are we to do with a hundred thousand Irish and German settlers and more arriving each day?

"Not to mention the Swedes, the Danes, the Dutch, and now the Poles coming in the thousands. Our cities are already teeming with this refuse. What are we to do? Send them back to their European tyrannies? Deny them the freedoms that we enjoy?"

"No, Thomas. The solution is to give them the same chance our fathers had. The chance to fight for the land. The chance to expand the nation, build homes in the new frontier, open up new settlements. Then the East can trade with the West instead of depending on Europe. We'll send them our manufactured goods, and then buy grain, furs, and corn back from them. And who knows what minerals, what gold or silver yet may be discovered in the West? And, with the railroads reaching farther out across the continent each day, it won't be long before we'll have strawberries and tomatoes in December right here in Massachusetts. Oh, what a bright new world it will be, my friend!"

"What doth it profit a nation if it gain the whole world but suffer the loss of its soul?" Mr. Browning asked. "Strawberries and tomatoes are small consolation for lost integrity."

"Oh, Thom! The Devil can quote scripture to his advantage. Besides, I believe Paul was speaking of the individual, not the nation."

Mr. Browning jumped up from his chair, brushing the antimacassar onto the floor with his arm. His face was red with a mixture of indignation and passion.

"A nation **is** it's people, by damn. It is composed of individuals. Seizing territory is theft by the people, or at least in their name. In my name and yours. Allowing slavery to grow is affirming as tolerable what we know in our hearts is an abomination before God. And you suggest that it would be glorious to fight a war based on these premises!"

"Gentlemen! Gentlemen!" Samantha chided. "I've brought you your toddies, and Mrs. Crump has a nice leg of lamb with mint jelly steaming on a platter in the kitchen. You mustn't get choleric, Father, and ruin your appetite."

"Sorry, my dear," Mr. Browning said, breathing deeply. "Just politics, you know."

"I suspected as much, Father. Dr. Broderick, don't you know better than that by now? You must have observed during these violent discussions of yours how Father's blood rushes to the extremities with a fury that it seems the top of his head must blow off. Or is it that you're looking for an apoplectic patient?"

"I apologize, sweet Samantha," the doctor replied. "You're absolutely right, of course. No more of that, right Thom? But come, Samantha, you haven't asked what I've brought for you."

"Oh, what could it be?" she exclaimed, as he pulled a small jeweler's box from the pocket of his waistcoat. "I can't wait to see."

The doctor handed her the small package with a mysterious smile. She opened it, and inside was an small reticule of maroon velvet.

"What can it be!" she said again as her delicate fingers pulled the drawstrings.

Then, with an unfeigned gasp of surprise she withdrew a delicate gold locket with a thin golden chain. The locket was filigreed with roses and a 'B' in Gothic script was raised in a ivory cameo on the front.

"Why it's absolutely lovely," Samantha exclaimed. "I've never seen anything quite like it."

"The cameo was from a ring of my late wife, Brad's mother. It is a 'B' which, of course, could stand for Browning. Or," he said with a significant glance at Thom. "It could serve for Broderick as well."

Thomas raised his glass of rum. Dr. Broderick reached over and clicked his own glass against his friend's. "To our families!" Thom offered.

"To our families," Matt returned the toast. And then to Samantha, "What is inside the locket, my dear? Won't you open it and see?"

Inside was a painted miniature of a handsome young man in a grey cadet's uniform with a high collar in dark trim. His visored cap was worn low, almost at the level of his eyebrows, and his gaze was steady and severe. His broad chest was accentuated by the long rows of buttons on his tunic.

"He looks quite fierce," Samantha said. And then added thoughtfully, "But at the same time he looks like someone you could depend on in a pinch."

"Well said, my dear," replied the proud father of the cadet.

"Why, goodness!" said Samantha, teasing. "That's our Bradford isn't it? Thank God he's on our side!"

Both men laughed appreciatively. Then Dr. Broderick added, "The picture was his idea. He wanted you to have it. But a miniature seemed so... what?" He searched for an appropriate word. "So, unadorned.

"So, I took the liberty of having the goldsmith fashion a locket. I wrote to Brad and told him what I was doing, and he suggested that I add the cameo from his mother's ring."

"I'm truly touched," Samantha said.

"I hope it was not presumptuous. But with Brad being at the Point and all, and no female visitors allowed. Well, I know how you, that is, how both of you felt... and I thought now that graduation is near... Well, you see... hurumph."

Samantha looked at the picture again. "He is quite handsome in the uniform," she said.

She had known Brad since she was a child. Although he always acted like an older brother, solicitous but distant, Samantha felt something more. She told him once when she was nine years old, "When I grow up I shall marry you!"

He had replied, "Dear Samantha, it's the man does the asking, you know. Even in this modern age."

Her answer was quick and to the point. "Then, I pray the day comes when you shall be bold enough to ask me!"

How casually and thoughtlessly we pray when we are children, Samantha thought.

"It seems so long since I've seen him," she said aloud. "Why he's become a real man, hasn't he?"

"And you're nigh on being a woman, Samantha," Dr. Broderick said. "Begging your pardon, Thom. I know fathers want their daughters to seem children forever.

"But I thought we might all go to the commencement in June. They'll be the ceremony, a rousing address by a noteworthy alumnus—maybe even General Scott—then the throwing of caps in the air. In the evening the Great Ball with the one who has been promised.

Happy, happy, happy pair!
None but the brave
None but the brave
None but the brave deserve the fair!

"Dryden, you know."

"Yes," said Samantha thoughtfully. "I remember, 'Alexander's Feast'."

"Indeed!" Dr. Broderick raised his thick eyebrows in surprise. "Quite so! Your knowledge does you credit. You'll be a fair companion for a gallant officer.

"Ah, Samantha," the doctor continued. "What a night that will be! The drums beating, the bugles sounding, then the Grand March of the cadets. *Eyes right*! and they'll pass us on the reviewing stand. The Stars and Stripes will be flying in the breeze. You're heart will do a little hand-stand then, I guess."

"And then as the sun goes down over the compound, you'll hear the men singing a verse or two of a wistful tune." Dr. Broderick leaned back in the heavy chair and sang in a deep baritone:

We'll bid farewell to cadet gray
And don the army blue.
Army blue, army blue
Hurrah for the army blue!
We'll bid farewell to cadet gray
And don the army blue.

"What a haunting melody!" Samantha said, gazing again at the picture in the locket. "It could almost be a love song, if you ignored the words."

Dr. Broderick and Mr. Browning exchanged knowing looks.

"See if Mrs. Crump is ready to serve dinner yet, Miss," said Mr. Browning. "That is, if you can tear yourself away from that handsome officer-to-be. I'm sure the good doctor is hungry. I know I am."

"Oh, Father," Samantha blushed and replied distractedly. "I was only thinking... Well," she said straightening her dress and regaining her composure. "Thank you for the wonderful locket. I shall write Bradford a note of gratitude for the picture and I shall say that I am looking forward to the Commencement Ball."

She went into the kitchen purposefully, leaving the men alone with their thoughts.

"Well!" said Dr. Broderick confidently.

"Well," said Mr. Browning more pensively.

"Seems like we had the right idea," Dr. Browning noted.

"Hmm, I don't know. I still think she may be a mite too young."

"Too young! Why Brad's barely twenty and he'll be going off to war!

"That's what I mean," said Mr. Browning.

"What? I don't get you."

"I don't mean she's too young to marry," Browning offered sadly. "But she does seem a bit young to be a widow."

Meanwhile, Samantha was helping Mrs. Crump gather the silver serving dishes and china to put in the dining room. All the while she hummed melodiously as she half-danced from the china closet to the dining room, to the kitchen and back again. Mrs. Crump could not resist a teasing remark.

"You seem quite enchanted by life today, my dear. Is it love?"

"Certainly not!" replied Samantha, with an imperious toss of her blond curls. "I'm just happy to see the doctor again. That's all."

"Did he bring you news of young Bradford?" Mrs. Crump persisted.

"Yes," Samantha replied. "It seems like he'll be an army officer in June," she added offhandedly, and then resumed her humming. *We'll bid farewellll to cay-dedt gray/And don the aar-mii blue!*

"What is that lovely tune you're humming, dear?" asked Mrs. Crump. "It sounds like a love song."

"No, it's not that," said Samantha reaching distractedly for the wine goblets. "It's not a love song."

But even as she said it, she was not sure in her young and changeable heart that was precisely true. He would make a handsome officer, and she smiled picturing herself in a white satin gown, her pale hand upon his blue tunic, the crossed swords of the young lieutenants gleaming above them, as they left the church as husband and wife.

CHAPTER 8

Tears and Apple Cider

Saturday morning was crisp and cold. The rooster's crow was a hard, clear sound which echoed across the courtyard. Frost sparkled on the grass, and the horse trough was covered with a thin pane of ice. In the stables Hezekiah was working quietly cleaning the stalls when Samantha came bustling in.

"I hear you back there," she called cheerily. "But I don't see you!"

Hezekiah looked over the half-door that separated the stall from the barn entrance. Samantha was wearing a full-length, brown woolen cape which fastenea at the front with a bronze clasp. She wore a brown bonnet with white trim. Her feet were shod in tooled leather boots. Hezekiah watched her as she undid the bonnet and shook out her golden curls. He watched the puffs of steam her breath made in the cool air.

"I know you're here!" Samantha called. "Now come on out!" She stamped her foot in mock anger on the straw-covered earth.

Hezekiah lifted the latch on the stall and stepped out with a sulk. He gazed at her feet.

"Here I am, Miss." He raised his eyes to her face pitifully. "Although, I suspect, it is not me yer lookin' for."

"Oh, Akley!" she yelped, placing both hands over her bosom. "Goodness! You startled me. You see, I was expecting..."

"Kevin, perhaps?" Hezekiah smiled suggestively.

"Well, I thought he might be grooming Napoleon. He does love my bay gelding, you know."

"It's a beautiful horse, Miss. That it is," admired Hezekiah looking over at the horse in the next stall.

"And Mr. Dillon told me, would you believe this, that he lived in a place in Ireland that had only one horse in the entire village! 'A one-horse town,' he called it. It seems there were several such. Yet, he works so well with horses, seems to communicate with them. So, I just thought..."

"Well, as you can see, he's not at it today. Would you like me to groom him for you, Miss?" asked Hezekiah.

"Well...," said Samantha pondered fingering the locket on the gold chain at her neck. "I suppose you could. That is, I don't suppose Kevin... um, that is, Mr. Dillon..."

"He's doing the milking today, Miss, and running a bit late, I'd say." Hezekiah didn't add that Kevin had been up to the early hours the night before, and had given Napoleon medicine and nursed him. Nor did he add that Kevin was in to check on the horse later this morning, or that Kevin had spent an hour combing and currying the bay before going off to do the milking.

"He's still got to fetch the eggs for Mrs. Crump," Hezekiah continued. "And then he has to clean out the roosting shed."

"Very well," Samantha replied with obvious annoyance. "You go ahead and do it. When you finish, saddle him for me as well. The bring him around to the front of the house. I'll be going riding later in the morning."

"Very good, Miss," replied Hezekiah tipping his cap with an air of both deference and contempt. She didn't even look in at her lovely horse, he thought to himself. That one's got something else on her mind.

Samantha was annoyed. She had hoped to see Kevin in the stables. She trusted Napoleon more with Kevin. She knew he felt genuine affection for the horse. She also hoped to flirt with Kevin a bit; maybe brag about her new locket. She had no other friend even close to her age with whom she could do that.

Hezekiah was her least favorite person to encounter before breakfast. Something about him, she thought. Something that disturbs. He seemed shy of her, and yet he sometimes gave her a bold look. He was obsequious, yet his manner barely hid contempt. It was as if he hated her and admired her at the same time. A mixture of feelings which perhaps even he didn't understand but which flashed across his features every time they spoke.

Up at the dairy barn she found Kevin sitting on a three-legged stool milking the last of the cows. Fourteen pails of milk were lined up in two rows on the far wall. "Pickles", the barnyard cat sat waiting for Kevin to spray a stream of milk at her, his usual practice after the last cow had been milked.

"Poor 'Pickles'," Samantha said. "She waits and waits with infinite patience."

"Aye," said Kevin without looking up. "She must be an Irish cat."

He continued his rhythmic motion and the milk sprayed in thin streams into the pail. "I haven't (squirt-squirt) seen you in (squirt-squirt) a few days (squirt-squirt)." His hands grasped the warty teats firmly and the cow lowed deeply with pleasure.

"Did you miss me, Kevin?" Samantha asked archly as he finished the milking and wiped his hands on this pants.

"You might say that. I haven't seen you since the doctor came to dinner. I've curried and groomed Napoleon four nights in a row now without so much as a look-in from you. I even slept with him one night when his breathing seemed a bit odd, and gave him some medicine to cure it. So, you might say you've been missed, and not just by me."

"Well, Napoleon and I shall go for a long ride today, and get re-acquainted. Besides it's only been four days. He'll have to learn to get used to my being gone. I won't be stuck on a farm forever."

"Where have you been then?" asked Kevin.

"Well, not that it's any of your business," said Samantha fingering the gold chain around her neck. "But I've been writing letters and looking at materials for a new dress. And then, of course, I've had several talks with our pastor, Mr. Martinsdale."

"Humph! And what's that thing around your neck?"

"It's not a *thing*, Mr. Ignoramus. It happens to be a finely crafted piece of jewelry fashioned by the Revere Shop from antique gold and ivory."

"I am sorry, Samantha, to show my ignorance." Kevin's voice softened. "And I apologize for my mouth. It's just that I... we... that is, Napoleon and I missed you."

"Very well," Samantha said primly. She came over and hugged him. "I forgive you. This time." She moved smoothly from the hug as Kevin's lips grazed her cheek, and patted his shoulder benevolently.

"You're a dear. It's just that I've been so busy and so happy these past few days. A whirl of events," she exclaimed, spinning on the straw as she spoke. "New clothes, a grand ball, invitations, plans to be made for June. Oh, Kevin, you haven't even asked to see what's inside the locket. Aren't you the tiniest bit curious? Look!"

She moved closer to Kevin. He could feel her warm breath on his face and smell the lilac water which scented her neck. He felt his stomach go soft and all his reserve melt away. He looked into her eyes with love, with adoration. But Samantha was talking away. She did not even glance up at him as opened the locket and displayed the miniature. He noted it briefly. A portrait of some kind. Confused and troubled, he returned his gaze to her eyes. Samantha's eyes glowed but with an enthusiasm which did not take him in.

"Isn't he wonderful! His name is Cadet Bradford Broderick, and he will graduate West Point in June. He will be a lieutenant then in the army. We will be married that same month in the First Congregational Church and his fellow officers will draw their swords as we leave the church and form a canopy of gleaming steel as we pass through. Isn't it exciting? I've always wanted a military wedding!"

Kevin nodded grimly. What could he have expected, after all? That a lady of her position would marry a hired hand? He looked again at the portrait of the young cadet in the locket. The differences between them were obvious. The high collar set off a proud chin. The face radiated health and self-confidence. Here was a man who knew where he was going and would rise to great heights in his society.

Suddenly, Kevin felt ashamed of his dung-covered boots, his milk-stained pants, and his torn and faded blue wool shirt. He felt like a dirty, ill-clad young boy, alone in a cold December night standing outside a great hall where ladies and handsome well-bred gentlemen danced to the strains of Mozart under crystal chandeliers. The young boy who had dreamed of one day being invited inside. But now the cold seeped into his bowels and he saw his own reflection in the glass. His ragged clothes, his uncombed hair, his pale hungry eyes. He would never be invited inside. How foolish he had been ever to think so.

Kevin knew now that no matter how long he stayed in this country, he would always be an outsider. The good land had already been taken, the social status already established, and the young ladies like Samantha long since spoken for.

"Aren't you happy for me, Kevin?" Samantha asked, oblivious to his feelings.

Kevin forced a smile. He closed the locket and kissed her hand.

Gallantly, he thought, moving a few paces back. It was as if he were not himself. As if he were someone else watching himself do these things.

"I wish you both well, Samantha," he heard himself saying. "I hope that you will be very happy together."

Samantha's cheeks flushed and her eyes brightened. Now she looked at him directly.

"Dear, dear Kevin. I shan't forget you. You gave me my first true kiss, you know." She smiled sincerely at him and took his hand. "And now you'll ever be my loyal friend, won't you?"

"That I will, Samantha."

"Forever, my dear Kevin," she said, her eyes brimming with tears.

"Forever," Kevin said, feeling his own eyes fill with the need to cry, but holding back, stifling his tears in pride.

When Samantha left, he let the tears come, streaming down his cheeks. He barely tasted their salt on his lips, the taste of gall was so bitter. His whole body shook in wrenching sobs. "Oh God", he cried. "Dear God, why must this be?" He buried his face in the straw so that no one could hear his cries, and his body rocked back and forth as if in pain.

For what Kevin had felt for Samantha these past few weeks was true. Make no mistake about that. Older folk might have called it "infatuation" or "puppy love." Adults create terms like these, verbal fictions, as a way of distancing themselves from emotions too disturbing to re-experience. They have settled into a less intense life and such youthful memories (if they still have them) are best disparaged, if they cannot be negated altogether. For if they should affirm them, no wife, no husband, would ever be satisfied. Because there is no love like that first awakening when one comes unknowing in the full energy of adolescent passion and confusion, in innocence and in trembling, to be consumed by a fever so that one's body aches with love, one's mind is preoccupied with love, and the whole world shines, glows, and reveals in transcendent beauty the reflection of one's love.

This love of youth, this first innocent love, should never be taken lightly. For, though mocked or ignored in adulthood, it is the love that is remembered most clearly in the cold days of old age, when the hair is gray and the face wrinkled. It is the memory of this passion that warms the heart and gives charm and grace, and sometimes even new beauty, to the face of an old man or woman.

And when that love has been offered freely, completely, and then rejected—Oh, the pain! The heart-wrenching despair that falls upon the one left behind. Then life seems at its bleakest. It is the deepest, grayest of all Decembers, and the light from the sun is too frail to offer any hope at all. One's heart has shriveled up inside and one feels small, inconsequential. One is indifferent to life outside, to the meow of the cat still hoping for a stream of milk, or the contented cows lowing in the barn at ease with their lives. They are one and the same because one cannot see them or hear them through the tears and the blind desolation.

At no other time in life is one as truly alone as when one's heart is first broken. All is dismal; all is desolate. All is irretrievably lost forever. Life is without joy, or hope. It is merely a long dark tunnel with no light, no gleam or hint of a better tomorrow.

CHAPTER 9

Drink to me Only With Thine Eyes

Hezekiah found Kevin in the barn sitting by the full milk cans. His eyes were dry but red-rimmed, and dirt streaked his face. Wisely, Hezekiah, made no comment on his appearance.

"Mrs. Crump needs a couple of these pails up at the house for breakfast," he said picking up the milk.

Kevin nodded indifferently. "Fine. I'm just going to sit here a bit and think. I'm not hungry."

Hezekiah's sharp eyes took in Kevin's forlorn appearance.

"I know just what you need, old Kevin. And I think I won't be eating breakfast myself this morning. Do ya know why?"

When no answer was forthcoming, Hezekiah continued.

"I've got two gallons of hard cider hidden down by the lily pond in the bush. I intend to get good and drunk today, and food would just take the edge off the booze. Miss Samantha is going off for a long ride on Napoleon, and Mr. B is off to Boston. So, they'll be no one to check on us for the next few hours. What do ya say, my friend? Are ya up for a good drunk?"

Kevin looked up. His mouth shaped itself into a tight grin.

"Damn me, Heck! Sometimes you have the most brilliant ideas. Two gallons! Why, you bet I'm up for getting drunk! I can't think of any single thing I'd much rather do, as a matter of fact. I'd like to get fallin' down drunk, don't-give-a hoot-drunk, tear-up-the-pea-patch drunk!"

"Well, I'm yer man then, Kevin," Hezekiah grinned back. "Ye can't keep an Irish down long 'specially when there's a drink offered. Right, boy?"

An hour later, Mr. Browning's carriage passed down by the river. Before leaving, he gave the boys instructions to cut two cords of firewood from the wood lot. Instead, they came up on the far side of the woods and watched his carriage disappear down the road. Then they walked down to where a small freshwater pond was fed by a spring hidden by marsh grass. The air was clear; the sky a startling, brilliant blue.

The water from the spring ran fast and cold over ice-covered rocks. A few yards away up on a bank, Hezekiah pulled away a covering of branches at the base of a large elm to reveal two wicker baskets. Each contained a gallon jug stopped with a cork.

"Here they are my friend!" he shouted to Kevin, holding the jugs up like trophies. "Teeth-aching cold but warm in the old breadbasket. The best hard apple cider in the sovereign Commonwealth of Massachusetts. You get the first taste," he said, coming down the bank and squatting at the base of an old birch tree.

Kevin grabbed one of the jugs and bit off the cork. He hooked the handle with his thumb and titled the jug back. The cider was sweet and cold like apple juice but, within seconds, he felt the warm glow of the alcohol as it hit his stomach and the warmth rose to his head. His face flushed and his toes tingled. He emitted a deep, "oooh-ahh" of both pleasure and astonishment and then started to return the jug to Hezekiah.

Hezekiah waved it back.

"Git yerself a good pull at it, Kevin. There's plenty more where that came from."

Kevin took another deep draught, then passed it on. "Where did you get this anyway?" Kevin asked. "Did you steal it from old man Browning?

"Naw," the other replied, taking a deep and satisfying drink and then passing it back. "I try not to steal from the old man. He's pretty sharp; counts damn near every hen's egg. I just gathered windfalls every chance I got. And I saved the bruised and wormy apples he wouldn't leave go into the cider press. Then when we had warm days, well... I got a bit of leaven out of the pantry, squeezed up a couple o' gallons of juice, dropped in the leaven and left it to work in the sun. It stopped working as soon as it dipped cold.

"Course there's dead flies and old worms and skeeters in it, maybe a beetle or two!" He laughed as Kevin paused in mid-tilt. "But the alcohol kills them so they won't hurt ya! Bet ya never thought when we were out in that damn orchard pickin' every day, that ye'd have this as a bonus. What a pain all that pickin' and pressin' is, especially when it goes to someone else's cider. Do ye remember them prickly afternoons were worked out there, with the bees abuzzin', and the damn ladder..."

Kevin remembered well the week they were picking apples out in the lower orchard. He remembered the tall ladders and the large wicker baskets. He remembered Samantha's eyes looking up at him as he picked in the high branches in the green-gold of the dappled light. He remembered the rich autumn odors of burning leaves and fallen apples, the hum of bees, and the cool breeze from the wood lot. He remembered thanking God for all his blessings. He had never been so happy.

Samantha wore a wreath she had fashioned of branches and leaves and wildflowers. She danced in and out of the trees until Mr. Browning came and told her that she was distracting the boys from their work. In fact, this was not true. Both Heck and he were picking as fast as they could in competition to show Samantha which one was the best. They had probably done more in fifteen minutes than most men could do in an hour. But now, watching her walk away, they were distracted, each in his own way. The work for the rest of the afternoon was desultory and forced.

"Yeah," Hezekiah said. "I can still feel the shape of the ladder on the soles of my feet."

"Remember how Samantha danced that day?" Kevin asked. It was more a reverie than a question and he smiled in recollection.

Hezekiah smiled, too. A quiet, satisfied smile. He remembered all right. He remember her dancing beneath the trees, her thin sun dress and petticoat clinging to her thighs, bare arms shining with a golden fuzz. He remembered her eyes heavy-lidded with the warm sun and the hypnotic flow of the dance. He remembered how her lips parted over her bright teeth as she breathed in the apple-sweet air. And he remembered his promise to himself.

"Did you ever..." he asked Kevin as they started in on the second jug.

"Did you ever, you know, shag her?"

Anger flashed quickly in Kevin's eyes, and then died in a confusion of loss, of pain, of sorrow. These were quickly replaced though the alchemy of fermented drink into the warm rush of comraderie for Hezekiah who was, after all, a fellow laborer, just a little ignorant, but not too selfish to share his jug.

"Huh? Shag? Oh, I gotcha," Kevin blushed as he guessed the meaning of the strange word. "No, I never did. She was savin' it, I guess for something finer. And now she's goin' to be engaged to some army lieutenant."

"An officer, pshew," spit Hezekiah. "Well, wadda ya expect? Too fancy by far for the likes of us. Oh sure, we're good enough to curry her horse, or to place her delicate foot in the stirrups. We're good enough to feed her damn cat or be an audience for her silly dancin'."

"Yer right, bucko," agreed Kevin. "Seesh too good for the like of ush."

"And what is she, anyhow?" Hezekiah continued. "A little snit of a thing. Miss High and Mighty. What's she got beneath them petticoats that any Crazy Jane or Sally the Fishwife don't have?"

Kevin leaned back against the peeling birch tree. His mind floated in and out of Heck's words, Ah well, he thought. Women were more trouble than they were worth. That's for damn sure. This was the life. Out in the woods with an old pal. A cool bubbling stream close by. The pond with its shiny coat of new ice. But, how could there be ice when it was so warm?

He licked his lips enjoying the thick taste in his mouth and remembered the autumn taste of crisp apples after working a morning in the field. He loved the warm, contented feeling in his belly which spread throughout his limbs, befuddled the sea of worry, and freed him of all care.

With Hezekiah, alcohol did not have the same soporific effect. His cerebral cortex was dulled and his higher thinking skills, never more than rudimentary, withered away. What remained, hard and clear was his snake brain. The primordial brain stem, the first evolutionary beginning of bestial instinct and urgings. And the more he drank, the less inhibited this snake brain became. He became fearless, unchecked by society or mores, by job or duty, feelings of gratitude or human sympathy.

He had not yet formed a clear idea of what he would do. He could not think that far ahead. He only knew that an opportunity would present itself and, when it did, he would be ready.

Meanwhile Samantha had ridden over the fields and out to the far side of town. She galloped Napoleon over the hard earth and the horse, pleased to have his head and his freedom after so many days in the barn, moved smoothly over the half-frozen fields. Samantha felt more free that she had ever felt in her life. She enjoyed the hard muscles of the stallion under her thighs. The sense of power, moving the animal this way or that with just a flick of the reins, filled her with pleasure. She finally slowed him to a canter and then a walk as they approached the Charles River Bridge. She dismounted and led Napoleon down to the side of the bridge to drink from the swift-flowing current. She watched the river flow toward the sea and thought about the months ahead.

Perhaps she would be leaving on a sea voyage to join her husband when the army moved to other camps. She once heard New Orleans mentioned as a place where there were large numbers of troops. She imagined walking the cobblestone streets of the Creole city, on the arm of a handsome officer. Her dress would be the latest Paris fashion and the envy of the other women. She imagined the romantic military balls, meeting colonels and generals, maybe even senators. The evenings of champagne and walks in the cool gardens under the eucalyptus and Spanish moss. She could taste the soft kiss which became ever more passionate, until her husband swept her into his arms. Then the slow moonlight carriage ride home, and... the canopied brass bed with the deep quilts. Ah, what would it be like? she wondered. Would he be a gentle lover?

She called Napoleon and gave a tug on his reins. She leaned her head against his muzzle and felt the soft delicacy of his ears. Slowly she mounted and when she had gained her seat, she tightened her knees against his flanks. They wheeled and galloped off in the direction of home.

Kevin and Hezekiah were singing the last in a series of songs about drinking, and gambling, bad ladies and lost loves. The sun had passed the meridian over two hours before as they traded back and forth, with Kevin supplying an Irish tune for each of Hezekiah's rambunctious American ones. Hezekiah, surprisingly, had an impressive repertoire.

"Just remember the chorus," Hezekiah said, laughing. "The other words are too hard to remember. I just know them cuz my ole Pa used to sing them." Hezekiah took up the tune in a lugubrious baritone:

> By the fierce flames of love I'm in a sad taking
> I'm singed like a pig that is hung up for bacon,
> My stomach is scorched like an over done mutton-chop
> That for want of gravy won't afford a single drop.

Okay, Kevin, now the chorus!

Love, love, love is like a dizziness
Won't let a poor man go about his business.

They both laughed and then took another slug from the bottom few inches of the second jug.

"Well, thish ish about gone. What will we do about moum smore, uh shom more?" asked Kevin.

"Don't worry," replied Hezekiah, eyeing his friend carefully. He did not think Kevin would be able to handle any more, but he did not say that. "There's plenty more," he said cavalierly. "As a matter of fact, you finish the rest of this."

"Are ye sure?" asked Kevin. "Are you per-fek-illy shh-sure?"

"That I am," replied Hezekiah.

"Well, sing some more of dat tune, about the lad what lost his love. Sing shum more o' dat. Sounds like my damn story."

Hezekiah complied as Kevin took another deep draught from the jug and lean back against the birch.

My great toes and little toes are burnt to a cinder
A hot burning glass burns a dish-cloth to tinder,
As cheese by a hot salamander is roasted,
By beauty that's red-hot, like a cheese am I toasted.
Love, love, love is like a dizziness,
Won't let a poor man go about his business.

He looked down at Kevin who had begun to snore with his mouth open. He nudged him gently with his boot. No response. He gave him a more substantial kick. Still no movement, other than a brief interruption of the snore which almost immediately resumed.

"Kevin, my friend, is there any drop left at all in the jug?" He snatched the jug out of Kevin's lifeless hand and drained the last few drops. "Sleep well, ya dumb Mick," he said. "Don't freeze to death out here in the woods.

"By this one and t'other, I'm treated uncivil," Hezekiah sang to himself. "Like a gizzard I'm peppered and then made a devil! Love, love, love is like a dizziness. Won't let a poor man go about his business."

He stumbled once or twice on his way back across the woodlot. But by the time he had reached the horse stables he was steady and coldly clear in his intent. All he needed now was opportunity and time.

When she came he would wait until she had the horse in its stable and then he would appear and offer to unsaddle it and cool it down. She would agree, of course, and when she turned to walk away he would grab her from behind and drag her over to the haystack on the side. She might let out a scream or two but the hay would muffle her cries. That, and the sound of the horses. But, if he had to make her completely and eternally silent before he had his way with her, he'd do that, too.

They were far enough away from the house that Mrs. Crump wouldn't hear. The old man was still in town. And Kevin, the dumb Mick was passed out at the lily pond. Typical Irish. Can't handle the liquor.

Afterwards, if she was still breathing, he would finish her. Then he would knock over the lantern by the tack room, and set the place ablaze.

He would be trying to rescue the livestock when Mrs. Crump arrived. He might, in fact, rescue the horses—which would make him a hero of sorts. But he would not have known about the girl, how could he? He had thought she was out riding. He had been chopping timber up in the woods and never heard her come back. Poor Samantha, and just as she was to become engaged to her fine officer! What a terrible tragedy.

Hezekiah knew about fires. He knew how they covered evidence. He knew when his father raised his hand against him, for the last time, and Hezekiah plunged the knife into his stomach, that nothing would be proved.

He knew when he silenced his mother's screams that Dr. Broderick would not find a trace of violence when he examined the charred bodies All cooked away, so to speak. The death of his two sisters could not be helped. He had thought of going upstairs for them but the fire was already out of control. Besides, I saved them the hard life of being orphans which, Hezekiah thought to himself, is a fate I wouldn't wish on a dog.

Hezekiah was strong from his work in the fields. He needed no weapon besides his oversized arms. Carefully, carefully, he thought, flexing his large hands. As long as I don't bash her skull, or break any bones, they'll never know. The fire will cover a multitude of sins.

He lay back against Napoleon's empty stall to fantasize just what various forms those sins would take. *Ah, yer don't like it, my fine Miss? Well, just pretend I'm yer bloody lieutenant just back from the wars!*

CHAPTER 10

Dung Beetles and Bloody Stripes

Among the steaming horse-droppings in the stables crawled a silent dung beetle. With his shiny back armored against most enemies, he moved single-mindedly about his business. His front claw-like appendages seized the hot dung. Greedily, he pulled apart succulent morsels to devour.

In ancient Egypt this beetle was sacred for reasons which remain locked in the unwritten sands of ancient history. The sacred scarab, the gold bug of Mr. Poe, which feeds on dung and breeds in the dark corners of barns and stables, has secrets which have not been plumbed in this age. Most do not want to look at it too closely, and who could blame them?

The beetle passed where Hezekiah was nodding sleepily. The beetle was aware of him peripherally but felt no fear. And Hezekiah, hearing the dry rustling of the insect, looked down at it out of the corner of his eye. Hezekiah was not averse to killing things, or even applying the most exquisite torture to flies, to captured mice, even to the litters of kittens which he was sometimes ordered to dispose of humanely. These latter he would often soak in kerosene and then light afire.

But the scarab beetle was something different. In it, Hezekiah recognized a dark and terrible force quite akin to his own, although he could not have said so. The single-minded persistence of the beetle, who would take his food and his love wherever he found it, even in the dark recesses of the stables or the barn. Crawling steadily, blindly, up over one hump of offal to another, searching, always searching for what a deep, primordial instinct told him to devour. To a reflective man, this might have seemed symbolic. It might indeed have given him a hint of why the Egyptians represented this creature in jewelry, in sculpture. Why it was found in so many tombs of ancient Pharaohs. But, for Hezekiah, no reflection was involved. He did not squash the beetle as he was wont to do with any ordinary bug. He let it crawl up his hand, looked at it carefully, and then allowed it to plod safely away to the darkness and the ordure of the stables.

Outside the barn the sun approaching winter solstice lost its final angle of inclination by the pond and slipped behind the trees. A cold, easterly wind began, carrying with it a breath of snow. The flakes fell softly on the lily pond without a sound. Further back in the salt marsh they hissed as they struck the water, and the marsh grass swayed in the breeze. Kevin stirred with the cold, scrunched his body up into a fetal position, and continued to sleep in the dreamless fashion of a young man drunk for the first time.

Samantha, catching a snowflake on her tongue, reined up her beloved Napoleon and looked at the sky. It had turned quite gray, and what sun remained was the color of weak lemon and fading quickly. The snow, falling so gently, so singly in small flakes, indicated a storm of considerable size and duration. The temperature dropped. A wind blew from the north-east, so she drew her cape tighter around her shoulders and urged her horse back to the farm. The horse needed little urging. He was hungry, tired, and anxious for the warmth of the stables. Only the tight rein of his mistress had kept him calm thus far. Now, given his head, he galloped gladly back across the fields, down the post road and up to the farm.

When Napoleon and Samantha clattered into the courtyard, Hezekiah came fully alert. The alcoholic haze completely left him, and his mind was clear with a predatory lucidity. His senses were fully alert. His blood flowed steadily and his heart beat rhythmically. He thought again about a weapon but then decided he didn't need it. She would do what he said. If not, his hands were sufficient.

Samantha dismounted and led the bay gelding into the stables. She talked softly to it as she walked ahead holding the reins.

"Good boy, Napoleon. Good, boy! You've given me an excellent ride. Now, we shall get you warmed up and fed, if I can find one of those foolish boys about."

"Here, Miss!" Hezekiah called as he appeared from behind the last stall. "Do you need a hand?"

"Goodness, Hezekiah, you've startled me again," Samantha cried, backing away from the sound of his voice. Napoleon whinnied and pricked his ears in Hezekiah's direction.

"If Kevin here, then?" Samantha asked.

"No, Miss. He's still back in the woodlot finishing up a job for your father."

"Very well, then," Samantha said. "Take his saddle off and dry him down real well. Then clean the saddle up with neat's-foot oil. I'm afraid it got a bit wet from the snow. After you've groomed him and rested him a bit, feed him some oats and water him."

"Yes, Miss. As you say, Miss," Hezekiah said as he unhitched the saddle and placed it on its wooden frame. He took the bit out of the horse's mouth, and pulled the harness from around his ears. The horse went by himself into the stall.

Hezekiah's removed the two saddle blankets which were wet from perspiration and the melted snow. He threw them up over the stall brace to dry and put a larger, dry blanket over the horse.

"You've been riding him hard, Miss," Hezekiah said matter-of-factly.

Samantha who had taken off her snow-covered cape and hung it on a tack hook, was now untying her bonnet. It, too, was snow-covered. The tendrils of hair damp with the melting snow curled prettily around her neck.

"Why," she said with genuine concern. "Is there anything wrong with him?"

"Well," said Heck, improvising his plan as he spoke. "There might be at that. Perhaps you'd better come take a look."

Samantha came into the stall, her defenses down, tired after the day's ride, and genuinely concerned about the condition of her favorite horse.

"The back leg, Miss. Take a look."

As Samantha bent down to have a look at where Heck pointed, he grabbed her awkwardly from behind. His lunge was sudden and brutal. Intoxicated once by the hard cider, he was intoxicated once again by the smell of her damp hair, by the silk rustling of her petticoat, by the golden tendrils at the back of her neck. He put his lips close to her ear.

"Now then, Miss, not a sound, I warn you. Just be very quiet and easy like and we'll..."

Samantha did not hear a word he said. At the first touch she was repulsed and then angered. Rage easily overwhelmed whatever fear she might have felt. She turned to face him, spitting out the words.

"You filthy, nasty animal! You get your hands off me!" She pushed him in the chest and he was forced backward. Napoleon whinnied and tossed his head. His rear hooves banged against the back wall of the stall.

Hezekiah, oblivious to her words or to the movements of the horse grabbed her wrist. He knew only one thing. He had finally made his move after so many months of waiting and fantasizing. There was no turning back. She was here, alone with him in the barn. The smell of her, the warmth of her body, the sensual rustling of silk and brocade filled up his senses. Even the sound of her voice, regardless of what was said, urged him on in a blind, inexplicable fury. It was not sex so much that he wanted. What he desired was to rip her fancy clothes off, to reduce her to a level lower than his, to have her there in the steaming muck of the stables, to tear out the soul and the will of her, and leave her battered and bleeding on the straw.

He grabbed her wrist and pulled her to him. Neither could hear what the other said. He could not hear Samantha's cold curses, nor could she hear his ugly words of lustful rage. But the horse knew, as horses do know these things, and Napoleon kicked out again, this time more accurately. His left rear hoof caught Hezekiah a solid blow on the thigh. Although it did not break the bone, it was sufficient to drop Hezekiah to his knees. Samantha tore out of his grasp, ripping her dress in the process, then ran out of the stall and into the arms of her father.

"Whoa, whoa! What, what is it, my love? I heard your cries and came just as soon..."

Mr. Browning heard Hezekiah moaning, trying to crawl out of the stall. The horse had already kicked him twice more, opening a cut on his cheekbone just below the eye, and again in the chest knocking the wind out of him. He would have run from Mr. Browning, but he was barely able to crawl.

A look at his daughter's ripped dress, the tears of anger and frustration teaming down her face, gave Mr. Browning all the answer he needed.

He dragged the whimpering Hezekiah out of the stall and threw him up against a post. He took a length of rawhide and tied the boy's hands securely to the beam. Then, after calming the horse who was still kicking against the walls of the stall, he picked up a large braided bullwhip from a hook on the tack room wall.

"I should just kill ye, ye rotten excuse for humanity. But when I'm finished with this, ye'll wish ye were dead."

He laid out the whip it's full length and then cracked it in the air.

"Samantha, ye'd better go back up to the house."

"No, father," Samantha said grimly. "I will stay. It was my honor he tried to steal. It is only fitting that I witness his punishment."

"It will be ugly, my girl," Mr. Browning warned. "You best go to the house."

"No uglier, Father, than what my life would have been like if he had his way with me."

"Well said, daughter." Mr. Browning looked at his daughter with new-found understanding and respect. She'll make a fine army wife, he thought proudly.

"Well, then. Let's have at it! I'll save a few strokes for you to give as well, my girl. It's only fitting that you should lay a few stripes on the back of him that attacked ye!"

The whip flashed through the air and ripped off Hezekiah's shirt. A large red welt appeared on his back. He screamed.

The whip came down again and again. Hezekiah's screams were high-pitched and girlish. He blubbered and begged. But Mr. Browning's strokes were accurate and steady. Never did a stroke land more than a few inches from the preceding one, so that the skin broke and then peeled off in long bloody strips.

Hezekiah turned once against his bindings trying to escape, and the whip tore across his groin. His bloodcurdling scream could be heard all the way to the lily pond. He vomited a spume of sour apple cider. He did not try turning his back away a second time.

Kevin awakened at the foot of the birch tree. He was covered with snow and shivering. The woods had grown darker and the snow was coming down steadily, small cold flakes blown by the northeasterly storm. He thought he had heard a scream off in the distance. A strange sound, high-pitched, almost feminine, and yet it did not seem like the cry of a girl.

He rubbed his hands briskly together. Where was Hezekiah? he wondered. He found the two empty jugs and checked each of them to see if any liquor remained. He had a pounding headache and his limbs seemed encased in lead.

He drank off the dregs of the second jug, but felt no hint of the warmth it had given earlier.

He stretched his legs and then windmilled his arms to get some feeling and warmth back in them. He cracked the thin patina of ice on the shallow creek and drank deep breathless gulps of the frigid water. Slightly restored to a semblance of humanity, he buttoned up his jacket and headed back across the wood lot to the farm. He tripped two or three times for, despite the cold and the long sleep, he was still significantly drunk.

Hezekiah had passed through pain and out the other side. His back was a soggy pudding of blood and straw and ripped skin. The bindings had raised deep welts on his wrists; his face and chest were covered with vomit and splattered with blood. But his mind had reached back again to that clear space; the cold snake brain which moved steadily, primordially toward a place it knew.

Mr. Browning, his face flushed, perspiration streaming down his cheeks from the exertion, handed the whip to his daughter.

"Give him one or two, daughter, that he may be reminded ever of the humiliation of this day."

Hezekiah turned his head. He spoke clearly through teeth gritted against the pain.

"I hope yer saving some of that for the Irish. For ye see, Master, he got what I only hope for. He had his slick Irish hands all over our little Mistress here and..."

"What, what is that, ye say?" asked Mr. Browning.

But before Hezekiah could elaborate, Samantha had cracked the whip over his head. The next blow caught Hezekiah high over the cheek, near the spot where the horse had kicked him, and cut the eye. Samatha slashed and cut carelessly, furiously, until her father seized the whip from her.

"Enough daughter, ye shall not kill him! He has been punished sufficiently."

"Now," he said looking into her eyes for the answer. "Was there any truth in what he said about the Irish lad?"

"He's a lying, nasty, despicable piece of trash!" Samantha screamed, trying to get the whip back from her father.

"And yet," said the father finding his answer in her eyes, "I think, there was some truth in him at that."

Mr. Browning held the whip sadly in his hand. Suddenly, he felt old, defeated. For, although tears streamed down her face, Samantha raised her chin defiantly. She felt no shame.

"It was not like that, Father. You don't understand. It was only a kiss. A little kiss, no more. And, that's been long since over."

The barn door opened and Kevin staggered in.

"Why, what's all this then?" Kevin asked bewildered.

"I was giving your co-worker a taste of the whip, Dillon," Mr. Browning said recovering his will and aware of a new rush of anger.

"It seems I should have saved a bit of it for you as well."

Kevin lurched and then straightened himself. He saw the bloody mess that was Hezekiah over in the corner. He looked at Samantha crying and was puzzled.

"We only had a few drinks," Kevin replied, still not guessing at the enormity of what had occurred.

"You'll get off my property and out of Cambridge now," Browning growled. "If you're found within ten miles of here, I'll have ye horsewhipped to an inch of your life, and then I'll have ye put into prison. Do ye hear me?"

He struck Kevin on the face with the handle of the whip knocking him against the door of the stable. As he raised his hand to deliver the second blow, Samantha jumped between them.

"No, Father, please. He's done nothing."

Enraged, Mr. Browning violently pushed his daughter away. Kevin raised his fist and, putting every fiber of every muscle he had developed in the months of farm work into the blow, cracked Mr. Browning on the chin.

The old man dropped like a stunned steer in the slaughter pen.

"Oh, Kevin, you've done it now!" Samantha cried.

"Oh, Father! I'm sorry. I'm so sorry!" She bent and cradled her father's head in her hands.

Kevin stood dumbfounded. He still did not guess at the cause of all this violence and anger. Surely, a couple of lads having a drink on a Saturday afternoon...

"Get out, Kevin, before he comes to. If he finds you here, he'll kill you or worse. Get well away from this farm, get out of Cambridge, cross the river. Forget that you ever knew this place."

"But, Samantha," Kevin muttered. "Surely..".

"Now, Kevin! Before he awakes. Don't you see? It's all been spoiled. You can live in this place no more."

Kevin remembered his mother telling him back in County Kerry to stay way from strong drink. 'There is only death and ruination in it,' she said. If this first experiment with John Barleycorn was any indication, Kevin thought, my mother was righter than rain.

Outside the snow already lay in drifts against the stables. The dry snow whipped by the wind felt like tiny razors against the deep welt on his cheek. His head had cleared and he was sober now. Angry, too, and feeling sorry for himself. He had no friends, no relatives, nowhere to go.

He looked over at the warm lights of the house, thought of the rich odors of Mrs. Crump's kitchen, pulled his collar up around his neck, and headed out into the storm.

CHAPTER 11

Christmas Gambol Oft Could Cheer

The snow lay in thick folds upon the elm trees and covered Boston Common in a flawless white quilt. Kevin's toes were numb and his boots soaked through as he walked beneath the trees. Two grackles chided him, following from tree to tree, as if to say: *You don't belong! Go on! Go on!*

He stumbled down the hill to where a path had been worn through the snow from Sunday idlers.

His stomach growled with an imperious vacuity as he approached the stand of roasting chestnuts. The smoke from the brazier hung in a gray-blue cloud in the air. Beneath this man-made cloud was a mustachioed Italian calling out his wares in a pleasant voice.

"Commma one, commma two, get them right away. Hot chestnuts hot, to warm up your day! A bag for da muff, one for da glove, too. A third one to take for da strolling and chew!"

People in their Sunday best, especially couples, stopped and purchased the paper cones of roasted chestnuts from the pleasant man who smiled broadly under his large woolen cap.

Kevin approached surreptitiously from the side so that he might warm his hands near the brazier.

"Here now, boy!" roared the vendor. "Get ya feelthy hands away." He grabbed Kevin by his arm. "What you try to steal from an old man, ha?"

"No, sir!" replied Kevin startled and stepping back, trying to squirm out of the man's grasp. "I wasn't trying to steal anything, honest. I was just trying to get my hands warm."

"Go to work then. Go get some work, ha! That's what will get you warm, huh! Get da muscles move and the blood a flow." He punctuated each of these remarks by squeezing Kevin's arm.

"Could you use some help, sir," Kevin asked meekly. "I could help you sell, maybe. Or I could use the tongs to get the chestnuts out."

"This is a one man operation, boy. It barely gives me da living. But I tell what what I do." He turned away briefly to serve a young man in a black frock coat accompanied by a pale women bundled in furs.

"Yes a sir. One pence, only. Two!" he said handing him the two paper cones of chestnuts. "One a for you and one a for the pretty lady."

Now, turning back to Kevin, he said sympathetically. "Do you have a hankerchief or a piece a rag?"

Kevin pulled a species of the latter out of his back pocket. The vendor told him to hold it open, and then dropped in four roasted chestnuts hot from the brazier.

"That will keep ya hands warm, *figlio mio*. And when dey cool a bit, dey will warm your insides, too. Now off with ya. Ya too young to be abeggin' in the park. Take a walk past da Frog Pond there, and go out to Beacon Street. Look alive, now!" the old man smiled. "*Va sano*! You might find one could use da hand shovellin' da rigs out of da snow, or hauling out da ashes. To work, *chi va forte*!"

"Thank you, sir!" Kevin said. "I'm beholden to you."

The warmth of the chestnuts revived him, but even more so the generosity and kindness of the Italian vendor. He felt tears come to his eyes. They were not tears of self-pity or despair, though. They were tears of gratitude that such good people lived in the world. He would remember this moment, he said to himself. He would remember that amid the hatred and prejudice, the cold and the indifference, there was still the generous heart, one which would see pain and relieve it, see fear and banish it, see sadness and respond with kindness and a smile.

Walking up Beacon Street he peeled one of the chestnuts and nibbled it. It had a somewhat bitter taste, like tannin, and he was tempted to spit it out. But he forced himself to swallow. He felt his stomach turn, and then settle. He ate two more which tasted sweeter and, though intending to savor the last one, he swallowed it hungrily. It was delicious.

He looked up as he licked his lips. 'Joy Street', read the sign. Surely that was a omen, Kevin thought. Surely, it would be lucky. He turned at Joy and Beacon and had gone halfway up the street when he saw an old woman carrying two overladen buckets of coal ashes out to the walk. She paused halfway to the street to rest. She wore a tattered blue dress that had seen better days and her thin red hair was covered with a red kerchief.

"Well, what in the name of Jasus and all the Apostles are ye lookin' at, ye leetle guthersnipe? Give us a hand here, can't ye? Jasus, Mary and Joseph, is there not a gentleman left in Boston?"

On closer examination, Kevin saw that she was not as old as she looked. Her pale skin was grimed with coal dust, but her blue eyes were lively and humorous. Thin, but wiry, and much the worse for labor. Kevin guessed she was probably in her twenties. Though not exactly good looking, she had an energy which was not unattractive

Kevin relieved her of the buckets and carried them over to the curb.

"Sure, me ol' man has got the curse of a hangover again," she confided to Kevin. "Whiskey will be the death of 'im. Do ye know why the Good Lord created whiskey, bucko?" she asked with a twinkle in her pale blue eyes.

"No," said Kevin. "That I don't know."

"So, the Irish wouldn't conquer the world," the woman laughed, a deep rich laugh that was infectious. Kevin laughed too, and she crinkled up her eyes. "So the Irish wouldn't conquer the world," she repeated again in the manner of her kind, since it had done so well the first time.

Her teeth were yellowed from the pipe. And Kevin could smell the whiskey on her, too. But the laugh lines around her eyes and her bold glance were refreshing to him. He lingered by the ash cans.

"So, you're Irish," Kevin said.

"What else would I be hauling ashes, burning garbage, scrubbing marble steps and shovelling snow from the walk. Not one of the Beacon Hill ladies out for me mornin' constitooshional!" She stepped closer to him.

Kevin laughed and moved back a step. She put her hand on the sleeve of his shirt and tugged him forward.

"Come 'er, bucko," she cajoled. "What's yer name, then?"

"Dillon," he said. "Kevin Dillon."

"Ah, I knew ye was one o' us. Yev got the map o'Ireland on yer face. County Cork, is it?"

"Kerry," Kevin said. "County Kerry."

"Wisha! Of course, didn't I say to myself when I saw ye coming up the road. There's a Kerryman. Not a penny in his pocket. If ye was a Corkman ye'd have some coins in yer pocket. But, I'll bet ye've naught but the rags on yer back."

Kevin nodded sadly.

"What, naught in yer pocket, then!" said the woman snatching at Kevin's pants with a leer. "Naught in yer pants?"

Kevin blushed. But meaning to push her hand away, he only made it worse and turned a casual touch into a caress. The woman smiled.

"Sure, as ye be a Kerryman, ye've got that all right. Ye've got somethin' there to blush about, hey!"

"Aren't you married?" said Kevin.

"Who said that! Oh, for the sake of my employmint with the High and Mighty, I am that. But how in the world could Kate Sullivan, kitchen helper, afford to pay a priest to hook 'er up with Patrick Casey, full-time reprobate and part-time footman? Married! God save us. Ye talk like ye just came from the Jesuit seminary. Where did ye come from anyway?"

"Ah, never mind that," she continued. "We'll go back to what's beneath them wool pants to blush at! I'm reminded of the story of the Kerryman and the Corkman who met on a bridge. One side of the bridge was in Kerry, the other side in Cork. Ye see, each spring the county councils would repair their own half of the bridge. But the six feet directly in the middle of the bridge, well, the Corkmen—always trying to save a shilling—said twas not their responsibility. Finally, the center part of the bridge became so weak it was dangerous, and the Kerrymen had a meeting of their council.

"Well," she went on, "some argued for repairing it; some argued against. Each councilman expressing his view. Finally, an old man named Dillon—maybe a relative of yours?" she said with a wink. "Anyway, this fine old oak tree of a man stood up. 'Put an end to yer blatherin', says he'. Yer worse than the old skinflints in Cork. What all this giff about a few damn feet of bridge anyway. Let's just fix it and be done. Why the fookin' section's so small, I could piss halfway across it!"

"The head of the council banged his gavel. 'Yer out of order!' he shouted. 'Yer out of order, Mr. Dillon!'

"'Of course, I'm out of order,' replied Dillon. 'If I wasn't out of order, I could piss the whole way across it!'"

Kevin was surprised into a burst of laugher and Kate joined in. He laughed so hard that his eyes began to water. Tears in my eyes, twice in the same morning. And both times for joy, he thought. It must be my luck's changing. He smiled at Kate with a mixture of wonder and delight.

She smiled back and pinched his cheek.

"There's me bucko!" she exclaimed pinching his cheek. "That's an Irish smile that will brighten up any colleen's heart, and maybe put a few pence in yer pocket as well. But fur now, go along the side there and when ye find the door to the storm cellar go on in. I'll sneak a couple rashins o' bacon down to ye and some biscuits. I'm guessin' ye've not broken yer fast today."

"No ma'am," replied Kevin.

"The name is Kate or Katie, if ye please. But I'm not a Madam and I ain't yer Ma."

"Thank you, Katie. I'd be beholden. I've had naught but a handful of chestnuts in two days."

"Then I'll see about an egg as well," she offered. "And maybe a hot cup o' tea with milk. Or would ye be liken some Irish coffee?"

"Irish coffee?" puzzled Kevin. "I thought I knew everything Irish. But that's one on me."

"Oh, I see ye've not been around the gentry here at all, bucko. Get down in the cellar wi' ye. And watch out for himself sleeping off his drunk."

She gave him a gentle shove in the direction of the side yard.

"Down to the cellar, Kevin. And be quiet now or they'll have the lot of us out in the streets!"

Kevin went around to the side of the house. He found two flat doors painted a forest green which opened upward from the cellar. They were closed with a padlock but the hasp was open. He lifted the top door quietly, squeezed inside, then lowered the door on its large hinge. He felt his way down the stone steps to the bottom. Once there, he could see by the light of the narrow windows a large coal bin to his left. Next to it was another, equally large, of stored wood, then another divided into sections of potatoes and squash and onions. Stacks of preserves stood on shelves against the walls in their jars. The cellar had a strong odor, not musty as he would have guessed, but fresh, like a truck farm or a produce shed.

Nor was it cold, despite the weather outside. For over to his right was something that Kevin had never witnessed before. A large furnace with enormous flames he could see through a metal grate, the flames blue-hot, and the heat from them rising and roaring through a series of large metal pipes to the floor above. The wealth that could feed the appetite of that furnace with daily coal was beyond imagining to Kevin. He thought it preposterous and wasteful. He could not imagine anyone wanting to keep a whole house warm. What were clothes and sweaters and quilts for? Why, in this house even the bedrooms must be warm as summer! He was both amazed and annoyed by the decadence.

Lying not far from the heat of this incredible blaze of the furnace was a ruggedly handsome man sleeping with his mouth open. Kevin took his time observing him. The man had a rough reddish beard in need of trimming, and brown curly hair. His herringbone suit, though of a decent cut, was gray with coal dust and his cravat was awry. The man was of medium build with strong-looking limbs and heavy shoulders. His boots were of good leather and, although dusty, had recently been polished.

So this is Casey, the footman, he said to himself. Well I'll just leave him be.

Kevin walked past Casey to the wooden stairs which led up to the kitchen. He crawled behind the stairs and sat down gratefully on a pile of flour sacks. His closed his eyes and had almost fallen asleep when he heard the creak of the door above him.

It was Kate with a plate of food in one hand and a candle in the other. She eased the door shut with her foot and started down the stairs. Halfway down she whispered hoarsely:

"Where are you then, kiddo? I've got some vittles for ye!"

Kevin crawled out from under the stairs and took the food from Kate. They sat down next to each other on the bottom step and he began eating ravenously.

"I like to see a man enjoy his food," Kate said.

"And I like to see a man enjoy his sleep," snapped a voice from over by the furnace.

Kevin almost dropped his dish in panic. He began to get up.

"Shush. Stay where you are. Sure it's only my Paddy wakin' up at long last."

Casey appeared before him. A tall man, over six foot, much taller than Kevin would have guessed watching him curled asleep by the furnace, He seemed to stretch himself and grow more substantial as he approached. He brushed off his suit and ran his hand through his hair.

"And what's this, then?" boomed Casey. "Are ye thinking of adopting one of yer own. Or is it a younger lover yer lookin' for?"

Kevin paled before the intimidating Irishman but Kate, nonplussed, replied, "Lower yer voice, ye old blathersnipe. Ye'll have the Madam down on us before ye know it. This here's Kevin Dillon from the Old Country and he's a bit down on his luck. I've given him a bit of breakfast, is all."

"Where do ye hail from, bucko?" Casey asked.

"County Kerry, Cahirsiveen," Kevin said.

"I know it well, a one horse town, but the people are decent enough," Casey replied grudgingly. "Better then most ye see here at any rate. I'm from Cork myself. Did ye ever hear the story of the bridge between Cork and Kerry? Well, it seems one day..."

"He's heard the story," interrupted Kate. "Haven't I just got through telling him the story myself?"

"Well, how could I be knowin' that, ye blabbering old sod!" Then turning to Kevin, "Ye wouldn't have a bit of a drink on ye?"

"No," Kevin said. "And I've not done too well with drink. It was drink, you see, that lost me my last position."

"Ah, then it's a favor drink owes ye now to restore your spirits and give ye back some of that which ye lost."

"How's that?" Kevin said.

"A hair of the dog that bit ye. Finish yer grub, mate, and we'll go out and see what two Irishmen can turn up in the way of refreshment."

"Yer not going off on a toot, Patrick Casey! Ye promised me you'd try to make something of yerself so that we could be together one day."

"And sure I will, Katie, me love, but not standing around in damp cellars, wearing the butler's hand-me-downs, and fetching the coach from the stable so Madam can ride to market. Sure, I'm made for better things, Kate darlin'. The bucko and I will go in search for work today. A man's work is what I need. Not this 'Yes Milady, No, Milady. Watch yer foot Milady.' Damn obsequious toadying! It's no work for a man. Toad-eating, tuft-hunting flunky-ism is what it is!"

"But at least yer safe. Ye have a place to eat and sleep and a bit of work to do."

"And so does the black slave have that, Katie, don't ye see? A man needs more. He needs some pride in himself, some dignity. Here I'm a servant of servants. I'll never be much more. And, if I have a son, his great ambition will be to be a coachman instead of a lowly footman like his father. I didn't come to the New World for that. There's plenty of that in the Old World.

"I'll have some dignity and respect, Katie. A position in the world or a piece of land I can call my own. I'll earn or steal or fight for a legacy for my son in keeping with the Casey name, or I'll die in the process. But I'll won't crawl in the dirt or follow after an English lady to keep her skirts from trailin' in the mud."

Katie reached over and embraced him. She held him tightly.

"I know how ye feel, Paddy. I respect ye for it. But I fear ye'll come to harm in this country. They have no love for us Irish and those that do not stay in their place are soon trampled."

Casey grinned cockily and picked Kate up in his left arm and swung her around.

"They'll not trample this Irishman underfoot, Katie!" He set her daintily on the ground and then put his other arm across Kevin shoulders, "And now that I have a strong Kerry lad by my side, they'll be no stoppin' me!"

Katie shook her head, smiling now in spite of her fears. He was irrepressible and she loved him for it. Casey turned to Kevin.

"Well, are ye with me, lad?"

"I am that," said Kevin. He handed his plate to Kate and thanked her sincerely for the breakfast.

"It kept my soul from fluttering out of my chest," Kevin said. "I am beholden."

"Then do the same for another Christian when ye have the chance," Kate said. She kissed him on the cheek and then turned to embrace Casey again.

"Good luck to ye both. I'll offer a novena to Saint Jude for ye."

"Make it St. Patrick," Casey said. "We're off to Christianize these American heathens and get a bit of respect from them, like St. Patrick in the ancient isles. We should have no need of St. Jude. Our task, I think, though difficult, is not impossible."

"If God wills it," Kate said.

"God's will is all one can pray for," Casey said, kissing her one last time and headed up though the cellar door. As he turned to leave, she surreptitiously placed a coin in his pocket.

"What now?" Kevin asked when they got back onto Joy Street.

"Well, have ye been through the Commons this morning?"

"Yeah, but no pickings there. It's cold and only a few couples out walking. I managed to get a few chestnuts from an old Italian who took pity on me."

"Ah, pity, is it? That's what's rotting the moral fiber of the Irish in this land. Hatred and contempt from the English, and pity and despair from the rest. Including our own women. We've got to do something, bucko. Get some kind of work that a man can do and be proud of."

They walked down Beacon Street talking of possibilities. At Park Street they crossed over to Tremont and headed north to Court. There they found a man whose team was tangled up because the outside horse had slipped on the ice. They stopped and helped him right the horse and untangle the harness. The wagon was loaded with expensive furniture.

The man, middle aged, with sideburns and a black frock coat, offered them a coin when they had done. Casey put up his hand in a gesture of refusal.

"We'll take no money for helping out a fellow Christian," he said. "But we would be grateful if you'd give us a few hours work. Perhaps you could use a hand unloading that furniture?"

The man put the coin back in his pocket. He got up on the seat of his wagon and looked down at them.

"Look, don't take this wrong. I've got nothing against you personally. I'm sure you're both fine lads. But I don't hire Irish, never have, never will. There's little enough work here in Boston for Americans. And besides, while I know you people are willing enough workers, you're too undependable. But I wish you both luck. Good day!"

With that he snapped the reins and took off down park Street. He did not wait for a reply or look back.

"Jesus, Mary and Joseph!" Casey exclaimed. "Did ye hear the mouth on that one! 'Undependable', says he. 'Don't hire Irish', says he. 'Don't take this wrong', says he. But who was it untangled his team when they were all balled up, I ask ye? Damned two-faced Americans! They're as arrogant and as hard-hearted as the Brits, I tell ye. Ye'd need a score card to tell them apart."

"I wish you had taken his coin," said Kevin.

"Damn his coin," Casey said. "I wish I had snatched him down off that seat and taken his whole purse."

"And given him a paste in the chops as well," Kevin said.

"That, too," Casey agreed.

By midday they had traveled down State Street, past the Customs' House to the waterfront. The dock area, although shabby in places, was undergoing major improvement. There were laborers with picks cutting out roadbed. There were carpenters and helpers putting up warehouses. At each site they passed, either Casey or Kevin asked for work. The answer was always the same.

There were upward of eighty great wharves, stretching in both directions. Long Wharf, Central, Commercial, India, Clarke, Lewis, Rowes. Each time they saw a foreman or someone who appeared to be in charge they offered their services. Each time they were turned away. Sometimes politely, sometimes contemptuously, but always firmly. No Irish. No Irish. No Irish.

They walked down broad streets crowded with merchants and seamen, craftsmen and vendors of seafood, and cloth and household goods. There were finely dressed ladies, bundled up in mufflers and furs, walking with their gentlemen. Not one took took notice of the waif-like Kevin or the pseudo-elegant Casey as they walked by.

The harbor and the water between the piers was a dense forest of spars, masts and sails, that stretched as far as the eye could see. They passed broad streets and elegant warehouse buildings. A sign near one of them proclaimed "Charles Bulfinch, Architect", a man Kevin heard had designed much of the area.

"I've been here before," Kevin said. "I could have told you we're wasting our time. They have their own longshoremen and they don't hire foreigners."

"Time is the thing we've got, bucko. What we don't have is a drink of rum or a piece of bread. We've not been to Central Wharf yet. That's the big one to the right of the Boston Pier. Its line of warehouses is the longest in America. Plus, later if they don't run us off, we can go up to the cupola there above the central arch and look out at the harbor. But for now, let's stop by this grog shop and see if we can get us a sip."

They went to the door of what looked like part of a warehouse. A thick oaken door, it had no markings, except the number twelve burned in with a hot wire. It was locked securely. They banged on the door. No answer. Finally, a man in a salt-crusted blue coat with the faded pipings of a first mate came over to them. He looked the worse for wear, his eyes bloodshot, and his cap torn.

"Looking for a drink, are ye, mates?"

"Aye, that we are, Sir," Casey replied.

"The name's MacBride, of the highland MacBrides. It's a damn shame what the Puritans will do to a fine town like this. It's like pulling teeth to get a drink on Sundays. They have the Blue Laws here, don't ye know? No drink can be legally sold on the Sabbath."

"Outrageous!" exclaimed Casey. "The Blue Laws, ye say?"

"Right on both accounts," replied MacBride shaking his head in sorrow.

"Still, if a man had a coin or two, and knew someone, well—I think that a drink might be found. It's a question of knowin', ye see, which is worth more than the coin. But without the coin, well, the knowin' is insufficient, if ye take my meaning."

"I do indeed," said Casey, feeling in his pocket for the coin which Kate had place so secretly and lovingly there that he might find it in an emergency. He felt a pang of guilt when he thought of how many floors she must have scrubbed to get it, of how she would have hoped that he might buy bread or cheese with it to sustain him in his search for work. But, it cannot be helped, he thought. When a man has nothing else, he needs a drink.

"I've money right here," said Casey.

"Well, what are we doing standin' around here jawin'? If ye'll walk with me over to the Barricado, we'll get us a taste."

They walked down to the "T" Wharf, an unusual pier which extended sideways from Long Wharf and ran parallel with the shore. They were headed for the Barricado which MacBride described as a sea wall built in the late 1600's out over what were the town flats. He told them that it was intended to be used for defense with a gun battery at each end, but shamefully had been allowed to decay. Now it was simply a tumbled down pile of rocks.

There they met another old sailor smoking a pipe. He had a fishing line dangling casually in the water, and seemed indifferent whether he got a bite or not.

"Here we are, Cap'n Jack, all stuck together on a Sunday with nary a drop to drink."

"I told ye before, MacBride, to take yer sorry Scot carcass off the pier unless ye had some money!"

"And, sure, it's money we have, my friends and I. And we'd like to share your company and some of that drink," replied MacBride ignoring the insult.

"Well, why didn't ye say so?" replied the other with a gap-toothed smile. He reached down and pulled out a bottle of rum from his seabag.

They drank until the bottle was empty and then MacBride proposed they should go off in search of more. Casey agreed, while Cap'n Jack seemed content to sit with his fishing pole contemplating the harbor. Kevin, however, was still eager for work.

"There's still a good piece of the day left. Let's see if we can make a bit of money," Kevin said. "Then we can have a bite to eat and another bottle of rum in the evening."

"Well," said MacBride. "That's not such a bad idea. Let's see what we can find."

Casey snarled good-naturedly. "Ah well, never let it be said that this Irishman turned down work. If you fellers can find it, I'll damn sure do it!"

They headed back towards Fanueil Hall, a motley crew, with the fire of rum in their veins. They had not gone a hundred yards when Kevin spotted the red-faced tavern owner who had, with his compatriots, left Kevin for dead in an alley some months back.

"Hold!" said Kevin stopping in front of him. "Do you remember me?"

"I can't say that I do, young man. Now if you'll excuse me," the man said trying to pass him.

Kevin grabbed the lapel of his coat. "You're not getting away that easy," he said. "Don't you remember a young Irish lad who came into your bar and ordered a drink? You told him no niggers nor Irish were allowed. And before he had a chance to defend himself you set upon him with three of your thugs."

"Is that a fact," said Casey coming over to the other side of the man.

"Don't like the Irish, and then use four men to beat up a youngster, hey?"

"It's my fight," said Kevin.

"No, no, he's mine," said Casey. Meanwhile, MacBride, spotting a policeman coming quick march down the street, discreetly crossed to the other side.

"Here now, what's all this?" asked the policeman.

"Hello, Sullivan! These two ruffians accosted me," replied the relieved tavern owner. "I was about to give them a taste of fisticuffs. Lucky for them, you happened along when you did."

"Why you, cowardly old washerwoman!" said Casey, preparing to hit him with a roundhouse right which would have knocked him into the harbor.

"Here, now. None of that!" said Officer Sullivan grabbing Casey's arm. "Back off now!" He stuck Casey a blow with his billy club on side of the jaw, and pushed Kevin to the ground. The policeman was a big man, over six feet and a muscular two hundred pounds. A former longshoreman and bodyguard, he was fearless and hard. He looked them both in the eye and they knew he meant business.

"Back off the both of you, or there won't be enough left of you to feed the crabs. Now, sir," he said turning to the tavern owner. "Are ye all right? Were ye robbed or molested in any way? Would ye like to press charges?

"Him press charges!" said Kevin from his position on the ground. "Why wasn't it him and his friends that beat me within an inch of my life and..."

"Shut yer trap," snapped the policeman, giving him a solid kick with his boot.

"No," said the tavern owner. "I'll not press any charges, I've no time for that. Besides, it's the Sabbath—which calls for charity even to the rogues."

"Ah sure, spoken like a true gentleman and Christian, Mr. Bates," said the policeman. "I'll give these lads a good talkin' to, and ye won't be hearin' from them again. That I'll assure you."

"Thank you, Sullivan," said the tavern owner. He reached into his pocket and took out a bill. "Here's a little something for your younguns."

"Ah, yer shouldn't, Mr. Bates. I'm only doing my duty." He put the money in his pocket with one hand and tipped his hat with the other. "Give my regards to Mrs. Bates, sir, and the rest of the family."

"I will, Sullivan. Good day."

"Good day, sir," smiled the policeman, tipping his hat again.

"Jasus, what kind of an Irishman, are you!" asked Casey rubbing his jaw which was slowly swelling from the blow of the club.

"Watch yet damn mouth, or the next time I'll break that jaw of yours instead of tapping it," replied Sullivan.

"Now look you here," the policeman went on. "Don't think that because my name's Tim Sullivan that I'm a dumb Mick same as you. I didn't just come over on the boat. I was born here. My parents came over in 1790. I'm a respected lawman and I've got six years of schoolin'. I know who's who and what's what. I know how to play my cards. My son might even be mayor of this city some day.

"You poor remnants of men are of no use to Boston. And ye might as well throw yourself in the harbor right now if you think you're going to practice such shenanigans as I just witnessed. Not on my beat, me fine buckos!"

"But that bastard struck..."

"That... gen-tle-man..." Sullivan replied enunciating each syllable,. "That gentleman happens to be Mr. Bates. He runs a decent establishment. He's a citizen, unlike yourselves, and entitled to the full protection of the law."

"And what about us?" fumed Casey. "We're human beings. Aren't we entitled to some dignity?"

"I can smell the rum on your breath, man. No drunk has dignity. And if it's sympathy your after, you've come to the wrong place. You have to fight for dignity in this country."

"Sure wasn't that what we wuz doin' when you came along," said Kevin getting to his feet.

"Well, lad, if your so anxious to fight, that can be arranged. It's better than going to jail or being coldcocked and tossed in the harbor. Follow me."

They headed back down toward Long Wharf where the new Custom House was located right at the water's edge.

"This here is the Custom's House," said Sullivan pointing to the building.

"Sure, your wrong," said Casey. "The Royal Custom's House is up near the State House."

"That's no longer used. This is the new one. A free, American one," the policeman announced proudly. "Built in 1837 on 3000 piles right up here on Long Wharf itself. Those columns there weigh forty-two tons each. It's an architectural marvel."

"How fascinating!" Casey remarked sarcastically. "And why do you bring us here, good sir. Is it the Grand Tour yer after givin' us? Or is there possibly work for my young friend and I unloading merchandise?"

"There's work for you, all right. The kind your type enjoys. There's work... fighting," Sullivan said.

"That's what the lad said he liked to do as well, if I'm not mistaken," the policeman continued. "Well, might as well get paid for it. No one can say that Sullivan does not take care of his compatriots."

As they approached the front of the U.S. Custom House they encountered a grim army sergeant. A short man dressed nattily in a blue wool uniform with large chevrons and service stripes, he seemed bored by his duty.

"What's this, then, Officer Sullivan," the sergeant asked.

"Some new recruits, Sergeant Harris. Some red blooded men willing to fight."

"Some bloody Irish, if I'm not mistaken," the sergeant sniffed.

"Anything wrong with that, Sergeant?" Sullivan asked drawing himself up to his full six feet.

"No, Officer Sullivan. Not at all. Go ahead inside, men."

"A moment of yer time, Sergeant," said Sullivan catching him by the sleeve. "That remark will cost yer a buck."

"What?"

"Ye get paid a bonus for the recruits, I know. So, a buck, my lad!" He held out his hand and the sergeant handed him the silver coin. "And next time, keep a civil tongue in yer head. Good day."

The sergeant met the men inside and led them to a small room. There he handed them an official-looking document.

"You're signing for a five year enlistment. Your pay is seven dollars a month, two of which will be withheld until the completion of your enlistment term. Is that understood?"

"Yessir," they replied.

"Your uniforms will be issued to you and your rifles. You are responsible for their maintenance. Any damage or destruction of them or any other property used by you in persuance of your duties will be deducted from your pay. Understood?"

"Yessir."

"Name?" he asked looking at Kevin.

"Kevin Dillon, sir."

"The sergeant printed Kevin's name carefully on the blank space at the top of the paper.

"Are you sober, Dillon?"

"Yessir," Kevin replied.

"Then, sign here."

By the time Kevin had looked over the document, Casey had been asked the same questions and was signing his. The document read:

I, Patrick Casey, do solemnly swear, that I will bear true faith and allegiance to the United States of America, and that I will serve them honestly and faithfully against all their enemies or opposers whomsoever; and that I will observe and obey the orders of the president of the United States, and the orders of the officials appointed over me, according to the rules and Articles of War.

Later, an examining surgeon would examine him briefly and swear that he was "free from all bodily defects and mental infirmity." The sergeant would also sign it testifying that he had "minutely inspected the Recruit, and that he was entirely sober when enlisted..."

Sober or not, Recruits Dillon and Casey were now in the army. Quick as that. In the morning they would leave Boston headed for points south where, within a matter of months, the Articles of War which they had agreed to so casually, would be irrevocably and brutally in effect.

CHAPTER 12

The Sea-borne Army

It was bitter cold on the deck of the ship and Kevin's woolen uniform, soaked through by salt spray, afforded no warmth. Kevin could remember few days in this New World when it was not damp and cold, or foggy and humid. How he longed for the tropics, those places the sailors spoke of where the sun shone most of the year, where the breezes were balmy, and the roses bloomed in December. He dreamed of brown-skinned girls walking in the parks at night in cool white dresses, of tall eucalyptus trees and colorful exotic birds.

The first leg of their journey had been long but relatively uneventful. They boarded a New York Central train in Boston which went west to Albany before it curved back south to New York City. After stop-overs in both cities they finally arrived in Philadelphia. The Pennsylvania Railroad was still under construction. And the tracks to Pittsburgh where they could meet the confluence of the Ohio, the Allegheny and the Monongahela had not yet been completed. So, they disembarked and began a forced march with full packs to Pittsburgh. Once there, with no rest, they were ordered to load barges with horses, cannon, ammunition and supplies which were waiting for them. Two days later they floated down the canal past Cincinnati then Louisville, until at Cairo they met the confluence of the Mississippi where they joined the 5th Regiment of Infantry. Together both the Michigan and Massachusetts units continued down the Mississippi on paddle-wheeler steamboats past St. Louis, Memphis, Baton Rouge and finally, after interminable but uneventful river travel, they arrived at the fabled city of New Orleans.

The army was allowed to get its land legs for the first time here. They were given a twelve hour shore leave the second day after the barges were unloaded on the docks. Ignoring his general weariness, for Kevin, like the other Irishman, was a recipient of the back-breaking labor of unloading the heavy field pieces, he headed out into the city. How different was this colorful Southern city from the staid grayness of Boston! Although still winter in New Orleans, there was a warm breeze. There were people in bright clothes walking in front of an impressive Catholic cathedral and they nodded politely at him as he passed. It was his first experience of any pedestrian even acknowledging him, let alone greeting him kindly.

A block further on was the Rue Bourbon where music and loud singing from the taverns was raucous and friendly. Ladies on the sidewalk twirled their parasols and smiled gayly. But Kevin was not distracted. He had enough of liquor and the problems it causes. Thank you very much. It was why he had not waited for Casey whom he knew would have wanted to accompany him. He had also, now that he thought of it, had enough of the ladies as well.

He walked up river for a while, past enormous oaks and magnolias covered with silvery-gray Spanish moss which glistened in the sunlight. He could see the river winding and sparkling beyond the trees and the clutter of wooden houses. He walked for a couple of hours, finally stopping at a cottage at noon when he saw a sign: "Vente de frommage." There he bought a delicious chunk of Brie cheese, a loaf of bread and a mug of a malt beverage. He went down to the riverbank where he picnicked, watching the driftwood float down the current and the barn swallows flash in and out of their nests beneath a shallow bridge.

He fell asleep watching the hypnotic flow of the river and the careful stitching of the swallows as they wove their way back and forth beneath the bridge, skimming the water for insects, and then returning to feed them to the dark mouths of their nestlings beneath the spars.

When he awoke the sun was angled gracefully on the road of dredged sea shells. He could feel the coolness in the air, but still found it difficult to believe it was winter. Indeed, he could feel the perspiration cooling inside his woolen shirt. The ditches alongside the roadbed were filled with wildflowers and a bird he did not recognize called *too-wheet, too-wheet!*

He thought he'd walk a bit more. As he left the road of clapboard houses and modest cottages and headed up river toward the plantations, he saw some impressive mansions now, with rambling galleries and gingerbread decoration. Houses with ornate iron fences, well tended lawns. Houses with turrets and gables and, like those in New England, the spectral widow's walks. And mixed in with them, the poor whites' shacks and the slaves' quarters.

Yet, even these architectural catastrophes had the purple and rose bougainvillea which wrapped around the walls, the gateways and the fences, which gave a grace and charm to even the most derelict of structures fashioned out of gray driftwood and pitch pine. And, something else they didn't have in New England: whether either rich or poor, there was an endless variety of color; there were houses painted blue and rose, deep yellow or even violet. Houses that announced themselves with a flourish, like painted ladies in Jackson Square.

There was a lushness, a sensuality to this city which Kevin had never guessed existed in the New World. Listening now to the cooing of doves and the smooth glissade of the river and the wind in the trees, his senses overwhelmed by the lushness of this place, he felt something akin to spiritual oneness with the world. And out over the city, as if in response to his feeling, rang out the churchbells for the Angelus. Delicate chimes from a small parish church, deeper clangs from a new Catholic convent, deep sonorous gongs from the great Cathedral.

He knew now what he had missed so much in his soul. This sense of connectedness with Catholicism, this sense of springtime in the soul which this city was giving back to him. He walked down a street so overgrown with camellias and jasmine and morning glory, that his senses were overpowered. The limbs of the oaks bent low and he was forced to bow his head when he passed. As he did, he made the sign of the cross and said quietly, "Thank you God, that I have lived to see this day."

And now, as the bells finished their chiming, another recognition, dim and faint came to him. Even in winter, he thought, it is green. Just like Ireland, this place is green. And he knew then, deep in his heart, that he would never go back North again.

He headed idly back downtown where he discovered Casey well on his way to becoming falling-down drunk. He was leaning heavily on the bar and arguing with the tavern owner when Kevin arrived. Kevin took him by the arm and guided him out into the sunlight.

"How much money do ye have?" Casey asked him.

"None to lend," Kevin replied. "Did you spend all yours?"

"Every penny," Casey replied. "And in spite of the fact of me giving him every cent of my business, the damned bartender wouldn't give me a drink on credit."

"He knows you're off in the morning," Kevin said.

"Well, in that case, he should have given me one for the road."

They had walked the block from the tavern back to the cathedral. "Let's go say a prayer," Kevin said. "For our own safe journey, and for the safety of all those dear to us that we've left behind."

He thought Casey might make fun of him, and almost regretted the suggestion as soon as he made it. But Casey, who had reached the maudlin stage of intoxication, thought immediately of his Kate, and tears streamed down his face as he took off his hat and followed Kevin up the steps to the cathedral.

"Ah, Kevin," he said. "You know just what is needed. A quiet talk with the Blessed Mother, who knows us all... and forgives us."

Kevin walked down the cool transept to the nave, he genuflected in front of the main altar, and crossed himself. Then, he walked over to the side altar of the Virgin Mary and lit a candle, dropping a coin in the metal box after he did so. He found it difficult to pray. It had been so long. He asked the Virgin to look after his parents, his sister and his brother. He asked her to give him strength in the journey and the battle ahead, that he not be cowardly, that he do nothing shameful, that he always serve her will and that of her Son.

He knelt at the foot of Mary's statue for several minutes breathing in the old familiar odors of beeswax candles and incense, the wood polish and linseed oil. An old woman saying her rosary lifted her head, glanced over at him, and smiled. Kevin smiled back. He felt that he had come home. That, finally, he had found a place in this New World that seemed right. But he knew that he could not linger.

Then Casey came and knelt beside him and began mumbling prayers under his breath. Kevin made the sign of the cross, leaned over to Casey and told him he would meet him outside. Once out in front of the church, he pulled out a cigar of Richmond leaf.

Inhaling the sweet tobacco, he felt invigorated, luxurious. Here he was in New Orleans when only a few weeks ago he had been languishing in cold misery. Here he was in New Orleans when only a year ago he had been dying of lung fever in a Boston alley. Here he was in the warm, Southern port getting ready to head south into what would be the greatest adventure of his life.

He had not thought about fighting, although he supposed that if he was told to do it, he would. He was more afraid of dying of hunger, or in prison, than of death on a battlefield. Like most of his race, Kevin enjoyed a good fight and, although he would have preferred to have been fighting for the freedom of his homeland than for a foreign army, he really didn't appear to have any choice.

Early he had imagined that the cause of this army was a just one. After all, the Americans had fought the hated British, obtained their independence, and then fought the English a second time in 1812. He had no idea when he enlisted of the specifics of the fight ahead, or its cause. He thought that the enemy was Spanish and that they were probably trying to re-conquer some of the lands to the south. His talks with Casey, while sometimes enlightening, usually left him more confused.

When he finally realized that he was to fight Mexicans, fellow "Americans," as it were, who had obtained their independence only two decades previous from the Spanish, his enthusiasm for the fight had dampened. Not only were these Mexicans fellow Catholics, but the army to which he now belonged was, the best he could figure out, one of imperialist conquest. Not a happy thought.

CHAPTER 13

No Ladies and Very Few Women

The steamer Alabama was headed south to Corpus Christi with Kevin and his mates aboard. It was to be a short trip, not more than a day, two at the most. Already there were a large number of troops at Corpus Christi. A few months before there had been a war scare, even a call up of the militia from various states following the admission of Texas to the Union.

"There were even reports that the Mexicans were getting ready to declare war," Casey said. "The Prussian ambassador said that they had moved thousands of troops to Matamoros on the border of the del Norte River."

"The Prussian ambassador?" Kevin asked.

"Yep. Can you beat that? Imagine anyone with sense listening to what a Prussian would say anyway? They did their best to help the English put down Washington's revolution."

"So what will happen now, do you think?" asked Kevin.

Casey lit a cigar and then looked over the stern where the water roiled in a white-green foam.

"It's hard to say. We're going to a camp in Corpus Christi. That's already south of the border and in Mexican territory. The Nueces River is the boundary. So, essentially we've issued a challenge to the Mexicans to declare war. If they don't, we'll probably move on down to the Río Grande del Norte where we know they have some troops, and see if we can't provoke something."

"So this is an army looking for a fight?" Kevin asked.

"Yep. And if a fight doesn't come, you can be sure we'll start fighting one another. Few of the native-borns have any use for us Irish, you know. And none of them have any use for Catholics. It's just a matter of time before someone pops off, and the fighting starts. That is, if we don't start killing Mexicans first."

"Mexicans are Catholics, ain't they, Casey?"

"Aye, that they are."

"How do you feel about killing them?"

"I'd rather kill the turncoat son of a bitch who railroaded us into the army."

"Yeah, his name was Sullivan, wasn't it?

"That's right," replied Casey, a bitter grin darkening his placid features. "You'll find there are different kinds of Irish. Ones like Sullivan are mostly Protestants who came over with the rest of the English colonists. Likely a Ulsterman and from a family that had holdings in the North of Ireland. His family, like he said, had been here a generation. The native borns don't seem to mind those kind of Irish quite as much as us. And his kind seem to have gotten ahead in this country. There are Sullivans and then there are Sullivans. Why, one fellow by the name of Sullivan even invented the phrase, 'Manifest Destiny'."

"What's that mean?"

"Why, Manifest Destiny means that the good folks in the twenty-eight states are ordained by God take over the whole continent. The Saxon race by virtue of their Calvinist faith are predestined to have the whole damn sheebang."

"That's the most ridiculous thing I ever heard of," Kevin replied.

"Be careful who you say that in front of, bucko. Be careful even of your own kind if they're wearing metal bars or stars on their tunics, or epaulets on their shoulders. There's even a couple of Ulster brigadiers in this army."

"You don't say!" exclaimed Kevin.

"Ah, but I do say, me boyo. Be not deceived. The people in the States are very selective in their prejudices. It's us peasant Irish who they don't like, you see. There's too many of us at one time, and—worst of all—we're Catholics in a country that was founded upon destruction of the hierarchy and all that goes with it. It's us Papists they hate and the brogue that goes with it. Talk like a Brit and throw away your rosary, and you'll do all right."

"I'll be hanged first," said Kevin.

Casey smiled. "Well said, bucko. Let's hope it never comes to that. But better to be hanged as a Yank traitor, than to be damned for turning against the Faith, or kowtowing to any mealy-mouthed Protestant lieutenant."

High winds and a winter storm held the Alabama outside the Aransas Pass most of the next day. It was uncomfortable on board. And, although Kevin and Casey were up on the deck, they were grateful when the steamer grounded the next day about a hundred yards off the coast of St. Joseph's and they were ordered to disembark. To Kevin and Casey it was a pleasure to wade ashore even in the cold January waters which splashed up to their chests. After the crowded troopship, the open spaces, the sparkling white beaches and live oak trees seemed like paradise.

Once they were landed on St. Joseph's, a steam lighter was dispatched from Corpus Christi to carry then over the last leg of the journey. What they encountered ashore was nothing like what they had expected an army camp would be.

Kevin had anticipated that there would be order: disciplined troops drilling and marching. But such was not the case. As winter had arrived in the camp, most formal activities had ceased. The site was damp, stinking from open sewage pits and the smell of mouldy and fouled clothing. To one side of the pier as he approached he saw a dead horse.

Its belly was covered with flies, and maggots were moving slowly through its cracked brainpan. Rats had nested in the intestines, and Kevin could clearly see a large female rodent nursing her young.

No sooner were they off the boat then a cold rain began. They were shown to their tent, a cotton affair, which leaked, and around which their two tent mates had banked earth to keep out the wind. Their new companions, welcomed them in a desultory fashion. The youngest, his face drawn and jaundiced, raised his head from an army blanket in a painful nod. The other, a handsome redhead in his late twenties who had a grace that bespoke good family, got up and offered his hand.

"Welcome, friends. Find a space for yer gear, and rest yer weary bones," he said in a soft brogue. His face was wan and pale, his movements leaden. "My name is John Murphy, I'm from County Mayo. That's McDowell in the corner holding his guts so they don't fall out. A long way from his lovely home in Galway where half the people don't even speak the English tongue let alone the barbaric Yank version of it. He's had the runs for the past three days."

"The runs?" Kevin asked.

"The bloody diarrhea, bucko. It's already killed two hundred of us or more. I had it myself but was lucky enough to run into an Indian gal who sold me a chunk of white cheese which bound me up good. And I've been careful ever since to drink either the goat's milk the Mexican's have, or the sasparilla at the grog shop. No water either. I don't know if the water was spoiled before the Yanks got here or not. But it damn sure is now with raw sewage seeping into every hole, and fouled pants being washed in the streams. Most of us will die in these camps before we ever see combat."

"Isn't there a doctor that could have a look at him," Kevin asked.

"Yeah, there's a surgeon. That's his tent you passed on the way in, with about two hundred men lined up in front. But what the hell. We do get paid tomorrow, and not in script either, in hard cash. We can go over to the grocer's tent and get us a bottle of whiskey and then take in a horse race.

"Horse race!"

"Hell, yeah! We have races every week, sometimes two or three a week. A lot of the officers have bought mustangs from Mexican horse traders, or captured wild ones from the herds that graze not far from here."

"Horse racing, gambling, booze. Sounds like my kind of place," laughed Casey. "And what about the ladies?"

"Well, in the words of one wit who said it better that I could: 'There are no ladies here at all, and there are damn few women.'"

Both Kevin and Casey laughed. Meeting a fellow countryman had softened the harshness of their first hour in camp. And, despite the moans from McDowell in the corner, they felt like they just might make it after all. A friendly face from one's homeland can have that kind of salubrious effect. Even hell, Kevin thought, might be tolerable if one could hear the brogue spoken there.

He looked around at his surroundings. There were canvas mats on the earth floor to keep off the damp. The tent was not waterproof and the cotton fabric seemed to absorb as much of the water as it repelled. Still, Kevin had slept in worse places. And, with a bottle of whiskey to keep off the chill, and a fire—it could be made tolerable.

"But there are women?" persisted Casey.

"Well," Murphy replied. "There are those who wash clothes. For that service they charge fifty cents a man, by the way, which is not cheap. If ye want any other services then the price rises accordingly. And most of them are as old as yer mother in most cases with chapped hands and the smell of lye soap about them. But, yeah, there are women. I just don't recommend any."

"Well then," Casey said. "Perhaps it might be worthwhile to go out on a scouting expedition outside the camp."

"It might be," replied Murphy. "And it might be wise to take your musket with ye when ye go and keep yer powder dry."

There were about two thousand men in the camp and, while some of the officers had a thatched mess, the enlisted men had to line up in the cold drizzle for the beans, bacon and biscuits which were served from a long canvas-covered table. By the time they got their food back to the tent, the beans were watery and the biscuits soggy. They managed, however, to light a small fire at the flap of the tent and heat some coffee in a lard can. They sat around drinking coffee and smoking while taps were sounded and the camp settled down for the evening. Kevin thought it was not half so bad. They told a few stories about the Old Country, and sang a song about Molly Malone who *wheeled her wheelbarrow through streets broad and narrow, crying cockles and mussels, alive, alive-o.*

The rain stopped at about ten o'clock and Kevin went out and stood beneath the stars. He had never seen so many, shining clear and cold, and close. And the camp itself was quiet with an occasional fire in officer's country and the tents shining in the light. "Alive, alive-o, alive, alive-o," Kevin sang softly to himself under the Texas skies. Whatever the future brought he was ready for it. Life was not so bad. He was seventeen years old and whatever was ahead would be an adventure.

Time passed slowly, but it passed. As in most army camps, while the days seemed interminable, the pages of the calendar flew by. On Christmas Day the Catholic soldiers attended Mass at a small Mexican church. Most of the soldiers were Irish with a few Germans mixed in, and they sat together with the small congregation, occasionally exchanging shy glances with the señoritas who sat with their parents or protective aunts. There were no young Mexican men at all in the church. In fact, Kevin had yet to see anyone, except horse traders and merchants, who looked to be fighting age in the village.

The Mass was in Latin, and Kevin felt the comfort of knowing that the same Mass, the same offering of the Body and Blood of Christ, was being commemorated in a small village in County Kerry, and in China, and all over the world.

When Mass was ended they were invited to join the other church members and have a bowl of tripe soup, called *menudo*, which most of them found so delicious that they asked for, and received, seconds. Kevin particularly liked the soft corn cakes, called *tortillas*, which were served with the soup instead of bread.

In the days that followed they were to spend more and more time in the little town. They got to know the priest and a couple of the Mexican families. They were invited to attend a small gathering on the Feast of the Three Kings where they were served a sweet bread decorated with fruit. Casey biting down hungrily almost broke a tooth on what turned out to be a tiny porcelain doll.

"What the hell," he growled pulling the offending object out of his mouth.

Everyone laughed, and the children danced around him shouting, "*Una fiesta con el Señor Casey! Una fiesta con el Señor Casey*!"

"It is a tradition," the priest told Casey smiling broadly. "Whoever receives the Christ Child in the bread, must make a party for the others. But you may also make a wish. It is very good luck to have found the Child."

"Well," said Casey his good humor returning despite a chipped tooth. "I'm very glad to learn that. Hmm. A fiesta, hey? Well, Capt. Magruder—at our camp—has been organizing a theater. It's suppose to be finished in a couple of days. Why don't I invite all of you to attend the first performance?"

The priest hesitated before translating for the others.

"What kind of play would it be? I have heard many stories about the so-called theater in the North. I don't know if I can recommend such entertainments as the Yankees are fond of."

"No, no Father. Nothing like that. It will be, how do you say in Spanish? Shakespeare."

"*Lo mismo*," smiled the priest.

"Huh?" asked Casey.

"Shakespeare is pronounced Shakespeare in Spanish," the priest said. "And I suspect it is the same in most countries."

"Ain't that something!" Casey remarked genially.

"And what is the title of the play, may I ask?

"Othello," Casey replied.

"I have lived too long, I think. *Madre de Dios*! Who would have thought I'd see Othello brought to a village in Cohilla to be acted by Yanqui soldiers?"

The others hung around the priest waiting for the translation.

"*El irlandés me dijo que les invita a una obra de Shakespeare. Othello.*"

"*Bueno! Qué divertido!*" the women said, while the old men smiled politely.

Off to the side, a girl of sixteen, plain and demure, had been looking at Kevin secretly for the past five minutes. He turned his head in her direction and caught her glance. She quickly lowered her eyes.

The next day, accompanied by Murphy and the now-recovered Jimmy McDowell, they went over to the newly constructed theater. Casey had been one of the volunteers on the construction crew and was proud of the work he had done. Even the reticent McDowell was garrulous in his praise.

"Jesus, Mary and Joseph. It's better than the Globe Theater of London. There's never been such a thing in the New World."

It was in fact quite an accomplishment: eight hundred seats, a raised platform stage with an interior and side entrances. There were marvelously painted sets, and even footlights. As they entered they could see a man and a rather ugly woman in costume who were gesticulating wildly. The man appeared ready to strike the woman, but then as she cocked her fist ready to strike back, he turned his back on her in disgust.

Kevin recognized Capt. John Magruder as the peacemaker who was trying to convince the couple to get along.

"I don't see what the problem is here, Lieutenant Porter. Would you rather have an illiterate washerwoman play the part? How would she know the lines?"

"I refuse to get on the stage with this hirsute barbarian playing the daughter of Brabantio. That's all there is to it. No, no, and no!"

"Well, you're a mite pale yourself to be cast as a black Moor," replied a rough voice testily.

"Enough, enough! Mr. Grant, you're the ugliest excuse for a woman I've ever seen. This won't be Shakespeare; it will be a farce and I won't be a part of it."

"Now, now, Lieutenant Porter."

"Nossir! I refuse. This was volunteer duty. I just un-volunteered."

"Who is the young feller dressed as Desdemona," Murphy asked in a whisper as they looked down on the stage.

"Lieutenant Grant," Casey said. "Ulysses S. Grant."

"If I was that Captain," Kevin said, "I'd look for a replacement quick. He's just about the ugliest woman I've ever seen."

By the time the play opened and Kevin and Casey had brought their guests, most of the kinks had been ironed out. Lt. Grant was replaced by an actress from New Orleans who was brought in especially for the role of Desdemona.

The troops were well-behaved except for a handful of drunks who were loud and insulting. One pushed his way to where the visitors were sitting and wondered aloud why "Messicans got seats among respectable people." He and his friends were escorted out quickly by a specially appointed sergeants-at-arms.

When the play was over, Kevin walked with Dolores, the girl whose eyes had caught his at the Three Kings party. The priest walked beside them and translated.

"What did you think of the play?" he asked.

"I do not have enough English to enjoy it," she said. Then she smiled. "But I find the company of yourself very pleasant."

"And yet you look sad," he said. "Even your smile is sad."

"It is so because all these men have invaded my country," she spoke passionately in Spanish. "I cannot be happy about that. And while you *irlandeses* respect Holy Mother the Church, the others do not. It will not be long before Catholic blood flows in the streets and the Church is violated by the invader."

The priest translated her words faithfully.

Kevin stopped and turned on the priest angrily.

"Did she say that, Father or did you?"

"Look into her eyes, my son."

Kevin looked into the girl's eyes and saw the tears, hovering, like a glass filled to the brim.

"It will not happen," he said. "I swear by my mother, that I will not let that happen."

"Then soon, my son, you will have to make a decision," the priest said. "You will have to decide which is most sacred to you. The oath you swore to serve this new land whose uniform you wear, or the oath you swore at the sacrament of Confirmation to defend your Faith against all her enemies even at the risk of your life."

"I hope it will not come to that," Kevin said.

"Live in hope, my son," the priest said. "But do not die in despair."

The priest took the girl by the arm and faced Kevin. His voice was sad but firm.

"We will say good night here. We thank you for your hospitality and your graciousness. I enjoyed the play immensely, and feel that there is hope for a country that has such obvious affection for the arts. I suspect, though, that it will be some time before the Yanquis learn that there are other cultures besides the Anglo-Saxon which are just as noble and far more ancient. And there will be much blood shed in the learning.

"Say good night to Dolores, my son. You may kiss her on the cheek if you wish. I know you find her attractive. Her full name is María Madre de Dolores, Mary, Mother of Sorrows. Her father and mother have both passed away. The name is appropriate, no? So make this first kiss your last.

"I do not want her to have any more sorrows at such a young age. We understand each other as men?"

"We understand each other, Father," Kevin said. He wanted desperately to add something, a gentle word or two for Dolores, but he could think of nothing to say.

The priest nodded and, with the girl's arm still firmly grasped in his, walked quickly away. Kevin stood quietly, waiting for the girl to turn, to give him one last greeting. She did not. He stood under the cold Texas skies and looked up at the stars. He did not know whether it was the smoke from the campfires or his feelings that made the stars dim, that made their light shatter into tiny pinpoints of blue and white, remote, meaningless and absurd. He only knew that suddenly he felt more alone than he had ever felt before.

He could not return to the tent. He knew the other men had seen him with the girl and would ask him about her. He could not bear to hear their ribald jokes. And, while Casey would be more understanding, neither could Kevin face the older man's pity. He made two full circles around the camp, nodded at the sentries as he walked, his thoughts buzzing in his brain like yellow-jackets around a berry pie at a picnic.

What the hell was he doing here in this godforsaken country? Whose side was he on, anyway? Why were they invading Mexico? And how could he justify to his conscience his participation in this largely Protestant army whose purpose was to take over the territory of a weaker nation. It would be the same as joining the English army to invade Ireland. An abomination. Maybe even a mortal sin. What would his mother say? He thought he knew, and could not bear to think of her judgment.

And the girl. Would he ever find a girl of his own? One who was not promised to another, or circumscribed by class or another culture, or by a tradition which would not let him in? Would he ever get beyond the kiss to an embrace? Would he ever have children, leave sons behind him in the world? Or would his seed be wasted, scattered on the ground like Onan's and his name lost in the sand?

These thoughts whirled through his teen-aged head for hours, until at the end of his third lonely circuit around the enormous camp, he came at last to his own tent. Everyone was asleep, and he lay heavily down on his damp army blanket and, fully clothed, fell into a feverish and fitful sleep.

The next day Kevin, too, had succumbed to the dysentery and fever which had plagued McDowell and others in the camp. Casey cared for him, bringing fresh water, with sugar and salt, to help the dehydration. He also spent what little money he had on goat cheese to bind him up. Still, Kevin was weak and even delirious for days at a time and it wasn't until February that he regained his strength. By then, conditions had improved. The tents had been raised up above the ground and set on wooden platforms which was a blessing because torrential rains soon followed. On February 6th, Captain Sibley and a small contingent were sent by General Taylor to reconnoiter the Matamoros Road and there was speculation that they would be moving out. But days passed and no orders were given to the troops. On February 24th, the day after Sibley's return, the army was put on 24 hour notice. The word carried like a wildfire throughout the camp that General Taylor had been given orders to advance to the Río Grande. The sergeant came by their tent.

"Ten-shun," Casey said when the sergeant raised the flap of the tent. The men began reluctantly began to get up from their cards.

"As you were," said the sergeant. "Tomorrow, General Taylor will be reviewing the troops. You will fall in for inspection in field dress at oh-six hundred. Any questions."

"Yeah. Is this it, Sarge? Are we movin' out against the Mexicans."

The sergeant was poker faced. "You know as much about this as I do. I just been told that the General wants to review the troops. Now get this place cleaned up for inspection, and get your uniforms spruced up."

"Okay, Sarge!" the men replied as one.

"God and all his angels and saints be praised!" shouted Murphy. "This is it! We'll finally getting out of this rathole!"

"Yah-hoo!" yelled Kevin.

"High time, too," said Casey. "You almost lost your mate, Murph. And I almost lost my young brother here in this Bleak House."

Kevin smiled. It made him feel good to be so adopted by Casey. The four men had developed a bond of comraderie over the past few months. Their exclusion from most of the gambling games offered by the "Americans" had given the Irish a solidarity that no other group had in the army. But, as Casey was fond of adding, there are Irish and there are Irish. Some Irish, especially the Protestant Ulstermen and those of the previous generation, did not consider themselves Irish at all, nor did they have a brogue. They merged with the Anglo-Saxon as if they were, in fact, compatriots. He later found out that most of these men were citizens of the United States. They were treated quite differently from him and his cohorts.

When dawn came the next day, there was no inspection and no review of the troops. It seems that General Taylor got into an argument with General Worth. Murphy who knew all the scuttlebutt came back with the news.

"Nothing going on today; no inspection, no parade. Everything cancelled."

"Why? What's the problem?"

The official word was that the weather had changed, and was judged too inclement for a parade. In fact, General Taylor in his orders of the day gave that as a reason for cancelling the review. But according to Murphy, the case was something different.

"The officers are fighting among themselves. It seems General Worth is just a Colonel but has a brevet as a Brigadier General. But Twiggs has seniority in lineal rank as Colonel. General Taylor designated Twiggs as senior officer which caused Worth to refuse to participate in the parade. To save appearances, General Taylor has cancelled the review."

"Jesus!" Casey said. "Could ya say that in Gaelic? It might make more sense. Yer a virtual tower of Babel."

"Catholics versus Protestants. Natives versus immigrants. Citizens versus non. And now brevet rank versus lineal rank," said McDowell. "This army better get an enemy to fight real soon, or we'll be killing each other."

"And don't forget Volunteers versus Regulars!" Casey said.

"How could I forget that."

"And the Texas dragoons versus everybody!" Kevin added.

The men laughed. The Texans! Trick riders who showed off their horsemanship to anyone willing to watch. Arrogant, strutting cowboys. They were also fearsome fighters and had an solidarity and *esprit de corps* which was the envy of many of the troops. They were arrogant and overbearing, though, and few of the regular troops could stand to be around them long. The Texans' hatred for Mexicans was legendary. On several occasions there had been reports of depredations against the peaceful Mexicans in surrounding areas. These were generally attributed to the Texas Rangers.

"Well," said Casey, "I'm glad they're on our side."

"The Texans don't have any side but their own," replied Murphy.

"Well," said Casey thoughtfully. "Perhaps that's the best way to be."

Kevin looked at Casey speculatively. Ever since they had both witnessed an Irishman getting "bucked and gagged", something in Casey had changed. He no longer felt as if there was even a possibility of being a true part of this army. He spoke about "Anglo-Saxon oppression and imperialism" to anyone who would listen. He also managed to get a pass each Sunday to go to Confession and Communion at the small village church where he would spend hours talking to the priest. Occasionally Kevin went with him, but the pain of seeing Dolores and not being able to talk with her quite distracted him from the Mass, and left him feeling less in the state of grace than he had been before the services.

The bucking and gagging had changed Casey, there was no doubt. In the months he had been here he had seen

Texans fight, even knifing one another, and receive only reprimands. He had seen "native" soldiers miss inspection, reveille, and even come back two days late on a 24 hour pass and simply receive restriction to quarters.

However, an Irishman who missed reveille one morning was ordered wear a crude sign around his neck which said, "Late and dumb!" as well as being forced to stand on a barrel from sun-up to sundown.

A Catholic who received a pass to go to Mass and later came back drunk from a unauthorized stop at a *pulque* shop had his hands and feet tied and was spread-eagled on top of a cannon for hours in the hot sun. Another Irishman, in fear of being late, ran past the sentry without observing the proper form, was placed in a hole in the ground with a wooden door thrown over it and kept there thirty days, fed three crackers and a glass of water each day.

But the worst of all was the bucking and gagging. This was the punishment he had witnessed of an Irishman who was impulsive enough to talk back to an officer. He was taken out to the parade ground and was tied up in a sitting position. Then a filthy gag made of dirty underwear was put in his mouth. His feet were then drawn up until the heels touched his buttocks. His hands were then twisted in front of his knees and tied with a rope. Then a stick was run under his knees and over his arms. In this excruciating position, the man was left until he passed out from pain. The company officer occasionally gave an order for the prisoner to be revived with water. This was done not from mercy, but so that the man should not, through unconsciousness, have a respite from the pain.

Branding with indelible ink was also common punishment for the Irish soldiers. One man who missed a work detail was whipped, then branded with a W to symbolize "Worthless." Another who came back from town drunk on two occasions was given fifty lashes and then was branded HD for "Habitual Drunkard."

Kevin knew that these punishments were humiliating and, like Casey, had trouble accepting them. But, even more disturbing to him were the soldiers who were executed—either shot or hanged for "crimes" which would not have been such under any just system. One man who did not properly salute a lieutenant was struck with a saber on the cheek. When he instinctively struck back, he was court-martialed and sentenced to be shot for "assaulting an officer".

He knew that there were many men who had already deserted and that many more would probably do so on the march. There was land to the West and no one to ask questions once you had gotten clear of the camp. Out West the gun was the rule of law, and anyone with guts and a willingness to work hard could trap, farm, claim a piece of land for himself with no one to dispute it except a passing band of Indians.

But somehow he felt that Casey had no intention of leaving the army for the life of a farmer. He was not the type of man to run away. He was mulling over injustice and was harboring a fierce resentment. He would not shirk a fight; that Kevin knew well. More likely, he was brooding over who the true enemy really was.

The few Mexicans Kevin had seen were peaceful, open, and kind-hearted. Those who knew what was going on, like the priest, were disturbed by the presence of the soldiers and knew that the purpose of the troop build-up was eventual invasion. Now, in Kevin's mind there was no doubt either.

The Catholic Irishmen were treated little better than animals by the officers, and generally ignored by the rank and file of American soldiers. They were not citizens, could not own land, would seldom make rank regardless of their abilities. So, what were they fighting for? Who was their argument really with? As the days passed, this question would occur to Kevin again and again. Less and less did it seem his fight was with the Mexicans. More and more they seemed to him like his own kind.

They, too, were Catholics. Catholics who had just thrown off the oppressive yoke of Spain, and now trembled on the eve of an invasion by a Protestant army with visions of Manifest Destiny. Hated by the Texans, considered an inferior race by the Anglo-Saxons, they—like the Irish—were held in contempt by Taylor's army. Poor, mostly farmers, wanting only to be left alone so that they could live decent lives, they were betrayed and invaded just like the Irish. More and more it seemed to Kevin, he was on the wrong side of this struggle. He looked over at Murphy.

"Yeah, those Texans stick together."

"Like I said, bucko," Murphy replied, narrowing his eyes. "They know which side they're on. You can hate them if you want, but what makes 'em so fierce is that they have no doubt about whether they're fighting for the right cause. Texans hate Mexicans. That's plain and simple.

"Now with us, it's not so plain and simple. It's apparent most of this American army hates Catholics. Most of 'em also think an Irish and a Mexican are two of a kind, and that neither is worth the price of a good hound dog. So what the hell are we doing? Let me ask you that. The only reason they even have us here at all is that they don't trust Negroes at their back with guns."

"Seems to me they're giving the black man more credit for spunk than they're giving us," noted McDowell.

"Seems like," Murphy said.

"Will you guys shut up!" Casey snapped. "That kind of talk just goes to prove them right. You all took an oath same as me. We're Americans in the American army."

"Who's an American?" Murphy asked. "Did you get to vote in the last election?"

"No."

"Are you a citizen?"

"No."

"And speaking of oaths, didn't you take an oath when you made your Confirmation to protect the Catholic Church against all her enemies? And if there's a choice between oaths, well—which has priority, your God? Or a country that doesn't think you're worth the price of a good mule?"

"Aghh. I can't argue with you, Murphy."

"Damn right you can't, because I'm right."

"Well, what are we going to do about it?"

"We'll wait and mark our time. When the day comes, we Micks will be the fiercest soldiers the Anglo-Saxon has ever seen. They'll not forget the Irish soldier in this part of the world. Not for a long time."

"I don't get your meaning, Murphy," Casey replied. "Hold now, take me with you."

"My meaning's clear enough for them that want to see it. And when the time comes... Well, as the good Lord says, them that is not with me is against me. And there's an end to it."

On Sunday morning, March 8, 1846, the dragoons and Capt. Samuel Ringgold's battery moved out to the cheers of the men and the strains of "Yankee Doodle" and "Hail Columbia." No passes were issued to the men so that neither Kevin nor Casey could see the priest or Dolores to offer a last farewell. In the following days the infantry brigades followed in what was to be a 150 mile march across uninhabited prairie to the banks of the Río Grande.

On Thursday, March 11, Kevin and his friends helped load the company wagon with 1,500 pounds of supplies—little enough for such a long journey and, likewise to the lively tune of "Yankee Doodle", they set out across the plains of Tejas y Coahilla, Mexico Territory, to the Río Grande.

Father and I went down to Camp
Along with Captain Goodin
And there we met the men and boys
As thick as hasty Puddin'.

Yankee Doodle sing it out!
Yankee Doodle dandy.
And the music and the step
And with the girls be handy.

CHAPTER 14

Guns on the Río Grande

The march was a long one but not particularly tiring or uninteresting to Kevin. For the first few days they marched at a strong pace across flat prairies with not another human being in sight. "Pioneers" were sent ahead to scout for water holes; the distance between such usually being the length of the day's march. They marched briskly, as a regimental drummer kept beat, occasionally breaking into song.

Kevin was in high spirits. Finally, he was going somewhere; a new place where something would happen. Any change, Kevin thought to himself, was for the better, even if it was to be a march into the cannon's mouth. Better to die with a musket in one's hand, he felt, than to give up the ghost in dirty sheets, choked to death by one's phlegm, dying in the filth of one's own excrement. Any end was better than that.

In some places along the way there were veritable oceans of wildflowers, yellow and purple which rose like waves over the hills. In other stretches there were the surreal shapes of cacti: the "barrel" cactus which some said you could drink out of, the "organ pipe" which looked exactly like its name, and the ubiquitous “beaver tail”. Occasionally they saw deer, rabbits, ducks and geese which the dragoons were allowed to hunt, and were a welcome addition to the officers’ stew. Other officers, especially the rambunctious Texans, rode after the herds of mustangs which grazed along the southern route. Many were able to lasso them and break them for personal mounts.

The two week march to the Río Grande took Taylor’s Army of Observation past the Nueces River, across Hogwallow Prairie, the Agua Dulce and San Fernando Rivers to the Santa Gertrudes Depot. There, they held up waiting word from General Twiggs’ advance guard as to the state of affairs.

“We’re getting close, now,” Murphy said, as they sat eating pieces of fat-back bacon and biscuit, washed down with coffee.

Casey moved the tin can, which held the water and coffee grounds, back from the flame so that it would stay warm without further boiling.

“Yep. Feller told me that a rider came in from Twiggs who said the Mexicans burned up some of the prairie up ahead, then took off. Next day Lieutenant Hamilton’s advance guard was stopped by a Mexican patrol who wanted to know what was their purpose.”

“Think he told ‘em?” Murphy asked.

“I reckon. Ain’t no point in lyin’. It’s pretty obvious we’re headed down to the Río Grande. And while this might be styled an ‘Army of Observation’, my guess is that our observing days are soon to come to an end.”

“So you figure that’s why we’re holed up?”

“Yep. I reckon the Old Man’s going to gather us all together before we make any more advances. Can’t take a chance. He don’t know how many Mexicans there are and what they might do. Best not to be so scattered out.”

Despite Casey’s prediction, however, their brigade set out the next day. The morning was cool but they could feel the warm wind blowing from the desert to the south. Grackles and jays, clown-like and noisy, followed them part of the way.

"Them birds don't have the sense they were born with," McDowell said.

"No, nor us either," Kevin said. "What the hell's the general got on his mind anyway? I thought we was goin' to stop back at the depot for a while."

"Looks like we're going to go a bit further. Hey. Speaking of the general, look over there!"

McDowell pointed toward a heavy-set officer, dressed in blue uniform pants, a rumpled white shirt, and a non-descript blue coat. On his head he wore a wide-brimmed straw hat. In his early sixties, with a grandfatherly twinkle in his eye, Talyor hardly looked the part of General in command of the largest expeditionary force in the history of the United States.

"That's old Rough and Ready," McDowell pointed.

"Jesus! He looks like my grandpa." Kevin knew that to be a compliment, albeit unwillingly granted. Kevin's grandfather, like Taylor, had the cut of jaw which showed strength and determination. Taylor might not look the part of a general, but he looked liked somebody who brooked no nonsense.

"Don't let the clothes fool ya. Look at the way he sits his horse."

Kevin watched him guide the powerful white stallion up and down the lines, crossing over to where the field batteries were and then trotting up to the staff officer where he quietly gave an order.

"Yeah, Kevin agreed. I see what you mean." And even as he said it, he felt sorry for the Mexicans. This was a man who showed determination in every move he made. Taylor turned and gave some orders to an artillery captain dressed in clean white ducks. The captain passed on the orders and a dozen caissons advanced past the brigade's flank.

Kevin did not know ordinance well but he was impressed by the shining 8 and 12 inch guns mounted on snug timbers which were wheeled quickly by. Kevin had learned in his months at camp that this army had the best artillery of any in the world. What's more, their field pieces were more mobile than those of Europe or Mexico, and their gunners better trained.

They marched into a live oak region with deep sandy soil which caused the caissons to become bogged down, and slowed up the column as the men put their shoulders to the wheels and helped the mules pull the heavy cannon out of the sand.

On and on, interminably they pushed the heavy cannon though the soft soil. Although the men complained, few of the Americans had any had genuine resentment about this detail. They knew that in the fight that was to come, these cannon would decimate the enemy and open up the paths of victory. If the group of Irishmen in Kevin's detail had other thoughts, they carefully concealed them. In Taylor's army, one cannon was worth a hundred men.

They camped at the edge of the oak grove that afternoon of the third day, so that they could get a early start. It was Tuesday, March 17, 1846. The Feast of St. Patrick, the patron saint of Ireland. A former Irish slave raised by the Romans, Patrick was to choose God over country, and return to convert the people who had enslaved him. Casey even had a silver medallion with St. Patrick's image on it. It was the only thing of value he did have. He fingered it thoughtfully in the firelight.

That evening, by the campfire, the Irishmen sang the songs of their homeland. And even the Anglos and the Germans, who had first mocked them, came to be quiet as the strains of Irishmen's sad and fierce songs echoed in the night air. And when all the songs were sung, the acrid tobacco smoked, and the hoarded whiskey drunk, the Irish joined together in the sad, defiant hymn of Hugh O'Donnel, the Gaelic chief. They each beat out the slow, dirge-like rhythm on the stocks of their muskets and they sang softly:

> The earth shall rot beneath our tread
> And flames wrap hill and wood
> And gun peal and slogan cry
> Wake many a glen serene
> Ere you shall fade, ere you shall die

My dark Rosaleen.
O my dark Roos-saa-leen.

Kevin made the sign of the cross and said a prayer for his mother, and for all the mothers of the Irish boys so far from their homeland. He asked that he be given the strength to do what was right. Then he fell asleep, peaceful as a child under the star-filled Mexican sky.

They awoke the next day, muscles aching and exhausted from their struggles with the cannon. But the desert lay ahead and there was no help for it. They had to get across. Foot-sore and weary, they marched hour after hour, through a seemingly endless stretch of desert terrain. They had crossed it by late afternoon, and stopped finally in the high chaperral or mesquite area three miles north of the Arroyo Colorado. There, Taylor ordered a halt to the column until all the brigades had closed up to supporting distances. He planned to concentrate his entire force before crossing the Rio Colorado.

The decision was a good one. General Francisco Mejía, the commander at Matamoros, had moved a force forward to confront him. Scouts reconnoitering had learned from Mexican pickets that any attempt of the Americans to go further would be challenged. The scouts' information was reinforced by the sounds of bugles which echoed back and forth from the high banks in the distance. The Mexicans were gathering their forces.

The "river" was in fact little more than a brackish stream, four foot deep and a hundred yards wide. However, the banks which rose above it were too steep for teams to cross. The Irish were called upon to form work parties to cut down the banks to enable the teams to make the crossing. Colonel James Duncan and Captain Sam Ringgold set up their batteries above them, prepared to give cover just in case.

For two days, Kevin and his friends cut timber and brush, hacked away at the riverbanks, and labored on the steep grade following the orders of the engineers. Although they heard bugle calls and drums, they saw no sign of the

Mexicans. Gradually, they had cut into the bank and graded it sufficiently so that wagons and horses could go down without endangering the loads of the drivers.

On March 20th at 10:30 in the morning Colonel Worth and his staff along with four light infantry companies crossed through the muddy water and clambered up the banks on the other side under the cover of Ringgold's and Duncan's batteries. When they had climbed to the top of the south bank they observed a few scattered Mexican cavalrymen galloping away. The drums, the bugles, the shouts on the other side, had merely been a ruse on the part of the Mexicans. They did not have a force prepared to oppose the American advance.

Four days later the army reached the junction of Point Isabel and Matamoros. General Taylor left Worth and the infantry there while he proceeded to the coast with the dragoons. When they arrived, they discovered that the Mexicans had set fire to the tiny village of Fronton de Santa Isabela on Point Isabel rather than let the Americans have the supplies that were stored there. However, the Americans had their own supplies coming. Late that afternoon transports arrived along with their escorts, and Taylor ordered work started on a fort to protect the stores. He garrisoned the base with two artillery companies, then left to rejoin the main force at Palo Alto, ten miles from the Río Grande. On the 28th they resumed their march and at noon the next day they came into sight of Matamoras, State of Tamaulipas, Mexico.

Curious crowds had gathered to see the gringo soldiers. There were old women in *rebozos* sitting up on roof-tops; there were the children shouting in the streets, and some young girls waved colored scarves. None of the villagers knew what was going on, but it was an exciting time for the inhabitants of this remote and sleepy village. In response to their new audience the marching band struck up "Hail Columbia' and the color sergeant unfurled Old Glory. Each regiment broke out their colors as well, and each company their pennants. The colorful and noisy American army had arrived to what seemed like a welcome-home crowd. There was little of war in the air.

After breakfast the next day Murphy and Kevin walked down to the riverbank. The picket told them not to get too close, so they hunkered down next to where the guard stood and looked down at the river. Some older women were down on the opposite bank scrubbing laundry on the rocks, rinsing it in the streams, and then setting it out to dry. As the sun rose they were joined by younger girls who, lifting their skirts and holding the bundled cloth in one hand, waded into the river. Their brown legs, bare to the thighs, glistened in the sun as if oiled. Their laughter was carried across the water and up the bank on the side where the Americans watched. The men especially liked the billowy cotton blouses, either bleached white or flowered, which the Mexican girls wore off the shoulder and which exposed the top of their breasts.

Neither the picket nor the Irishmen spoke of these things. They simply watched quietly from the opposite bank. Kevin was afraid to move lest he scare the girls off. He could tell by the heavy breathing coming from Murphy, that his companion was dazzled and delighted by the glimpses he had of the round shoulders and the firm brown legs of the señoritas.

Finally, Kevin moved. The discomfort of his position and the warmth of his groin forcing him to his feet.

"My God," he said. "I don't know when I've ever seen a lovelier bunch."

"There is no lovelier bunch," said Casey. "At least not in this world."

The picket snorted. "You two have been too long on he march, that's plain to see. Damn brown-skinned Catholics. Sluttish women and lazy superstitious men. Damn waste of ammunition and time comin' down here to help the Texans. I just hope we hurry up and get this damn war over with."

He walked away looking for his relief. Kevin turned red in the face and balled up his fist. He was speechless with rage at the man's remarks and was headed after him to give him a thrashing. Murphy rose to his feet and grabbed Kevin from behind.

"Hold off, bucko," he warned. "There's not much to be done for the likes of him. His kind burned the women healers in Massachusetts and called them witches. They forbade dancing and singing, and called Holy Mother Church the Whore of Babylon. Ye can't change the likes of him. So, ye best ignore it."

"But it's his side we're to be fighting on," Kevin exclaimed.

"Ah, well, ye see, bucko," Murphy temporized. "We're not fighting yet are we? It's a beautiful day. Now, I can smell a goat cooking on the other side. And I wouldn't wonder if one of them young ladies might not serve us a generous portion in exchange for a coin or two. What say we go down and ask?"

Although pickets were instructed to shoot Americans swimming across the river to the Mexican side, there was no such prohibition from the Mexicans. Young women could and would swim across the river, and there were many who came to sell roasted goat, *aguardiente*, or *cigarillos* to the Americans. Many lingered behind after sundown. And, despite the shots that occasionally rang out along the riverbank, an occasional soldier in blue would swim across to make a rendezvous with a young lady, or to have a night on the town. Four men had drowned by the first week in April, and two had been shot by pickets. But for many of these men, the chance at a evening with a pretty señorita was worth the risk.

Kevin and his friends were content to signal across to ask for food or drink, and then wait for a young girl and her friends to deliver it. They ate the rich goal meat stewed in its own juices called *birria*, which was mixed with chiles and garlic. They drank *pulque*, a foul tasting drink made from fermented cactus, which nevertheless had a terrific wallop. They also drank *aguardiente*, a rougher tasting drink which was even stronger. They served themselves portions of stewed meat using corn *tortillas* as edible spoons and plates. As the days passed they learned more than a few Spanish words, and found themselves smiling a lot at the señoritas who took, it seemed, as much delight in Irishmen as the Irish did in them.

They met some of the Mexican men as well, and smoked tobacco with them rolled into the *cigarillos* which, to their surprise, many women smoked as well. Some of the Mexicans even spoke English, having lived in Florida or Texas, places where there were large groups of English speaking settlers. Most of them had no hard feelings against the gringos, but they were disturbed that they would come south in such numbers. They feared, they said, for the safety of the villages, for their churches, for their women. The Irishmen sympathized. And it was not long before the Mexicans learned that the Irish were not like other gringos and they began to trust them and tell them of movements of their own army.

The days of leisure did not last long, however. At the end of the month all Irish soldiers were ordered to be "engaged on Engineer fatigues." This consisted of construction of a star-shaped earthen fortress with walls nine feet thick. It was an onerous detail. So, difficult was the work and so oppressive, that each man engaged received a gill of whiskey at the end of the day.

Despite the whiskey ration, however, the work irked Casey. It was becoming more and more obvious to him what the agenda of the American army was. The construction of the earthen "Fort Texas" was a red flag to be waved in front of the Mexican bull.

"They intend to construct a fort, right here, opposite a major Mexican town, in Mexican territory. Their generals won't stand for that. The people wouldn't let them. It's a damn insult."

"And that's the whole point, ain't it?" replied McDowell.

"How do you mean?" asked Casey. "That Taylor hopes to provoke them into a fight?"

"Ain't it obvious? If they don't fight now, they wouldn't be men at all."

"What do you think about it all, Casey?" asked McDowell.

"I'm thinking the same thing that Murphy was thinking when he talked about those Texans a while back. The Texans have their war and they're fighting it. Likely, when they get what they want, they'll go home. I don't like the Texans, but I appreciate the way they stick together and the way they fight for what they believe in.

"But we don't have any fight against these Mexicans. If anything—our fight should be with them, not against them. They're Catholic, so are we. They're being attacked by an Anglo-Saxon army which hates the sight of an Irishman and works him like a damn slave, beats him like a dog, and talks about him like he's dirt."

"You're right," Murphy said. "And it's about time we did something. I've got a few ideas of how..."

The lieutenant on command came over to where they were standing. He whacked Murphy on the rump with the flat of his sword.

"That's not getting the fort built, boys. Come on, come on, back to work."

Murphy gritted his teeth and bent over his shovel. He continued filling the canvas sacks with dirt to that they could be carried up the ladder to form the nine-foot earthen walls. He worked steadily and quietly until the lieutenant left.

"He's one on my list," Murphy said biting off a chaw of tobacco from his plug. He settled it into his jaw before he continued. "But never mind, his day will come." He spit a long stream of brown juice which completely smothered a black, stink beetle which was crawling up the half completed wall.

"Now, listen. It don't make sense to talk here. We'll meet tonight out by the river bank. I know of some other fellows who are of a like mind with us. One of em's name is Jackson. George Jackson from Pennsylvania. He ain't Irish so he's trusted with picket duty. But he's told me he's had his fill of this army. He said he won't shoot anyone going over, and he plans on going over himself."

"How come?"

"Seems like he's had his fill of the abuse of folks like us. Says he sympathizes. Says his people, the Quakers, had to move to Pennsylvania in the old days to escape the kind of persecution he sees us going through. Says he can't stomach a war against Catholics."

"This ain't gonna be a war," Casey said. "This is gonna be a slaughter. I already had a look through the lieutenant's field glasses that he left on the parapet. These people ain't got a decent piece of artillery that I can see. Shit, the army could hole up in this old dirt fort for the next ten years if it wanted to. And if it decided to attack, those Mexicans would stand a chance in hell."

"All the more reason for going over," McDowell smiled.

"How do you mean?"

"Ain't we Irish always on the side of the underdog? There ain't no honor in fighting on the winning side."

"There ain't no honor in getting hanged, neither," said Kevin.

"Boy," Murphy snapped. "Ain't you ever read you Irish history? Ain't you ever heard of Robert Emmett? He was captured by the British while fighting for Irish independence. They took him to a London prison to hang him. His last words were, 'Don't bury me—let my bones bleach in the sun—until I can be buried in free Irish soil.'"

"So that's us, huh?"

"Well, Kevin me boy, I don't know about you. But I'd rather have my free bones bleaching on Mexican soil, than be slaving in a blue uniform without honor, without respect, without manhood. I'd rather die with a gun in my hand fighting, than bucked and gagged or whipped to death for acting like a man and standing up for myself."

"A gun in your hand, or a noose around your neck," Kevin said.

"Ah, it's unlikely they'll be any nooses, boy. An Irishman will fight like a beast at bay. Besides, there's no war on yet. I don't think they'd be hanging anyone who deserted. But even so. I'd rather risk that then continue this shameful work."

By the following week over thirty men had swum to the other side and permanently left Taylor's army. On Sunday, April 12th, a tall, broad-shouldered and muscular man by the name of John Riley received a pass from his commanding officer to attend a Mass which was to be celebrated by a Mexican priest on the north bank of the river.

Riley, who some said was a former artillery officer in the British army in Canada, had more than he could stomach of Taylor's expeditionary force. Despite his obvious skills and background, Riley—an Irish Catholic—was only a private in the American army and was placed on the demeaning work details along with his less gifted compatriots. A superior soldier in every way he, nevertheless, was not trusted with any responsible position and, as Taylor's army approached the day of reckoning with the Mexicans, he and his co-religionists been singled out for new kinds of harassment. A friend had a rosary snatched off his neck. Another's scapula was ripped from the shirt on which it was pinned, and cast into the campfire. Men were warned about praying aloud.

This particular Sunday, Riley himself had to beg for permission to receive the sacraments for the first time in six months. Only reluctantly had permission been granted. The Irishmen had, in fact, completed most of the work on the fort, and it was due in no small part to the energy and hard labor of Riley and his compatriots. His company commander, Capt. Moses Merrill was to remember him as "having a good character." Unlike some of the Irish, he would add, "I never had to discipline him."

Good character notwithstanding, Private Riley, had shovelled his last spadeful of dirt for Uncle Sam. He crossed over the Río Grande, right under the nose of a Pennsylvania picket who swore he did not see him, and joined the Mexican army.

Called at first the Foreign Legion, the new branch Riley formed consisted of Irishman from the American army who had crossed over like himself, as well as Scots, Germans and other Irish who had been living in Mexico for a number of years, and were sympathetic to the Mexican cause.

If the Americans did not recognize the abilities of this six-foot-two redhead with a knack for command and an instinctive understanding of artillery tactics, the Mexicans did. The thirty-five year old Riley and the forty-two year old Mexican general, Mariano Arista, hit it off at once. Both were redheads, tall, used to command, self-confident and intelligent. Both were Catholics. Both had lived in the northern U.S.; Riley in Michigan, Arista in Cincinnati. They both understood the force that was arrayed before them and the kind of men who would be needed to confront it. Arista immediately promoted Riley to the rank of artillery lieutenant, and placed him in command of a brace of cannon. He then sent a column of 1,600 mounted soldiers across the river to cut off the supplies to Fort Brown.

On April 25, 1846, an American scouting party was attacked by a Mexican cavalry unit on the disputed left bank of the Río Grande. In this scuffle, eleven Yankees were killed , six wounded and sixty-three taken prisoner. General Taylor rushed this news to Washington where President Polk had already decided to declare war against the Republic of Mexico. The entire army was assembled to hear the news from General Taylor.

Hostilities had begun. Anyone leaving the army now would be a deserter under the Articles of War, and the penalty for such desertion after commencement of hostilities was death by firing squad. Murphy and McDowell, Casey and Kevin, had missed the narrow window which would have allowed them to change sides before the war had begun. Now, any decisions to cross over would mean death: on the field of combat, if fortunate—lined up against a wall, if not.

The Irishmen were under no illusions. Despite the impressive cavalry maneuvers they had seen on the Mexican side, they did not believe the Mexicans had much of a chance. There was no way a country of seven million could compare in resources and training with a country of twenty million. Despite the doggedness of her infantry, the courage of her cavalry, the Mexican army could not stand up against the American cannons. It was only a matter of time.

To simply desert from the American army at such a time would be dangerous, of course. Still, the American west was large and few people asked questions then on the frontier. Armed and healthy, a young man with grit and energy would have a chance.

But to desert the American army and not run away, but remain, choosing to fight on the Mexican side, was a kind of wild and desperate chivalry which had not been seen in history for generations, and would never be seen again.

This latter was the decision which Kevin and his countrymen were about to make on the first of May, 1846, a chilly spring morning, when General Taylor moved out with troops to obtain supplies at Point Isabel. The Irishmen had been left behind to complete work on the fortifications. They sat on top of the forward wall eating their lunch. Down below them they could see Mexican cavalry going though maneuvers. Behind them, over a quarter mile away they could see some twelve and six-pound cannon.

"Jesus, a dirt wall," Casey said, tamping down his seat. "You know General Taylor must figure we don't have too much to fear from the Mexican artillery," Casey said.

"Well," McDowell replied. "I figure these walls could be breached, all right. You'd just have to move the cannon up a lot closer than what they've got. Then keep your fire trained on one spot."

"So, what do you think?" Murphy asked. "Are we goin' over?"

"Was there ever any doubt?" Casey asked. "The only question is when and how."

"Wait," Kevin said. "I've got another question."

"Yeah, kid?" McDowell turned and looked at him. They all waited. Kevin banged his boot against the outside of the dirt wall. He wanted to ask why they were throwing their lives away. Why they would leave one army to join another of a people whom they did not know. Why, if they were going to leave the American army, they just didn't hightail it west to San Francisco. But suddenly his mouth was dry. He could not bring himself to speak.

"Aw, nothing, I guess."

"You don't have to come with us, kiddo," Casey said. "You make your own decision."

"Where else would I go, Casey?" Kevin asked. "You fellers are the only family I have. Where you go, I go. What the hell would I do here if I knew you fellers were on the other side? I couldn't shoot my rifle in that direction for fear I might hit one of you."

"That's the way, bucko! And, who knows? We might survive this war. We might all own a little piece of land someday, marry up with fine señoritas, and have children. This is a big country, bucko. The Americans might get tired of chasing around down here. They might sign a peace treaty and go back up north."

"Especially if the Mexicans give 'em Texas," McDowell said.

"Which they've lost already anyway up to the Neuces," added Murphy.

"Now here's what we do. Tomorrow morning just after sun-up, this señorita I been meeting with these past couple of weeks, name of Yolanda Martínez, and her brother Óscar are going to be down on the riverbank. George Jackson will have sentry duty. He doesn't get relieved 'till six. We'll tell the Sarge we're volunteering to sleep up here tonight. We'll offer to man the two eight-inch guns in case the Mexicans decide to attack now that the Old Man has taken off with most of the army."

"I think it'll work," McDowell said. "I already heard Major Brown talking to the captain and saying that he was worried about an attack."

"Can you trust the Mexican girl?" Casey asked, lighting a *cigarillo* and squinting his eyes against the smoke.

Murphy spit a stream of brown juice off the nine foot wall and just missed a green and gold lizard sunning himself on a rock below. He turned to Casey and glared at him.

"I'd trust a Mexican quicker than I trust any of these slave owning bastards in charge here," he snapped. "Besides," he added, softening his reply and smiling shyly. "She's going to be my wife."

Casey looked him in the eye. He started to say something but then caught himself and put his hand out.

"Well, have you thought about who yer best man will be?"

Murphy shook the hand offered to him, and then McDowell and Kevin joined in, shaking his hand, patting him on the back.

"I figure you to be the best man, and McDowell to be godfather. And if it's a boy, I believe I'll name him Kevin. I always was partial to that name. It was the name of my youngest brother who died of a fever in the old country.

They all grew quiet then, thinking of Ireland, knowing that they would likely never see her green hills again. The looked down at the river flowing along its green banks, at the sheep grazing idly as if there were no war coming. The breathed in the cool damp air of the riverbank and watched a flock of barn swallows flash in and out of the trees. They could hear the mourning doves calling to one another off in the distance and their calls echoes across the water.

"Sure, one could make a home here," Murphy said. "One could grow strong sons. And in time they might go back across the sea and run the bloody British out."

"That'll be the next war for sure," Casey said.

"If we survive this one," McDowell said.

"But it will be a war for those of Kevin's age, the youngsters," Murphy said. "Not mine. I'll raise a family here and live in peace, if they let me be."

"It seems like a small enough thing to ask," McDowell said. "To raise a family and live in peace."

"Small enough, I reckon. But we won't get it without a fight."

"Well, hell, when did an Irishman get anything without a fight?" McDowell asked. "Come on, let's get our gill of whiskey and drink to the battles to come."

They climbed down and got their whiskey ration poured into tin cups. Then, they picked up their rifles and headed down to the riverbank. Casey passed *cigarillos* all around and they sat and watched the river turn golden with the late glow of the afternoon. As they sat there quietly enjoying the warm rush of the whiskey and the harsh sweetness of the Mexican tobacco, a buck and two does came quietly down the water to drink.

The buck spotted them and stood like a statue, letting the females drink and never taking his eyes off the men. The Irishmen did not move. They did not speak. Not one of them reached for his rifle. Finally, the buck came forward a few steps, took a quick drink, and then wheeled quickly herding the does before him. When he had reached the top of the bank on the other side, he paused, tossed his antlers defiantly, and then disappeared into the brush.

The four Irishman sat by the river, still not speaking. They watched the gold of the river fade to blood red, then purple, and then darken to oblivion except for the occasional silver flash of a small fish. The air grew chill around them but they did not notice. None of them said a word. Nor could they have said a word for they had not the language. But Kevin would remember in the days that followed, that it was the first time he knew what trust was and the first time he had ever truly been at peace in the company of men.

He knew that he had a bond with these rugged soldiers who had chosen to fight for the losing side. And it was a bond which went beyond religion or race or homeland. A bond which negated the importance of victory or honor. But he could not, nor would he ever be able to articulate what it was. And when less sympathetic men, more callous men, would ask about it he would lie. But he would never wonder after about his decision, nor question the fact that this night on the riverbank was the happiest he had ever been in his short life, or ever expected to be again.

CHAPTER 15

Green Fire in the Blood

The river was colder and deeper than Kevin had guessed. Since neither he nor Casey could swim, they had paired up with Murphy and McDowell each on one side of a charred log which had floated down from the burned village to the east. Kevin was fine until the sandy bottom dropped off beneath his feet and he realized that one slip would send him under where he would be dragged downstream by the current, beyond the reach of his companions, the life choked out of him by the turgid flow of the silt-laden waters.

He thrashed his legs so violently in his efforts to stay afloat and push the log further from the shore, that Murphy snapped at him.

"Just hold the log, boy! You and Casey both. Let me and McDowell do the work. Much more of that thrashing about and ye'll have the whole bloody camp down on us!"

"Yessir," Kevin said, imagining now the snap of bullets from the shore behind him, the lead slap of a discharged ball smacking his exposed neck, cracking the bone. He tried to shift around so that he could get a look at the shore.

"Jasus, and what is it ye think yer doin' now?" asked Murphy giving him a sharp look.

"Nothin', " Kevin replied and concentrated on simply holding on to the log without moving. It was hard to do. The fear had given him an adrenalin surge which made it torture for him not to engage in some activity. But he hung on, not moving a muscle, as they inched their way across the river.

The trip seemed interminable, and they were pulled by the current five hundred meters west of where they had intended to meet the Martínez girl and her brother. Casey, who liked the rest of them had followed Murphy's order to bring their muskets, had a look of incredulity (which would have been amusing to see under other circumstances) when his feet finally touched the sandy bottom on the other side and he was able to release his death grip on the log and adjust his musket sling.

"Jesus, Mary and Joseph! I'd rather fight three battles with nothing but a bayonet than have to cross another river like that one."

Murphy laughed. "Then I suppose that means you're here for good, Casey!"

"Good or bad, we're all here for the duration," Casey replied. "Unless you can give me one good reason for swimming back again."

They all turned and looked back to the other side. They had swung beyond the curve of the river and could no longer see the earthworks of the fort. But they could see the drift of the smoke from the early camp fires which had not been banked; they could hear the clanking of muskets and swords and the whinnying of horses as the Americans got ready for their day.

Looking back, Murphy had no feeling of regret. He knew that there was nothing left for them on the other side; that there never had, in fact, been anything. He felt no solidarity with Taylor's army; he had no comrades in arms, no one upon whom he could depend except his Irish companions.

Murphy raised his fist in a Fenian salute. "Sinn Féin!" he said to his three companions.

They all shook hands, Roman fashion, clashing the wrists, the way Cassius did with Brutus on the fields of Philippi.

"Sinn Féin!" they said in unison. And the Gaelic salute of brotherhood and solidarity, "Ourselves Alone!", echoed there above the rush of the Rio Bravo, above the caws of the querulous crows of early morning, and the rumbling of caissons as the American cannon was moved from the fort out onto the Santa Isabel road.

Kevin felt tears spring briefly to his eyes but he quietly blinked them back. "Ourselves Alone." Yet, he had never felt less alone in his life. He had merged this morning with three others into a solid unit. He felt that he, Casey, McDowell and Murphy were like Roman centurions on the frontier soon to join up with the main phalanx of the legion. But unlike the soldiers of Rome, he and his fellow centurions were well-armed with modern weapons, homogeneous in their faith, and in top condition. Their own solidarity, he believed, would prove stronger than that of any army. Moreover, they were all suffused with a passion more sentimental men in a gentler time might have called love.

For when men separate from their families and are cast ashore on alien land far from their own hills and shores, there is no stronger call than that of blood and the God who was worshiped by their fathers. And in the Irish blood which flowed through these men's veins was mixed that of the Spaniards who crashed on Irish shores when the Armada of 1588 was lost in a violent storm. Spanish sailors and officers had married the widows of fishermen who lived on that rocky coast.

The two strains, Irish and Spanish: stoic, fearless and passionate, convinced beyond thought of the power of the Virgin whose image lived in their houses, and through whose intercession, had now combined to bring (far beyond their knowing or the world's) these four men now to another place, far beyond their homeland, and yet so close here again in spirit to the Virgin whose Son they worshipped and whose bells they now heard tolling from the village church.

Yolanda and Óscar Martínez had seen the men crossing. And now, Óscar, after giving a low whistle so as not to alarm them, approached the clearing when the Irishmen stood, checking to see if their powder was dry, whiping their musket barrels and bayonets with the ends of their shirts.

"*Buenos días, señores. Bienvenidos a mi pueblo*," announced the Óscar Martinez, a young man of evident breeding who had the light skin of a Spaniard but the high cheekbones and flashing dark eyes of the Indian. He wore a linen shirt cut in the latest fashion and a pair of whipcord riding pants with the high leather boots of an equestrian. In his hands held an expensive felt sombrero which he flourished as he greeted them.

The men turned as one, with McDowell brandishing his weapon, and Murphy making a motion for him to put it up.

The young Mexican was nonplussed. He opened his hands to show that he carried no weapons and then smiled even more broadly. "*Qué bueno que ustedes traigan sus carabinas*!"

Murphy nodded his head.

"*Los necesitarán*," Óscar continued. "You'll need them."

"I told you!" Murphy said triumphantly to Casey after translating for the others. "I could tell by looking at their artillery that they'd likely be short on infantry weapons as well. He calls this a carbine, which it damn sure ain't, but its probably better than anything he's seen."

Then he turned to the Mexican and bowed apologetically. "*Me disculpa, por favor. Le presento a mis amigos, Señores Casey, McDowell y Dillon. Y me llamo Murphy*."

"*Mucho gusto en conocerles, especialmente a usted, Señor Murphy*," the young man replied with a bow. "*Su servidor, Óscar Martínez, a sus órdenes*."

Casey shook Óscar's hand, and held it for a few seconds in genuine pleasure while the others nodded politely, friendly but distant, unfamiliar with the customs of the new land, and somewhat intimidated by the young man's elegant bearing.

So quietly, so gently that they had not even suspected she was among them until seconds after she was there, Yolanda Martínez stepped out from behind a willow tree whose low branches had concealed her while they talked to her brother. She stood beside him now. Except for the tilt of her chin, which was a bit prouder than that of her bother's, the two were alike as twins.

"*Les presento a mi querida hermana, Yolanda*," Óscar said, reaching behind him and taking her hand.

"*Buenos días*," Casey said smiling foolishly. "*Mucho gusto*."

The others, including Kevin, bowed shyly as swans and mumbled greetings in English.

"Jasus," whispered McDowell to Kevin. "Every damn one of 'em is either a goddess or a princess."

Kevin nodded in agreement. He had yet to see an ugly Mexican girl Although he supposed that such a species did exist, time had given him no evidence of it. Yolanda approached them now with a dazzling smile which took each of them in before she demurely lowered her eyes. When she raised them again she was looking only at Murphy. And he had taken her hand and walked a bit away from the group.

She was a natural beauty. Her hair, thick and luxurious, was twisted in a thick braid which reached her slim waist. She was clothed in a white blouse which was low cut and accentuated her full breasts. Her blue dress of pleated linen clung to her hips and stopped below her knee an inch above the top of her kidskin boots.

She turned and spoke briefly to her brother. Then she raised herself on tiptoe to give Murphy a hug and a light kiss. Kevin was stunned by the gold flash of her thigh. He was imagining a tender kiss just at that sweet spot, just brushing his lips across it, when the brother's voice startled him back from his reverie.

"Caballeros," his dark eyes flashing briefly in Kevin's direction and then including them all. "*Con su permiso*." Here he gestured toward the town. "*Vamos a mi casa donde voy a explicar lo que ustedes van a hacer*."

"He wants us to go with him to his house," Murphy translated. "There he'll explain what we do next." He stood next to the girl and waited until the others joined him.

"You speak this lingo pretty good," Casey said, his voice of mixture of envy and admiration.

"Yeah, so-so. I studied for the priesthood in the Old Country. My Old Da's crops failed though, and the money ran out. You can guess the rest."

He smiled and gave the girl's shoulders a squeeze before he continued. "I also discovered I had a fondness for the lasses. Anyway, my Latin teacher in the seminary was a Jesuit from Barcelona. Good man. He taught me a bit of Spanish as well, but I never thought I'd have the chance to use it."

"God works in mysterious ways," Casey said.

"His wonders to perform," Murphy added, finishing the quote.

"Amen," Kevin added watching the feline movements of the girl climbing up the bank, her short dress pulling with each step the pleated material up across he thighs.

"He's a lucky bastard, ain't he?" McDowell asked.

"Huh? Oh yeah, yeah, he's lucky all right," said Kevin. Then looking toward Murphy, he added, "But he's a good man, too, and he deserves the best."

The exchanged glances. From then on each of them knew that Yolanda Martínez would be as safe with them as if she were in a nunnery. The future bride of their compatriot was off limits, in thought as well as action, and they softened their hearts to friendship and brushed away the lust from their minds, and the leer from their glances.

Their walk through town was uneventful, although Kevin expected at any moment to be challenged or shot at from behind one of the low slung houses and storefronts that lined the main avenida. People were scurrying to and fro in the streets. A steady stream of people, many of them Indians judging by their thicker bodies, broader noses and high cheekbones, carried baskets of fruits and vegetables to the north side of the plaza, safe from the reach of enemy guns.

Their caravan occasionally passed a soldier coming from his home or an overnight rendezvous with a señorita, buckling his belt, or casually gripping his worn musket by the barrel as if it were a broom, and him on his way to sweep the street and not rejoin a regiment poised for a major confrontation.

But, although Kevin's stomach soured and his sphincter tightened, nothing happened. They kept their muskets slung behind their backs as Óscar suggested, and they quickly arrived at a non-descript house not far from the plaza. The worn stone facade looking out on a dusty, unpaved side street had little to recommend it except the front door. The door, eight feet high and thick, was fashioned of madrone, and had an intricate coat of arms carved in bas relief surrounded by delicately crafted oak leaves. It looked incongruous there, as if it might have been stolen from a baronial mansion or an English church and set here as a trophy amid the crumbling mortar and stone.

Óscar rang a bell and amidst a flurry of barking both high and low, desperate and sonorous, an ancient Indian woman came to the door. There were two dogs beside her. The first, a wiry terrier with a high yipping sound did handstands and cartwheels around them as they stepped in the door. The other, a mastiff, big as a small pony, woofed solemnly twice, and then at a sharp word from the master, settled for sniffing them each suspiciously as they passed. Unsmiling, the Indian woman said something in her own language to Óscar and turned away.

Yolanda gathered the terrier in her arms where he snugged close to her breasts and left off his annoying yaps and yips.

"Our dogs," she said smiling. "The little one, Celosa or The Jealous One."

With that she made her apologies and disappeared into the interior.

"And the brute, whom my dear sister failed to introduce, is called César. He is at most times master of the house, although on occasion he defers to me. *Pasen ustedes*," he added, stepping back politely.

As the door closed behind them, the Irishmen left the sounds and smells of the dusty hubbub of Matamoros for an other-worldly delight of sound and sense. Inside was a courtyard with a lush garden of magnolia and white hibiscus. Blue songbirds and green parakeets, canaries, and gray lovebirds sang from wicker cages mounted on the balcony which rose above them. Everywhere was bougainvillea, rose and violet, glistening in the morning dew with a phosphorescence which was unworldly. A handsome fountain, carved intricately of stone, sprinkled water among a pool of lilies.

"It's a paradise," Murphy said to his host.

The others, too moved to speak, were engaged in a dumb show of oohs and ahs as they jostled each other for a look, now at the parakeets, now at the fountain, now at the bougainvillea-adorned balcony.

"It's only a small patio," Óscar demurred. "Come. I want you to meet my uncle."

They crossed the flagstone walk and entered a dining area whose floor was inlaid with blue tiles, and whose walls were covered with multicolored tapestries of hunting scenes. There was a large mahogany table in the center polished to a high gloss. Surrounding it were high-backed wooden chairs covered in plush velvet. The centerpiece was a burnished copper bowl containing an arrangement of white, yellow and pink roses interspersed with ferns.

Although the shutters to the street were closed to keep out the noise and dust, the room was not dark. It was lit both by the soft light of the patio and the stronger eastern light of the kitchen which was to the right of the dining area. Close to the kitchen entrance was a table with an ornate glass mirror above it. The table and the mirror frame were intricately carved of the same dark wood as the other furniture.

"*Qué pena*!" said a mocking voice, high pitched like that of a cranky old woman. "*Una estupidez, no? Usted, cómo la ve?*"

They all turned and looked in the direction of the sound. It was a large parrot with blue, green and red feathers, swinging on his perch, in an enormous cage suspended next to the table. The bottom of the cage was littered with bits of chicken, apples, and melon.

"This is our parrot, Malinche. She is very sarcastic. She imitates the voice of a woman from Madrid who was the daughter of the governor in colonial times. They were not amiable people but we thought there was no reason why the parrot should perish in the struggle for our independence."

"*Qué milagro*!" the parrot squawked.

"She only knows a few words," Óscar remarked as he adjusted the tie the maid had brought him, then slipped on a handsome velvet jacket. "Thank you, Rosa. Perhaps you might cover the bird so that we can eat our meal in peace."

"Please sit," he said with a courtly gesture.

Almost immediately another servant, a young Indian girl of about twelve, brought in plates of fresh limes, tomatoes, chopped onions, cilantro, jamaica, and small green chiles.

"We will have some *menudo* first, which is one of Rosa's specialties, and then you will meet my uncle. He will tell you where your countrymen are. I know you will be anxious to join them. For now, please enjoy our hospitality."

Yolanda, who had disappeared when they entered the house, returned now in a dress of blue velvet and ruffled lace. She carried a tray with bowls of water which she set out before them. Each bowl had rose blossoms scattered across its surface.

Kevin who was thirsty from his hike from the river was about to pick up the bowl and drink it, when he saw his host dip his fingers in it, rub them briefly, and then dry them with a towel. Shame-faced and blushing from his near faux pas, he followed his host's example.

"*Lavabo inter innocens manus meus*," Murphy said.

"Ah, Latin. The true language of Christians. Appropriate, too, my future brother in law. You do, in fact, wash you hands among the innocent."

No longer amazed at anything Murphy said or did, Kevin smiled. Yolanda, who now had the terrier in her arms again, set the dog down and sat next to Murphy, touching his arm gently as she did so.

Kevin leaned back in the plush chair and waited to see what would happen next in this strange new world. He did not have long to wait. Rosa returned bringing a tray containing small crystal glasses, a large bottle of yellow liquid, and some small saucers of cut lime and salt.

"This is a drink of my country," Óscar said. "Perhaps you have not tried it? We make it from the maguey cactus, those spiky plants you've seen along side the road. It is not as smoky as your whiskey, but it has—how would you say it—the mule's kick?"

"That's for me," Casey exclaimed watching thirstily as his host poured the *tequila.*

"And you see, if one puts the salt so," said Óscar sprinkling some crystals on the back of his hand. "Then takes the limón thus," followed by a lick of the salt, a suck on the lime, and a quaff of the liquor, "one has a savory drink."

By the time Kevin had managed to accomplish the same feat, Casey, who was unimpressed by such niceties as far as liquor was concerned, had already consumed three shots. It burned all the way down his empty stomach and felt like liquid smoke in his veins. Before any of them could drink more, however, Rosa and the girl returned with steaming bowls of soup.

"This is *menudo,*" their host told them. "It is made from tripe which is cooked many, many hours along with elote. It is very healthful and rich, very good for the digestion. It is the recommended food whenever one is—how do you say *crudo*? hung over? But it is also good after such times as a early morning swim in the river.

"We usually take it with the onion and celantro sprinkled, so!" he said demonstrating with his own bowl, a sprinkling of each. "And if you are *much' hombre*, a little of the green chile as well."

Murphy translated and then answered McDowell's question about "what the hell is tripe, and what does he mean if we're real men we'll eat a damn chile."

"Tripe is cow's intestines," Murphy explained. "And the chiles are hot enough to burn the roof off your mouth—if you're not used to them. I had some in Louisiana, and I've heard some of these Mexican ones are even hotter. I suggest you not try to prove your manhood."

"Ha!" McDowell exclaimed. "Anything this Fancy Dan can eat, I can eat, too. What's a damn chile to an Irishman? He popped a half dozen of the small chiles in his mouth and bolted them down. Then he snatched up a second handful to eat more leisurely.

"But I forget myself, sir," Óscar said addressing Murphy and studiously ignoring McDowell. "You would, perhaps, like to offer up a grace in your language."

Murphy thanked his host and cleared his throat. He suppressed a smile at McDowell who now was foolhardily masticating the mouthful of chiles.

"In the name of the Father, the Son, and the Holy Spirit. Amen."

They all made the Sign of the Cross and reverently lowered their heads.

"Bless us, Oh Lord," intoned Murphy. "And these Thy gifts which we are about to receive from Thy bounty through Christ, Our Lord. Amen."

"Amen," replied Casey and Kevin.

"Ah-men," echoed Óscar.

"Holy Mother of God!" roared McDowell snatching up his finger bowl and downing the water and rose pedals at a gulp. He reached over and did likewise with the bowls in front of Casey and Kevin. In doing so, however, he tipped over a full serving of hot menudo on the terrier which was hiding under the table.

Celosa came out from under the table, yipping and snapping with rage. Rosa entered at exactly the wrong time. For Celosa, unable to determine the guilty party, decided to bite the maid who had kicked her once or twice in the kitchen some months before.

"Ai, Yai! Chicharrón perrita! Huichichotl, chiloauwautl. Ai, cielos. Ai, ai!"

Rosa's screams and curses in a unintelligible mixture of Nahuatl and Spanish brought César who had been dozing peacefully by the door. He charged into the room banging the parrot's cage as he did so, knocking the cover off.

"*Qué pena*!" said the bird in her sarcastic voice. "*Una estupidez, no*?"

"*Ai, yai. Diablito, ai*!" screamed Rosa as Yolanda tried to get Celosa to release her grip on the maid's dress which she had now ripped clear up to the calf in a her rage.

"No, Celosa," begged Yolanda. "Down, girl, down! Bad dog!

"*Y usted, cómo la ve*?" asked the parrot. "*Una estupidez, no*?

"What kind of deviltry is this!" exclaimed McDowell, his red face apoplectic and his breathing heavy and strained, while his eyes were shining with the dullness and perplexity as those of a cow in the midst of her own slaughter.

"Just the simple Mexican chile," Murphy laughed. "You can't say no one warned you."

McDowell turned to Murphy with a mixture of perturbation and self-pity. "I'm poisoned I tell you! My whole insides is burning up and my mouth feels like it has lives coals in it!"

"*Qué pena*!" said the bird. "*Una estupidez, no*?"

"Sometimes we find that a bit of bread or tortilla is better than water in such a case," Óscar suggested in polite Castilian.

"What! What does he say! Infernal trickster. Am I man? I'll show him."

As Yolanda belatedly rescued Rosa from the terrier and took her to the kitchen, the young Indian girl returned with a basket of corn tortillas. Guessing the guest's plight, she rolled one quickly and handed it to the stricken Irishman.

He chewed it quickly, ate two more after that, then quaffed the bowl of tripe and *elote*. The girl hurried out and returned with another bowl for him, and a replacement for Kevin's which had spilled in the fracas. McDowell's breathing finally returned to normal, and he began eating the second bowl slowly. After a few spoonsful, he raised his head sheepishly.

"Holy Mother of God and all the saints preserve us! We won't have to worry about the Yankee cannon if we can just get them to eat a few of these things."

"*Qué milagro*! replied the parrot.

Everyone laughed and McDowell finally joined in as well, laughing good-naturedly at himself until Óscar raised his hands in a gesture of seriousness.

"We would not want the gringo soldiers in on this secret, my friend. For even now as you sit here, you feel the fire of those chiles in your blood. It is the fire of the sun, which has passed into you now. Notice how freely you breath, how clean your blood feels, how your true strength now reveals itself to you. You know now that you are alive. You feel a new power in your loins."

Casey, now on his third bowl of soup, knew that this was so. He looked for the first time into the Mexican's eyes, and the Mexican—never blinking—returned his look candidly. McDowell felt a new bond with him as he released his gaze. And Óscar, for his part, smiled in comraderie, took a handful of chiles, then passed the bowl around. Each man took a couple in solidarity but ate them carefully—having learned from Casey's example—mixed with spoonsful of *menudo* and bites of *tortilla*.

When the meal was finished and they all enjoyed a good cigar and another tequilla, they were ready for war against any pale-blooded enemy. Any man who did not have, as each of them did, green fire in his veins.

CHAPTER 16

The Seige of Fort Texas

"May I present my uncle, Major José María Calderón."

The Irishmen rose to their feet as one when the artillery officer entered the room. Dressed in a dark blue cloth coat, with crimson collar, cuffs and piping, the lanky Mexican exuded confidence and authority. He held himself erect in a flawless military bearing and acknowledged the men's greetings with a curt nod.

Kevin was impressed by the officer's hawk-like visage as well as by the uniform. The officer's close-cropped hair and slim face were set in sharp relief by a stand-up collar decorated with a yellow exploding bomb on each side, signifying artillery. The two dozen brass buttons down the front of the coat, each with a similar imprint, the Turkey-blue trousers with crimson piping, could be compared in elegance with no uniform he'd seen before. No American officer had comparable dress blues, and their own enlisted men's outfits seemed hopelessly drab by comparison.

"Please sit," the Major said. "I hope you have enjoyed this simple meal? Yes?" he continued after everyone had mumbled their thanks. "Well, there is much to be done.

Today I will introduce you to Lieutenant Riley who will be your immediate superior. You will be assigned as gunners."

He looked around at the group, then focused on Murphy. His smile, though strained, had a trace a friendliness.

"My niece tells me that you speak Spanish?"

"*Sí, Señor,*" Murphy replied.

"Fine. Then, **Sergeant** Murphy, I suggest that you go to the commissary officer and order uniforms for your men. You may appoint a corporal as well. Since it is May and the weather is warming up, you may ask for the summer uniform issue.

"Once you have your uniforms, you will report to the paymaster and give him your names and new ranks. You will also advise him that you have brought your own weapons and that Major Calderon has ordered you receive a premium for this contribution to our cause."

"Thank you, sir," Murphy replied.

"No need for thanks, Sergeant. But if thanks shall be said here today, let me thank you and your countrymen for making a decision to help us in our hour of need. From now on, I shall consider you one of us and, if God wishes us to survive this conflict, I look forward to welcoming you in my family."

"Now, after you have dealt with the commissary and the paymaster, and you have drawn ammunition, your will go to the main plaza. There you will ask for Lieutenant Riley of the Saint Patrick's Company. He will be somewhere close by arranging for tomorrow's cannonade of Fort Texas. Any questions?"

There were none. And the officer, still unbending, repeated his curt nod.

Murphy called, "Attention!" and the men rose to their feet and saluted. Major Calderon returned the salute crisply, then turned and quietly left the room.

By two o'clock that afternoon the men emerged on the streets of Matamoros clad in white canvas trousers, dark blue coats with the same crimson piping and stand-up collar they had admired on the major. The brass buttons gleamed on their tunics. McDowell, however, objected strenuously to the cap. It was a dark blue cloth barracks cap, piped in crimson, with a prominent red tassel handing down the front.

"I feel like a Scotsman in this thing," he complained.

"I'd say you looked more like an organ-grinder's monkey," Casey teased.

McDowell aimed a blow at his shoulder. Casey ducked the blow easily and then held up a finger.

"Watch it, boy! There are severe penalties for hitting an corporal."

"At least we don't have to wear those kepis which I saw some of the Mexicans wearing," Kevin remarked.

"I still feel a bit of fancy-man in the hat, although I'll admit the rest of the outfit is quite stylish," Murphy conceded.

"Hell, don't let the hat bother you, Sergeant Murphy," Casey consoled. "Once we get on with Lieutenant Riley, he'll probably let us replace the tassel with a shamrock. The Saint Patrick's Company! Can you believe it?"

"Hooray!" yelled Sergeant Murphy.

"Hooray!" they all responded. "*Viva México*! Long live St. Patrick and all his warriors!"

The four artillerymen continued down the road to the plaza, heads erect, marching in perfect lockstep, welcoming the stares of the townspeople, the admiring glances of the ladies, and nonplussed by the barking of stray dogs. Murphy's sergeant stripes were as broad as his biceps and Casey's two chevrons gleamed in the afternoon sun. Their canteens clinked rhythmically as they walked along, and their muskets bumped with solid assurance against their shoulders as they headed down the dusty street to the plaza.

When they reached the *zócalo* there was a flurry of activity. Orders were being shouted in Spanish, there was the creaking of leather and crash of wood and metal as a battery changed position and the horses strained against their tack. A shell screamed overhead and crashed into an abandoned vegetable stand.

"Muévanse! Muévanse! Lárguense de aquí!" shouted a tall redheaded lieutenant over the din.

Another shell smashed into a barricade that had been erected on the north side of the plaza. A group of soldiers huddled close together under the cover of a eucalyptus tree until jostled fiercely by the lieutenant and, accompanied by oaths in English, Gaelic and Spanish, they were induced to help the placement of the moving battery.

"Hallo, there!" Murphy shouted over the din. "Are you Lieutenant Riley?"

The tall Irish officer turned quickly at the sound of the voice. His scowl turned into a welcoming grin.

"That's me. The Major told me that your were coming. Murphy, isn't it? Glad to have you and your men aboard."

The sweating redhead, his uniform covered with black power stains and his face flushed with heat and exertion, offered Murphy his hand. He returned the salute of the others with a casual gesture.

"Not much time for formalities, I'm afraid. But I'm glad to see you. We need all the men we can get. Good to see that you brought you're own muskets as well. A shame you couldn't have smuggled out a couple of Duncan's cannon."

"How is the artillery, sir?" Murphy asked.

Riley shook his head sadly.

"In a combat situation I'm afraid we'd be badly damaged unless we manage to get in under their guns or behind them. No way to deal with them. Their range is far superior.

"However, this is a siege situation and we have half a chance. What is Taylor leaving behind in the fort?"

Murphy, who had kept his ear to the ground throughout the construction, had the facts readily available.

"About five hundred men under the command of Major Jacob Brown. There are two 18 pounders, and then Braxton Bragg's field battery."

"Good work," said the officer obviously impressed. "Well, I could have guessed the 18 pounders. That's what's been reaching us most of the day. Bragg's men are pretty good, too, but I'd be much more worried about him in the field than I am when we've got him in the fort. His field pieces won't do us much damage here.

"Is the layout of the fort the same? They haven't changed anything since I worked on it in April?"

"Nossir," answered Murphy, uncertain of the purpose of the question. "The gun emplacements are basically the same. They'll keep the 18 pounders where they are."

"And the officer's quarters?"

"Same location, sir," smiled Murphy as Irish lieutenant's strategy dawned on him.

"Good! I intend to personally lob a shell right into the lap of Major Brown. He built his own tomb with Irish slave labor."

He turned and shouted some orders to a group of men loading boxes of ammunition. Murphy and Casey exchanged glances of admiration. Kevin was too stunned by the noise and the smoke to make sense of anything that was going on. And McDowell, clenched and unclenched his hands on this musket; anxiety threatened at any moment to overcome his composure.

"Okay. I'm moving some of these batteries closer," Lt. Riley announced. "We've got some new redoubts where they can be set up at close range. Tomorrow at dawn we'll bombard that damn fort of Brown's until it's a pile of dirt. That is, if we can get close enough without getting killed in the process.

Murphy's crew was assigned to help man a 16 pounder in a redoubt northeast of the plaza. The rest of the day and most of early evening they spent securing shot, cannister, shell and balls. Murphy, who was the only experienced gunner, explained what their work would consist of.

"Okay," he said pointing to a cannon that easily weighed over a ton and had been moved on a wheeled carriage pulled by eight horses into the redoubt. "This here is a sixteen pounder."

"Looks more like sixteen hundred pounds to me, Sarge," joked McDowell. "Mexican's must weigh things different."

Unsmiling, Murphy continued with his explanation.

"Actually it weighs well over 2,000 pounds. The designation refers to the approximate weight of a solid iron cannon ball. The diameter of a 16 pound shot, or cannon ball, is 4.8 inches. The next biggest, like the two in the fort that you've seen, they're eighteen pounders. And over there, he said, pointing to where a mixed Mexican and Irish crew of over twenty men were working with Lieutenant Riley, is a 24 pounder. It is called that because of the weight of its 5.5 inch shell. Got it?"

The enormous and immovable rusted cannon which he referred to look more like a relic than a functioning weapon. Plus it was well behind the plaza, about two hundred meters away.

"Will that thing even work?" Casey said.

"All Lieutenant Riley needs is one good shot. And he's one of the best there is. Worked as an artillery officer for the British. If there's any justice at all, and it's my belief there is, you'd best say the prayers for the repose of the soul of Major Brown."

The men nodded their silent agreement. Behind them, officers and soldiers whipped mules and horses reluctant to pull the heavy artillery into place. One cannon had fallen into an *arroyo* sometime earlier and its cast iron barrel had cracked. It lay there now in the sand pointing its useless trunk into the sky. A horse, which had fallen with it, lay splayed out, his legs akimbo in rictus, his hooves pointed skyward.

Flies were everywhere, as well as persistent sand fleas and gnats. A thick black smoke filled the air and the odor of dead horses, of sweat, and of charred wood and burnt flesh. The skies rumbled, and the ground shook from the enemy's cannon. Kevin thought to himself that he had a glimpse of hell. He did not know that he wished to see more.

Murphy, the would-be priest, teacher, charmer of girls, and now instructor of artillery, continued his lecture as if he were in a Jesuit classroom.

"Your job, Kevin, is that of swabber. You take this here pole with the sponge on it, and run it down the bore, like this. So. That's to make sure that there are no sparks left from the round just fired.

"Casey, you're the ramrod. You take one of these cloth bags of gunpowder, put it down the muzzle, set it with this pole, then follow that with the whatever projectile McDowell hands you, according to my order. You seat it with the ramrod behind the powder charge. Then, after I've adjusted the elevation and range, the charge is ignited by a flash of priming powder through the vent hole here. Got it?"

The men nodded their agreement.

"We'll have more boys coming along to help us with the loading and priming so that I can direct my attention to some of the other emplacements and also so that I can observe the effect of our fire and order changes when necessary."

His lecture was interrupted by the arrival of Lieutenant Riley.

"Ten-hut!," the sergeant ordered.

The men came to attention and saluted. Lt. Riley had a short telescope in his hand.

"Thought you might be able to use this, Sargeant Murphy, since you have a forward position. You can keep me informed on the accuracy of our fire."

"Yessir," Murphy said. "I was just making assignments and answering some of the men's questions. They're new to artillery."

"I see. Any question I could answer for you men?

"Yessir," Casey said. "What are all these other things stacked up next to the cannon balls?"

"Good question. Well, first of all, Corporal, the cannon balls you're talking about are technically called shot—if they're solid. Like those over there. The second stack—about the same size you'll notice—will be a little lighter to handle. They are called shell, since they are hollow balls filled with explosive which will blow up upon impact. There's also grapeshot, clusters of iron balls, and cannisters, which we only have a few of, which are filled with musket balls or pieces of scrap metal. They'll rip up a whole platoon of infantry."

"Pretty impressive," Casey said.

"We'll do them some damage, right, sir?" McDowell asked.

"We'll do that, son," the officer replied.

Kevin observed, however, the worried glance that Murphy and the officer exchanged. They both knew that the effective range of their shell was about 350 meters; the shot, about 500 meters. The American artillery, by comparison, could reach 1,000 meters often with deadly accuracy.

"We'll tear 'em up, waa-hoo!" shouted McDowell.

"Carry on, Sergeant," the lieutenant said. "Good luck to you, boys. Do honor to your new flag now, and to the mothers that bore you."

"Yessir," the men replied, saluting the tall lieutenant with the shock of red hair whose blue eyes gleamed in the darkening dusk.

The gun crew did not get much rest that evening. Three more Irishmen joined them, and another Mexican officer who spoke English came by to supervise the loading of ammunition.

The new arrival, Captain Francisco Moreno, was Riley's immediate superior. Born in Florida, which was formerly Spanish territory, Moreno was darkly handsome and smoothly efficient. His affection for the Irishman was apparent and he spent most of the night with Riley supervising the gun emplacements, encouraging the men and seeing that the horse-drawn limbers, or caissons, loaded with ammmunition chests, made their rounds efficiently to all of the batteries.

Kevin did not sleep at all that night. The constant shouting of orders, the whinnying of the horses, and the intermittant fire from the fort precluded rest. So, when the sky began its slow lightening in the east, he buttoned his coat and stood up to inspect the cannon. A dog howled protractedly from a house back in town and mourning doves cooed softly.

"Up and ready?" came a voice behind him. He turned to see the tall liuetenant. His uniform looked clean and fresh. His cheeks still glowed pink from the razor and his blue eyes were bright as if he had slept a full eight hours.

"Yessir, I couldn't sleep," Kevin said apologetically.

"They'll be time enough for that after the fighting is done," Liuetenant Riley said. "Time eternal for some," he added ruefully.

Behind them the bugle sounded and the rest of the gun crew got quickly to their feet and saluted the liuetenant.

"Okay, men," he ordered returning their salute with crisp one of his own. "Let's get at 'em! Sergeant, see to your crew.

"Yessir," Murphy replied. "Dillon, help get the first shot, then ready your swab. McDowell, back him up. Corporal, ready the charge."

"We're close enough here," the lieutenant said. "We're under their guns at this point. They'll be shooting over your heads into the square. Your piece should cause considerable damage, and you know best where to aim, Sergeant. You and your men built those fortifications and know the weak spots. If we place our shot well enough, they just might decide it's not worth keeping."

The bugle rang out again and a color guard approached the forward bunker with a guidon. Behind them in the plaza, there was a drum roll and another blare of the bugle as the Mexican colors—a golden eagle with a snake in his talons mounted on a field of green, red and white—was hoisted by white-gloved soldiers.

Everyone in the bunkers came to attention. When the flag had reached its apex, they saluted, and then returned to their tasks as the color guard distributed smaller flags to the bunkers and a priest blessed the cannons with holy water. Minutes later the order was given.

"Fire!" And the bunkers gave forth an eruption of fire and sound such as Kevin had never imagined in his short life. The ground shook like an earthquake, and the air rushed out in a vacuum. Smoke was everywhere and the concussion was enormous. He felt that his eardrums had burst. Across the river he could see the dirt fly up in great cones as the shells hit. But there was no time to think as he swabbed the barrel and then stepped back so that Casey could place the charge. KAA-BLOOM! KAA-BLOOM! The sound echoed a dozen times as other batteries fired their charges as well. High above them on a silk flag which was now flying over the redoubt, the Mexican eagle danced in the smoke, his great beak wrestling with a brown snake.

The bombardment continued, uninterrupted for five hours. The men stopped only for a drink of warm, brackish water. A shell had burst next to the ammunition park and killed a half dozen horses hitched to a caisson which had just been loaded with gunpowder. Their desperate, high-pitched whinnys rose above the sound of outbound shells. To Kevin it seemed like it had taken the horses hours to die and his brain still echoed with their horrible cries.

Another shell had landed in the center of the northeast redoubt, killed the crew and disabled a twelve pounder. Kevin felt weightless and ethereal. He had already worked in the past five hours, harder, faster, and more efficiently than he had ever thought possible. In spite of the fact that incoming fire was steady and close, and that he could hear the whine of the enemy shells during every pause in their own firing, he had not been afraid. Besides what could he had done with his fear anyway? There was nowhere to go. No place to run.

He was more afraid of looking like a coward in front of his fellow Irishmen than he was afraid of the enemy guns. But mostly he had no time to think. No time to imagine and, thus, no time to fear. It was loading, swabbing, loading, moving shot, and following shouted orders.

They took a break at midday. An Indian girl brought them some tortillas, salt and limes, along with fresh water. It was not much of a meal, but neither did they have much of an appetite. Their stomachs were tight, their ears ringing, and their throats parched with the heat and acrid smoke. Each time the cannon roared it pulled with it all the air from the bunker and left the men gasping, breathless. They inhaled great gulps of air now, as they received their tortillas from the girl, and she filled their canteens.

“We’re giving them hell!” Murphy encouraged them. “You mates are the best gun crew in the field.”

"I just want to see that damn fort crumble back into the dirt it came from," Casey said.

"And all them sonabitches in it," McDowell added, chewing on a tortilla.

"Good job, men!" called Lt. Riley approaching their bunker. "No, no, as you were, Don't get up," he added as the men made to rise. "Let's see your glass, Sergeant."

Riley opened the telescope and looked across the river.

"We're having some effect," he noted looking through the glass. "No doubt of it. We've haven't breached the wall, but we've disabled one of the 18 pounders, I think. We've also placed a couple of rounds inside, close to where our Major Brown might have been at breakfast, hey?"

"Yessir," Murphy grinned.

"Okay, take five. Then re-stock your ammunition. When you've replenished your stock you may fire at will. We'll keep up the bombardment as long as we have visibility, Sergeant, or until our guns, like Joshua's trumpets, cause the walls to crumble."

By nightfall, the Mexicans had lost another cannon, this time the ancient 24 pounder, without making any significant breach in the walls. But the Americans had failed as well in their attempt to set the town ablaze with hot shot. The exchange was a draw. General Ampudia ordered the batteries secured at 7:30 PM and the Irishmen took their rest. The Americans, relentless, continued their firing upon the town for another four hours and it wasn't until midnight that Kevin felt the day had finally ended and that sleep might be possible.

CHAPTER 17

Springtime in New York

There are jonquils in the fields next to the West Point parade ground, the ice has melted on the pond, and the first tender buds have burst forth on the elms. The air, though chilly, already has hints of warm winds from the south. The ground is muddy where it has thawed and fat, red-breasted robins have appeared on the Commandant's lawn.

Cadet Bradford Emerson Broderick, U.S. Military Academy, has just received a letter from his betrothed, Semantha. Arrangements have been made for them to marry the day after graduation. Already the news of the war has changed the outlook at the school. President Polk has announced to the nation that "American blood has been shed on American soil" and forces are being raised to support Taylor's forces at the border. The Commandant is ecstatic with the news. For him it means that West Point will stay in business for quite a while. For the past year his job and the school itself had been languishing, waiting for a reluctant Congress to appropriate funds. There had even been speculation that the Military Academy would be closed down. But now, news of the war has put an end to all that.

For Cadet Broderick, though, the most important thing is the promise of a quick promotion that the war, any war, offers. Instead of a year as a lieutenant, two more as a captain, five as a major, three more as a lieutenant colonel, and colonel—if lucky—at retirement, he had a chance at brevet rank of captain with the year. Colonel by the war's end. Then, who knows, maybe a generalship in Washington. Plus, he had a lovely bride-to-be waiting in the wings.

Samantha was a pretty thing, he mused, opening the back of his pocket watch where he kept a painted miniature of her. Although now that he thought of it, she was only a farmer's daughter. A rich farmer's daughter, of course, and that might not hurt if the end of the war brought the opportunity for a career in politics.

There was something sticky about what went on at the farm last summer though. He looked at the fine features of Samantha in the miniature. The forthright eyes, the hint of a smile. The full, sensual lips. What was it his father had said? Something about the hired boy? Or was it boys? Who had cornered her in the barn until old Browning had come to her rescue with a pitchfork. Hmm. Where was that letter?

Ah yes! Here it was. "Jedadiah Ackley, the homely one, you know," his father had written. "Drunk he was, too. Also, the young Irish lad they took in, you remember? By the name of Kevin Dillon. Shows you just how ungrateful the Irish are. Took him in when he was half dead and nursed him back to health. Gave him a good job and found. Some reward!

"Anyways, my good friend Thomas arrived in time; no damage was done to your future bride; I doubt she was even touched. Thomas ran them both off with a pitchfork, as I said. Good thing for them that he didn't have the musket handy. He should have turned them over to the magistrate, though, if you want my opinion.

"My sources at the Customs House in Boston inform me that both of them have since joined up. Dillon some time ago. Ackley just about the time war was declared. Thank God we have officers like yourself in the service who know how to discipline the likes of these! Though if you ask my opinion, our army is better off without them."

Cadet Broderick made note of the names. Kevin Dillon. Hezakiah Ackley. He took out his leather covered pocket notebook and wrote them down. I'll see to it, he said to himself, that they not have an easy time of it, if they are in the vicinity of any command I'm attached to.

But Samantha. What was she doing alone in the barn with them? Certainly not being discreet. She must have done something to encourage them. No boy would have the guts to just come on to the boss's daughter without so much as a wink or a nod that it might be welcome. And Samantha did, now that he thought of it, have a saucy eye.

He picked up the watch again and looked at the miniature of his soon-to-be bride. A saucy eye, indeed! And those full lips. He closed his eyes and imagined himself in the barn with her. The warmth of the horses and the rich smell of hay and oats. He imagined her surprise as he took her there on the floor of the barn, and the dark eyes of the animals as they watched, and the warm breath of the skinny Irish kid watching hungrily in the shadows.

Neither the graduation nor the marriage ceremony took very much time. There was an brief address by the Commandant and by Brigadier General Roger Jones at the graduation. Secretary of War William Marcy was scheduled to speak but recent events had keep him in Washington. It seemed that, even as President Polk was delivering his war message, another battle was taking place down on the Mexican border.

Two battles, in fact, the general told the cadets. The Mexicans had laid seige to Fort Texas and, while they did not take the fort, they killed the brave Captain Brown who had so gallantly defended it. General Taylor had since named the outpost Fort Brown in his honor.

When General Taylor returned from Point Isabel with his troops after picking up supplies, the Mexicans crossed the Río Grande and attacked him at Palo Alto. According to reports, although his train was temporarily immobilized,

Taylor's forces rained devastating artillery fire on the Mexicans which resulted in heavy enemy losses.

The following day at a place called Resaca de Palma, the Americans attacked a superior enemy force and soundly defeated them. The Mexicans retreated in disarray back across the Río Grande to the city of Matamoros with Taylor hot on their heels.

The cadets' hats flew into the air as was the tradition at graduation but this time there was the added elation that they were not only officers in the army, but officers in a victorious army which was even now in the field routing the enemy. Everyone was anxious for their orders and happy when the lieutenants' bars were pinned on their collars, the speeches over, and they could compare assignments.

"I'm to join up with Worth's division," said one shavetail lieutenant.

"That's part of Taylor's army. The first brigade, I believe," replied another in a knowing voice.

"How about you, Broderick?"

Broderick's face was downcast. He read his orders twice to make sure.

"I've been assigned to General Wool, he's getting up some volunteers in Illinois."

"Volunteer's? Tough luck. It's hard enough to command regulars. Those volunteers give liitle damned respect," said the knowledgeable one shaking his head. "But say, who is your commanding officer?

"Colonel William Harney."

"Harney? Harney, the Commander of the First Dragoons?

"Yeah. Is that good?"

"Hell, yes, my good man. Why Harney's just about the toughest s.o.b. in the army. Voluneers or no volunteers you've got a commander that will back you up against the men and will give the enemy hell at the same time."

He patted Broderick on the back. "I'd say you've done a bit of all right. You could do a lot worse that Harney. Plus, Old Harney's a Democrat, just like our President."

The newly-created officers drank whiskey thoughout the night, exchanging views on their assignments, drawing maps of the movements of the army, discussing the prospects for promotion. It was well after 3:00 AM when Lieutenant Broderick went to the hotel room he had rented in town and set out his dress uniform for the wedding the next day.

The pop of buggy whips and the sound of trace chains outside his window woke him early the next morning and, after splashing some cold water on his face and rinsing his mouth out with a pull from the whiskey bottle, Broderick shook himself awake like a gruff bear coming out of winter hibernation. He opened the door to the "shave and a haircut—two bits" knock of his best man, Lt. Robert Beebe.

Lt. Beebe was enthusiastic, his face shining with good health and sobriety.

"I've been up since dawn!" he exclaimed. "What a day. The birds singing, the troops all out shining their swords so that they can give you a good send-off. What! Are you just now getting up?"

"Shut up, you damn teetoteler. You'd think **you** were getting married for God's sake!"

"Touchy, touchy! Well, I suppose that's the sign of a good dragoon lieutenant. Irascible, mean as a rattlesnake that's been stepped on. But say, how do you think that personality will set with that pretty young thing setting down there in the buggy waiting on you?"

"Damn! she's here already?" exclaimed Broderick pulling open the drapery and looking down on the street. Samantha was sitting in the buggy surrounded by young lieutenants smiling gaying, while Mrs. Crump tried to look both stern and nonchalant.

"You'd better get down there quick. She's already charmed the honor guard and everyone of them is ready to take her to the altar if you've got cold feet."

"Christ," said Broderick. "The way I feel now they're welcome to it. This getting married business was never my idea anyway."

"Ah, but think of the advantages, my good man. Always having a woman there when you need her. The young sons who will carry your name for coming generations, and the grandchildren to whom you can tell of your exploits in the war. And it's not as if our occasional forays into town have appeased your carnal desires. Or, have they?"

Broderick looked down again at Samantha. A remark by one of the lieutenants had brough a blush to her cheek. The wind whipped her petticoats showing showing a trim and delicate ankle. Her blond hair was lifted in the wind. He felt a warm flush of desire, and smiled to himself. He returned to the bedside table and took a deep pull on the bottle of whiskey.

"Help me get into this damn uniform, Lieutenant, and stop babbling! We've got a wedding to go to."

The wedding ceremony itself took no time at all. There was one moment when he turned to his friend with a look of utter despair. It all seemed so final somehow. But Samantha looked radiant and he could tell from the looks of the other officers, including the Commandant with his dumpy wife, that they envied him. Samantha was the most beautiful girl in the church—bar none.

His hand was damp when he took hers and there were butterflies in his stomach when he said, "I do." But he could not help feeling exultation as he and his new bride passed though the crossed sabers at the door of the church and her eyes misted with pride as she looked into his.

Here he was, an officer in the U.S. Army, with a new wife, a new command. An officer in Harney's Dragoons, the toughest outfit in the greatest army on the face of the earth. His stuck out his chest and strutted rather than walked to the buggy that would take them to the hotel for the reception and wedding supper.

There were not a lot of relatives or family friends, only Mrs. Crump and Thomas Browning on Samanta's side, and Dr. Broderick on the groom's. But the young officers and instructors from the Point made up for it. Some of them had bought their fiancées and there was much ado about the bridal bouquet and who would catch it.

From the men there was a great deal of war talk, and occasionally some ribald jokes about married life. Broderick spent little time with his new bride, preferring the talk of his fellow soldiers, the trips to the punch bowl, and the occasional nips of whiskey outside.

By eight o'clock the Commandant and the senior officers and civilian instructors had left. By ten, many of the young officers were under the weather. One had mauled Samantha and torn her bridal veil. Another had started a fight and upset the wedding cake.

"I think maybe it's time we left," Samatha whispered close to his ear.

"Just a little bit longer," Broderick said puffing on a cigar and continuing his conversation with his friends.

"Maybe you should listen to the lady," Lt. Beebe said.

"Maybe the little lady needs to learn that the husband is the commander of this particular platoon," Broderick snapped. "Let's go have a drink."

It was after midnight when the last of the guests had left, and Broderick and his new bride went into the honeymoon suite.

Broderick, his faced flushed, was about to offer to carry Samantha across the threshold, but thought better of it. He was a little unsteady on his feet. He unlocked the door for her but then went ahead of her to light the gas lamp and pull down the quilt on the bed.

"Well, here we are at last. I know you wanted to leave early but it was my last night with those fellows. Tomorrow we'll all be off and some of us will never meet again."

"Tomorrow, but you never said..."

"Tomorrow, girl. I'll be off. So we'd better get at it, hey?" he said unbuckling his sword and setting it next to the bed. He gave her a knowing wink.

Samantha put her hand to her throat. "I'm sorry," she said, blushing. "You'll have to tell me what to do. I mean I've never, you know. I mean should I go into the dressing room first? You'll have to tell me."

He took off his blue tunic and unloosened his belt. He shook his head, amazed by her stupidity.

"We're married, girl," he said in a condescending tone. "Didn't your Mrs. Crump tell you what that means? Come here!"

He cupped her chin in his hand and kissed her hard. "I've waited too long for this to be put off by girlish tricks." He pulled her bodice and exposed the top of her breast. He pulled the breast out of its snug nest and kissed it. She gave a gasp and then blushed. Broderick laughed at her and pulled her roughly down with him on the bed.

All her senses were charged. She dreaded what was to happen and she desired it at the same time. She felt like one of those loose girls Mrs. Crump had told her about. She felt a warmth between her legs, a thrill of fear, too, coupled with desire. She made no attempt to interfere as he unbuttoned her dress. She caught the scent of bay rum and tobacco and whiskey as he bent over her, his breath coming fast, his desire rising.

Layer by layer he removed her gown, her petticoats, until all that was left were her chemise and her stockings. When he did not remove the last of these garments, she raised her eyes to look at him. He had removed his collar and his shirt. His pants were down below his knees but could go no further because of his boots. She was fascinated by the breadth of his naked chest, the darkness of the hairs which curled down the line of his stomach and below. Her stomach fluttered as much from desire as from the odors of stale cigar smoke and whiskey. She wanted him to stop. She wanted to say that this was not how she expected it to be. She wanted him to take off his boots. She wanted to say she needed to use the bathroom, which now she suddenly did.

She turned her head into the feathered pillow so that she would not have to look at the nakedness of him, nor the lust in the glazed eyes. She stretched her body out straight and put her arms to the side. The rough texture of his chest brushed the nipples of her breast and she was both aroused and frightened.

He rolled down her stockings to her calves and then pulled up her chemise to her waist. His knees forced their way between her legs to spread them as he raised himself on top of her. She felt something warm and very hard come up against her moistness and she pushed against him, certain that she was too small for what he was trying to force into her.

"No," she pleaded, "Please, not yet. Please."

Her eyes pleaded with him. "It... you can't. It's too big."

His eyes were glazed over with lust and drunkennesss. He laughed and then slapped her hands away. "Come on, girl, don't be playing games with me." Then, with a thrust of his hips, he entered her and she felt a stab of pain but his mouth covered hers and stifled her cries.

In seconds she had forgotten the pain, as waves of sensation began to build in her and her own natural lubricants began to work. He started a rhythmic thrusting of his hips and she closed her eyes and felt the warmth rising in her. In spite of herself her hips rose to meet his, to move in the compelling rhythm. Then he called out: "That's it, girl! You know how to do it!" and she turned from him flushed by humiliation. As if he thought she was one of those women! And she bit the pillow so she would not cry out, and she lay perfectly still as he continued thusting angrily now, like a mad bull, breathing heavily into her ear, repeating ugly, vulgar phrases, calling her a slut, a whore, and worse until finally an explosion of hot liquid filled her and he rolled off, already half-asleep, and she pulled up the quilt against the cold, shivering as the damp, viscuous semen leaked down her thigh.

She lay there in the dark overcome with loathing and dread. She looked down at him sleeping with his mouth open, a thin trail of spittle coming out of the side of his mouth. He made a snorting sound and then turned over on his side. She jumped out of bed and put on her chemise and two of her petticoats. She walked over to the chamber pot and vomited up an acid stream of vegetables and wedding cake and punch. Then she sat on a leather chair across from the bed and wiped absently at the sticky fluid on her thighs with the edge of her petticoat.

She thought of the beautiful white dressing gown with lace cuffs which she had intended to wear on this special night. It had been her mother's. And she had pictured herself, beautiful and angelic on this special night. Now she would never wear it. She thought of the tender kisses she had dreamed of ever since she was a child. She thought of the times with Kevin when they had kissed in the barn and there was something holy and innocent in their stolen love. She wished desperately she could have that again. She thought of the candlelight, the romantic talk, the tenderness and beauty she had expected on her honeymoon night with her husband. How special that was supposed to be! A stupid girl's dream, she thought. I should have known better.

And then she felt so desolate, so alone, that she cried, deep bitter, gulping tears of frustration and loneliness and despair, biting down on her wrist so hard it would draw blood so that he would not awaken and do something to her again.

Oh, Kevin, my own my first, my true love! she cried softly. Is this how you felt when you were sent away into the cold world. Is this how you felt when you saw love die? And she cried herself to sleep, mingling tears for Kevin with tears for herself. Tears for lost love, for childhood gone, for shattered dreams.

The next morning Broderick awoke in an angry mood with a hangover from the whiskey. He got up and filled the wash basin with the pitcher and splashed his face noisily. He looked at the pale figure of his wife sitting in the leather chair in her petticoats. She was curled up in the chair, one leg turned under her so that the muscle of her thigh showed clear under the taut material of the chemise.

He walked over to her and pulled her roughly to him. She twisted away.

"What, what! None of that now. You come here, you little devil."

He dragged her to the bed by her wrist and pulled up the petticoat. She desperately tried to pull it back down, frightened and awkward in her movements.

She looked into his eyes and she saw the will. She saw the crude early morning lust there which would not be denied. And she saw the cold, unrelenting anger that was an integral part of sex for him.

"You're my wife, girl. If you don't give it to me, I'm just going to take it anyway. So, why not make it easy?"

She shifted her weight to get away from him but it just brought her closer. His hand curved itself into her neck to stop her movements and he felt her stiften in resistence to his touch. He ignored her unwillingness and brought his mouth down to her lips.

"I'm not as tender as your little Irish boy, huh?" he asked.

"Who?" she blushed. She had been thinking of Kevin when Broderick touched her. But how could he had have known? Did she call out his name in her sleep? She blushed with embarrassment and guilt; she trembled like a lamb caught in the wire as the wolf come slowly closer.

Broderick was irritated that she wouldn't yield to him but he was more patient this time. He reached under the chemise and began stroking her thigh, whispering to her softly, tenderly, as a cavalryman would to his nervous mount. He knew how to handle horses and he knew that a woman liked stroking. Finally he felt her open, he found the moistness between her legs and moved his fingers slowly into her, feeling the velvet of her lips, and the warm wetness as she moved against him in spite of herself.

"At least take off your boots," she said.

"Shush, girl, shush," he answered. "Don't talk back to me. Just be a good, quiet little girl."

And then he started kissing her throat, her lips, her neck, his hands stroking her, and this time when he entered her she did not feel pain but a warm fullness that made her tingle all over, and he called her "baby" and "little girl", and an inferno of emotions erupted in her, and she moved against the hardness of his muscled body as he thrust deep into her, and now she moved with him as his tempo increased, and it drove her to a moment of explosive pleasure, again, and again, and then a violent shudder as he came and then relaxed into her, breathing hard and warm into her ear.

"Now, how was that, little girl? No puny Irishman could give you anything like that, hey?"

He rolled over on the mattress to look at her. He ran his hand up her thigh and she shivered with the pleasure of it. He moved his hand over her belly.

"You've got enough seed in you now to grow something you can be proud of."

She smiled in spite of herself. She was exhausted and filled with emotions she could not understand. She hated him, but she loved how he made her feel.

He kissed her hard on the lips and got out of bed. She watched him as he walked across the floor, the solid lean buttocks, the muscled thighs.

"You're mine," he said wiping himself off with a towel and proceeding to dress in his field uniform. "I don't want you ever to forget that."

"I won't," she said in a small, quiet voice.

"And I don't want to hear any more stories about Irish boys or field hands out in the barn."

Chastened, she said nothing. She got up and helped him pack the remainder of his things. Then she dressed herself before the porter arrived to carry her bags.

He hugged her to him roughly and they said goodbye as the New York stage carrying the other officers arrived.

"You'll maybe have a nice healthy son for me after that last bit," he smiled. Then he climbed onto the stage and exchanged some ribald remark with another officer. The men laughed together and did not look in her direction.

He turned to her just as the stage began to pull away.

"By the way," he said. "When I find him, your little Kevin Dillon and his friend will wish they never heard your name. Consider them dead men, my love."

He smiled again and waved a casual goodbye as the stage pulled out in a cloud of dust.

"The bastard," she thought to herself. She felt the tender ache of her muscles as she walked back to the hotel. The chafing of her legs against her petticoats reminded her of one more thing. "He never did take off those damn boots," she said to herself. "The bastard."

CHAPTER 18

The Hecatomb of Palo Alto

The main body of the Mexican forces under General Arista had already left to cut off the Yankees on the Point Isabel-Matamoros Road. Kevin and his compatriots crossed the river the next day with General Mejía to continue their bombardment of the fort—this time with the addition of a howitzer which appeared to have some effect. At least the shells were landing inside the fort.

Kevin was beginning to enjoy the rather mindless work of loading and, during his breaks, observing the other units work. He watched the shells hit the fort, and the trajectory of the howitzer which lobbed shells over the earthen walls. Most of the return fire from the fort was still directed toward the town and the redoubts. The occasional shot which came toward the Irish was over their heads.

But on the morning of May 7th this pleasant duty came to an end. They were ordered to leave off shelling and march several miles east to join up with General Arista's forces who were sealing off the Matamoros Road with the intention of intercepting Taylor and his supply train. The next morning the Irish and Mexicans were drawn up in a double line a mile in length across the Matamoros Road at the pond of Palo Alto.

The Mexicans had the numerical advantage in troops: Arista's 3,700 against Taylor's 2,290. And Arista's flanks were secure: a swamp on one side, a wooded knoll on the other. It seemed an ideal position and an easy Mexican victory.

However, Arista foolishly gave Taylor time to move his artillery (including two eighteen pounders) and his men into position. Then, after more delays, the feckless Arista ordered a long drum roll announcing his attack. Arista's men opened fire with their cannon from a range of seven hundred yards. But the Mexicans lacked high explosive shells and the solid cannon balls struck the ground in front of the Yankees, bouncing along so slowly that they could be easily side-stepped by the delighted American cannoneers.

The Americans didn't waste much time laughing, however. An attack was an attack, and on Taylor's order the American artillery responded with a vengence. Out in front went the batteries of Ringgold, Duncan, Ridgeley and Bragg, raining fire upon the Mexican lines, one round a minute with shot and shell, cutting the Mexicans to pieces. Arista, unable to use his infantry, ordered a calvary attack but Ringgold's canoneers annihilated them.

Some of the Mexicans approached Ampudia and asked if they could make a bayonet charge but they were told that it was suicidal.

"It is suicidal standing here, Señor," answered a Mexican sergeant. "They are slaughtering us like cattle."

"Return to your positions," Ampudia ordered.

All around were men dead or dying, and the Americans, safe behind their cannons, continued to pour devastating fire on the Mexicans while they themselves were untouched.

Meanwhile General Arista arrived, galloping along the lines, being implored by the men to either lead them in an attack or retreat. The hooves of his horse crushed a skull of a dead man in the front ranks. The bodies were so thick on the field that it was impossible for the horse to step over them.

The horse shied and nearly threw the general. Beyond him on the other side of the chapperal the cannons flashed and roared. The guns fired non-stop it seemed and there was no escape from them. And all the while, toward the rear, there was a steady procession of wounded dragging themselves to cover. But there was no cover from the terrible guns and Arista had no flying artillery to answer Ringgold's or Braxton Bragg's. Finally, when the chapperel caught fire and the Mexican general had no visibility to even sketch a plan, he ordered his men to withdraw out of artillery range. They pulled back, leaving over five hundred bodies dead on the field, and another hundred or so wounded.

All night Kevin could hear the crying of the wounded and dying. He could hear the slurping sounds of the coyotes feeding upon the dead bodies, and the fearful flutter of wings and ripping of beaks as the turkey buzzards gobbled human flesh.

He found Murphy, his face blackened by power but otherwise unhurt. Together they walked around the camp which was lit by a dozen grass fires. The acrid, oily smoke of the burning creosote got in their eyes, and tears streamed freely down their cheeks.

"Do you know what this is like?" Murphy asked.

"Dante's Inferno," Kevin replied through his tears, walking among the wounded and despairing men. The lucky ones were piled up on wagons to go back to Matamoros. Others could still be heard moaning out in the fields.

"That, too. But what I was thinking of was a hecatomb. The ancient Greeks used to offer up a great slaughter, usually of oxen, to their gods. That's what we were like out there. Hundreds of oxen, slaughtered by the Yankee cannon before we even had a chance to fight back. Dumb, helpless beasts sacrificed to some unknown god, greedy for blood."

They found McDowell and Sgt. Murphy next to a cart of wounded men. McDowell had the lower part of his jaw blown off by a shell. All his teeth were gone and blood streamed from the makeshift dressing.

"I'm trying to make him go back to Matamoros with the wounded," Murphy said. "But he won't go. The surgeon who had the medicine chests has disappeared. There are no medicines, no drugs here. Why, there's not even a good bandage!"

"Nyaaa, nyaaa," McDowell said, shaking his head and pulling back from the wagonload of wounded.

"Hell, let him stay with us if he wants to stay, Murph!" Casey counseled. "Better to die with your friends then alone in some damn lice-infected cot."

"Why did the generals give Taylor time to get set up? Jesus! Didn't they know he had two eighteen pounders, and the biggest we've got out here is twelve? And no damn canisters or shell! Christ, it's one thing to lose men in battle, but to have them slaughtered before they even have a chance to fight. My God! These Mexican generals ought to be shot."

"Be careful what you say, Murph. We're the greenhorns here."

"Hell, I'm not saying anything the Mexicans aren't saying. Damn, some of the officers are accusing Arista of treason. The men are completely demoralized, and this is just the beginning."

The next morning the Mexicans took their position on the far sides of a *resaca* or a dry river bed. Actually, a place where a branch of the Río Grande had once flowed centuries ago. This time the Yankees attacked with cavalry and some of the Irish under General La Vega were able do a bit of damage to the American horsemen. However, they had no support from Arista who seemed unaware a battle was even going on. When his forces finally arrived, they were too late to prevent the capture of the guns and the loss of General La Vega.

The Battle of Resaca de Guerrero, or Resaca de Palma, as the Yankees called it, was over before Murphy and his men could do anything. When they saw Arista's lancers fall back in disarray they knew it was over, and headed to the rear. There they encountered Lt. Riley who ordered them to help get one of the two six-inch guns he commanded back to Matamoros to cover the retreat.

The return of the troops was ignominous. This time there were no tri-colors flying, no music playing, no priests to bless the cannons. The demoralized soldiers came in flocks swimming across the water, or floating on caissons, bedraggled and bloody. There were no townspeople to greet them; no church bells rang. There was only the dust, the blood, and the silent weight of defeat which hung over them like a dark cloud.

Kevin, Murphy and Casey set up and serviced the six-inch gun back in the plaza of Matamoros, firing every once in a while at the Fort to cover the soldiers' retreat. They were soon joined by Riley and his crew which consisted of John Little, James Mills, and Thomas Riley, all but Mills having been born in Ireland.

McDowell rested against the buwarks nursing his wound. He could not speak. But Casey had secured him some strong drink which helped with the pain, and Murphy had promised to take him to the Martínez house in the evening where he could be treated. He had already sent word to Óscar to try and locate a surgeon, or at the very least a dentist.

The afternoon dragged on with troops coming across the river and intermittent fire from the fort which was desultorily returned by the batteries in the town. Taylor's army did not seem to anxious to pursue the Mexicans across the river—which was fortunate, Kevin thought. If he had, the Mexican army would have surely been destroyed.

When night fell they got permission from Lt. Riley to accompany their friend to the Martínez home. There, Óscar had brought a dentist who managed to wire McDowell's jaw and give him some tincture of opium for the pain. The bivouacked there for the night and joined Lt. Riley the next morning.

"How's your friend," Riley asked looking dubiously as McDowell's swollen and bandaged jaw and his glassy eyes.

"He'll make it, sir," replied Murphy. "He can't talk yet, but he can still fight."

"Hmm, if you say so," replied Riley skeptically. "However, I think the fighting is done for the time being. General

Arista is having a parley with Taylor, proposing an armisice. I don't think he'll have much luck but it will give us a bit of time to lick our wounds."

"Will we surrender the town, sir?" Murphy asked.

"That's a foregone conclusion, Sergeant. There no way we can hold it. Our only hope is to get further south, to some city that is already strongly fortified. But before we can even do that we need to rest and treat our wounded. We'll have a long march ahead of us."

Murphy didn't ask anymore. He gave the lieutenant a brisk salute which Riley returned smartly.

Kevin felt reassured somehow. Not by what was said by the officer, but rather by what was not said. Riley exuded a quiet confidence that seemed to imply that somehow this was only a temporary setback. Kevin felt that underneath the lieutenant's dust and the smoke-stained uniform beat a heart unwilling to accept defeat. It firmed Kevin's resolve as well, and he returned with the others to his post, stunned, but with a new confidence and faith.

CHAPTER 19

And Streams in the Desert

On the afternoon of May 17th, General Arista gave the order to abandon the city, just one day before the American army's crossing of the river to occupy it. The Mexicans retreated upriver about ten miles, jettisoning five cannon and much of their baggage into the Río Grande. They also left behind many of their wounded because they were unable to care for them. Then they turned inland, this army—reduced now to about 2,500 effectives by casualties—with a train of nearly a thousand dependants and camp followers. Their destination was Linares, about two hundred miles to the southwest, through cactus desert and mesqite, following dirt trails.

Day after day the soldiers plodded on. The sun seared the sparce grass to a golden brown, and the tramping feet of the men, the hooves of the horses, stirred up choking clouds of dust. The only sounds were the clanking of near empty canteens, the rattle of the trace chains, and the creaking of the wagons. Now and then a horse would snort his disgust, or crack an ankle joint. Nobody talked. Each needed to preserve what little saliva and breath he had.

For Kevin the march was mind-numbing. He could not even will himself to think. No fantasies, no glimpses of another life, nothing came into his mind except the dull blankness of going on, one step in front of the other, hour after hour in the blazing sun. Kevin had been hungry many times before but he had never been so thirsty. The sun sapped his strength. And he felt the dehydration as it dried his blood, his tissues, and caused blinding headaches. By the second day, Murphy had showed him the trick of carrying pebles in the mouth to stimulate saliva, and that helped for a while. But only for a while.

The sun broiled down and there was no relief. White skulls of cattle lined the trail, and choking dust covered everything. The sweat turned it to mud on his skin and in his hair. That night the whinnying of the horses was continuous as they went without water and Kevin could not sleep. He felt desolate and lost. Under the immensities of the constellations and the stars, he said a quiet "Hail Mary." He prayed for the safety of his parents, his brother and sister. He was not afraid. Each of the battles was a terrible thing but most of the time in combat he was too busy to be scared. And when the men were ripped apart by Yankee shot and shrapnel, he was filled with rage and hatred for the enemy. Now he just felt lost. Alone on a desolate plain in a land far from home. But of one thing he was certain. When the sun came up hope would be born anew. He would make this new land his home. A place he would fight for, would gain respect and honor in. A land that would welcome him as a Catholic warrior and a hero.

But when morning came, the sun emerged like a ball of fire in the east. He was already sweating by the time he had hitched up his rucksack and joined the rest of the men. He did not feel like a warrior, or a hero. Nor did he feel like he would live long enough to be given the chance to prove he could have been. It was hotter than he had ever imagined the earth could be. By ten o'clock Kevin was staggering. Toward noontime, he fell. Casey helped him to his feet and they stumbled forward until Kevin could get hold of the end of a wagon.

"Just lean on the wagon," Casey said. "Walk along and lean on it whenever you feel like you're going to fall. Say a 'Hail Mary' now and then, and ask the Virgin to give you strength. God never gives us more than we can bear.

"But whatever you do, don't fall out. They won't stop for you, you know. If you fall out here, you'll die."

Murphy came up behind him and gave him a sip of brackish water from his canteen. "You'll make it, boy, never fear," he encouraged him.

Then he pointed to McDowell who was marching ahead.

"Look at that feller, with half his jaw gone now. Don't it make ye feel ashamed? Come on, show some grit."

The afternoon dragged on. The creak of the wagon wheels, the rattle of the trace chains, and the interminable dust. Kevin fell again, and then again, but managed to right himself and grab onto the wagon. But toward late afternoon, just when Kevin had fallen for the third time and the wagon had gone ahead leaving him behind in the dust, the skies clouded over. The air temperature dropped sudddenly and a cool breeze stirred the canvas top of the wagon.

Then suddenly, miraculously, the skies opened up in a torrential downpour. Kevin tilted his head to the heavens and gulped greedily the cold water that literally poured down. It was like no rain he had ever seen! It was a monsoon, the beginning of the Mexican rainy season.

"They call it a *tormenta* ," Murphy called to him laughing. "Hell of a name, huh? Only for us there's no torment about it. Fill up your canteen. Get anything you can find in the wagon, too, that will hold water. It won't last forever."

Drybeds, or *arroyos* ran in torrents like new-born rivers, and each gully was choked with brown water. Several soldiers were laughing and dancing in water up to their thighs in an *arroyo* which moments before had been dry as bone. Among them Kevin noted a soldier who had been limping from a shrapnel wound in his leg, but who now kicked up a stream of water. He saw his friend, McDowell, too, splashing in the stream and he seemed to be shouting in pleasure.

"Dank, Gawd," McDowell cried in a slurred but understandable voice. "Oh, dank Gawd."

They splashed each other and filled their hats up with water and drank from them whooping and laughing.

Murphy smiled and put his hand on Kevin's shoulder.

"It's just like the good book says, bucko. 'Then shall the lame man leap as a hart, and the tongue of the dumb sing; for in the wilderness shall waters break out, and streams in the desert.' Isaiah, chapter 39 verse 6."

The lightning flashed perilously close to the wagons and great rips of lightning split the skies. The thunder was incredible. Its percussion unlike anything in Kevin's experience except perhaps artillery. As a matter of fact, now that he thought about it, it sounded like Taylor's eighteen pounders were were just over the next rise. But, no, it was only thunder. But what thunder! The very earth seemed to tremble and the skies reverberated.

The storm lasted fifteen, maybe twenty minutes, and then—as suddenly as it came—the storm moved on. They could see the rain clouds further east, but where the army was, the ground steamed in the sun, the birds sang happily in the *palo verde*, and the drying crystals sparkled on the barrel cactus and Spanish sword cactus.

A Mexican soldier came up behind him and slapped him on the back.

"You see, *irlandés,*" he said smiling. "God is on our side. The blessings of Providence come to us now."

Kevin smiled back. For the first time since the war began he felt hopeful. He felt that what the Mexican said might in fact be true. Despite the long march, the bedraggled army with its Indian women and poor pack horses, there was a spirit here of forbearance and solidarity. They were a long way from winning: one draw, one major defeat. But the army was basically intact. And there was another army ready to join them further south, as well as many fortified cities ready to offer them protection. Moreover, this was their country and their holy religion they were defending against an invader. Kevin lifted his head and quickened his step. Just then a shot rang out, followed by a cheer.

Kevin raced ahead to see what was going on. When he reached the knot of men, he saw a Mexican wielding a large skinning knife on a fallen antelope. The tawny hide was stripped off in minutes and the remainder of the small animal looked much like a skinned goat. Some Indian women came up then and carried it off.

A buck-toothed and banty-legged Irishman by the name of Kerrigan, whom he had seen before with Lt. Riley's artillery, was slapping his musket in satisfaction.

"Well, we'll eat tonight like kings!"

"You brought him down? Kevin asked.

"Damn straight! One shot in the neck. Snapped the neck, too, it did, just like a dry stick."

"Not much to him was there?" Kevin remarked, thinking about the small, skinned carcass he had seen the Indian women take away.

"Well, I reckon that the Mexican antelope is smaller than the pronghorns up North. Less to feed on in these parts, plus it's gone through the same dry season we have. But those Indian women will make a stew out of it. It'll feed half the battalion.

Kevin was skeptical that the small antelope would furnish food for twenty men, never mind the hundred that constituted half of a battalion. But he held his tongue. It was just possible that he'd be included in the feast.

"Which battalion is that?" Kevin asked.

"What! The Irish Colorados', o' course. Riley's own. You're one of us, I'd suspect."

"Dillon's, my name," Kevin said offering his hand. "Kevin Dillon."

"Pat Kerrigan."

"A Kerry name, ain't it," Kevin asked with a smile.

"That it is," Kerrigan returned, showing his yellowing buck teeth in a broad smile. He looked at Kevin a bit closer. "Dillon, is it? The Dillons from up by Cahirsiveen?"

"The same," Kevin said with a smile.

"Well, well, Kerryman, bring your friends", he said, slapping Kevin on the back. "You're more than welcome to our feast."

They camped that night by the side of a dry arroyo which still had some runoff flowing in it from the late afternoon rains. There the Indian woman had with some tubers, some chiles, water and antelope meat, created a savory stew. The meat was well-cooked and tender, though stringy. And, Kevin, spooning the pot liquor produced from the onions, chile and meat felt revived and invigorated by the rich broth. To his surprise, over a hundred men, Irish cannoneers, Mexican officers and non-coms who had been invited to join ate heartily and had their fill.

They cleaned their bowls with corn tortillas which the woman had also made, and some of the officers passed around cigars which were shared. It was the first opportunity Kevin had to sit down with Mexican officers and he was impressed by their fastidiousness, their good manners, and their dress. Despite the fact that they had been marching through dust and 120 degree weather for three days, the officers were properly dressed and spruced-up. They had taken advantage of the day's rainwater to scrub themselves. They had unpacked clean clothes, had their uniform brass polished, and their boots shined.

Though they sat on tree stumps and ammunition boxes (Kevin and the rest of the men sat on the ground with their plates on their knees), the officers acted as if they were in their parlors.

They began talking softly of the plans for the march and their intentions. They nodded politely from time to time to an orderly who brought them tortillas and coffee. At one point General Ampudia asked Lt. Riley the name of the marksman who had brought down the game. When Riley told him, he asked the soldier to be brought to him

When Kerrigan approached in a tentative way, the general told him to come closer in polite, unaccented English.

When Kerrigan did so, the general handed him a gold coin.

"I hope you will not be offended, Sergeant Kerrigan, if I make you a small present for our dinner. Let's hope it will buy you a good time in the *cantinas* of whatever town we finally come to rest in."

Kerrigan, as delighted as any man could be under the circumstances, smiled broadly. He was at a loss for words.

The older general, General Mejía, nodded at him and smiled as well.

"*Gracias, mi sargento irlandés*!" he said.

Kerrigan straightened in pride. He thanked the generals profusely, saluted, and was dismissed.

Generals Ampudia and Mejía then resumed their conversation in Spanish with their adjutants and the other officers while General Arista quietly looked on. It became apparent, listening to them, that Arista was no longer in charge. It seemed to Kevin to be too soon for any order to have come from the capital relieving him of command, and he asked Casey about it.

"My guess is that all of the officers know that Arista screwed up. Their reports, along with the generals' dispatches, have been sent by a rider to Mexico City. Ampudia will no doubt be the commander as soon as the orders arrive. He's just showing his colors a bit early, that's all. And no one's about to call him on it. Least of all Arista, at this point."

They slept well that night, a belly-full of good food, their faces and bodies cooled by the desert night breezes and the water from their canteens. But the next morning the march began again in earnest and it was more of the same. A sweltering heat that dried up every pore of their bodies. Each exposed bit of flesh had become reddened and blistered.

Two of the draft oxen had been killed the night before. The Irishmen, it seemed, weren't the only ones who felt that they deserved meat. And, although Arista wanted to court martial the men responsible, Ampudia intervened and said that the animals could not be maintained anyway. There was no feed and not enough water for both men and beasts. His view prevailed. Four pack mules, along with the Indian women and some of the pioneer company, took the place of the missing oxen pulling the heavy caissons and carriages but even so, the column was slowed.

That afternoon the sky opened again. This time is was not the *tormenta* of a few minutes time which had both rescued and delighted the men the day before. This time the storm, described by the Mexicans as a *chubasco*, turned the trail into a muddy swamp. The caissons bogged down, the surviving animals collapsed in fatigue unable to pull further. The men pulling the six inch guns fell in the mud and were unable to move the carriages. As night fell, the rain continued in torrents, hard pellets of rain, not drops, while sheets of lightning lit up the skies and thunder rolled like bowling balls across the sky, and bolts crashed into the nearby trees and wagons.

Many of the horses and mules ran off and were lost in the surrounding wilderness. They would not be recovered.

The next morning found the dragoons dismounted, carrying the saddles of their horses. The Irishmen, too, had new burdens. With the loss of the oxen the day before and the mules at night, they now had to take turns pulling the heavy guns across the sandy soil. Although their shift was only for a half hour each time with a three hour rest, it weakened them. But no one had it easy.

The cavalrymen carried horse blankets, bridles and reins, as well as saddles, canteens, and saddle bags. The Indian women carried heavy skillets, wicker baskets of corn, pans, dried clusters of red and green chiles, ropes of garlic, and sides of oxen meat wrapped in damp cloth, or they helped the men with the cannons.

The infantry carried muskets, some with splintered stocks and bent barrels to be repaired when they came to a town with a blacksmith shop. They struggled down the muddy ruts with cartridge boxes, ammunition crates and powder kegs. Others were impressed by the ambulance drivers or the calvery officers to carry tack, saddles, stirrups, and even wagon wheels. Many of the men were ragged, with only a piece of shirt on their blistered backs, and cotton pants tied by twine. Some had no boots and their feet were bloodied by cactus spines, or swollen with infection. Still they marched on.

On the 28th, the weary, footsore troops and their camp followers reached the small town of Linares. There at the Well of Todos Santos they rested, waited for word from the capital, and for the generals to make their plans.

It wasn't long before riders came from the capital. The great news for the Irishmen was that their first payroll had arrived. They joined their new friend Kerrigan who had treated them when they first got there with his gold coin to cigars and drinks in the local *taverna.*

This night they ate like kings at a eating place called La Casa Grande which they had often passed but not had any money to stop in.

"How much money do you have, Casey?, Kevin asked.

"More than the damn Yankees ever paid me, bucko! How about you?"

"Seventeen pesos," Kevin said. "That's about sixteen dollars. Hell, I'm rich! That's the most money I've had since I left the old country!"

Sargeant Murphy had two month's pay, about thirty-two pesos and Kerrigan, a sergeant for less than a month had a bit less. Still, neither saw fit to brag about their additional earnings.

They entered the cool, stucco building which served as a restaurant in the small village of Linares. The walls were whitewashed and clean. The dirt floors swept. Inside were two long rustic tables running down the center with benches at either side. There were smaller tables in the back. At these some Mexican officers were seated. They looked at the Irishmen briefly and then returned to their meals.

"Officer country, over there," Murphy remarked. "Let's settle in right here."

Behind a raised counter, a small beef and two tiny *cabritos* roasted on spits. The friendly, mustachioed owner came from behind the counter to serve them.

"Amigos! No están con los Yanquis? Tal vez son irlandeses?"

"Así es. Irlandeses que luchan por la Patria."

"Qué bueno! Hoy tenemos hoy molletes, carne asada, empanadas, cabrito al pastor..."

"*Y su especialidad?*" Sgt. Murphy asked.

"*Filete gambrino*! " He explained to Murphy that this was a filet of beef stuffed with a corn fungus called *huitlacoche. "Muy, muy, rico*."

"What's moo-ey, moo-ey mean? Cow?" Casey asked.

"Sounds like it," Sgt. Kerrigan replied. "Moo-ey, moo-ey, rico. A rich cow. The best." He turned to Murphy and said knowledgeably, "You're ordering the beef, I reckon?"

"Why, you pick right up on this Spanish, Sergeant!" Murphy replied. "Does everyone want the beef?"

They did. And when it was served they ate ravenously, washing the food down with vast quantites of homemade beer. Sgt. Murphy did not feel it necessary to describe the "stuffing" of the beef was corn fungus, or that moo-ey moo-ey did not mean cow. Nor did he see fit to advise his men that along with their pay came news that Arista was replaced not by Ampudia but by Mejía who was very ill from the march, and of proven incompetence. He had a feeling both omissions were of no import.

If they enjoyed their meal, nothing would be gained by telling them of their special ingredients. And as for General Mejía, he had a feeling he wouldn't be in charge long. For now, rest, good food, and getting his men back in shape for the fight was his only concern.

"How's the food, men?

"Great!" they answered between mouthfulls. "Good pick, Sarge."

"How you doing, Kevin?"

"I'm fine, Sarge. Just great!" He looked up from his second plateful of beef to wink at the owner's daughter who was removing empty plates of beans from the officers' table. "I feel human again. I think I'm beginning to like this country."

"I hope so, son. it won't be long before we have to fight for it again."

"Hell," Casey said. "We're all ready to fight for it! Just give us the position and the artillery. We'll show em what we can do."

The rest of the men grunted through mouths full of food in agreement. "Damn right!"

"We're ready, Sarge!"

"I have a feeling you'll get your wish before long," Murphy said. "Eat up, now. You'll be needing your strength."

In the back of the restaurant the Mexican officers conferred. Like Murphy, they knew that Mejía's days were numbered. They knew that Ampudia would take over, at least for a time. But they also had new information: The government of Mexico City was about to fall, and the irrepressible and devious Santa Anna was waiting in the wings to assume command of the entire nation. They were troubled, these men, by the shifting sands of their country's political machine.

Men of honor, responsive to the call of duty, educated, and fearless, they were the embodiment of the Mexican officer class. They had no great love for the peasants or Indians, or even for the mestizo noncoms who served under them. Nor were they really much enamored of the Irish sitting down to dinner this close to them. But they were men of honor and duty who loved their country. They had already seen these soldiers, who trusted them to lead, used as cannon fodder and ripped apart as a result of ineptitude, conflicting orders, and manipulation by ambitious generals and politicians. They did not want to witness it again.

CHAPTER 20

Massacre at Monterrey

On Sunday morning, September 20th, 1846, the mists clung to the turrets of the churches. The dark, brooding mountains which surrounded Monterrey provided the city with an ambience of fairyland castles where medieval knights must soon appear. Drawn up in colorful array the Mexican Army's green and red pennants floated over tents and houses, barricades and forts. The bishop and several priests moved among the men in full vestments of silver and gold giving Holy Communion to the soldiers. All was quiet except for the gentle murmuring of the priests: "*Ecce, agnus Dei*!" "Behold the lamb of God" as they offered the host.

Kevin had never seen such a place. It reminded him a little of Ireland, the ancient castles, the rolling fields, the small nondescript houses, the ubiquitous priests. But it was much bigger than any city in Western Ireland and, if the impressive cathedral behind him was any sign, a lot richer. Instead of potatoes, there were wide *milpas* of ripe corn, half of them already harvested, and there were carefully-tended fields of sugar cane.

The houses, too, were more impressive than the Kerry countryside. Instead of sod or wattles, they were mostly of stone and more secure against ordinary assaults. Many were loopholed for musketry and the *azoteas*, or flat parapeted roof tops, provided excellent defense positions. The doors and shutters were of thick oak and formidable. The narrow streets easy to barricade.

Monterrey was a natural fortress, impregnable. Capital of Nuevo Leon, this city of 12,000 had resisted a siege by the royal troops of Spain during the Mexican War of Independence. Now, garrisoned by 7,000 troops and more than forty cannon, it was a perfect Gibraltar. Northward from the city proper, at a distance of about 300 meters stood an unfinished church surrounded by the bastioned walls of the citadel. Here Dillon, Murphy, Casey, McDowell and fifty other Irishmen manned the 12 and 16 inch guns. With them were 350 Mexicans commanded by Col. José López Uraga.

Extending 70 meters on a side and mounting a dozen guns, the Citadel covered the junction of the roads leading into Monterrey from the north and east. Between the Citadel and the city itself were houses and gardens, crossed by the Ojo de Agua Canal which went east and south where it emptied into the Rio Santa Catarina. The Marín-Monterrey road crossed this stream at a fortified bridge called La Purísima.

This late in the rainy season the land was lush and green. The stalks in the milpas whispered in the wind, the verdant trees added their shade to the cool valley, and hibiscus and roses spilled over in bloom. The air echoed with the sound of doves calling to each other from either side the mountains, their brooding voices marking their territory.

Kevin felt secure behind the black masonry of the Citadel. In front he could see any advance of the enemy for miles. The elevation gave his cannon considerable range, and although he did not have canister, the shot was more than sufficient if well-aimed. Neither he nor his fellow gunners intended to waste ammunition.

Behind him, to the southeast, was a four-gun redoubt, La Tanería, which got its name from the tannery located nearby. To the south and west were a chain of fortifications, the one nearest to the Tanería being Rincón Diablo, or the Devil's Corner. General Ampudia, he reflected, had planned well. The soldiers and engineers had spend the past month building, reinforcing, tearing down, moving, and building again, various redoubts, gun emplacements, and forts. Kevin was glad that the general had finally settled on the present arrangement.

And, if the artillery fortifications were reassuring, the Mexican lancers who even now were saddling up after their morning devotions, were inspiring. They wore bright scarlet coats with silver buttons, and snow-white belts. Their horses, too, were richly arrayed with silver and finely caprisoned leather. They were, thought Kevin, like knights of the Middle Ages getting ready to go off on a Crusade. Sitting erect in their saddles, their brass helmets topped with flowing black and red plumes, their lances decorated with ribbons of green and red, these warriors took his breath away. He watched as their lines came together, perfectly formed, while they waited for the commands of their captain.

The Bishop blessed them with holy water and then, taking his mitre from an attending priest, made the Sign of the Cross over the troops. Another priest raised a bronze censor and the air was filed with the sweet odor of incense. Then a order was given by their commander and, chanting a song Kevin could not hear, they moved down toward the Marín road.

"Ah yes, they're a wonder to behold!" came a familiar voice. "They're as pretty as painted toy soldiers in a rich child's closet."

Kevin, who had been dreamily leaning over the parapet, turned quickly and saluted when he saw the officer.

"Lt. Riley! Good morning, sir."

"Good morning, Private. Is your sergeant about?

"Yessir, Let me take you to him. He's over on the north side."

Sgt. Murphy was unaware that anyone was approaching as he continued giving one of the gunner's mates an earful.

"Just how the hell you goin' to load that shot with a damn broomhandle? I'll take that broomhandle and shove it where it won't be comfortable. Now get down the road there and cut ye a good sapling. Ye feeble excuse for a soldier!"

The object of his wrath was a teenager who face was as red as his hair. He could not stop blushing, nor looking foolish as he held desperately onto the short-handled broom he had intended to use as a tamper. His face was even redder now as the sergeant applied a foot to his backside and sent him sprawling in the dirt.

"Easy, Sergeant, easy," Riley ordered. "The poor lad's on our side, ye know. Let's not start treating our men like the enemy!"

"A lunkhead is a lunkhead, sir," Murphy responded not missing a beat. "He'll get us all killed if he's not given a bit of a reminder."

"Hmm. You may be right." Then, turning to the boy. "Well, don't stand there, boy! Hop to! The Yanks are just over the rise. They'll be here by mid-afternoon."

"Is that the information, sir?" asked Murphy. When the lieutenant nodded in the affirmative, he continued. "Well, it's none too soon if you ask me. We'll finally have a chance to get even. Right, lad?" he asked Kevin, thumping him on the arm with his meaty fist.

"Private, go see to your gun," Lt. Riley said to Kevin. "I have things to discuss with your sergeant."

Kevin saluted and left quickly with a spring in his step. He was exultant. Finally! They were going to fight. He could not imagine a better time nor place. Seven thousand men in top condition, forty, maybe fifty guns, with the command of all the high ground and fortifications in or near the city. Why, it would be a massacre for the Yanks! And that would be only righteous comeuppance for the horrors of Resaca de Guererro and Palo Alto.

He was understandably anxious to fire his gun. All the weeks of waiting, of stewing over the shameful slaughter and the terrible desert march. Then the months stuck in the village and the weeks that followed carrying rocks, chopping wood, building one redoubt on Monday, only to move it to another place on Tuesday. But now here they were. The hour of glory, the hour of victory.

"They'll be here by mid-afternoon, the lieutenant said!" he called over to McDowell. "Pass it on."

"Yaa-hoo! You hear that!" McDowell shouted to his neighbor. "The Yanks will be here by afternoon!

"You all hear? They'll be here by noon!" yelled another, as the news in its altered state made its quick circuit of the Citadel.

Meanwhile, Sgt. Murphy and Lt. Riley had a different kind of conversation.

"Here's the deal, Sarge. We're in very good shape. We've got over three hundred men here and López is one of the toughest s.o.b.'s in the Mexican army. We also got a dozen guns up here. We can hold this place until doomsday. But there's a problem as I see it, and no one seems to want to listen."

"What's the problem, sir. I mean if we can hold this place to doomsday, and the Yanks have to get past us to take the city. Well, hell, sir. It means we can't lose."

"That's where you're wrong. The Yanks can't go through us, that's for sure. But they can go around us. It would mean that Taylor would have to divide his army to do it. The Mexicans are betting he ain't that crazy. I'm guessing that he is.

"I think some of these guns should be moved to the Tannery, and some more to the those two hills west of town, Federación and Independencia. The Tannery, that's Col. Corrasco and the Querétaro Battalion, it only has three guns for Chrissake. What if the Yanks sweep around to the east and take it?"

"I see what you mean," Murphy said, assuming the last question to be rhetorical. "How about the hills? How are they defended?"

"Well, on top of Independencia is a small fort with about fifty men and two light guns. Down the slope is the Obispado with Berra's four guns. Federación only has two small works."

"So, what do you think?"

"Hell, López didn't want to move any guns at first, but after I explained the possibilities, he approached General

Mejía, and General Mejía agreed. He's down there at the tête-de-pont at the Purisima Bridge. Ampudia saw the possibilities but he said that he's moved all the guns he's going to move today. He says for the Yankees to take the town they'd need an army of twice what they've got. Even then it would be a bloodbath."

"And?"

"And... Ah, hell! I think he's right. It will be a bloodbath for sure, if Taylor is crazy enough to come at us. But what's his choice? He ain't going back to Texas, I don't reckon. He'll come on all right, and take his chances."

At 2 o'clock that afternoon about half of Taylor's army of 6,000 marched out onto the plain before the city. A Mexican lieutenant anxious to avenge the defeat at the Resaca gave a premature order.

"Fuego!"

And the Black Citadel opened fire from three miles away. The cannonade echoed across the Sierra Madres and the flash and boom of the artillery kept the enemy at a distance.

"Hold your fire," Lt. Riley ordered. "They're out of range. Jesus, what stupidity! Corporal, go see the Colonel. Tell him that, if the enemy approaches no closer, we might send some men to flank them with the ten-inch mortar and a couple of howitzers."

"Yessir!"

Less than an hour later the Mexican howitzers and Irish mortar opened up from a concealed quarry on the Yankee flank. But as far as Kevin could see it was no more effective than the opening volley from the Citadel. By nightfall the Americans withdrew.

At sunrise the next morning 200 Mexican cavalry from Jalisco under Lt. Col. Juan Nájera went out to intercept the flanking movement of the Americans to the west of the city. Kevin could hear musket fire and then artillery fire as the Yankees opened up their field batteries on the Mexican cavalry.

"Damn, Sarge! The cavalry is getting whipped over there," Kevin said, frustrated that there was nothing which could be done from inside the fort.

"Don't worry, bucko. The Yanks will get theirs yet. Right now, let's just take care of what's in front of us."

As far as Kevin could see, there was nothing. But, as the sun rose above the mountains and the rocks colored azure and pink in the morning sun, he saw the dust and then the mass of blue marching to the northeast. The cooing of the doves faded as the heavy tread of foot soldiers kicked up the dust. The apparent movement of the U.S. force was to flank the Citadel with the goal of attacking the weaker Tanería.

"Lt. Riley," Sgt. Murphy said. "What are your orders?"

"I'm waiting on Colonel López, and you'd best do the same. No early fire this time. Let's see what they'll do. I think they're just faking. They wouldn't be crazy enough to come under our guns."

"Teniente Riley," the Major called.

"Mayor!" Riley snapped a salute. "*A sus órdenes*!"

"We will wait to see if this movement is just another Yankee demonstration. We know they are attacking to our left. They have made contact with our cavalry and a significant force is attempting to take Federación. If, however, the Yankee general is foolish enough to divide his army and attack the right as well, we will enfilade him.

"*Sí, señor*!"

The Mexicans and Irishmen leaned against their guns and watched the slow movements of the bluejacketed Americans. The column came to a halt. Lt. Riley observed them through his field glasses.

"Jesus, they've sure got a mess of generals out there. More brass per foot than West Point. Looks like their having a parley. Wait! Damn, I can't believe it! They're marching forward into our guns. Here they come!"

Across broken ground 800 men streamed to the left of the Citadel. Lest there be any doubt now about their intent, they let loose a loud huzzah! and brandished their bayonet-tipped muskets.

"Huzzah! Huzzah!" the Americans shouted as a drum roll moved into a steady beat and a piper started Yankee Doodle.

The Mexican colonel gave his order:

"*Fuego! Fuego*!"

"*Mátenlos, malditos yanquis*!" the gunners shouted lighting their fuses.

The already-primed guns bellowed forth as one, and the Americans fell in bunches, like clumps of grapes from the vine. Still they came on. Kevin helped reload and did not take his eyes from his canon until the third volley. Then he paused to look down through the smoke at the scattered limbs of soldiers and the craters formed by the shells.

Below him and to the right of the wall he saw a sixteen-inch shell burst in the mist of a platoon. He watched numbly as a man's leg, severed from his body, was sent spinning in the air where it smacked another soldier in the face rendering him unconscious.

"God have mercy on us!" Kevin said and crossed himself quickly.

He turned back to his gun and loaded again as McDowell swabbed, and the Corporal set the primers.

"What is it?" McDowell asked, noticing the sudden pallor of Kevin's face and the trembling of his hand as he loaded.

"You don't want to know," Kevin said. "Just keep swabbing, Mac." The guns on the east side of the Citadel were firing directly down on the Americans now, but the Yanks still kept coming. Kevin knew that his gun alone had killed twenty or thirty. There were eight guns trained on the Americans and all of them were firing steadily, ceaselessly. It was Resaca de Guererro all over again, only this time is was the Americans who were suffering. Why didn't they pull back? Were they crazy?

Finally, at about 8:00 AM, most had retreated. But a group of about seventy men kept going and drove on into the Tanería. General Majía, however, from his position on the Purisima Bridge became aware of what was happening and sent the 3rd Light Infantry to reinforce Carroso with one light gun. The Americans came under such murderous fire that they lost more than one third of their officers and men. Still they kept on.

By noon the Americans had taken the Tanería. They manned the three guns within against the Mexicans in the city and, by late afternoon, they had captured thirty prisoners. Kevin looked down from his post at the field below. He had never seen so many dead. More than three times the number of dead and wounded at Resaca de Guererro or Palo Alto. A rich mixture of officers—even generals—among the casualties. The Americans had captured a small redoubt with three guns. Kevin estimated the cost in Yankee casualties at well over 300 men. A high price.

And only three guns captured, out of the forty or fifty the Mexicans had. He made a quick calculation. It didn't take much figuring to guess that Taylor would run out of men before the Mexicans ran out of cannon. A sudden volley of shots roused him from his reverie. Today's fighting was not over yet.

Anxious to remove the Americans from even this toehold, the Mexican cavalry made another charge from the southwest at dusk. But they broke off their charge, and were driven back into the city by American artillery. Tomorrow would be a long day, Kevin reflected. Neither side had given up much, and what they had reluctantly conceded was at a price heavily paid in blood.

As the sun began its journey behind the mountain, the firing abruptly ceased. Within minutes Kevin could hear the doves again, echoing clearly across the two mountain peaks. As if nothing had happened. As if this was just another day in the beautiful Sierra Madres. As the smoke cleared, the dust rose into the sky where it mixed in such novel proportions that the sunset was orange and pink, gold and purple, and then towards the end, a dark bloody red. Kevin had never seen such a sunset. He had never known such beauty in an evening sky. He continued to watch until there was just an emerald speck of light above Saddle Mountain and then he turned back to the real world of the battlefield.

Below him, the ground was littered with bodies and parts of bodies. A mangy yellow hound had come onto the field in the closing darkness. Now, he carried a man's arm in his mouth. It was too heavy for his jaws to support and he dropped it. Then he picked it up and dropped it again. Angry, the dog began growling, shaking the arm in his mouth, trying to loosen a chunk of flesh.

Casey picked up a musket. He took careful aim. It was a difficult shot, from an awkward angle and at the extreme of the musket's range. Darkness in the mountain fortress was falling quickly. Slowly, he squeezed the trigger. The dog fell like a bundle of rags. The Mexicans raised a cheer. And from behind the walls of the Tanería, the Americans answered gratefully with one of their own. It was the first time in the war that either side had acknowledged their common humanity, the solidarity of the living against the scavengers of death. When the cheers died down, the men lit their campfires. It was time for rest. Time to tend to the wounded and pick up the dead.

But as darkness fell on this bloody Monday, the skies opened up, and there was a violent thunderstorm. The temperature dropped, and a freezing rain fell. Kevin could hear below him the drowning sounds of men unable to turn their crippled bodies away from the rain which poured down their open throats. Then he heard the creaking, jolting wagons, and the clink of the trace chains as the ambulances prowled the fields searching for those still alive.

He pulled his collar up against his neck and crawled beneath the cannon. There was no place which was completely dry, and no place comfortable for sleeping.

"It's going to be a long one, Kev," McDowell said, crawling under the lower part of the cannon. "I doubt we'll get any rest tonight."

Kevin agreed. He shivered in the cold mountain air and felt the water dripping down his back. He wondered what kind of battle tomorrow would bring. He wondered whether he would stand firm at his post, regardless of the outcome. He thought of the dog and the man's arm. He thought wearily of the long hours before dawn.

Minutes later, Kevin pulled his legs up against his chest and, amid the wild mountain winds, the driving rain, the howls of wolves searching out the corpses, fell deeply, dreamlessly asleep. The winds died down and Venus appeared in the sky, then Orion, the hunter. The wolves slunk away from the fields and retreated to the hills where they howled for hours at the unapproachable, merciless stars.

CHAPTER 21

There is a Tide in the Affairs of Men

Kevin awakened to the sound of musket fire over on Independencia Ridge. It was Tuesday, September 22, 1846. The Texas Rangers along with two infantry regiments had snuck up the hill in the pre-dawn hours. Now as sunlight touched the red and white banner on Libertad's flagpole, the Mexicans opened fire. An infantry duel of musketry ensued but, within minutes, the Obisbo had opened artillery fire in support and the Americans fell back.

A half hour later the scene changed again. This time the Americans surged forward carrying with them a dismantled 12 pound howitzer to Libertad. They overcame the small defensive position there, and then turned the howitzer on the Obisbo below. By late afternoon, after a determined but unsuccessful counter-attack, the Mexicans abandoned this position as well and moved back to defend the city.

Kevin and his cohorts watched the action from the turrets of the Citadel, powerless to help. They spent most of the day servicing the guns, replenishing shot, and observing the movements of the troops, now forward, now backward. It was, he thought, like a battle between a scorpion and a centipede. The artillery with its stinging tail, the infantry with its hundred legs. It was exciting for Kevin to watch; it felt a bit like being at a rugby match. But it did not feel like war. It was too remote.

"Hey, Sarge! When do you reckon we'll see some more action?"

"Can't say, Kev," Murphy replied chewing on the stump of a cigar, then spitting a brown stream of juice. "Looks like the Yanks learned their lesson yesterday about coming too close to this here Citadel.

Kevin turned at the sound of victorious shouting from the western side. He could see the stream of Mexican soldiers retreating down the hill and fleeing toward the city.

"Damn! Why don't they let some of us go out there and help? They've already lost the Obisbo and Libertad Hill."

"You're right, bucko. We need to be doing something. Despite our victory yesterday, things seem to be unravelling. The generals need to make a decision pretty soon and not leave us holed up here. Reminds me of that part in Julius Caesar when Brutus advises Casius to fight. Goes something like this:

> The enemy increaseth every day;
> We, at the height are ready to decline.
> There is a tide in the affairs of men,
> Which taken at the flood leads on to fortune;
> Omitted, all the voyage of their life
> Is bound in shallows and in miseries.
> On such a full sea are we now afloat,
> And we must take the current as it serves
> Or lose our ventures.

"That's about how it is now, Kev. I know that Lt. Riley can see it. I just hope that the Mexican generals realize it as well."

Then, as if realizing that he may have said too much, he bit down on his cigar butt again and frowned. "Say, if you're finished your work, why don't you go over to the east side and take a look. Report back with what's happened."

Kevin was glad of something to do. The worst thing about this war, he had already decided, was the waiting around for someone to tell him what to do. As long as he had a job to do, he was fine. But the waiting wore him down.

On the right side of the Citadel, however, everything was quiet. General Taylor had indeed learned a hard lesson the previous day and was keeping his men well clear of the Citadel's guns. Still, Kevin could see there was at least a brigade of U.S. troops inside the Tanería and, although they were outside the effective range of the Irish and Mexican guns, a Mexican lieutenant occasionally gave the order to fire a round or two. It kept the Americans heads down, made then nervous, but accomplished little else.

He returned to Sgt. Murphy and reported when he had seen. Then he settled down to smoke a pipe with a wizened vet by the name of Francis O'Connor. Kevin did not smoke much, but there was not little else to do and it passed the time.

"Mr. O'Connor, what are you goin' to do when this war's over?"

The old man shook his head. He squinched his eyes against the smoke that a sudden breeze had blown back into his face.

"I ain't sure this war will ever be over, the way these folks are fightin'. Hell, we should have finished them off yesterday. Now they got us sittin' here like eagles on a mountain top watchin' the rest of the boys get wiped out."

"General Taylor's a long way from home. His supplies are bound to run out," Kevin offered.

"Maybe. Maybe not. He could have supplies coming in by ship from Vera Cruz for all we know. At any rate the way this here army keeps backing up we'll be in Panama or maybe even Venezuela by next year, and Taylor will be in the Halls of Montezuma."

Kevin laughed. The old man was a lot like his own grandfather and most Irish farmers He believed that if you predicted a bad crop, then God would give you a good one. It didn't do to think positively. You were tempting fate.

The next day by 11 o'clock Kevin could see smoke rising behind him from the direction of the central plaza. When Lt. Riley arrived with his field glasses, Kevin was able to overhear the latest details.

"It looks like the Americans are in the city," Riley was saying. "No large concentrations, but there's some street fighting going on and some private houses being blown up by set charges."

"Sounds like the work of the Texas Rangers," Sgt. Murphy grumbled. "Any sign of guns, sir?"

"Looks like there a mortar or two. One is ours, I'm sure. The other one might be, too. Let's see. Damn! There goes a chunk off the Cathedral. Looks like the Yanks have the other mortar."

"Damn!"

At four o'clock the men in the Citadel had their dinner. They had worked up an appetite, cleaning the guns, lounging around, watching the battlefields below and exchanging comments. The dinner, although a simple one, crema de *rajas con tortillas*, tasted to Kevin like manna in the desert. The mixture of cream and peppers was unusual, he thought, but tasty. And the cool well water that washed it down was as good as any beer he had ever drank.

Lt. Riley was called away from his meal by a Mexican adjutant and informed that the Governor of Nuevo Leon, Francisco Morales had asked Taylor to permit the civilians to withdraw from the city. Taylor refused.

"*Y qué pasará*?" Riley asked.

"*No lo sé. Ahorita hay una junta*."

The "junta," or meeting, of the staff was to consider terms for the withdrawal of the army.

Riley was furious. When he approached Col. López he did not even show the courtesy of a salute.

"Goddamned, Colonel! The men will not permit it. They simply will not permit it."

Colonel López looked at Riley and raised a quizzical eyebrow. He showed no emotion beyond that of perhaps mild annoyance at the Irishman's discourtesy.

"*Teniente*?"

"*Discúlpeme, Señor,*" Riley said, bringing himself to attention and saluting. His salute was carefully returned by the Colonel who now gave him a wary look.

"It's just that... Well, hell Colonel, we've licked 'em. We killed two or three hundred yesterday if we killed one. You can't ask the men to quit. You can't ask them to just walk away from victory."

"The men will do as they are ordered, *Teniente*," the Colonel said quietly. "And so will I. And so will you. To do otherwise is treason."

"Treason! Dammit, Colonel! I'll tell you what's treason. Giving up this city without a fight is treason. Asking these men to surrender before they've been licked is treason."

"*Teniente! Coronel! Alto!*" the adjutant interrupted as he approached with General Mejía.

"*Caballeros,*" the general said grimly. "*Pasen ustedes.*" They went into the temporary headquarters where they encountered the other generals who were grimly going over some papers on the desk. General José María Ortega and General Tomás Requeña were studiously ignoring the governor who was trying to explain what dangers that faced the civilians under his charge.

General Mejía spoke. "In deference to *su señoría, el gobernador*, I will speak briefly," he said with just the slightest hint of irony. "The bulk of the American army has withdrawn from the city for the time being. However, they have troops within mortar range of the Cathedral. They have also secured all the major fortifications of the city."

"Excuse me, sir," Col. López interrupted. "Not the Citadel."

"*Bien dicho, coronel.* Not the Citadel, as you say. However, this Citadel which your gallant troops have defended has now become superfluous. The Americans have penetrated the city. I repeat, they have *penetrated* the city. They have also captured the interior guns."

"Well, what do you propose?" growled General Ortega. "That we give them the city. My men are ready to fight. Most of them have not even got their uniforms dirty. If we fight the Yanquis street by street, house by house, we shall drive them from our soil once and for all."

"At what cost, sir?" the governor interrupted. "How many innocent lives will be lost? Not all of us are soldiers like yourself."

"Are you not a man? Would you not defend your homeland against the invader?"

"Gentlemen, please!" General Mejía interrupted. "Thank you, general. You have eloquently expressed your point of view. However, it is only one point of view."

"There is another, *mi general*? Ortega snarled.

"*Sí, general. Lo que el jefe dice*. What General Ampudia says has more weight than your emotional speeches. Although the general would like us all to come to an agreement on what he proposes."

"Of course," quipped Gen. Requeña. "So he does not look like a coward or a fool back in the capital when the news reaches Santa Anna. And pray tell, what does my *jefe*, Don Pedro, suggest."

General Mejía ignored the sarcasm. He cleared his throat and spoke in the calm voice which had always characterized his meetings.

"He says that the Americans are within range of the Cathedral. He says that he is sworn to protect civilian lives and that many women and children have taken refuge in or near the Cathedral. He says that he has proposed to surrender the city on the condition that he be allowed to withdraw his men and munitions."

"Traitor!" shouted General Ortega.

"Incompetent imbecile!" added Requeña.

Both general and staff officers joined with curses and epithets in a mixture of bewilderment, anguish and frustration.

Riley, in deference to his superior whom he knew would argue his position, sat quietly. Only his clenched jaw and whiteness of the knuckles on his sword indicated the depth of his outrage.

"This is the worst betrayal ever witnessed in the history of the Mexican army," General Ortega said softly. "How can Ampudia even suggest it."

"I suggest you be careful whom you call traitor," General Mejía said in an equally soft voice which did not, however, disguise the menace in it.

"Let me also remind you that yesterday Colonel Berra disobeyed Gen. Ampudia's order to hold the Obisbo. He led a glorious charge out of the bishop's palace and, as a result, had his troops decimated. He squandered a major link in the defense of the city. His men, those who were not killed outright by his stupidity, withdrew to Monterrey instead of returning to the Obisbo to wait for reinforcements.

"This is what comes from not obeying a superior's orders. And now, you, sir, want to call our *jefe* a traitor? Think twice, sir."

"What does he want us to do?" General Ortega asked.

"To simply support his request for a withdrawal. We will sign a paper saying that this was a decision reached after discussion among all of us. The Americans' losses have been heavy. They will be ready to make concessions. If Taylor refuses, you Requeña, you Ortega, and the governor will form a commission to discuss terms."

"*Demonios*!

"*Ya basta*! That's an order, General," Mejía snapped. "This meeting is over. You are dismissed."

The next day Ampudia's proposal was presented. As expected, Taylor refused it, then countered with one of his own for the surrender of the city and the army. Later in the day the commissioners from Monterrey and their American counterparts, General Worth and Henderson, and a young Colonel by the name of Jefferson Davis, met to finalize terms. It was late afternoon, September 24, by the time they had hammered out the agreement.

The American commissioners demanded the immediate surrender of the city, all weapons and all property. The Mexicans insisted on keeping their personal arms and a six-gun field battery, as well as 21 rounds of artillery ammunition. Instructed by Taylor to conclude an armistice (his troops were exhausted and he could not complete the seizure of the town without heavy losses), the Americans agreed. An eight-week armistice was signed with the stipulation that Ampudia also surrender the Citadel and withdraw all forces from the city and retire beyond the Rincónda Pass.

On the morning of September 25th, Kevin and his crew responded to the bugle call at reveille and fell in for muster. There had been no deaths in the Citadel and only minor injuries during the three-day battle. All of the men were in good condition, well-rested, clean. Dressed in their colorful red and blue artillery uniforms, they appeared as if it were the first day of battle rather than the last.

Colonel López addressed them in a soft, well-modulated voice.

"My countrymen. I wish to thank you all—individually and collectively—for the fine stand you have made here at the Citadel. You have made the enemy pay a terrible price for his invasion of our territory. You have fought with courage and determination and you have brought honor to yourselves and to this army.

"My dear Irishmen who have joined our cause, we salute you as well. You have been steadfast at your guns and you have honored our flag and that of St. Patrick.

"Today, I have some sad news. Because of the enemy occupation of the city, I have been ordered by my commander to surrender this fort and its cannons."

There was an audible gasp from the men, followed by expressions of dismay and incredulity. The junior officers put up their hands to signal order, and the Colonel continued.

"We will, however, honor our *bandera*. There will be a drum roll and an eight-gun salute as the Mexican colors are lowered from the flagstaff. The officers will retain their swords and the men their muskets.

"The 4th Infantry will form in companies and march out carrying the national colors in the vanguard. The Colorados will follow carrying the banner of St. Patrick. Hold your heads high, like the victorious army you are. We shall fight another day! *Viva México*!

"*Viva México*!" returned the men. "*Viva México*!" shouted Kevin and the Irishmen along with them, as tears of frustration and pride streamed down their faces.

A bugle sounded, the drums reverberated in a tremulous roll, the cannons sounded over the Marín Road as the eagle and the *nopal* came slowly down.

They marched out with heads erect, past the bloody and dirty Americans who quietly and respectfully lined the road. There were none of the usual gibes or catcalls the Americans were so fond of in times of victory. If before they had doubted the valor of their Mexican adversaries, now they had learned. The road to Mexico City would not be an easy one. The Mexicans would fight them every inch of the way. And, while the generals would make mistakes, like the one that cost them the city today, the Yanks now knew that the Mexican soldiers and their allies were formidable opponents, and it would not do to underestimate them.

Among the Irishmen in the U.S. Army, many of them, who saw the proud banner of St. Patrick unfurled, its green and silver glistening in the morning sun, would leave the victorious Stars and Stripes to serve under the new flag in the weeks ahead. The withdrawal parade of the Mexicans and the San Patricios would bring well over a hundred new converts to their side, enough to form another company. So strong was the honor and spirit this army this army showed.

When the division approached the gates of the city, a regimental band started playing. Women came out into the streets and touched the banner of St. Patrick. Others made the Sign of the Cross as the ensign passed. Kevin struggled with mixed emotions of relief, pride and sadness. Relief, because had come through his third battle unscathed. Pride, because, although the generals had surrendered, he and the rest of the men felt undefeated. Sadness because it seemed as if courage and steadfastness and the righteousness of a cause were not enough to insure victory. And that once again they were in retreat. This last feeling turned to bitterness as they reached the city limits.

Over the sounds of the marching and the creaking of the caissons, Kevin could hear firing from the Citadel. Already renamed the Black Fort, it had been invested quietly by the enemy as the Mexican troops left the city. But now, as Kevin and the silent army headed south toward the Rincónda Pass, the Americans announced their victory. Kevin counted the cannon blasts—twenty-six, twenty-seven, twenty-eight. One for each state. And he shook his head angrily. Behind him the Stars and Stripes rose slowly above the fortified city and waved triumphantly in the noonday sun.

CHAPTER 22

Colonel May's Dragoons

Five months had passed since Monterrey, and Lt. Bradford Broderick had not yet seen action. On the high plateau of Agua Nueva, six thousand feet above sea level, he could feel the bone-chilling wind penetrate his wool uniform. His horse snorted beneath him and pawed the earth. It was just daylight, February 20, 1847, and the Dragoons were lined up in front of General Taylor's tent. Broderick knew that his was the most elite outfit in Taylor's army and felt that this morning the general was going to give them a chance to prove it.

Under the command of Lt. Col. Charles May and in the company of Ben McCulloch's Texas Rangers they were being ordered south on the San Luís Potosí road to scout for enemy troops. A message had come several months before from General Scott advising Taylor to transfer half of his command to him in order that a U.S. invasion from the coast could be adequately supported. It was message that General Taylor considered "too preposterous to be entertained." That was actually the second message. The first message sent by Scott had been intercepted by Santa Anna. Now, it was reported that Santa Anna was making a forced march with twenty thousand men across the desert and mountains between San Luís Potosí and Saltillo to intercept and destroy Taylor's army. Lt. Broderick and Colonel May's Dragoons were to travel down the road towards Santa Anna's army and report back on the progress of the Mexican forces.

The Dragoons and the Texas Rangers continued along the road for about six miles until Lt. Broderick heard shots and the troopers were ordered to halt. An advanced platoon of the Second Dragoons had captured a young Mexican lancer and were questioning him as Broderick approached.

"*Dónde está el ejército*?" Col. May's translator asked. "*Dónde está Santa Anna*?"

The Mexican trooper shook his head. "*No lo sé.*"

"Tell him we'll kill him, if he does not tell us." Col. May said. "Tell him we'll first cut off his balls."

The sergeant translated the message and accompanied it with a lewd gesture. For a second something like fear cross the eyes of the young trooper and then a black defiance took its place.

"*Eso no sirve nada, señor. Es inútil. No sé donde está el ejército.*"

"He says he doesn't know, sir." The sergeant translated. "He says it's useless to cut off his balls; he still won't tell."

"Turn him over to McCulloch and the Rangers. I guess Ben knows how to use that bowie knife he keeps strapped to his waist."

Lt. Broderick and his friend Lt. Beebe took their canteens and walked over to where the forward platoon was resting. One of the troopers was sitting by the side of the road writing in a journal. When he saw the officers he started to rise to his feet.

"As you were, trooper," Lt. Beebe said. "What's that you're writing?"

"A journal, sir. I've been keeping it since Resaca de Palma."

"You were there, hey?" Lt. Beebe remarked, delighted at the opportunity to question a veteran. "What's your name, Private?"

"Sam Chamberlain, sir. First Dragoons."

"So you were there, eh? Resaca de Palma. What a show, eh? What was it like for you Dragoons? I heard Charley May's boys led quite a charge."

"A wild charge, sir, like the kind you read about in romances. A gallop of a quarter mile right into the mouth of the Mexican cannon. A glorious charge. But then, unfortunately, a wild charge out again with little to show for it except several dead troopers."

"What the hell are you talking about, Private!" interrupted Lt. Broderick. "Everyone knows that Capt. May captured a Mexican general with that charge and several cannon. He received two brevet promotions for it. That's why he's a Lieutenant Colonel. Be very careful what you say now."

"Let him speak, Brad. You weren't there, remember?" he added with a trace of sarcasm.

"Neither were you, if I recall, Lieutenant."

Before the private could finish his story, however, they could hear the high-pitched screams of the captive Mexican cavalryman. They all turned to the sound of the screams, and then wheeled back as they heard Col. May approaching on horseback.

Both lieutenants came to attention and saluted. The private, however, insolently took his time and first closed his journal and put away his pen, before rising to salute his commander.

"Didn't they tell you boys about fraternizing with enlisted men? Or are they teaching some new kind of social consciousness at the Point?"

"Yessir! Nossir!" the officers responded in unison.

Private Chamberlain allowed himself a slight smile and he tapped his journal with his pen.

"Private, you can return to your post. Lieutenant... what's your name?" he asked turning to Brad.

"Broderick, sir!"

"Well, Lieutenant, you head over to where Ben McCulloch and his Rangers are making that boy a girl, and tell

McCulloch—if he's got no more information at this point—to go ahead and put the Mexican out of his misery."

"Sir?"

The Colonel cast a whithering look down on the young lieutenant. Exasperated by the failure of the officer to understand a simple order, he enunciated each word carefully as if he was speaking to a child.

"Tell Mack to quit playing with the Mexican and PUT-HIM-AWAY! You got that?"

"Put him away. Yessir, I got it," Lt. Broderick replied and hurried off to relay the order.

The Colonel wheeled about on his large gray and galloped off in the direction from which he had come. The private had returned to his position on the ground, his journal open again. Over his shoulder Lt. Beebe could clearly read the words: *Put him away*.

"You ought to be careful with that book of yours, Private Chamberlain," he said.

When the soldier looked up, Beebe gave him a grim smile. "By the way," he asked. "Who was it that really captured those cannon and the Mexican general at Resaca de Palma?

"Colonel Belnap and the 8th Infantry took the guns. They captured General La Vega as well. Captain May rode hell for leather away from the cannon as soon as he realized how perilous it was being that close to the enemy. You probably won't read that in the history books, sir. But it soothes my soul," he smiled, tapping his notebook, "to know that it's written down somewhere."

Lt. Beebe heard the single shot ring out that spelled the end of suffering for the tortured Mexican. It occurred to him that this war had many stories which would be conveniently forgotten when the histories came to be written.

"Be careful, soldier," he told Pvt. Chamberlain. Then he mounted and rode back to meet up with his comrade.

The Dragoons set out again after the Mexican was disposed of and,within an hour, the advance guard spotted a ranch at the bottom of a hill due south of them. They observed several men running from the ranch into a ravine.

The bulk of the command attacked the hacienda and occupied it while Lt. Sam Sturgis gave chase to the retreating Mexicans. He did not return and was assumed killed or captured.

Colonel May ordered the hacienda fortified and had his men use the Mexican prisoners as workers, preparing breastworks, rounding up the cattle on the ranch to be butchered for food, and watering and feeding the horses. Lt. Broderick was ordered to supervise some of the Americans charged with setting up the few six-pounders they brought from Washington's command.

By sundown they had roasted several sides of beef and were enjoying a great barbecue. As they were eating, a lookout raised an alarm. On the horizon about a mile off the men could see the dying sun glancing off the lances of several horsemen. Col. May, convinced that he was being approached by the main body of Santa Anna's troops gave orders for the captured Mexicans to be killed and for the excess animals to be released. He ordered the rest of the men to mount and be prepared to ride. Lt. Beebe saddled up. If he was surprised to see Lt. Broderick head over to the corral and begin ordering men around, he didn't show it. He waited until Col. May pulled out his field glasses and was intent on observing the dust clouds to the south before riding over to confront his friend.

Broderick and a handful of men from his platoon were herding the Mexican prisoners over to the corral. The remainder were scattering the cattle as Lt. Beebe approached.

"What the hell are you doing?" Lt. Beebe asked.

"Getting the prisoners ready to be shot. You heard the Colonel."

The volunteers seemed more than eager to carry out the task as they hustled the prisoners into the wooden enclosure with occasional blows from their stocks of their muskets. A sergeant from the regulars, however, came over to protest.

"Sir, I ain't sure that what we're doing is right."

"What!" fumed Broderick. "You're not sure? Just who the hell are you, Sergeant? Are you the commander of this outfit? Are you the company officer? Just who the hell are you to question an order. Now get over there and have your men load and prime their muskets. Await my order to fire."

"Christ, Brad! This isn't right," Lt. Beebe argued. "You can't just kill unarmed men like that."

Just then a bugle sounded. The scouting parties had returned and, while they had not encountered enemy troops, they had located a site where a large troop of Mexican cavalry had been camped.

Colonel May rode up on his big gray.

"To horse! To horse!" he called to his men.

Broderick caught the reins of his horse, a palomino, which the sergeant had fetched as soon as he heard the bugle call. He had mounted and was in his saddle next to the Colonel in seconds. Beebe still stood beside the corral gate.

"Lieutenant Beebe," Col. May ordered. "See to those men. I want them put away."

Both the Colonel and Broderick galloped away in a cloud of dust headed south. The command, however, was moving back to Agua Nueva, the buglers blowing the call to withdraw in defiance of May's orders. May was screaming, trying to determine if someone had countermanded his orders or if he had been simply misunderstood.

"The wrong way! The wrong way! Who gave the order to that bugler?"

Finally, exasperated, he turned to Broderick and said, "Oh hell!" and together they rode north after the Dragoons, back to Taylor's camp.

"Sir," inquired the sergeant, still at the gate of the corral. "What shall I do with the prisoners?

"You heard the order, Sergeant. We were instructed to put them away," Lt. Beebe said. "So close the corral gate and let's get the hell out of here."

The sergeant grinned. He shut the gate and said, "Don't you fellers run away now!" Then, he ordered his men to mount. They followed May's troops back the way they had come. In the distance they could hear the rumble of gunfire and as they reached the Paso de los Pinos, where May feared an ambush. They heard the Colonel give the order to take up a gallop and the sergeant's troop followed suit. When they finally arrived breathless back at the Agua Nueva camp, the only real fire they had received on the way was a couple of stray rounds from some of Taylor's nervous pickets.

The four hundred men under Colonel May rode straight to General Taylor's bivouac. Private Chamberlain had his foot over the pommel of his saddle; his perennial notebook was opened and propped on his knee. Lt. Beebe noticed that he had pen in hand. The private grinned over at him.

"I wouldn't miss this for the world," he said smiling at the lieutenant's raised eyebrow.

General Taylor walked over to a log fire in front of the tent. He was dressed in a loose-fitting pants and what looked to be a nightshirt. He shook his head in mild exasperation at the breathless colonel.

"Lt. Col. May reporting, sir. I wish to say, sir...

"Doggone those pickets making all that racket," the general said with quiet sarcasm. "I knew that it was you coming all along, Mister May."

CHAPTER 23

The View From Buena Vista

It was Washington's Birthday and no one in Taylor's army was ignoring the significance. At nine o'clock, word had come that an advance screen of Mexican cavalry had appeared before General Wool's position. It was a beautiful, clear, sunny morning, and the army had gone into a state of readiness. Lined up in formation they listened enthusiastically as the regimental band played "Hail Columbia" and other patriotic tunes. At 11:00 AM Taylor rode his white horse in review of the troops who greeted him with wild cheers. His popularity had risen with each successive victory, and many of the men had come to the conclusion that he was unbeatable. The volunteers especially liked Old Rough and Ready because he seemed one of them. Dressed in a straw hat, blue cavalry trousers with a stripe down the side and a nondescript and loose fitting blue jacket, he looked like a volunteer himself instead of a general officer in the regular army.

"Christ!" muttered Lt. Broderick maneuvering his horse through the crowd as he followed behind the general's staff.

"What a bunch of rabble these volunteers are. And none of them has been in a battle yet. God knows what use they'll be."

"None of us has been in a battle before either," Lt. Beebe reminded him. "Except for the First Dragoons."

"Yes. That's true enough. And some of those are not much at obeying orders," Broderick replied.

"Christ, remember last night? The bugler calling for retreat when Colonel May had clearly ordered a charge? Speaking of orders... What did you do with the Mexican prisoners last night?"

"I put them away, as ordered," Lt. Beebe replied pleasantly.

"You had them killed then? Well, at least someone can follow an order."

"I didn't say I had them killed. I put them in the corral—that's *away*. And that was the Colonel's order. Put them away, he said. So I did, and then I left them there."

"But that was not the order!" Broderick spluttered in outrage..

"That's how I interpreted the order, my friend. Besides, following orders precisely has never seemed to have caught on in this army. General Taylor was ordered to give half of his troops to Scott. He didn't do so. Thank Christ! What would be doing now with Santa Anna hot on our trail with God knows how many troops?"

"But orders are orders," Lt. Broderick remonstrated. "You knew what May wanted you to do. You purposely avoided following his order. And you're not a general."

"Neither is your beloved Col. Harney, who is not here today by the way. Why is he not here? Why are we serving under this nincompoop May? Because your Colonel Harney is in Washington to be court-martialed for not obeying orders. At least I ignored an order for a good reason: so as not to be a murderer of unarmed men. Your Colonel Harney ignores orders to secure himself a bit of glory in the dispatches. This time it backfired on him!"

Lt. Broderick was about to answer angrily in defense of his leader, when four Mexican lancers came into the camp under a flag of truce With them was Mexican Surgeon General Pedro Vanderlinden who bore a message from Santa Anna.

Gen. Vanderlinden ignored Gen. Taylor, riding past him without a second glance. The Mexican emissary, in his experience of how commanders dressed, thought Taylor could not possibly be an officer—let alone a general. He gave the letter instead to Gen. John E. Wool, a brigadier general in full dress uniform. Wool, a stern and proper man, with a receding mane of gray hair, and a cold blue-eyed stare, accepted the note and, at a motion from Taylor, opened it.

"Read it to me, General, if you please," Taylor said.

"It's in Spanish, General. I'm not fluent in that tongue."

"Major Bliss!

Gen. Taylor's adjutant rode over and accepted the note from Gen. Wool. William W. S. Bliss was not only adjutant and chief staff officer, he was also in the opinion of everyone who knew him the brightest intellect in the army. He had been hand-picked by Gen Winfield Scott to be the brains behind the colorful but uneducated and often wrong-headed Gen. Taylor. It was a good choice. Loyal to Talyor and discreet, he often compensated for Taylor's most glaring weaknesses. When the war was over, he would marry Taylor's daughter become the general's favorite son in law.

"Yessir!" The Major saluted.

"Translate this for me, son."

Major Bliss hesitated briefly, skimmed over the elegant Spanish, and then raised his head. He recited in a clear unhurried voice the message from the enemy.

"His Excellency the Commander-in-Chief of the Mexican Army to the General commanding the American Forces. Greetings! You are presently surrounded by twenty thousand men, and cannot in any human probability avoid suffering a rout and being cut to pieces with your troops; but as you deserve consideration and particular esteem, and as I wish to save you from a catastrophe, and for that purpose hereby give you notice, in order that you may surrender at discretion ..."

"Jesus," Lt. Beebe said. "Hasn't Santa Anna ever heard of a run-on sentence?"

"Shut up and listen," Broderick said.

"...under the assurance that you will be treated with consideration belonging to the Mexican character, to which end you will be granted an hour's time to make up your mind, to commence from the moment when my flag of truce arrives in your camp; therefore, think carefully but respond with alacrity to this concession which will not be repeated by your adversary who greets you in the name of God and liberty. ANTONIO LÓPEZ DE SANTA-ANNA. Commander-in-chief of the Mexican Armies. General Quarters. Paseo de Carnero. 22nd day of February 1847."

"Bill, is that mealy-mouth Mexican saying what I think he's saying?" General Taylor asked his adjutant.

"I believe so, General," Major Bliss replied. "He's essentially saying that you're surrounded by twenty thousand men and you may surrender at your discretion."

"At my discretion! Well then, tell that two-faced Mexican son of a bitch that I'll see him in hell at my discretion!" Taylor said, his anger and his salty wit rising to the occasion. "Besides he hasn't got any twenty thousand men; he lost six thousand of 'em on his forced march from San Luís Potosí. Old Ben McCulloch spent the damn night in his camp and just reported to me. He knows more about the Mexican army than Santa Anna does."

Major Bliss, however, aware of the obligations of history, even if his general was not, penned the following lines for the general's signature:

22 February 1847

General,

In reply to your note of this date, summoning me to surrender my forces at discretion, I beg leave to say that I decline according to your request.

—Gen. Zachary Taylor, U.S. Army

"Ah, Major Bliss," said Taylor when he received the note for his signature. "Perfect Bliss! What would I do without you?"

Then, with a smile and a flourish he signed his name, handed the reply to the Mexican officer, who saluted and rode off with his entourage.

"I was wondering what happened to Ben McColloch last night," Lt. Broderick said. "The Texas Rangers returned but McCulloch and one of his men were still missing when we turned in."

"Another feller that doesn't know how to follow orders," Lt. Beebe smiled. "This old army's full of them."

For the next two hours the Americans watched as the Mexicans moved their army up the mountain and around the valley with the apparent intent to flank the American left. About three o'clock in the afternoon the Mexican artillery under Gen. Ampudia opened fire. General Taylor dispatched a battalion of the Indiana brigade as well as the Kentucky cavalry to meet the attack and until nightfall there was sporadic fire and inconclusive maneuvering between the two forces.

That night the troops on both sides lay next to their weapons, without fires, in the bitterly cold and windy heights. There was a slight drizzle, and at six thousand feet in the mountain valley, the two freezing lieutenants got little sleep.

"What do you think will happen tomorrow, Bob?" Lt. Broderick asked.

"Well, Brad, even if its only fourteen or fifteen thousand troops that Santa Anna's got, we're still outnumbered three to one. Not very good odds."

"Then all the more honor when we beat him; all the more glory if we die," Broderick replied seriously.

"You know, that's true. We can't lose. If we die, we'll be the army that took on a force three times our size. If we fight gallantly and win, we'll receive promotions and maybe a mention in the dispatches. I wonder about the men, though. I wonder how they feel tonight."

"The men are not important, Bob. They'll do what they're told. When its over, the volunteers will go back to their farms, the regulars will finish out their hitches."

"How about the Irish? I mean they're not even citizens most of them. If they die tomorrow no one will care. If they survive the war, they go back to digging ditches if they're lucky, and living in coal cellars."

"The Irish on our side, you mean. I hear Santa Anna's got a whole artillery battalion of Irish on his side as well," Lt. Broderick said.

"I heard that, too. I guess we'll find out for sure today," answer Lt. Beebe. "Say, why the hell would someone do that, Brad? Just leave a victorious army to fight on the losing side."

"One of those things we'll never know, I guess. Every race has their story. But the only history that gets read is the one that's written by the victors. And the Irish, poor bastards, ain't won a war yet. Maybe losers just kind of gravitate to one another. I never did care much for Micks anyway. I wish they'd all desert so I'd have the please of killing them along with the Mexicans."

"Any Mick in particular?" asked Lt. Beebe who had heard the story of Kevin Dillon and Hezekiah Akley when Broderick was in his cups.

"Could be, Bob," replied Broderick. "There just could one I'd especially like to see killed."

At dawn the men heard reveille sounded from the enemy camp. Then from further off in the hills it sounded again a few minutes later. Then from the plateau where Santa Anna's camp was located, a bugler played it a third time. At two-minute intervals the Mexican commander had ordered the bugles to sound reveille in order to emphasize the enormous size of his forces and intimidate or at least unnerve the Yankees.

Then as the sun rose, the Americans could see the Mexican force had gained the very top of the mountain overlooking the valley where the Americans had camped. On the plateau Santa Anna ordered some of his infantry and cavalry to display themselves to the enemy while company bands played religious music. Priests in colorful Advent vestments blessed the cannon, and the smoke from their incense filled the air.

The first attack by the Mexicans was at The Narrows, or La Angostura, a narrow passageway between a network of gullies on one side, and a plateau intersected with ravines on the right of the Saltillo road just south of the Buena Vista Ranch where Taylor's supply train was stationed. It was quickly repulsed. But up on the plateau Santa Anna's forces were more powerful. They broke the both the Arkansas and the Kentucky cavalry regiments which retreated in confusion. And the volunteers of Indiana, after losing ninety men in almost as many minutes were ordered by their commander to retreat which they did willingly and with great dispatch. Lieutenants Beebe and Broderick, along with Captain Enoch Steen of the First Dragoons and Colonel May of the Second, waited impatiently for orders.

Major Bliss left the general's side to take a closer survey of the field. The remnants of the Indiana volunteers had been reorganized and were again on the attack but they were faring badly. He returned to report to Taylor.

"I'm afraid we're getting badly whipped, General."

"I know it, Bill," Taylor answered. "But the volunteers don't know it. Let them alone and we'll see what they do. Meanwhile..."

Taylor spotted young Jefferson Davis of the Mississippi Rifles.

"Captain Davis! Take your men and rally the 2nd Indiana. Hold that left flank, Jeff! I'm depending on you, son."

"Yes sir, General. You can count on the boys from Mississippi!"

"There's a real officer, Bill," Taylor said admiringly to Major Bliss. "If I had half a dozen like him the war would be over tomorrow."

Bliss, knowing a rival when he saw one, kept his peace.

Suddenly his attention was caught by a cloud of dust in his peripheral vision.

"General, check your glass!"

The general looked through his telescope to where Bliss was pointing, and almost dropped the glass in alarm in alarm.

"Colonel May! Captain Steen!" he shouted. "Take the Dragoons and head back to Buena Vista. It appears that the Mexican cavalry is trying to circle around us."

He pointed in the direction of a large body of cavalry which was indeed already half a mile beyond Taylor's position and headed to the American supply depot at Buena Vista Ranch.

The Dragoons took off for Buena Vista figuring that they could head them off by using the road. They did. But upon their arrival they found Col. Humphry Marshall of the Kentucky Cavalry and Col. Archibald Yell of the Arkansas Cavalry yelling conflicting orders at their men.

"Mount up, and charge!" yelled one colonel.

"Stay dismounted! Check your fire until they come closer," yelled the other colonel. "I'm the superior officer here."

"Jesus, here we go again!" Lt. Beebe said to Broderick. "Brevet rank versus lineal rank. These bastards have been doing this in every camp I've been in. I didn't think they'd resort to it in the middle of a battle. And there goes Colonel May to put his two cents in."

While the argument raged among the colonels, Captain Enoch Stern of the First Dragoons rode up and yelled savagely:

"There's too much damn jawing around here and not enough fighting! Here come those damn lancers. First Dragoons, at the ready..."

Stern drew his saber, and his men followed suit. There was the metallic slither of steel leaving scabbards multiplied a hundred and thirty times, a brilliant flashing in the sun as one hundred and thirty troopers drew their weapons. Then the order.

The sun was glorious, radiant, shining on the raised lances of the Mexican cavalry, caparisoned in red and silver, as they bore relentlessly down on the camp. The dragoons shifted slightly so that their point was on the Mexican color guard. Captain Stern clearly intended to attack at the center, thus splitting the Mexican force in two.

For Lieutenant Broderick it seemed that there was no sound, no time. Like those intense moments before a great storm, the atmosphere was heavy and thick. Then, the order:

"First Dragoons forward! Ho!"

Far away he could hear the crashing of the infantry volleys, and the steady thunderous duel of the artillery brigades. But it was as if that were occurring on another planet. For Broderick there was only here: this unplowed field before the nondescript ranch house of Buena Vista, the slap of the scabbard on this left thigh as his palomino cantered forward, his left hand tight on the reins to restrain his eager mount from a premature gallop, the sweat on his right hand where he held the saber as if it were his very life. And then the final order:

"First Dragoons, at the ready... CHARGE!"

A swift gallop then into the forest of Mexican lancers, the clash of sabers, the jostling of mounts, and the contact with the enemy in which everything was forgotten as he yelled so violently and struck so forcefully that he felt as if he were not in his body, but a part a force greater than any single human, indestructible and deadly.

His horse wheeled and pivoted with the slightest pressure as if it knew where to stop, where to move on, where to turn and meet the enemy. Broderick could not hear the clash of steel or the whinnying of the horses. He could not hear the cries of men, their limbs hacked away, their necks broken by the relentless sabers. His arm was like a machine, independent, incessant, as he swung down again and again at his foe, slicing and slashing.

He was in a fury, oblivious to any blows which came his way. Twice during the charge he had a lance pierce his jacket. The second time it opened a wound in his side that spurred him to such a fury that he cut the offender's arm off with a single saber slash. Now, in close contact, the Mexicans lances were useless and they, too, had resorted to the sword. But their lighter weapons were thrust aside by the heavy sabers of the Americans and again and again the Mexicans fell to the earth.

Although the lancers were some of the tallest of the Mexicans and their mounts the sturdiest, they were still no match for the Dragoons. Many of the Americans were muscular six-footers, and all of them had well-fed and intrepid mounts. Less than seven minutes had passed as Broderick hacked and slashed at any enemy uniform or horse that came near him, but already he felt their resistance giving way. Then, from behind him, like a great wave borne upon an offshore breeze, came the Second Dragoons and the Kentucky cavalry with bugles blaring. The Mexican force, already divided and confused, galloped off in several directions hotly pursued by May's Dragoons and the cavalry.

"Yahoo!" yelled one of the troopers in Broderick's outfit as they reined in to let the reinforcements take the pursuit.

"Yahoo!" the troopers echoed, and they gave Capt. Steen as welcoming cheer as he rode back and ordered them into formation.

"We whipped Santa Anna's best today, boys!" Capt. Steen assured them.

"We sent 'em to hell, sir," called one trooper from the formation. "At least most of 'em. The rest we'll leave for Charley Day if he ain't too out of breath jawing to catch 'em."

Lieutenant Broderick was laughing with relief and in high spirits. Lt. Beebe's face was ashen, however, and he could not stop shaking from the adrenalin rushing through his body.

"We did it, Bob! God dammit!" Broderick yelled to his friend as he brandishing his saber. "We broke them damn lancers and sent them running back to Santa Anna. We beat their best!"

Beebe looked over at his friend. His cap was gone, his hair matted with sweat and blood, his coat torn and his mount foaming from heat and exhaustion. Broderick's eyes gleamed liked those of a madman.

Gradually Beebe stopped shaking. He felt the muscles of his horse under him, and looked down at the broken lances, the deep ruts and hoofprints in the sod. Suddenly, he felt a chill.

"Lt. Broderick" he said, unable to look at the craziness in his friend's eyes. "I believe it's going to rain."

Meanwhile, the other American units had not fared as well as the Dragoons. Santa Anna had enveloped the American left, decimated the Arkansas and Kentucky regiments, and destroyed the Second Indiana. He had also established a strong position up on the plateau and the 16 pounders of the San Patricios up on the sierra wrought havoc on the Americans below.

"We are whipped," General Wool told Taylor at one point.

"That's for me to determine," Taylor replied, quietly and without emotion.

Meanwhile, the Mississippi Rifles and Braxton Bragg's artillery formed an inverted V and waited until the Mexicans with Gen. Pacheco's 1,500 cavalrymen were seventy yards away. Then they all fired at once. When the Mexican line crumbled, the Mississippians used their vicious bowie knives to finish them off in hand-to-hand combat.

Seeing that the Mexicans were now vulnerable, Taylor ordered the 1st Illinois to attack the upper reaches of the Plateau but he underestimated the numerical superiority and the desperate determination of Santa Anna's forces. Under the command of General Lombardini the Mexican infantry emerged from a broad ravine in groups of twenty, then thirty, then hundreds, and the Americans fell back in retreat.

The sixteen pounders of the renegade Irish company was inflicting heavy damage and their green flag annoyed Taylor considerably. Unable to bear it any more he ordered the First Dragoons to charge that position. It was a mistake. Although the Dragoons came close to the position and wounded a few gunners, they were beaten back with heavy casualties. Among them, Lieutenant Robert Beebe, graduate of West Point, Class of '46, Lieutenant Broderick's only friend. A canister formed of waste rock and dirt from the ridge had smashed into his face, shearing half of it away and leaving him unrecognizable.

As the first drops of rain that Lt. Beebe had predicted began to fall, the American artillery opened up on the Mexicans to protect the retreat of the Kentucky and Illinois regiments. They were not in time, however, to save the lives of several courageous officers including Henry Clay, Jr., the son of the U.S. Senator whose consistent protests against what he considered an aggressive and untenable policy toward Mexico had cost him the presidency. Ironically, the son would die for a cause his father did not believe in.

The attackers kept coming from the ravine, hundreds of them, astoundingly, and the Mexican artillery kept up a thundering cannonade.

Some men from the San Patricio company actually left their guns at one point and seized two six pounders abandoned by the Americans who no longer had enough soldiers left alive to man them, or horses to pull them.

At this critical moment, when everything seemed lost for the Americans, Braxton Bragg arrived with his flying artillery. This unit received its name because the rapid mobile batteries could be set up and deployed within moments. They had already commenced opening fire when General Taylor and his adjutant arrived at the scene.

"Am I glad to see you, Captain Bragg! Keep it up. Maintain this position at every hazard. If they move you, we are lost. Be assured you have my full support."

Bragg looked behind him. Then to both sides. There were no American troops to be seen, either on his flanks or at his rear. O'Brien's and Washington's cannons had been lost or abandoned. The closest infantry was a hundred yards and they were in retreat.

"Who will support me in this position, General?" Bragg asked.

"Major Bliss and I will support you, sir," replied the intrepid Taylor, exposing himself to enemy fire on his white charger. "By the way, what are you using, Captain, grape or canister?"

"Canister," General.

"Single or double?"

"Single."

"Well, double shot your guns and give 'em hell, Bragg!" the General shouted over the roar of the Mexican barrage.

Bragg's next salvo staggered the Mexican line, but still the enemy kept coming—inexorably, blindly. His next three salvos cut them down in sheaves and, as the smoke cleared and the dying thunder of the cannons echoed a final time across the hills, the rain came down in torrents. It was 7:00 PM, Sunday, February 23, 1847, and the Battle of Buena Vista was over.

As Taylor ordered the surgeons to attend to the wounded, he was filled with despair. He had held the field but in the process had lost a third of his command. There were 673 confirmed dead, 387 wounded, and 1,500 missing or otherwise unaccounted for. He was almost out of ammunition. While he expected that reinforcements would arrive later that evening as well as a supply train, he did not feel confident should the Mexicans resume their attack the next morning. All of his troops except Jefferson Davis' Mississippi Rifles, the Dragoons and Bragg's artillery, had at least once turned their backs to the enemy. While there were many individual cases of bravery and intelligent command decisions, on the whole the army had performed quite badly. Taylor felt that he had little to be proud of. He returned to his tent saddened and troubled and, despite his exhaustion, slept fitfully, wakening often to the dolorous sound of the rain on his canvas tent.

CHAPTER 24

The View From the Other Side

For Kevin and his compatriots it had been a long, bloody and exhausting day which had been foreshadowed by a month of wanton deaths and debilitating marches. Even the elation he felt at the end of the battle could not compensate for the aching bone-weariness.

The month before, the Engineers, the San Patricios and other artillery companies proceeded by the cavalry, had left San Luís Potosí on the road to Saltillo. Each day thereafter an infantry division had followed: Don Francisco Pacheco's, Don Manuel Lombardini's, Don J.M. Ortega's. The total force was 23,340 men. Knowing that they would encounter a much smaller American force and, knowing, too, that this forced march would give them an element of surprise, both the Mexicans and the Irish were confident.

Besides the soldiers themselves, there were over 1,500 camp followers, mostly women. Among them was Cécilia Hermosillo, a nineteen year old girl from Marín whose father, mother and brother had all been killed at Monterrey. Céci and her aunt, Mónica, cooked for the men and helped load cartridges. Since the end of the summer, Céci and

Kevin had seen a great deal of each other—always under the supervision of Tía Mónica, which only served to intensify their feelings.

She spent many hours by the campfire in the evening with Kevin while he, notebook in hand, learned the Spanish words for each item of equipment, each morsel of food, and ultimately for the feelings he barely knew how to express in his own language. His mind, young and supple, absorbed the Spanish quickly, and the scornful laugh of the aunt when he mispronounced a word merely acted as a spur to his progress. By Christmas he was not only fluent in the minimalist vocabulary of the army, but he had even approached the priest to intercede for him with Tía Mónica so that he and Céci could be married. He was deeply in love with her, even though they had not yet spent more than two minutes alone, nor exchanged more than a kiss on the cheek. Despite Santa Anna's order that the women stay behind, all of them—including Céci and her aunt— continued on the march as soon as Santa Anna and his lancers departed.

From the very beginning, however, the march was a disaster. Coming across the mountains several soldiers died of the cold. Others, collapsing from fatigue, had to be left behind.

At Encarnación, the Mexican lancers encountered an patrol of Kentucky cavalry which had been sent forward to scout the Mexican position. The seventy-one Americans, surrounded by five hundred of Santa Anna's best lancers, surrendered without a fight. This was a tremendous boost to the Mexican morale as the troops watched the prisoners being escorted ignominiously to the rear. And the march went on.

Coming down from the high sierras the skies opened up and a freezing rain deluged them for over a week. Kevin heard that over two thousand men, many of them poorly-fed and scantily-clothed Indians recruited from the south, perished during that terrible week.

When the Mexicans at last reached the base of the mountains on February 5th, they encountered a valley of cultivated land which stretched for over thirty miles. This should have been a comfortable time for the army, and would have been except for the fact that one of the commanders decided to order a rest for his division without notifying anyone to the rear. Since each station could accommodate only one division at a time, the other divisions were ordered by Santa Anna to march backward for a day to retain the proper interval. More died in that return march.

Next, they encountered the desert. Since Santa Anna had months earlier ordered the water caches along the route destroyed so they could not be used by the Americans, his own men were now without access to water along the desert stretches. The thirst and the agonized suffering of the men increased a hundred-fold in the desert, but the fact that four hundred horses and pack animals died was a more pressing concern for the Mexican general. He ordered the small water ration for his men to be cut even further so that the more valuable stock would survive the journey. Over four thousand men and women either died or were abandoned after falling from heat stroke and dehydration during this phase of the march.

On Sunday, February 21, 1847, Santa Anna was about sixty miles from Taylor's camp. His men were suffering from exhaustion, muscle cramps, and debilitation caused by water loss and the strenuousness of the march. Santa Anna, unwilling to slow his pace, ordered the cavalry to continue on without stopping for water. At this point he again ordered the women to turn back; again they refused. The infantry, after a ten minute break during which time they were allowed a small ration, continued their forced march at arrive at Angostura on the morning of February 22nd.

Of his command of 23,340 men which had left San Luís Potosí, Santa Anna had only 15,142 effectives remaining when he reached La Angostura, most of them enervated, exhausted, and suffering from horrendous muscular cramps and headaches caused by dehydration. Still, they were the survivors: the toughest, the most spirited, the ones with the most grit. They didn't come this far to be defeated. Though they had come through a horrible death march, if properly rallied, properly led, their superior numbers could defeat the Yankees.

On the 22nd, after General Vanderlinden delivered the surrender demand which the Americans rejected, the recently-promoted Captain Riley and the other artillery officers gave orders to their crews to unlimber their guns. Because the Mexican cannon had such limited capabilities, Santa Anna himself supervised their placement. He ordered fourteen pieces of artillery to form the center in support of Lombardini's and Pacheco's infantry. Chief of Artillery General Antonio Corona and Chief Engineer Ignacio Mora y Villamil chose the position for the three 16 pounders which were to be manned by the San Patricios. On the left were Col. Santiago Blanco's elite Regiment of Engineers.

General Mejía began the attack with a feinting movement against the American right which Taylor met with the 2nd Kentucky, some cavalry and a section of artillery. Maneuvers, nothing more. Santa Anna testing and Taylor responding. At about 3:30 PM there was some periodic rifle skirmishing but neither side gained any advantage and as night fell both sides rested.

As night fell, the Mexicans held the high ground, they had superior numbers and the dominating position. As Kevin went to bed on the night of February 22nd, listening to the sporadic gunfire, he felt sure of victory.

The morning of February 23rd was beautiful. It was a clear, sunny, mountain morning with a soft breeze blowing across the fields below. Kevin and his crew had been up since 2:00 AM readying the guns. At 8:00 AM, after the initial assault by Ampudia's brigade, Capt. Riley approached.

"All right, men," Riley announced. "We've got the 16 pounders. I guess all of you know what an honor that is."

"Hell yes, sir," Sgt. Murphy answered. "And we've got the high ground. We'll enfilade most of the American line."

"You're right, Sergeant. Okay, listen up! Gen. Ampudia is already advancing. I want you to give support. Eliminate those six and four pounders that are giving the American attackers their protection. Let's drive those sons of bitches off this plateau."

Kevin could not see much of the battlefield after the firing started. It seemed like there were at least three battles were going on simultaneously. He could only follow the one that was in front of him and—due to the smoke—not much of that. He was running on an energy reserve he didn't even know he had. That and the flow of adrenalin. He took turns swabbing and loading as if in a fever.

He was like a specter; his eyes piercing the smoke of the battle as the ground trembled beneath his feet. He was in the service of a metal monster which spewed death and vomited metal. As the afternoon wore on, Col. Francísco Rosendo Moreno was wounded. He was the Mexican commander of the San Patricios and his fall inspired the men to even greater effort.

"Cannonade those bastards off the damn plateau! They got the Colonel and half the crew of the far gun. They've also blasted the hell out of the Engineers!" Capt. Riley shouted as the Americans continued their attack.

The San Patricio battery, situated on a ridge where it commanded the entire plateau, now became deadly and even more precise than before, hurling grape and canister, and using even the rocks from the mountainside to serve for the shrapnel which was in short supply. By late afternoon they had repulsed a desperate attack by the American Dragoons and wiped out two enemy guns crews.

Above their cannon fluttered the green flag of St. Patrick with its silver cross and the harp of Ireland. As the enemy gun crews below them retreated, abandoning their cannon, the men lifted up a cheer.

Riley called over to the Engineers. "There you are, *amigos*. There's your vengeance! Go get them."

Several of the San Patricios followed the Engineers down the slope to the abandoned enemy position where they picked up the American flag, several guidons, and wrestled two brass six-pounders back up to the heights. When the American infantry tried to intercede, they were badly mauled by the Irish cannon.

Kevin was at the end of his reserves, however. He knew they had delivered a serious blow to the Americans and should follow their advantage. However, just then the American flying artillery began pounding the ridge, and the San Patricios lost several more men including a lieutenant and two corporals.

About six-thirty an unseasonably heavy rain squall swept the field dampening the powder and effectively ending the artillery barrage. The firing came to an end on both sides. Kevin looked around him for the first time. Beneath the sound of the high-pitched whinnying of the dying horses, he could now hear the moaning of the wounded. He watched as they removed the bodies of the Irish gun crews. At least a third of the eighty Irishmen defending the ridge had been killed or wounded. A lieutenant as well as two sergeants on the first gun had been killed during the Dragoon attack. Two corporals and seventeen privates had been killed during the final attack by the flying artillery. The Colonel, two other corporals and two more privates had been injured earlier.

The rain poured down now, and the blood ran in rivulets across the stone face of the ridge where it collected in puddles beneath the cannon. The fighting was over. The Americans had no infantry support for their artillery, so they would not mount another attack. The Mexicans, who had initiated the fighting throughout the day, did not have the will or the stamina for another assault. And so the day ended.

Shortly after 7:00 PM the sky lightened briefly, the rain stopped, and a beautiful rainbow spanned the valley. Then the sun dropped behind the mountain and both sides settled down to another cold, damp night.

"Well, we did it. Right, Sarge?" Casey asked. "We held our positions and gave 'em hell."

"Sure did! All you boys did a fine job. Plus, we got a few extra cannon here," he added, pointing to a captured 4 pounder and the two brass 6 pounders that the Engineers had retrieved. "But we lost a lot of men in the process."

"How many, Sarge?" Kevin asked.

"Looks like about twenty-seven killed or wounded. That ain't a lot when you consider how many the Mexicans lost, but there was only eighty of us to begin with... Ten-hut!" he interrupted himself as Captain Riley approached.

"At ease, men. Well, we finally won a battle. I know we won this one. Every damn infantry regiment that tried us ended up retreating."

"The dragoons, too!" Kevin added.

"You're right, son. The damn Dragoons, too. Hell, we even destroyed one artillery company. Good work, men."

"That last bunch really hurt us, though," Casey added.

"That was Braxton Bragg," Murphy noted.

"Well," Captain Riley said. "I guess he could have hurt us a lot worse than he did, but the rain dampened his powder just in time..."

A soldier screamed once and then murmured, "Ah please. Don't let them take the damn leg, eh? Give us a break."

Captain Riley signaled the stretcher-bearer carrying a young Irishman to follow him. He whispered words of encouragement to the wounded boy.

"Yeah," Murphy said wearily dropping down beside the cannon. "I guess we won all right. Hoo-ray. Hoo-ray. But I ain't real hopeful about tomorrow."

He looked over at McDowell who, along with half a dozen other soldiers, had already fallen asleep beneath the cannons.

"What we need here, Kev, is a good fire and some grub. Do you think that girl of yours could help us out?"

Before Kevin could go in search for her, Céci had appeared on the ridge. She ran up to him breathlessly. Hugging him and crying, she spoke rapidly, the words flowing like a balm over the weary soldier.

"*Estás vivo, gracias a Dios! Gracias a Dios*! Thank God you're alive!

"*Estuve muy preocupado por ti*" Kevin said, embracing her. "I was very worried for you."

"And I for you, my love," Céci said kissing him.

"*Ganamos esta vez, sin duda*," Kevin said.

"*Sí, ganamos. Qué bueno! Por fin!*

"*De veras. Por fin ganamos. Y se merecen esta victoria.* Truly. Finally we've won."

"*Ves el arcoiris?*" Cécilia said smiling happily.

"*Cómo?*" Kevin asked. *Arcoiris* was not one of the vocabulary words that he had learned during his fireside studies.

"*Los colores del cielo*," his *novia* replied, pointing to the sky over the field where a perfect arch of color had appeared.

"Ah, a rainbow! *Sí, lo veo*," Kevin replied happily.

"It is a sign, Kevin," she said. "A sign of our victory and our love which will last forever."

"*Bien*, Céci. I know you are right. Now, if you would be so kind, my love, go see what food can be found. I will prepare a fire."

When Céci returned he had a blazing camp fire going of dry madrone wood. Céci brought beans and *tortillas* and, unfortunately for Kevin's secret hope and fantasies, she had also brought her Aunt Mónica who would lie down between them as night fell to preserve the chastity of her charge.

The Americans groaned in pain and cold throughout the night. The more seriously wounded were evacuated to Saltillo. The dead were removed more slowly since there was no hurry. Lt. Broderick could not wait for the stretcher bearers. He had gone out to the field and picked up his friend's body. He would let no one help him. And when finally the gravediggers came to relieve him, he cursed at them and had to be restrained.

"I will kill every damn Irishman I see," he said at one point to nobody in particular. "I will make those bastards pay. God damn me, if I don't."

Firewood was scare in the American camp and such fire as they had were not sufficient to dry their clothes or to keep the cold mountain dew from penetrating their blankets. Only Lt. Broderick, fueled by the fire of his rage, did not feel the damp. Only Lt. Broderick did not shiver with cold and trepidation of the dawn which would certainly bring a more deadly battle.

The Americans could see the Mexican fires burning brightly throughout the evening. They envied the Mexicans their fir and madrone trees on the heights which allowed them to spend a warm and cozy night.

They envied them their position, too, and their large force, even though fresh American troops had continued to arrive during the afternoon and evening.

On both sides there were counsels of war. On both sides the generals debated the feasibility of continuing the battle the next morning. For both the losses had been heavy; the margin of victory dubiously narrow. An independent umpire would have said that there were three battles that had been fought on February 23rd: one the Mexicans had won, one the Americans had won, and one that was a draw.

As dawn came slowly over the Sierra on February 24, 1847, the Americans shrugged off their damp blankets and cast nervous glances up at the heights. The Mexican campfires were still smoldering, but the army had gone. Lt. Broderick brushed the sleep from his eyes and then stared. The Irish who had guarded the ridge were gone. The Mexican cavalry gone. The infantry... all gone. The men muttered among one another first in confusion, then in wonder, then in delight.

"Thank God Almighty!" someone yelled. "We've won. The Mexicans have given up the field!"

And so it was. Santa Anna had lost over two thousand men. The remainder were exhausted beyond the limits of human endurance. His food and water were low. There was a hope that he could replenish his supplies at Agua Nueva, rest his men for a few days, and lure Taylor into making an attack at that time. But, this hope, too, would be shattered. Taylor, after caring for his wounded, returned to Monterrey with his victory. He had won his last battle against the Mexicans, and on his high road to the Presidency of the United States there would be little opposition.

Now it was General Winfield Scott's turn. Leading the largest amphibious force in the history of warfare, including elements of the U.S. Marines, he commenced bombardment of the city on March 22, 1847. After five days of shelling by the army and the navy, during which 750 shells fell on the city every twenty-four hours causing over 1,100 Mexican casualties—many of them civilians—the city capitulated. The road to the capital from the east was now opened and the second front of the invasion of Mexico began.

CHAPTER 25

We Shall Receive no Letters in the Grave

I'd like to pause here in the middle of the war, so to speak, and tread water. For those of you who are distressed when the author sticks his nose in a story you are reading, I offer the following in apology: This is primarily an historical account which offers only a passing nod to the conventions of the novel. I will, when Kevin is actually involved again, return to my relatively unobtrusive role as the modest (but omniscient) third person narrator. However, this next chapter concerns the second front of the war. General Taylor is now safely out of it and will go on to become President of the United States based on his war record. The war in the north is essentially over now. The next phase of the war will involved the largest amphibious invasion in history, second only to the D-Day invasion of the beaches of Normandy. The bombing and shelling of Veracruz, followed by the subsequent conquest of that city, will position elements of the American Army poised at the heartland of Mexico under the command of General Winfield Scott. When he begins his march toward the capital we will return to Kevin Dillon and his cohorts. In the meantime, a digression.

The mid-1800's was one of the most literate periods in the history of America. Walt Whitman, Henry David Thoreau, Ralph Waldo Emerson, Edgar Allan Poe, Herman Melville, Henry Wadsworth Longfellow, James Russell Lowell were not only writing and publishing, they were read by vast numbers of Americans. Reading as a pastime had never been so popular or widespread. As a result of leisure time brought on by industrialization coupled with the availability of inexpensive newspapers and journals, the expanding readership of Americans made them the envy of the world. The "democracy of print" had given rise not only to the common reader but to the common writers as well.

There were tales of Gothic romance, religious tracts, political diatribes, sentimental tales, and with the advent of war, hundreds of books, articles, reports, journals and letters. Not all of these found their way into print, but a surprising number of them did. In 1848 Harpers Brothers alone boasted twenty-two presses which printed 6,000 volumes a week.

The Mexican War was the first in which the war correspondent was actively employed on a large scale. The combination of the telegraph (which had been invented two years before), the penny press, and a large mass readership, caused many young reporters to volunteer for duty so that they could write on-the-spot dispatches. In addition, hundreds of officers and an equal number of enlisted men tried their hand at authorship.

Many of the newspapers from the period are preserved on microfilm. But the journals and pulp books have long gone out of print and the letters, for the most part, have disappeared. Still, a handful of bibliophiles have salvaged some of this material. One such is Owen D. Kubik. Were it not for Mr. Kubik's collection of fine and out-of-print books in a small shop in Dayton, Ohio, we would not have this digressive (but enlightening) chapter. Mr. Kubik has done his best to collect every scrap of paper, letter, journal, pamphlet and book from the period and has graciously given me access (at a handsome price, *querido lector*, for book dealers are not philanthropists!) to some of the choicer bits. I give you here a potpourri of letters and clippings which, though they may seem haphazard, are carefully chosen to advance the narrative to the point where Kevin and his companions can logically join us once again. Come with me now as we discover in the back of Mr. Kubrik's little shop in Dayton, Ohio, a box labeled "Mexico, 1847." We open the box and carefully remove the brown-edged brittle papers one by one. This is what we read.

12 March 1847

Landing at Vera Cruz

...If you suppose that we write at an elegant desk, with gold pen, and superfine post, you are just off the track. But thus: Half buried in soft sand—our left elbow "dug" in so as to form a support—for a desk we are using a huge old book, stolen (we fear) from a Mexican Ranche. What? Holy Mother! "La vida de Santa Maria"... I scribble in the midst of sweets and bitters, of heaven and hell, and to vary the monotony around, am obliged at intervals to drop my pencil, throw myself flat on the sand, to escape being chucked off by fragments of shell, or "cock" my ear at the whistling of a grenade, in order to get clear of its course.

—Thomas Mayne Reid, Correspondent, *Spirit of the Times.*

26 March 1847

Vera Cruz, Mexico

...I shall never forget the horrible fire of our mortars... going with dreadful certainty and bursting with sepulchral tones often in the center of private dwellings—it was awful. I shudder to think of it.

—Diary of Col. Ethan Hitchcock.

Letter to the Editor

Re: Volunteers

I have no wish to participate in such "glorious" butcheries of women and children as were displayed in the capture of Monterrey, etc. Neither have I any desire to place myself under the dictation of a petty military tyrant... No Siree! As long as I can work, beg, or go to the poor house, I won't go to Mexico, to be lodged on the damp ground, half starved, half roasted, bitten by mosquitoes and centipedes, stung by scorpions and tarantulas—marched, drilled and flogged, and then stuck up to be shot at, for eight dollars a month and putrid rations.

—*Cambridge* (Mass.) *Chronicle*

March 30, 1847

18 April 1847
Lt. Bradford Broderick
B Company, 2nd Dragoons

Finally, we saw some action. Col. Harney has been having trouble with the army brass ever since we left Corpus Christi. First, he was charged with leading an unauthorized foray to the Bravo del Norte, then with disobeying orders. The result was that he missed out on the big fight at Buena Vista. Lt. Beebe and I saw some action, though, and managed to repulse a troop of Mexican lancers. We held the field but suffered very heavy casualties, including Bob Beebe, my best friend. Irish deserters manning the Mexican artillery caused many of the deaths. Harney swears he'll avenge those deaths. He feels responsible because he did not lead us, but left us in the hands of Col. Day.

Yesterday, Gen. Twiggs or "Old Davey" as he's known to the men, called for reveille at 4:30. Col. Smith was sick so Col. Harney was detached to lead his brigade. We marched for about four hours to a large hill called La Atalaya when all of a sudden Mexican troops appeared. We attacked up the south-east slope after being given the order, "Attack 'em to hell." Anyway, ol' Harney took it literally and we get strung out halfway to Cerro Gordo chasing them until we got pinned down. We pulled back that night.

Next day the men dragged a 24 pounder up La Atalaya, following a path that Capt. Rob't E. Lee of the engineers figured out. Smart fellow that Lee! My guess is we'll hear more about him. But anyway, that morning —must have been the 17th, Harney was still in command of the 3rd and 7th Inf., Smith's red-leg infantry and of course our own Dragoons. Hell, you should have seen ol' Harney. Rising his sword over his head, he yelled, "Run those lousy bastards down!" And we did. We overran their breastworks and had Cerro Gordo in our hands before the other brigades had even taken the Jalapa Road. The Mexican general was killed; a brave man by the name of Vásquez who fought in the front lines with his men. Sgt. Thomas Henry of the 7th Inf. ran up the Stars and Stripes and Capt. John Magruder turned the Mexicans guns on the enemy. Hell of a day.

If Taylor and his crew were thinking about court martialing Harney, Scott will be thinking of making him a brigadier after today. I sure am proud to have fought with him this day.

Col. Harney is a tall man, with a bit of a squeak to his voice especially when he gets his temper up. He's a redhead and they say that's a type with a temper and he's no exception. He says that if he catches up with the Irish deserters he'll do them worse than any of the Mexicans. He says they have no honor. That's my opinion, too. I wonder if the boy that worked for Mr. Browning is among them? What was his name? Dillon, wasn't it? Kevin Dillon, if I'm not mistaken. I know he was in the army and that there were quite a few desertions after Monterey from Taylor's army.

We'll catch up with them soon. Tomorrow we march inland on the Jalapa Road. From there I am told you can see the volcanos of the Aztecs. Before the summer is out we shall be camped in the Halls of the Montezumas. Mexico is ours!

Your loving son,

—Brad

United States Senate
Washington, D.C.
2 March 1847

...If I were a Mexican I would tell you, "Have you not room in your own country to bury your dead men? If you come into mine, we will greet you with bloody hands, and welcome you with hospitable graves."

—Sen. Thomas L. Corwin, 29th Congress, 2nd Session

Mrs. B. E. Broderick
Cambridge, Massachusetts
(Illegible, 1847)

My dearest husband,

The last I heard of you was the letter to your father which you wrote from Corpus Christi. I hope that all is well with you. Imagine you in the Dragoons! I always thought of the Dragoons as so, I don't know, Napoleonic, not at all like an American group. But there you are. I am just a silly woman. Not too silly, though, to bear your child! Your son is now three months old. He's healthy as a horse and putting weight on like one, too. Your father is very happy in his role as Grandpa. He has gotten your old oaken crib out of the attic refinished in time for our lad.

Since I did not hear from you, I named him Kevin. It is an old family name, and goes back to my great grandfather. I asked your father if he thought that you would have any objections and he said that he thought not. We felt it was important to have the baptism and christening this month now that the weather has broken, as it may be a year before you are back this way.

Your father told me that you might be serving under Col. Harney. The newspapers have had some awful stories about him. They say he's risked men's lives at the Rio Bravo and will be recalled. Father says it is just political. They don't like him because he's a Democrat and is favored by President Polk. The Whig paper has said that he was accused of ravishing Indian girls during the Florida campaigns and the hanging them in the morning! They said that in St. Louis he beat his female slave, Hannah, to death. Even if half the things they say about him is true, he must be a terrible man.

I hope you will not become so brutal or so callous. Our son needs a father whom he can respect. I know that war does terrible things to human beings, not only to our enemies but to ourselves as well. For your soul's sake and that of our son's try to be a man of honor and restraint.

Your loving wife,

—Samantha

The President of the Mexican Republic to the Catholic Irishmen engaged in the Army of the United States.

The circumstances of war have brought you to this beautiful country. The American government engaged you to fight against a country from which you have received no harm. Your companions have after the battle received and shall only receive the contempt of the United states and the scorn of the nations of civilized Europe that, quite surprised, see that government seek engagements for their battles in the same manner as they look for beasts to draw their carriages.

Sons of Ireland! Have you forgotten that in any Spanish country it is sufficient to claim Ireland as your home to meet with a friendly reception from authorities as well as citizens?

Why then do you rank among our wicked enemies?

By conquest you can take cities, towns, but never possess two feet of ground unmolested as long as there is a Mexican. The last of the Mexicans are determined to fight without release for his country and his God.

But our hospitality and good will towards you tenders you what by force you can never possess or enjoy—as much property in land as you may require, and this under the pledge of our honor and our holy religion.

Our sincere offers have already been realized with many of your countrymen, who are living as brothers among us. Rely on what I offer you in the name of our nation; present yourselves like friends and you shall have country, home, lands; the happiness, which is enjoyed in a country of mild and humane customs; civilization, humanity and not fear, address you through me.

HeadQuarters Orizava the12th April 1847

—Antonio López de Santa Anna

And now Old Zack's at Monterrey
Bring out your Santa Anner
For every time we raise a gun
Down goes a Mexicaner.

—Popular song.

Cerro Gordo

April 18, 1847

After the battle we sorted the corpses and among these we observed the body of a young and handsome though coarsely attired female, apparently not more than eighteen years of age. Perhaps she had been the wife of one of the soldiers, and had stayed during the action. Perhaps they were newly married, and had been spending their honeymoon amid the horrid din of war. One could scarcely help wondering which among that number of ghastly corpses had been her husband. For among them he must be; it would be impossible to picture him flying on the road to Jalapa, and leaving behind the bleeding corpse of his young and beautiful bride.

—Diary of Pvt. George Ballantine

July 6, 1847

Peace Commissioner Nicolas P. Trist

My dear sir:

Looking over my stores, I find a box of Guava marmalade which, perhaps, the physician may not consider improper to make part of the diet of your sick companion.

Yours very truly,

—Winfield Scott

We love to indulge in thoughts of the future extent and power of this Republic—because with its increase is the increase of human happiness and liberty... What has miserable, inefficient Mexico—with her superstition, her burlesque upon freedom, her actual tyranny by the few over the many—what has she to do with the mission of peopling the New World with a noble race? Be it ours, to achieve that mission! Be it ours to roll down all of the upstart leaven of old despotism that comes our way!

—Walt Whitman
Brooklyn Daily Eagle, July 7, 1846.

It is not surprising... that the Irish are ignorant and, as a consequence thereof, are idle thriftless, poor, intemperate and barbarian... Of course they will violate our laws, these wild bisons leaping over the fences which easily restrain the civilized domestic cattle, will commit great crimes of violence, even capital offenses, which certainly have increased rapidly of late.

—Theodore Parker, Sermon.
"The Moral Condition of Boston."

The diffusion of knowledge, and especially moral and religious knowledge is the only foundation of national virtue. On the other hand, general ignorance is almost universally attended with general corruption, as is fully exhibited in the Catholic countries...

—Universal Geography For the Use of Higher Class in Schools (Boston, 1835).

We may condemn, we may argue against the tendencies of a race of men of higher organization, bolder hearts, more enterprising minds, of superior thews and muscles, and stouter wills, to supplant weak and emasculated tribes—good authority can be evoked to show how wrong all this is—homilies to this day are written against the pilgrim fathers for ejecting the savages from the primeval forests of the North; but, until the eloquence of ethics can melt human nature and mold it anew, we apprehend the world will wag on much after the old fashion. No scrap of philosophy, nor moral essay, nor political discussion will countervail... an army of Anglo-Saxons.

—Editorial page, *New Orleans Picayune*

The Mexicans are Indians—Aboriginal Indians. Such Indians as Cortez conquered three thousand [sic] years ago, only rendered little more mischievous by a bastard civilization. The infusion of European blood whatever it is, and that, too, infused in a highly illegitimate way, is not enough, as we see, to affect the character of the people. They do not possess the elements of an independent national existence. The Aborigines of this country have not attempted, and cannot attempt to exist independently along side of us. Providence has so ordained it, and it is folly not to recognize the fact. The Mexicans are Aboriginal Indians, and thus share the destiny of their race.

— Editorial, *New York Evening Post*

Men gladly hear of the power of blood or race. Everybody likes to know that his advantages cannot be attributed to air, soil, sea, or to local wealth, as mines and quarries, nor to laws traditions nor to fortune, but to a superior brain, as it makes it more personal to him.

—Ralph Waldo Emerson, *English Traits*

No man in his senses ever believed, fully and fairly, the {Roman Catholic} doctrine of transubstantiation. Let us not be misunderstood; there have, doubtless, been many who thought they believed it, but owing to the prejudice of education, their minds at this point were dark, and saw things that were not as they thought they were. So often do we see an individual inflicted with mental imbecility on some particular subject.

—Sermon of the Rev. Elijah P. Lovejoy.

The whole ceremonial of the Romish church, the doctrine, the gorgeous ritual, are adopted precisely to meet the inclinations and circumstances of all the ignorant men and women in our land.

—*American Quarterly Review.*

Irish with us means a class of human beings, whose women do our housework, whose men dig our railroads... The vicious Irishman always attracts attention. He is soon felt in a community of order as a disturbing character.

—H. Giles, *The Christian Examiner.*

To my friends and countrymen in the Army of the United States:

The President of this Republic, in hope of giving every advantage to the foreigners in the American army, through a feeling worthy of his high station both military and civil, and through motives of the purest friendship towards the misguided inhabitants of other countries who have joined the United States to foolishly embark on this impolitic and unholy war, once more offers you his hand & invites you, in the name of the religion you profess, the various countries in which you first drew the breath of existence, of honor and of patriotism, to withhold your hands from the slaughter of the nation whose thoughts or deeds never injured you or yours.

Irishmen! I call upon you for I know your feeling on this subject well, for the sake of that chivalry for which you are celebrated, for that love of liberty for which our country is so long contending, for the sake of that holy religion which we have for ages professed, I conjure you to abandon a slavish hireling's life with a nation who even in its moments of victory treats you with contumely & disgrace. For whom are you contending? For people who, in the face of a whole world, trampled upon the holy altars of our religion, set the firebrand upon a sanctuary devoted to the blessed Virgin, and boasting of civil and religious liberty, trampled in contemptuous indifference all appertaining to the dearest feelings of our country...

—John Riley, Captain
San Patricio Battalion
Army of Mexico.

Corporal Kevin Dillon
First Militia Company
of San Patricio
June, 1847

Dear Mother,

Much has happened since I last wrote. Gen. Winfield Scott and the Americans have made a naval landing on the coast and are moving a large army inland. They now greatly outnumber our poor army and are better armed. We fought a brief battle at a place called Cerro Gordo and were woefully outnumbered and outgunned. Now we are headed inland to the capitol to defend it as best we can from the Yankee advance.

The lovely girl I mentioned, Cécilia, was killed in the battle. We were unable to recover the body and had to leave her to the care of the enemy. Which is like leaving her to the tender mercies of the coyote and the vulture.

The good news is that the number of Irishmen and others joining our cause grows larger each day. Despite the American victories their leaders continue to treat the Irish like dogs. They are considered inferior in camp, useful to clean latrines and polish the officers' shoes. In battle, they have proved their courage but are not recognized for it. Anglo-Saxons get the medals and promotions. Irishmen get scornful glances, contempt, and the feel of the lash if they don't jump quick enough.

We've had eighty more join us since my last letter to you. Most of them are overjoyed to find priests in our ranks. They go to Confession as best they can with the language barrier, receive absolution, and then Holy Communion. It is a great comfort to them. Many had not received the sacrament in over a year. The speak often of the atrocities committed by the invading army, the girls ravished, civilians shot, and churches robbed. It shames them that they were unable to do anything to prevent these things.

The Mexican people are warm and gracious. They are very polite to us and tolerant of the many mistakes we make trying to learn their language. I could live very comfortably in this country after the war is over, and I'm hoping that it will be over soon. The Americans may, in fact, march on Mexico City but they could never hold it. Also, according to the Irishmen who have recently left them, the feeling seems to be that most are tired of the war, including the generals and the citizens up north, and will sign a treaty of peace very soon. The fighting goes on, it seems, only to insure that the best possible treaty will be made. The Americans are greedy for territory, especially that of California and will, no doubt make that territory a part of the terms.

I miss my lovely Céci! To think I will never hear her voice again this side of the grave. Although I never even kissed her except on the cheek, never spoke much beyond those few words I know of greetings and of thanks, I loved her dearly and I know that she loved me. Our eyes spoke volumes when she brought a drink of water to my cannon, or when she looked across the firelight at night where she sat with her aunt and sister. I hope she went to her death knowing that she was loved.

The Mexicans are a noble people who have suffered greatly. Despite the horrors and deprivations, their generosity and grace never wavers. Their music around the camp fires at night reminds me much of Ireland. How happy they would be if left alone to work out their own destiny without the fear of the Protestant invaders!

Mexicans, like us, are a people of music and poetry. They hold the same things sacred: family and honor and an unshakeable belief in the power of the Virgin who must look down on us now with pity and sorrow.

I believe that God never gives us more than we can bear. There is a reason for this pain which we suffer. If nothing else than to let others yet unborn know the horrors of lust for the land of others, and the blood which it costs to take it. It is blood which will never wash off, and will stain the hands of the Americans for the next hundred generations. I hope some of them learn why. I had hoped someday to have a son to write my story, but now it seems that is not to be. So pass it on to the young ones who are still with you. Let them know that their brother fought in a far off land for freedom, dignity and for the faith. And if I die, know that the Irish have a stake in this country and that our family will always be welcome here.

I don't know how or when this letter will reach you, now that the Yankees have taken the seaport. I trust God to find a way. Give Pa a hug for me, tell the young uns to behave, and tell Pa that, if it's God's will that I come through this war, I'll be sending for all of you to come live with me and raise a good crop that will feed us all on the fertile plateau of Jalisco.

Your son,

Kevin

CHAPTER 26

A Thing That None But Fools Would Keep

The San Patricio Battalion along with scattered elements of Santa Anna's Army of the East fled from the coastal regions through Jalapa, to Puebla and then down the national Highway to Mexico City. They were in retreat from the yellow fever as much as from the Yankees. Transmitted by the female *Aedes calopus*, a mosquito of the lowlands, it reduced a healthy man to a whimpering, jaundiced, and vomiting sack of emaciated flesh in days. Few survived. There was no known cure and most who contracted it were left behind; the lucky ones to hemorrhage and die quickly, the unlucky ones to die a slow and painful death of dehydration. The only satisfaction the men had was that General Scott's men in their relentless pursuit must have been suffering as well.

When they reached Mexico City at the beginning of June, the San Patricios met with Mexican officers to sign papers to serve an additional six months in the Mexican Army. There was cool *limonada*, a drink made from limes not lemons, at a table set out among eucalyptus trees in a small park, tortillas, and *birria* or goat meat stew. After the men had signed their papers they sat beneath the trees and considered the future.

"You think this war will last another six months?" Kevin asked Sergeant Murphy.

"I don't know. I figure if we can hurt them enough in one good fight outside of Mexico City, the Yanks might sue for peace. Hell, what are they going to do even if they manage to capture the city? If Santa Anna can't control the capital from a few hundred miles away, do you think Polk could do it from Washington? Too many folks in this country just don't take well to being run. That's why they drove the Spanish out in the first place."

"Yeah, but giving the Yanks enough of a hurt could be a problem. This feller Scott got twelve thousand fresh troops and more coming every day. We got maybe eight thousand who've been fighting this war since it began. And now that Santa Anna's put down the latest uprising in the capitol, maybe a couple of battalions of National Guard troops who are green as shamrocks.

"Well, sure but..."

"And, on top o' that, they got one unified command, while we got Santa Anna and Valencia with neither one able to agree with the other on strategy and both wanting to run the whole show."

"Damn it, bucko, hold on a minute! I didn't say if we lick 'em," Murphy reasoned. "I said if we put a hurtin' on them. If we make 'em pay a heavy price for every inch they got... well, then we stand a chance."

John Riley, tall and trim, wearing a Mexican infantry uniform with the gold oak leaf of a Major on his collar approached the group. The men from Murphy's platoon began to rise, saluting as they did.

"As you were, *caballeros,*" Riley ordered as he joined them. He squatted on his haunches next to Murphy.

"You got the right idea, Sergeant. Put a hurtin' on them is all we need to do. Santa Anna has already informed me that amnesty for those of us who defected from the U.S. Army will be a precondition of any peace treaty he signs. So, if we do our duty and give the Yanks hell, we might see the end of this war by September. The Yanks don't want Mexico. Just California and Texas. Santa Anna will probably agree to let them have it, too, provided he can save face and get a decent price.

"Well, fight we will, Major, and give them a hurting that their mind could have not imagined till now. We'll throw our banner in their faces, for though they may cry 'traitor,' we'll not be traitors to the vow we made at Confirmation, to defend our Faith against her enemies."

"Well said, Sergeant. Very well, I'll be off to see about our orders," Major Riley said, getting slowly to his feet. "Good day, men."

"Good day, sir!" the men replied, rising with the major and giving him a formal salute.

"Boldly spoken," said McDowell to the Sergeant.

"And truly felt, I'm sure," grumbled Casey beneath an ash tree as he drew heavily on his pipe, spittle and burnt tobacco ends making a sickening sound.

"And if we fall, sir?" McDowell said, ignoring Casey and turning back to the sergeant. "If we die before Santa Anna has made his deal?"

"A pox on Santa Anna and his deals! Neither he nor his deals were the reason we joined. What he does or doesn't do is not the point. If we be men, there is only one course and that's to make the price of our deaths a dear one for the Yanks. If you have fear, Private, and which of us does not, remember the words of the Bard: 'Reason thus with life. If I do lose thee I lose a thing that none but fools would keep: a breath thou art, servile to all the skyey influences.' This is a time when it will be golden to die, twice blessed both by our Holy Faith and by the green banner of our race which ever allied itself against the invader and in the name of freedom. We'll not be forgotten, and thus we will not die."

"A paradox!" Casey smiled with delight. "Now I know why you were chosen to be sergeant. The mystery is solved. You are headed for the general staff where you can spend time drafting the rationalizations for Santa Anna's failures."

"Watch it, Casey."

"Ah, yer too quick for me, Sergeant. Like the feller with the shells and the pea. I'm not sure where the pea is now. Correct me if I'm wrong. But if history is written by the winners, what kind of immortality do you think we'll get from the Yankee historians? Deserters, they say, and drunks, most likely. Bloody murderers at the end, too, of their own brethren."

"In the end," Murphy pronounced, "the truth will out. *Magna est veritas et praevalebit.* Great is truth and it shall prevail..."

"When no one cares if it prevails or not," Casey ended the quote.

"And that's the whole point, you dumb Mick!" Casey continued. "So, we're not going to just give them a hurtin'. We're going to fight this next damn battle to win. And if anyone shows a sign of weakening, if anyone suggests surrender, we blast em. If'en we run out of ammo, we fight with bayonets. And if'en the bayonets snap, we throttle their throats with our hands. How does that strike you, Sergeant?"

"It sounds..."

"Because by God if you've learned nothing from soldiering at all you had better have learned this. The man who fights like he's only going to put a hurtin' on ye, is a man whose going to get hurt. Ye have to fight for the whole thing, all or nothing. Kill or be killed. If we win, all well and good. And if we lose well we'll never know it, but our names will honor our lives long after we're gone, and our bayonets will have carved a dozen Yanks for Satan's platter for every one of us who goes to Saint Peter. How say you now, Sergeant?"

"Well said, Casey. Well said, indeed. I say, Amen. How say ye all?" Murphy asked of the Irishmen who had now gathered around in a large group attracted by the intensity of the argument.

"Huzzah! Hazzah! Drive the Yanks to the gates of hell!"

Some of the Mexicans had gathered curiously around. Kevin led another chant.

"*Viva México!*" he shouted. "*Muerte al General Scott y los invasores!*"

"Viva México," the other soldiers echoed, saluting with glasses of limonada and smiles. And for a moment it seemed to all of them that they would transcend the problems of feuding generals, of green troops, of exhausted veterans, of limited supplies, and of the inexorable enemy moving his cannons closer and closer to the city they had sworn to defend to the death.

Summers in Mexico City are different from the summers in the north. The sky darkens in late afternoon just as the tropical heat has become suffocating and intolerable. The winds rise, storm clouds move quickly blotting out the sun, the temperature drops precipitously, and a sudden calm descends over the land.

Then there is the shattering tear of lightning which rips across the sky, slow dynamo flashes over the mountains, thunder more explosive than an artillery shell bursting ten meters away, the wispy hairs of dark clouds coming closer, and then the rain.

There are seldom gentle rains in the Valley of Mexico. Rain usually begins with large drops, sometimes mixed with ice crystals as the temperature drops twenty degrees in a matter of seconds and then, as if the heavens opened up a cistern with the stored waters of the Caribbean and the Pacific, the deluge begins. Rain comes in torrents, blasting the canvas tents to the ground, pulling up stakes, turning over wagons, converting dry arroyos into raging torrents in which many an unwitting soldier will drown. The lighting is a pyrotechnic *tour de force* unequaled in any artillery barrage or fireworks display on the Fourth of July or Bastille Day. And the thunder shakes the earth.

By July the Mexican camps had become treacherous bogs, ruts made by the wheels of caissons were now rivulets; uniforms were darkened and mud-splattered, and tempers flared.

"Christ, what a life!" Sergeant Murphy exclaimed as the rains predictably flooded the Irishmen's tent, water flowing up over the trench carefully dug earlier that day and deepened for the purpose of preventing the very thing that was now occurring.

"First you suffer from intolerable heat, the poisonous spiders with their red bellies, the diamond-backed snakes, the scorpions, the relentless sun that seems magnified by the Creator like a small boy's glass as he tries to set fire to a pile of leaves..."

"And we're the leaves," brooded Casey, sucking at his empty pipe.

"That we are, Casey! Tossed this way and that by the whim of our commanders. But just when you think that you're going to pass out from the heat and humidity and would give your soul for a cool bath, along comes this chilling wind like an answer to your prayer, that freezes the sweat to yer skin. 'Ah, be careful what you pray for', my good mum often said. Ah, blessed relief this cold wind, you think, until the lightening starts and hits the bridle link killing your best horse, and the thunder that would scare the bejeezus out of the most sanguine Scot, thunder the likes o' which occurs in no civilized country on the face o' the earth. Jesus, Mary and Joseph! It sounds like the Yanks have fired off every twelve inch cannon ever manufactured..."

"And right behind our tent at that!" said Casey.

"By the bye," he added, seeking to lighten the mood. "Did you never hear why old Santy Anna steps out of his tent in full uniform during the lighting?"

"No, Kevin" said eagerly, ever the straight man. "Why does he?"

"Because he thinks that God is taking his photograph!"

"Hah! Ain't that the truth! A war fought by idle gentlemen using the dregs of Europe and a bunch of hapless Indians as cannon fodder."

Just then there was a lull in the rain and Murphy pulled back the canvas tent flap and looked out.

"A magnificent night, is it not, bucko?"

Kevin took in the cheerless night of muddy company streets, collapsed tents, two horses struck by lightning in a tangle of harnesses, wet men cursing at each other as they tried to untangle them, others grousing as they tried to raise a wet tent in the wind.

"Oh, yeah, magnificent," he said. But to himself he thought, How stupid everything is! What an absurd life!

He turned back to the tent and put his head in his hands. He wished he could dream, have a fantasy, or even picture Cécilia again. But his mind had become blank in these last two months of boredom, routine tasks, and forced close quarters. There was never a moment alone; never a moment for reflection or peace. But, ironically, neither was he kept truly occupied. Oh, there were the routine tasks to be done: grooming of horses, cleaning of cannon, working the leather bridles and harnesses with neet's foot oil. But always someone by his side, commenting, cursing, complaining or malingering. And always a sergeant or an officer shouting orders in Spanish, or countermanding an order given by another officer or sergeant five minutes before.

Life in the tents in the evening was no longer pleasant either. The songs and the warm fires had given way to coughs and sneezing, the catarrh of *la gripa* and other respiratory infections that came with the rainy season and hung on day after day. Clothes were sodden during the afternoon, damp and muddy at night. Even the best of soldiers did little more than complain.

As July passed into August, and August began to deepen, Kevin had little to do but clean his musket until it shone like silver, and sharpen his bayonet which already had an edge that could shave a cat's whiskers without the cat feeling it. Love had left him. Not only the warm memories of Samantha and Cécilia, but the summer images of roses and eucalyptus, of walks in the woods, of gentle afternoons and firefly-lit evenings. Life was damp, colorless and wretched. He caressed the cold barrel of his weapon, tested the fixed bayonet with the edge of his fingernail. He only had one fantasy these days and it came unbidden and inexorable as a wet dream to an adolescent boy. But it was not a fantasy of sex. Instead, he saw himself plunging his bayonet into the groin of an enemy soldier, felt the rotation of the stock in his arms as he turned the weapon, twisting the long knife. He heard the crunch of the bone shattering, smelled the sweet warmth of the blood that streamed forth when he pulled out the bayonet, and heard the satisfying viscous suck of the irreparable wound.

He could have this fantasy any time, day or night, asleep or awake, on guard duty or eating breakfast. Always it came with a passionate longing; always when it came it kept him enthralled, although it was the same dream over and over: the quick thrust to the groin, the twist of the metal cracking the bone, the withdrawal to the satisfying thurp of wet flesh closing on its engorgement of blood as the knife was withdrawn.

Those who have never experienced war think that what turns a man into a homicidal fighting machine is merciless training in which the soul is hardened, or fear when the battle is in earnest, or when the hot blood and adrenalin are easily mistaken for courage. But it is none of these things. What makes a man a killer are the hours, days, weeks and months of boredom and anxiety, with the terror licked away by the incessant tongue of monotony, and courage and glory eroded by dreary days of cold and dark clouds, orders given and rescinded, nights of half-sleep in a damp and evil smelling tent.

An idle mind, mothers used to remind their children, is the devil's workshop. But to the mind already made insensible by lack of use, forced into a systematic pattern of non-thinking (the condition of every soldier in a front line camp when an expected battle does not materialize for months) is more than a devil's workshop. It is a forge at which the devil presides with hammer, anvil and tongs, where the soldiers' synapses are melted to a white heat, billowed by primordial fears and unconscious rage, until the snake brain which remains is something deadlier than any weapon of gunpowder or steel. It is why in the end the rifleman in the platoon is the ultimate weapon in any war. It is why he will charge into the mouth of a cannon.

Now, as the rain ceases, almost as if a faucet were suddenly turned off in the sky, Kevin sees beyond the stream which borders the camp, where the women are coming with baskets of muddy clothes to wash. The air fills with the murmur of mourning doves, the raucous clatter of crows, and the gentle whirr of hummingbirds, their green breasts twinkling like neon in the evening light. The world returns to itself after a rain in Mexico. Everything returns with a crystal clarity: the bougainvillea, rose and sparkling violet, against the stone wall of the alcalde's house. There is the startling clarity of Spanish vowels crisp and clean as the sergeants give orders for the policing of the camp. The green fields to the south glisten and wave with the ripening corn, and to the north, the pastel colors of the stucco houses sparkle in earthly contrast against the dark wet stone of the somber cathedral. Kevin stirs as if awakening from a dream and shudders.

Kevin was as close to losing his soul that August afternoon as he had ever been. Something had broken in him during those months of emptiness and boredom which he had managed to keep whole up to then, despite the death and destruction, despite the loss of love. But now in these last days only the tiniest fiber of it still vibrated in his deepest core. And that vibration had become so dim and faint that he was hardly aware it existed. But just then, one of those happy accidents occurred, one of those fortuitous events that never seem to happen in novels or histories because they are so ordinary, so banal. Still, they do happen in real life and despite his frequent forays into fantasies of ugly and thoughtless violence, there was still something real in Kevin. It is that which makes us follow him now out to the bank of the river where the women are washing the soldiers' clothes. Suddenly, there is a shout and a woman snaps a wet shirt at a brown and black cur that had been sniffing around her basket.

"*Lárgate de aquí, perra!*" she screeched. "Out of here, bitch dog!" And the half-starved hound scrambled through the mud to land breathless and grovelling at Kevin's boots. It was a pitiful remnant of a dog: sunken eyes rheumed with fever, coat mottled and dry with the ribs sticking through from a hunger which had been lifelong and intractable. She had given birth to a litter of pups once and the litter died. Her poor breasts had shriveled and puckered from lack of milk. She was a throwaway in a land that could barely feed itself and now, with invading armies descending on the capital, devouring and destroying the crops as they came, was not even able to do that. She was not a dog but a blight, a scar on the earth, with not enough meat on her bones to make a broth for the stew pot.

But suddenly Kevin is seventeen again. An Irish lad whose long wrists and bare ankles show he has already outgrown the Mexican uniform he donned a year ago. An Irish lad far from home who kneels down now in the mud and calls the animal to him. She comes, tail between her legs, quivering. Who knows what Kevin sees? Surely not a scrounging bag of bones. She looks up at him, golden eyes flecked with rheum and fever, but burning now with gratitude and hope of affection. And Kevin in his loneliness does not turn away. He smiles and strokes her ears gently, and looks deep into her golden eyes.

"Ah, my sweet colleen," he whispers. "All alone in the world, hey? Without a friend, a kind word, or a bite to eat, hey?"

She licks his hand, then places a ragged paw on his thigh.

Kevin sighs deeply. His sigh is a mixture of sorrow, pity, weariness and defeat. What could he do for a dog in the middle of Mexico on the eve of a battle which would probably be the end of him and his small band. What was the point? But then, slowly, like the light breaking through the fog on a Kerry wharf, the feeling is replaced by hope. For a moment he is home again on a hillside looking out at the sea. He strokes the dog again almost absent-mindedly. Something to care for, something to cherish. And something loving next to him at night, to push away the dream of the bayonets and death.

He gets to his feet and turns back towards the camp. The dog, used to rejection, lays down in the dirt and looks after him with her sad eyes.

Kevin turns. "Come on then, if you're coming. Let's see if we can find a bite to eat!"

Revived by the tone, rather than the alien language which she could not comprehend, the brown dog followed him with an almost puppyish spring to her walk, although still guarded, still cautious, and several feet behind the boy.

The camp was more lively now that the rains had ended. The setting sun glowed golden among the tents, and burnished the steel of the weapons with a red glare. Cooking fires had been started and the air was rich with the odors of corn, goat meat, and boiled coffee. At his tent, a group of men led by Murphy were singing an old ballad as they watched the stew simmer on the fire.

"In Dublin's fair city, where the girls are so pretty
Was there that I first met sweet Mollie Malone.
She wheeled her wheelbarrow, through streets broad and narrow
Crying cockles and mussles, alive, alive-o
Alive, alive-o-o, alive, alive-o-o
Crying cockles and mussles, alive, alive-o."

Murphy left off singing and got to his feet as Kevin came into the camp.

"Jasus, Mary and Joseph! What is it ye have there, Kevin, my lad? Looks a bit too stringy for the stew pot."

The dog carefully sidestepped the sergeant and walked over to where the singing continued unabated by her presence.

"Alive, alive-o-o, alive, alive-o-o
Crying cockles and mussles, alive, alive—oo."

"Ahoo ahoo, oo, oo!" moaned the dog.

"Alive, alive, oo, oo," sang Casey in a high tenor .

"Ahoo, ahoo, oo, oo," chorused the dog.

"Sure and begorrah!" cried McDowell. "Dillon's found himself the only singing dog in Mexico!"

"And she's ragged as a fishmonger, herself, isn't she?" Casey asked. Then stooping down to stroke the dog, "Aren't you, now, my Molly Malone?"

The dog swung her tail happily at Casey's words and looked over to Kevin for his approval. Kevin nodded his head and smiled.

"Ha! Well, Molly Malone, it is, hey?" said Casey.

The dog continued wagging her tail as Kevin sat down beside them. They sang until the stew had boiled, and then ate from the common pot with the newly christened Molly eating her portion off a corn tortilla. When she had finished she curled up sleepily but alert at the entrance to the tent. The San Patricios had another recruit.

It was well that they did because the Mexican Army was suffering their perennial problem: too many chiefs and not enough Indians. By mid-August the Americans were twenty-five miles south of Mexico City and planning an attack on the capital. There were four possible routes to the city and Santa Anna did not have sufficient troops to defend them all. He decided to divide his command and place General Valencia's army on the American flank while he took a position at El Peñón, a 450 foot hill defended by thirty pieces of artillery and seven thousand men.

By August 18th the Americans had arrived at the Pedregal, a lava field south of San Angel, and Churubusco, a fortified convent. The lava field, a black expanse of chunks of black rock, boulders and ravines, was such erratic and unmapped terrain, that it was considered a natural defense, difficult for a man on foot to traverse without breaking an ankle or a leg in the process, impossible to cross on horseback or with cannon. The Americans appeared to be making a sweep towards the south around the lava field. General Valencia's shift of his troops south of San Angel at the northern end of the Pedregal effectively checkmated this move.

As darkness approached on the evening of August 18th, General Valencia received orders from Santa Anna to withdraw the main portion of his troops to the crossroads between San Angel and San Antonio. Santa Anna's concern was to protect the highway to Mexico City in case the Americans should find a way through the Pedregal or around Valencia's force. This position would cover both possible American routes.

Valencia, however, was not interested in withdrawal. He wanted a successful battle and subsequent victory over the Americans which would solidify his reputation as a brilliant general and future leader of Mexico. A withdrawal to join up with the other defense forces would place him more directly under Santa Anna's command, and thus any victory would resound to Santa Anna's credit.

Besides, he had a commanding position on a high premonitory overlooking the road to the village of Contreras and the Padiera farm, areas which the Americans must pass through. The only way the Americans could enfilade him would be to cross an impassible ravine and bring artillery through the equally impassable lava field known as the Pedregal. He felt secure that even the wily Yankees could not accomplish those kind of miracles.

CHAPTER 27

Carnage at Churubusco

In the early morning hours of the 19th of August, Captain Robert E. Lee commanded a group of 500 men and engineers who slowly and meticulously carved a path through the "impassable" lava field to approach the rear of Valencia's position. American rockets and mountain howitzers kept the Mexicans' front occupied. By nightfall, American infantry was within two hundred yards of Valencia's camp. Informed that the Yankee's had crossed the Pedrigal, Valencia laughed in scorn. "No! No! You're dreaming, man. The birds couldn't cross that Pedregal."

Meanwhile, a brigade under General Pillow made a demonstration before the other end of Valencia's camp. This movement, interpreted by Valencia as the main American attack with a tentative and weak force, convinced him that victory was within his grasp. When he received another relayed order from Santa Anna to withdraw, he scornfully refused. As darkness fell, he sent a message to Santa Anna that all he needed to do was mop up the remnants of the Yankees in the morning. His victory was assured. Santa

Anna, angry and incredulous at Valencia's arrogance, cautiously withdrew his own forces to the safety of San Angel.

In the meantime, Captain Robert E. Lee with only lightning flashes to illuminate his perilous journey, walked back through the treacherous lava field in a driving rain. He must get word to General Scott of the perilous position of the exposed small American force, as well as the possibility of a resounding victory if they were quickly reinforced so that they might attack the unsuspecting Valencia at his most vulnerable point.

Picking his way carefully among the dark boulders, talking care with each step over the slick uneven black rock, knowing that a one slip could tumble him into a chasm, that a careless move could crack his ankle in a chuck hole, or snap his leg in a fissure, Lee arrived miraculously back in the American camp. It was 11:00 PM on the night of August 19th. He advised General Scott of the disposition of the American forces who were isolated and would be vulnerable to Valencia's attack in the morning. Given a brigade quickly, however, he could turn the tables on the cocky Mexican general.

Scott ordered reinforcements to follow Captain Lee back across the Pedrigal using the route he had discovered. By 1:00 AM he had guided the Americans back across the dark and treacherous lava field in a driving rain, each man holding on to the one in front of him so as not to get lost. By 5:00 AM they had scaled the "impassible" ravine behind Valencia's camp and, following a single musket volley, charged the camp with fixed bayonets.

Within seventeen minutes Valencia's army broke ranks and ran. General José Mariano Salas bravely tried to rally the cavalry. However, the horses and men, surprised and confused now by an attack from the American gunners in front, broke and ran, trampling their own retreating infantry in the process. In less than a half hour, General Valencia's army had ceased to exist as a viable force. It's remnants scattered, most of them headed for the safety of the Convento de Churubusco, a Franciscan monastery.

All that remained of an organized Mexican Army now were the defense forces of Santa Anna. These consisted of the combined Mexican National Guard, the San Patricios, and a few veteran units from the Puebla retreat. These Santa Anna ordered to defend the bridgehead of the River Churubusco and the fortified Convento beyond.

Kevin hadn't slept well despite the fact that he had found a mostly dry spot in the interior of the old monastery. Undeterred by the damp and cold, a brigade of mosquitos buzzed in and out of his ears throughout a good portion of the evening. He had slapped himself silly, and by dawn his ears were ringing so he could not be sure whether it was artillery he heard or the remnants of the latest August storm. He got up and, keeping his blanket around him for warmth, went out on the balcony to relieve Sergeant Murphy.

Doves were cooing in the arches of the century-old monastery and the Angelus bell was ringing in the church next door. The bougainvillea dripped with moisture and the air smelled fresh and clean. The sergeant was leaning over the balcony rail looking at the wooden firing platforms which had been erected a few days before.

"Morning, Sarge!" Kevin called, still shivering despite the blanket.

Murphy gave one last glance at the scaffolding and at the landscape beyond, then he turned slowly toward Kevin. Still as skinny as he was when he joined, Murphy thought, but he's proved himself a man. There was a weary confidence to Kevin now which had not been there before. The eyes that gleamed palely in his thin face were confident and sharp despite his being freshly awakened. Only the dark circles under them bespoke the strain of the days and the night of waiting.

"Something's happening out there," Murphy said, pointing out past the cornfields to where the Rio Churubusco murmured through the farmland of Coyoacán. Kevin looked in the direction Murphy pointed. The land was green and fertile, marked out in checkerboard squares each twice the size of the New England farms Kevin had known, and five times the size of the ones farmed by his kin in Ireland.

It seemed rich land to Kevin, broad expanses of maize waving green and gold-tassled in the morning sun. Each parcel marked off by a dirt path or by maguey plants and cacti planted as borders. And all of the land as far as he could see was irrigated by a complex series of muddy ditches and dikes which carried the lifegiving water and rich silt of the Rio Churubusco to each of the farms.

He looked out over the red roofs of white-washed adobe houses. Several had vegetable gardens planted behind them. Some of the better ones were surrounded by walls covered with bougainvillea vines with their red and violet blossoms blooming feverishly from the August rains and sun.

"Looks pretty peaceful to me," Kevin said.

Murphy rolled a cigarette from leaf tobacco and corn silk. He carelessly twisted one end and lit it from his tinder box. He shook his head and took a deep drag on the harsh smoke before he spoke again.

"See those puffs of smoke over there. The small ones rising in the air?"

Kevin looked but could barely make them out in the haze of the morning air. Although there was no wind, the air was thick and brown towards the south.

"That's musket fire, if I don't miss my guess. And that's dust from men or horses that obscures the smoke. I think that's an army beneath it, theirs in advance or ours in retreat. I ain't sure which. Not that it makes much difference. It will all come to the same thing. A fight that's on its way here soon enough."

And now Kevin saw it. A cloud of dust to the southwest, beyond the rain-swollen river where the land rose to the San Angel heights and then dipped to another valley of not-so-rich farmland bordered by ancient lava fields. Kevin could see the brown cloud topped by scattered puffs of white.

"See it now?" Murphy asked.

"Yeah," Kevin said and he felt his stomach tighten with anticipation. He shivered despite the fact that the sun was now well over the horizon and the air was becoming humid and close even up here on the parapet.

"I'll have one of the señoritas bring you up some grub, bucko. You'll have plenty of time for breakfast. It'll be some time before the action starts. Hell, the generals haven't even got here yet so there's no hurry. But you'd better eat your fill, my good lad, because they'll be the devil's ration of lead and powder before we have a chance to eat again."

Murphy kept his word, and within a half hour an Indian girl, whom Kevin knew to be his own age but already married to a Mexican gunner, came by with a half dozen *tortillas*, black refried beans, fresh tomatoes and *aguacate*. Kevin thanked her and then leaned back against the parapet. He made the Sign of the Cross, gave thanks, and then began to eat slowly and with relish.

He had taught himself in the last few months to eat this way, tasting each separate flavor, savoring each bite. A Mexican cannoneer named Humberto, observing Kevin bolt his food on one occasion, had given him advice which Kevin remembered and applied.

"We Mexicans have a word, *aprovechar*, which means to 'take advantage'. You must not miss an opportunity. And so with eating you must not miss the opportunity to savor the smells, to taste each flavor, to chew so as to recover all the nutrients of the earth, the sun, the water, the corn, the frijol. When we say *Buen provecho, irlandés*, it is not just a wish that you have a good appetite. All of us in Mexico have good appetites, *verdad*?

He laughed at the double meaning and Kevin joined him.

"Unless you are too old," Kevin said.

"And even then," Humberto replied. "My grandfather liked brown sugar even in his nineties."

Kevin laughed again. He smiled now recalling it. Every meal should be a small *fiesta*, Humberto had told him. Every *chile*, every *frijol*, a laugh in the teeth of fate.

He ate more slowly and with true enjoyment the simple food of the village of Coyoacán. When he finished he wiped the unglazed piece of pottery with a scrap of corn *tortilla* and chewed it slowly relishing the warm flavor of the corn and tomatoes grown just two miles to the south. The sun drew the dampness from his clothes and the food restored him from his former weariness to a state of calm alertness. He felt ready for whatever the day would bring. He wondered briefly where his dog had gone off to. She had left sometime in the night, while he was slapping wildly at the mosquitos, in search of a safer place.

Now he heard a cheer followed by a clatter of hoofbeats below. He walked over the front of the monastery and looked down over the newly-erected earthworks in front of the church. He saw a troop of horse led by a Mexican general who rode proud in the saddle. Behind them, marching across the damp land which bordered the cornfields, came a regiment of cavalry, some artillery and a large infantry unit which was mostly out of view behind the six foot corn stalks. The general moved with grace and conserved energy. There was no hurry, no wasted movement. He moved casually among the defenders at the breastworks, checking the cannon, ordering additional artillery put into place.

Just then Kevin's dog, that had been begging successfully among the cooks below, joined him on the balcony of the Convento.

"Hello, Molly!" he smiled, noticing the easy, self-satisfied swing of her butt as she approached him. In the past few weeks her eyes had brightened, her once shabby coat had developed a healthy gloss, and her ribs were fleshed in. One would not call her fat, or even chubby, few creatures in the Mexican Army were—including the generals. But she was healthy-looking and sleek. She had also gained a measure of independence and, after giving Kevin a perfunctory lick on his outstretched hand, she walked over to the side of the monastery to look at the entrenchments below.

"Well, Molly," said Major Riley as he stepped out on the balcony. "Think we've picked a good spot for our last stand?"

The dog barked and jumped up, putting her forepaws on the commander's chest. Kevin jumped up, too, and saluted the red-headed major who had led them safely through so many battles.

"At ease, soldier!" he smiled returning the salute. "Off with you, Molly! Go check on the cannons." The dog obediently dropped down and trotted off in the direction of the guns.

"Did they give you something to eat, son."

"Yessir. *Tortillas*, some beans and tomatoes."

"No meat, hey? Wonder why the hell they didn't butcher those cows? The general staff knew there was a fight coming this way."

"Because it's Friday, sir?

"Ah, sure it is! Wasn't I just writing in my journal this morning. Friday, August 20, 1847. I have a feeling this will be a day recorded in the annals of history. And no meat is appropriate, is it not? A Catholic army on the day of an attack by the Saxon heretics needs no red meat. We've got the warm unleavened bread of the Host inside us."

Riley made the Sign of the Cross and then gave Kevin a smile. He came next to him and stood looking out over the parapet.

"Well, what do you think of the layout, bucko?" Riley asked. "I know your dog approves. Or are you just admiring the view?"

"Actually both, sir," said Kevin, his confidence grown through many battles and also from the rapport the San Patricio officers and men had developed. The officers, especially Riley, who had been promoted on the battlefield three times, fought with a ferocity and an indifference to danger which made them seem common soldiers with uncommon valor.

The accoutrements and honors of rank were acknowledged, but the mutual respect among fighting men in a common cause made the relationship much different from that of the American or even the Mexican Army.

Kevin had been looking to the south, fascinated by the Rio Churubusco, full to its banks with August rains, glinting in the morning sun as it ran with its series of canals flowing east from the mountains of the southwest between mounded banks of maguey and a thousand fields of corn and sugarcane like chess squares of green felt. From there it descended eastward and emptied into the flower-strewn lake of Xochimilco, an Aztec wonder that Kevin had not yet had the opportunity to visit but whose northern banks he had seen from atop the parapet.

Below and to the right, where the highroad to Acapulco crossed the stream, was a bridge. The far end of it had been reinforced with earthwork embankments which rose fifteen feet from the bottom of a wet ditch to the top of a parapet. It was across this deep ditch, up to the parapet, in the face of a half dozen Mexican cannon backed by infantry that the Americans would have to pass before they reached the fortified monastery.

The Convento where he and Major Riley stood was about a quarter of a mile north of the fortified bridgehead, or *tête-de-pont*, as it was called by the generals. Beside the monastery (*convento* in Spanish) was the hundred year old Church of San Mateo where he had attended Mass the night before and received Holy Communion. It, like the Convento, was surrounded by massive adobe walls four feet thick and twelve feet high. It seemed unassailable. But, just in case, Santa Anna had ordered General Rincón to build earthworks outside the walls with emplacements for seven guns. Further, behind the walls of the church and the monastery, scaffolding had been erected with firing platforms for the infantry muskets.

"God Himself couldn't have chosen a better place for us to defend," Kevin said softly.

"Aye, you're right, bucko. It is good ground. And it was God Himself, in one of his many incarnations, after Whom the place was named. Churubusco. It's a Spanish bastardarization of Huitzilipochco, the place of the war god, Huitzilopochtli. A word that was apparently as hard on the Spanish tongue as it is on the Celtic."

Kevin smiled in appreciation of Riley's wit and erudition. One couldn't help but admire the man. The quality of officers among the Mexicans, he observed, had improved, too. Whether due to attrition, or simply the fact that those who were in charge of the final defenses of Mexico City were the best, he did not know.

"Who's that general down below, sir?" Kevin asked.

The major looked in the direction Kevin pointed. It was the soft-spoken officer whom Kevin had noticed earlier moving surely and easily among the men. There was no hint in him of the Spanish grandee; he looked mestizo, muscular, darkened by the sun and days in the saddle. Yet, he moved with the quiet grace of one born to be a leader.

"That's General Manuel Rincón," Riley answered. "He's a cool one. Don't seem to know the meaning of the word fear. He also has an engineer's eye. He'll have the Convento, and General Pedro Anaya will be commander of the entire works. Anaya's another one with brass balls. He won't give the Yankees an inch of real estate as long as there's a shell left to fire."

Kevin looked out over the firing platform and then towards the church. The two positions supported each other and could in turn give protective fire to the *tête-de-pont*, or receive support from that quarter should it be necessary. The only way the Americans could possibly overrun the position would be...

"There's only one way we could lose," Riley interrupted his reverie.

"Not enough men left to defend, or..."

"We run out of ammunition," Kevin finished his thought.

"Or we run out of ammunition," Riley agreed sadly. "Our stores are low, as you well know. So Rincón has given the order. We don't fire until they're 20 meters distant. We don't spend a single ball without a specific target. We make every one count. Pass that on."

"Yessir!" Kevin replied with a salute as the major turned and walked off. But he couldn't help a wry smile. Riley was an artilleryman and his comment about not spending a single shot without a target showed how out of touch he was with the infantry role in the war. With only seven functioning cannon defending the Convento, most of the San Patricios would be infantrymen today. Kevin among them. He had brought his own musket when he deserted the U.S. Army. Manufactured at the Harper's Ferry Armory, it was a large English-designed flintlock weighing twelve pounds. This "Brown Bess," as it was popularly known, fired a ball $^3/_4$ of an inch in diameter. It's smooth bore was of .75 caliber and it had a powerful kick. His shoulder had a perpetual bruise from it but he had become so inured to the pain that he no longer winced when he fired. Not that it made much of a difference. The effective range of the musket was less than sixty yards.

There would be no question of obeying Riley's orders about holding their fire until the enemy was well within range. The San Patricios were well-disciplined and intended to make the Yankee attack costly. However, as far as choosing specific targets for their shots, well—that order would be more honored in the breach. The Irishmen, knowing the wild inaccuracy of these weapons, would deliver a concentrated barrage against the enemy, one every twenty seconds, the time it took to load and recharge the muskets. If the Yankees were pigheaded enough to keep coming, the Irishmen would exact a terrible toll despite the limitations of their muskets.

By 10 o'clock the cannon were loaded and ready. The San Patricios manned three and were commanded by Major Riley. General Rincón and his troops manned the remaining four, as well as providing the infantry backup. Junior officers hurried back and forth from the scaffolding to the parapets, from the monastery to the church, from the earthworks to the wooden gates of the compound, giving orders, checking the guns, ordering the limited store of ammunition distributed among the various companies.

To the south Kevin could hear the spluttering of musketry more clearly now, along with the shouts of the wounded, the high-pitched whinnying of horses, and the reports of cannon like distant thunder growing closer and more ominous.

McDowell joined Kevin on the ramparts. His face was strained with anticipation. The old scar from the Palo Alto attack gleamed wetly on his face, pulsing with excitement.

Kevin, too, was anxious for the battle to begin; his eyes had a fierce glow that belied his thin good looks and made him seem what he was, a dangerous young man ready to kill with all the ugliness and brutality that he had trained for.

"Beejesus, if we don't win this one, we'll never have another chance, Kev. And we can beat 'em this time; I know it."

"Yep," Kevin said not wanting to disagree at this juncture despite the fact that he had privately accepted the fact of his death. "We'll make them wish they never left Massachusetts, by God!"

Lieutenant Romero came up behind them. He was the officer who would supervise the musket fire from the platforms.

"*Cállense, soldados!* Never mind all that chatter. Put your attention on your arms. Make sure they are loaded and ready."

"Pompous ass," McDowell whispered as he walked away.

"Sure, he's right, though." Kevin said. "Might as well get loaded and primed."

"How about yourself then?" McDowell drawled.

"I'm ready," Kevin said, bring his weapon to a smart port arms. "I've been on duty since dawn."

McDowell stood up and took out a cartridge from his ammunition pouch. The cartridge consisted of a pre-measured charge of powder wrapped in paper along with a 3/4 inch ball. McDowell stood his musket up, barrel facing the sky. He then ripped open the paper cartridge with his teeth. He poured the powder down the barrel with a steady, practiced hand, dropped in the ball, using the cartridge paper as a wad, and then seated the ball with a ramrod. It took him less than fifteen seconds. He then poured a pinch of gunpowder from his powder horn into the pan—this was the primer. Five seconds. Ready! It needed only the drop of the hammer to release the spark from the flint.

Kevin smiled in admiration at McDowell's dexterity. McDowell liked to complain as much as any soldier that Kevin knew, but he was a fighter and one of the best. His hatred for the Yanks for ruining his face back at Palo Alto was legendary among the Mexicans as well as the San Patricios. The scar distorted his visage and made his attempt to smile back at Kevin frightening.

"Jesus, McDowell." Kevin said, shaking his head. "I'm glad you're on our side."

10:30 AM—For now there was nothing to do but wait. The men inside the monastery were sweating from the heat, anxious to begin. They were restless, too, anxious to say or do anything to settle their nerves. But talking had ceased after firm orders were passed down from General Rincón. Here were no bands to play, no bugles or drums, no loud *Vivas*! "Maintain yourselves in a state of alert readiness. *Silencio.*" The idea, Kevin guessed, was to get the Yankees to underestimate the unit's strength.

The Mexican tricolor flew boldly over the Church of San Mateo, also called the Church of María de los Angeles by some of the local soldiers. On the ramparts beneath the Mexican standard flew one of the San Patricios' banners. Embroidered by the nuns of San Luís Potosí, this battalion flag was of dark green silk. On it glittered a silver cross and a golden harp. Along the border were appliquéd silver shamrocks.

Atop the monastery walls flew another Mexican flag of green, white and red with a golden eagle rampant holding a serpent in its outstretched talons. Beneath it flew the banners of the Independencia and Bravo Battalions of the Mexican National Guard. Between these latter standards flew the pride of the nuns from the Convento de Carmen. Especially designed by Major John Riley and meticulously sewed by the good sisters, this was a triumph of combined religious and martial artistry. It's dimensions were six feet by eight feet, and it was made of fine green silk and bordered with gold tassels. On one side was an appliquéd gold harp surmounted by the Mexican coat of arms with a scroll painted "Libertad por la República Mexicana." Underneath the harp was the motto: "Erin go Bragh." On the other side of the banner was a painting of St. Patrick holding in his left hand a key and in the other a staff resting on a serpent. Underneath this were the words: "San Patricio."

A National Guard captain had given the order to have this banner removed from the monastery as it was larger than the Mexican flag and thus not appropriate. However, General Rincón countermanded the order. "The Irish standard bears the Mexican *escudo*. Besides," he added with a smile, "both St. Patrick and ourselves are crushing the same serpent."

10:45 AM—There were now approximately 1,700 defenders behind the fortifications of the monastery and church. General Scott was advancing toward them with approximately slightly over 10,000 troops. Valencia's army was effectively destroyed. Santa Anna was leading his 7,000 men back toward Mexico City, presumably to set up a defense of the capital. But Kevin and the rest of the men at the Convento were not aware of these figures. They only knew they were outnumbered and needed to make every shot count.

11:00 AM—General Bravo with two companies of troops from Valencia's defeated army reached the reinforced bridgehead. They were a ragtag group, dispirited and confused, without order or discipline. Several scattered as soon as they reached the river; others collapsed from injuries or exhaustion.

"Jesus, Kev! Look at that lot!" McDowell called from his post in a loud whisper. Kevin glanced to where McDowell was pointing, toward the *tête-de-pont* at the river. The Mexican column at the bridge was a confused mass of muleteers, camp followers, servants, wagons, artillery, infantry and cows and mules. They were bunched together, slamming into the earthworks, crawling over each other as they churned the muddy approach to the causeway into a swamp. Several soldiers were trampled by retreating cavalry. One cannon was hopelessly bogged down in the mud and abandoned by its crew.

"Jesus, Mary and Joseph!" muttered Kevin. "Are these our reinforcements? We're better off dying on our own without that lot. All they'd be after would be grabbing the last of the food and water. Don't look like there's any fight left in that sorry bunch." Meanwhile, however, Santa Anna moved two regiments up to the northern bank of the river to protect the retreating troops and salvage what he could of their train, especially the ammunition. In addition, he ordered fresh troops to reinforce General Pérez's brigade at the *tête-de-pont*. Santa Anna and the rest of his army then withdrew to guard the approaches to Mexico City. He sent word to Rincón to hold the Convento as long as was humanly possible. Rincón, unlike Valencia, knew how to follow orders. For once, Santa Anna's faith in a commander was well placed.

Thus, the situation was not as desperate as it appeared to be. Neither Kevin and his compatriots nor the Mexicans knew that. They all assumed that they were hopelessly outnumbered and that death was imminent. Having been through many battles together they had no feelings of despair or even regret. They were silently determined to make it as costly for the Yankees as possible.

But if the defenders were mistaken in their estimate, so were the Americans. They had assumed that Santa Anna had fled to the capital leaving only a token force in an old monastery to delay the inexorable advance of the blue tide. The American attack, now imminent, would be precipitate and unplanned.

"Man the ramparts!" Captain Moreno ordered.

"Man the ramparts!" Sgt. Murphy echoed, as the men ran to cover their positions on the walls, the scaffolding and the firing platforms.

"Muskets primed and cocked!" ordered the sergeant.

"Man the cannon!" General Rincón said in a clear voice, and his junior officers shouted it down the line as the men of Bravo and Independencia Companies along with the three gun crews of the San Patricios jumped to their positions. All of the orders were oral, no bugles sounded in order to prolong the ruse of a token force.

11:45 AM—"We are the last defensive line before the capital," General Rincón addressed the men in a clear voice which carried up over the ramparts. He was seated on his horse, a gray stallion which pranced each time the general punctuated his remarks with a spur. The hoofbeats clattered in the walkway where once monks read their breviaries.

"General Santa Anna has two regiments to the east of us. General Pérez has another brigade at the bridgehead. The Americans are coming on, thinking there are only a handful of us fighting to defend which appears to be a ruin of an old *convento*. They shall be surprised, and not, I trust, pleasantly." He permitted himself a small, tight smile which his adjutant perfectly mirrored.

"We fight to defend our homeland. We fight on this holy and consecrated grounds to defend the Church they would desecrate. We fight that future generations may know the price of our honor and our birthright. It is blood. Some among you are Irish who have joined our cause. Today we are all one people, one army. I can think of no greater tribute than to say to you as to all of my men, Soldiers of Mexico, do your duty! *Viva México!*"

"*Viva México!*" the men responded. But the cheer was subdued. This was not Angostura with tens of thousands of troops, of regimental bands, priests in vestments, and colorful lancers in Napoleonic dress. This was a last ditch stand behind the walls of an old monastery at a dusty crossroads, miles from glory.

There would be no medals cast for the heroes of Churubusco. No bands would play for them. No one would write of their exploits in the dispatches. Their history would be written in blood, their own and that of the invaders. It would soak into the dry dust of the roads, the black soil of the cornfields, the baked adobe of the walls. And when it was over, and the last of the dead had been tossed into the *barrancas* without a shovelful of earth to protect them from the crows and buzzards, few would remember what happened here or would care to recall. History is written by the victors. But even the victors would regret August 20, 1847 and, if they could not erase it from their memories, they would insure that the story would go no further than their generation, that nothing would be written in the school books for their children to be reminded.

12:00 Noon—"Get the rhythm, by Jesus!" yelled Sergeant Murphy. "Too-rah-loo-rah-loo —Bite the cartridge.

Too-rah-loo-rah-lay —Powder and ball —Rah-loo-rah-lay —Tamp-rah-loo-rah-lay —Prime, hammer back! Fire!"

The first American assault came from the cornfield opposite the convent, not from the bridge as the defenders had expected. A brigade under the command of General Twiggs avoided the *tête-de-pont* and crossed further down river. He intended to surprise the Mexicans at the monastery and make short work of them before moving on to the capital. It was a mistake born of arrogance and the Americans answered for it. The first Mexican volley mowed down three dozen, while the Irish accounted for another twenty.

"Too-rah-loo-rah-loo—Hey!
Too-rah-loo-rah-loo—Hey!
Rah-loo-rah-loo—Hup!
Prime, hammer back! Fire!"

The Americans came out of the fields of head-high corn bewildered, staggering haphazardly into the withering fire of the Mexican and Irish muskets. Expecting a quick victory, some dragging scaling ladders that were tangled up in the corn plants, they fell with expressions of surprise, anger and confusion. *This shouldn't be happening!* their faces seemed to say. *The Mexicans were beaten! What is going on?* For many of them, these thoughts were their last.

For Kevin it was an experience unlike any other. He had delivered musket volleys before, but never more than two or three and then the enemy was upon him and he was forced to retreat or defend himself desperately with a bayonet. But now he kept ripping cartridges and stuffing power and shot with his bent and clanking ramrod, priming, then firing, so many times that he had lost count and the barrel was red hot. He did not aim, he simply fired in the general direction of the blue forms coming through the smoke, stumbling over the bodies of those already dead and dying. He watched the enemy troops sweep forward and back as through they were a field of grain, blown forward by the wind and then cut down by the scythe. And he felt the same satisfaction that he did cutting hay on the Cambridge farm so long ago. Despite the terrible heat, the sweat running down his brow and into his eyes, despite the smoke and the flies, the smell of cordite, of burnt flesh and charred cartridge paper, there was a satisfaction which came from clearing the field in front of him, sweeping the obstacles away with a deadly instrument.

When the Americans' last rush failed, their commander wisely ordered a withdrawal to re-assess the situation. Up on the ramparts of the Convento, Indian girls brought gourds of water to Mexican and Irish soldiers and the men eased their muskets down.

"Christ Almighty!" McDowell yelled. "Hot damn! We gave em a lickin', didn't we? What are ya doing there, Kev! Goddam! Come on down here, bucko! Get down, I say!"

Kevin smiled looking down at the black face of his comrade, boyishly ludicrous with smudged gunpowder. Kevin was unaware that he was still standing on the platform fully exposed to enemy fire. His legs trembled from the adrenalin rush of the fight, and his breath came in short bursts like the locomotive panting of a woman about to give birth.

He had not thought it possible that this small group of men could force the Yankees to retreat. He had no hope of success. He had just kept firing, firing, determined to kill as many as he could before he finally dropped. But now the unexpected had happened. The Yankee line had broken!

1:00 PM—But no battle is simply one battle. It's several. Besides that of the musketry on the ballustrades, there was also the battle of the Mexican and San Patricio gunners who delivered such a deadly and accurate barrage that the American artillery had to pull back, leaving behind twenty-four dead gunners and fourteen horses.

Meanwhile the American 6th Infantry, Scott's crack troop which led the attack against the *tête-de-pont*, were forced to retire butt end first. It regrouped a second time, and a second time it was repulsed. Kevin could not see this. He could comprehend little of the battle except the action on the ramparts and in the cornfield in front of him. But now, looking back toward the south, he could see the flashes of orange-colored flame from the cannons at the bridge-head. He could hear the screams of soldiers and the neighing of horses beneath the steady earthshaking reports of the big guns. Finally, his trembling legs could support him no longer and he dropped down beside his friend.

"You know, Kev," McDowell said with a mixture of sadness and wonder, "you notice some funny things during the volleys. Sometimes you wish you didn't, but you do. This last volley, you know? Just before the Yanks pulled back? Well, there was these two fellows, about the same age as you and me. Probably comrades, you know? Anyway, our volley caught one of them with four shots—as if they was aimed—two in the face, one in the neck and one in the chest. Jesus! I saw him clear as I see you now. There was a puff of wind and then for a few seconds no smoke where he was standing. And then he fell. And, you know, his friend—well, he wasn't hit at all. He just turned slowly, looked once at his comrade, and then tore off back through the corn. Now you'd think by all that's right, at least one of those musket balls was meant for him. But fate is a funny thing, ain't it?"

Kevin put his hand on his leg to stop it from shaking but his leg was trembling, too. He felt the bile rising up in his throat, gagging him. But before anything could happen the sergeant appeared at his post.

"Anybody been hit? You hit, Dillon? No? Well, come on then, boy. Look lively! Come on, up and at em. Them Yanks ain't all dead yet. Some of em is just playing. And I hear General Scott got another ten thousand just over the hill when we get done with these. Get them muskets loaded and primed. Together, now!"

Kevin and the others scrambled to their positions and carefully picked up the rifles, avoiding the red hot barrels. They checked their pouches. There were no ammunition cases for them to refill them with, so they merely counted the remaining cartridges.

"Together now!" roared the sergeant. "Too rah loo rah loo, Hup."

When they were loaded and primed, the sergeant ordered them to simply cover the field and not fire until further orders.

But now the Americans had changed their tactics. Another division had crossed the river via the Coyoacán-Mixcoac Road and then swung northeast to cut off Santa Anna's troops which they assumed were withdrawing to the capital. Santa Anna countered by rushing 2,000 men to answer their threat. He then raised the stakes by sending a troop of cavalry to threaten the American left. The Mexicans took cover in a series of ditches and opened a devastating fire which the Americans under General Shields could not handle. They broke and sought shelter among some buildings. Kevin watched as the mortars blossomed among the buildings until one of the structures glowed a cherry red. He watched but did not cheer as some others did, when the Mexicans picked off the Yankee soldiers, as one by one each traded suffocation in a smoking inferno for the clean death of a musket ball or bayonet.

1:30 PM—In any other war, the battle would have been over. The four-pronged American attack (three prongs of which each constituted a mini-battle) had all been repulsed. However, the Battle of Churubusco had yet to run its course. The American Army was a thousand miles from its nearest supply line. There was no turning back. It had to fight on to the capital or die. The Americans may have met an immovable object at the Convento but they had no option but to re-group, recover their second wind, and try again. Taylor had snatched victory out of the jaws of defeat at Buena Vista, perhaps Scott could do the same at Churubusco. At any rate, there was no choice; he had no place to retreat to. At his front and to the sides were the enemy, behind him lay alien territory, where a retreating Yankee could hardly depend on sustenance or aid.

2:00 PM—Gradually, an enveloping move by General Shields managed to outflank the Mexican left, and he was able to move his men up the road. About the same time, reinforcements from the 5th and 8th Infantry arrived from Coyoacán and forced the twenty-foot wide ditch, scaled the parapet and took the *tête-de-pont* in hand-to-hand fighting. Sheer force of numbers prevailed and they overwhelmed the Mexican defenders capturing 192 prisoners, three pieces or artillery and ammunition. They took up one of the four-pounders immediately and turned it on the monastery.

Meanwhile Captain Duncan moved two more cannon up to the highway where they could bombard the Convento from the northern end in safety. For fifteen minutes the Americans pounded the convent with shot and shell.

Another infantry assault was attempted but repulsed, just barely. The Mexican/Irish fusillade was at half force.

"*Qué diablos pasó?*" Sgt. Murphy asked referring to the half-hearted response. "What the hell happened?"

"No ammunition, sir," replied McDowell. "Half of us were out of ammo at the last order. Some of us who were out of flints lent our last cartridges to those who needed them. But that's about it for the muskets, Sarge, unless we get some supplies."

"Jesus, what next?"

Just then there was an explosion in the southwest corner where General Anaya was supervising the cannon. The general along with Santiago O'Leary, a tough veteran of Angostura and two other San Patricos, was thrown violently back against the wall. A store of gunpowder had been hit by an enemy round and exploded. The general, badly burned, was quickly dragged back inside the monastery proper.

Kevin had two cartridges left but only a small piece of flint. He decided to wait until the enemy were actually approaching the parapet and then fire directly into the chest of the closest man. Looking down he could see an American officer shouting orders from a large short-tailed bay. He seemed remarkably poised to Kevin, drawing his reins while his horse made sharp, dance-like movements. Behind him a sergeant major relayed his orders as the drivers of the leaders and wheelers flourished their whips, bringing the cannons to new positions.

The guns were impressive, their gaping mouths rising slowly now as the gunners adjusted the trajectory, and the limbers arrived with more shell. Kevin knew that he was looking at his death and yet there was a beauty in the precision of the horses, the solid bulk of the guns, and the ballet-like movements of the gunners who served them.

Reluctantly, he tore himself from this aesthetic musing and set his bayonet. He had only two cartridges left and he wanted to make them count. He had guessed their plan. They would bombard once more and then would come an infantry attack, and among the foot soldiers the boldest and strongest would be in the forefront with scaling ladders and fixed bayonets.

"*Rápido! Muévanse!*" General Rincón had given the order for one of the Mexican cannon to be moved to the northern side of the Convento which was undefended and taking the brunt of the American bombardment. Kevin followed the gunners and watched the approaches as they set up the cannon.

There was a deep-throated growl, and then to Kevin's left a blur of brown-black fur as Kevin's dog, Molly, attacked the first of the Americans coming up a scaling ladder to Kevin's blind side. Kevin wheeled and shot the man cleanly through the chest at a distance of ten feet. He quickly grabbed another cartridge, tore it, primed, and loaded again. He fired at a group of men recovering the ladder below. Quickly, he reloaded his last cartridge. By now the Mexican cannon was in place but its trajectory was too high to inflict any damage on the approaching infantry below. Moreover, the defenses on the southern side had been weakened by the removal of this cannon.

"Molly! *Otro lado!*" And Molly flew across the other side just it time to be clubbed by an American captain scaling the wall. Kevin wheeled and fired but the charge did not ignite. Simply a flash in the pan. The captain clubbed one of the gunners next and Kevin charged him with his bayonet. An enlisted man reached the parapet right behind him and turned to the captain's aid. He smoothly countered Kevin's bayonet charge and then lunged his own knife toward Kevin's exposed belly. The blade caught on the loose folds of Kevin's coat, and Kevin twisted once, pivoted, and brought the butt end of his musket hard against the soldier's jaw. He heard the satisfying crack of bone, and then Riley's order.

"Withdraw! Back inside the *Convento. Retírense. Rápido! Rápido!*"

A Mexican bugler also sounded the notes of the *retirada* and the men abandoned their exposed positions on the parapet. The soldiers already inside the Convento fired a volley above their heads to give them covering fire. To his right Kevin could see the gun crew on the north side abandon their useless cannon and head back to the safety of the monastery. Pieces of masonry and rock were whizzing in the air where the American guns had shattered sections of the wall. Bits of metal from American canister ripped through two of the gun crew, the shrapnel throwing chunks of bloody flesh into the smoky air. Kevin stopped for a second to see to Molly. She was unconscious and a trickle of blood like a red thread came from her mouth. He pulled her into the shade of one of the cannons and then dodging a Yankee ball, ran back, tears blinding him, for the safety of the monastery, choking on the thick air, gasping for breath, feeling his back naked, vulnerable to the chunks of metal and stone raining upon the parapet.

General Rincón had sent messages twice to Santa Anna requesting more ammunition. He could not hold the convento without it a moment longer. The second messenger finally got through and one small wagon arrived with few cases. Saved! But a quick examination of the contents revealed that it was captured ammunition, and not the proper caliber for the Mexican muskets.

"Useless!" Rincón unleashed a volley of curses. "*Malditos cartuchos. Diecinueve adarmes.*"

Riley checked the cartridge boxes. "Nineteen *adarmes*. That's the same as .75 caliber, my general. My men will be able to use them in their muskets."

"Well then take the malditos *cartuchos*, Mayor."

Riley quickly organized a platoon to pass out the boxes of ammunition to the men still on the parapets. Below, he formed two firing lines in the Convento grounds to cover the retreat back to the monastery. He ordered the remainder of his men to conceal themselves behind the large cypress and ash trees in the garden and work as snipers.

Re-armed, the remaining San Patricios on the parapets fought fiercely, firing in the face of an enemy as close at ten feet away. The forward column then engaged the Americans with bayonets as the reserves loaded and fired behind them. The dead and wounded were now as numerous as those still fighting on the parapets and balconies. The blood stood in deep puddles and men slipped and skidded, sometimes sliding off the balconies to crash on the rocks below.

In the interior courtyard the San Patricios were faced with Americans scaling the garden walls, not in ones and twos, but a dozen, twenty at a time. One of the Mexican guardsman tried to raise a white flag. Captain Patrick Dalton, a San Patricio who had taken command of the interior, tore it down. A second white flag went up on the ramparts. Jack Kelly tore it down. The San Patricios had no intention of surrendering. But to the Mexicans, without ammunition, surrounded by the enemy, resistance was futile. A third time the white flag was raised. This time, Captain Dalton cut it with his sword and shouted:

"The next man who raises a white flag will answer for it with the point of my sword."

2:30 PM—The front gate of the monastery was finally blown open by a powerful cannonade. The ground trembled and the air was sulphurous. Caisson were blown apart, horses killed, and for twenty minutes the monastery grounds erupted as great holes were torn in the lawn. Earth and mortar, jacaranda and eucalyptus exploded in great rips and geysers. Rock doves and Inca doves cascaded down from the rooftops in great numbers stunned by the bombardment. Dead soldiers were scattered throughout the gardens, many without arms or legs, some decapitated.

Still the firing went on. The earth was plowed with cannon shells, the bodies of the already dead pulverized by fortuitous shells. And now the infantry in an unrelenting assault, trampled down the remaining plants and flowers, firing indiscriminately, bayoneting the wounded, charging over the discarded knapsacks, cloth-covered tin canteens, haversacks and masterless scabbards. Broken muskets and bent ramrods, exploded limber boxes, swelling bellies of dead horses, abandoned tack, torn blankets and trousers and coats, blood, bone and torn flesh carpeted the monastery grounds.

And now, finally, an American captain tied his own white handkerchief to his sword and waved it at his troops.

"Cease fire, men! Cease fire. It's all over. My God, let's put a stop to this."

Mercifully then, the firing ceased. The remaining San Patricios and Mexicans, with only bayonets and empty muskets were surrounded by hundreds of enemy troops. The battle was over. A cool wind came up from the northwest and clouds scuttled across the sky.

And then not a sound was heard. There were no cheers from the American side. No cries of lamentations from the Mexican or Americans. The wounded, who were strewn across the garden twenty minutes ago, now were churned into a mass of blood and dirt, unrecognizable. The sky darkened with storm clouds and the rain, first in large drops and then in a torrent, came down on the field.

3:00 PM—Through the wet leaves of the walkway, General Twiggs and his aides approached the refectory of the monastery where the wounded General Pedro Anaya lay on a table. Attending him were General Rincón and two Mexican captains. General Rincón helped his wounded fellow-officer to a sitting position as the Americans approached. The officers presented their swords to the victorious Americans.

Twiggs accepted the swords and then passed them to his aides. Then he looked around him as if expecting something more.

"General," Twiggs asked. "Where is your ammunition park?"

Anaya replied, "*Si hubiera parque, ustedes no estarían aquí.*"

An aide translated. "He says, General, that if he still had ammunition, you wouldn't be here."

Outside the wind picked up. The roof rattled and the windows shook and lightning flashed across the ski, thunder boomed, and the rain turned into hail, stones as big as grapes falling and bouncing indifferently among the mutilated corpses in the garden.

CHAPTER 28

Judgment at San Angel

Twenty-four hours later Kevin regained consciousness. He had fought on even after shrapnel had pierced a lung, but a blow to the temple from a musket stock had finally taken him out of the war. Minutes later the Convento was taken and Kevin, along with 2500 of Santa Anna's soldiers—including more than seventy San Patricios—were rounded up and captured.

Sergeant Murphy was holding a foul-smelling damp cloth to Kevin's head. Kevin pushed the hand away with a gesture of disgust. He tried to raise himself up but a blinding pain caused him to lie back down again.

"Easy, lad, easy!" Murphy said. "You had one hell of a knock."

"Where in bloody blazes are we?" Kevin asked looking around. There was the press of many unwashed bodies, a damp dirt floor, the oily smoke of camp fires and, over the beds of the wounded, some canvas stretched on poles to keep out the sun.

"Tis some kind of stockade they've arranged for us. They've stuck about a thousand prisoners here, and another fifteen hundred down the road. More prisoners than they want or can do much with, if they want to get on with this war."

"So, what's happening?" Kevin asked shaking his head to try to restore mental alertness.

"Well, they're treating the Mexicans pretty good. They let their women folk bring food into them, and fortunately the Mexicans share with us. If they didn't we'd soon starve. The Yanks haven't even offered us a chunk of bread.

"This morning Scott and Santa Anna signed an armistice, and they've been releasing Mexican officers upon their parole not to bear arms against the Yanks."

"That's sound pretty good, Sarge," Kevin said hopefully. "So there's a chance for us to get out of here yet?"

"Well, if Santa Anna makes our release a condition of any peace treaty, it could go well for us. My guess is that he might very well do that if the time comes. But right now I don't think he'll sue for peace. The Yanks took a lot of casualties yesterday. That's why they agreed to the armistice so readily. They need a chance to rest up and re-group. But Santa Anna, too, is playing for time. He intends one last battle for the city. The war's not over yet."

"So, what do you think will happen to us, Sarge?"

"Well, Kev, I think they'll let most of the wounded go home." Noting Kevin's look of surprise he quickly amended that. "The wounded Mexicans, I mean, not the Irish. They don't have any way of caring for the Mexicans and can't spend the time worrying about it. They'll return them to their own people figuring that they're out of the fighting anyway.

"The rest of us they'll likely send to prisons in the vicinity. Major Riley said there's quite a few that have been cleaned out either by our men or by theirs. We'll probably end up in one of them, get court-martialed at some point, and then a prison term for the duration of the war. Easy duty. We'll sit out the end of this fiasco. Reflect on what we'll tell our grandchildren about seeing the elephant."

"Is that the worst..."

"No, bucko." Murphy put his hand on Kevin's shoulder and his voice softened. "The worst is that they could line us up in front of a firing squad for desertion and bearing arms in the Mexican ranks. That's surely a possibility."

Kevin raised himself on one elbow feeling the sharp pain recede only to be replaced by a cold premonition. The look he gave the sergeant was one of bleak acceptance.

"I said could, boyo, not would. Now lie easy. Let me get you some water."

Kevin shook his head. "No, no. I'm all right. Tell me, truly. What are the odds?"

"Against us standin' in front of a firing squad? Well, there's been a lot of desertions in this war, nigh onto 10,000, I'm told, from the American side. I don't recollect that any have been taken before a firing squad. Ain't even heard of any being court-martialed. A few were shot out of hand back at Matamoros, a couple more at Monterrey. But them was just before a battle. Most of the rest, those that were caught, just got whipped, put on KP, and returned to duty.

"Now, you figure we got an armistice today. So, they're mulling over what they might do. But if Santa Anna resumes hostilities, the Yanks might just muster us out and send us north. They won't want to be wasting time with court-martials."

"And they might just shoot us where we stand! Isn't that so, Sergeant?" complained a voice with a Massachusetts accent.

"Who's that?" Kevin asked twisting to see. The pain tore at his ripped lung and left him gasping for breath.

"Easy, lad. Easy. I was just about to say that you won't be too lonely. An old pal of your's from Cambridge is here as well. Name of Hezekiah. It seems you both took a hankering to the same girl once, he's been telling me. Well, he's gone and got himself captured along with the rest of us."

Kevin stared incredulously at the unkempt figure before him. Hezekiah Ackley had never been a pleasant young man either in looks or personality, and two years of camp life and drinking had done nothing to improve him. His heavily pockmarked face was red and puffy. His narrow-set eyes, once merely furtive, had become frightened and desperate. He glanced over his shoulder periodically as he spoke as if afraid someone would stick a knife in his back. His voice, though strained, was defensive and petulant.

"I might of got captured with the rest of youz, but I ain't one of youz. Tell him, Kevin, for God's sake. I'm not Irish; I'm not Catholic. And I never took up arms against my own country."

"Well," observed Murphy sardonically, "although I wouldn't recommend your tailor, it does seem you're wearin' a Mexican uniform. Or is that for a costume ball?"

Although tight at the shoulders and short in the arms, the Turkey-blue coat with crimson collar, cuffs and piping which Ackley wore, bore the distinctive features of the Mexican uniform. His mud-splattered white canvas pants, which had obviously seen better days, were regulation Santa Anna.

"Yeah, well, I can explain that. See... we wuz at a theater house in Puebla and we had a few drinks, see? And a few laughs, ya know? So, me and a fella came across this Mexican gal, a pretty lil' thing. 'Course she was with her brother or uncle, but that don't amount to spit. So, I says to Hank, that's Henry Longheimer, I says, Hank, how would it be to have some of that?

"Well, the gal give me the eye a couple of times in the theater. You know how these gals are down here. They got them roguish eyes which say what they want clear as speech. So, I got my bottle of *mezcal* out of my coat and we have a few slugs and then follow them out to the street when the play's over."

Murphy, who was in love with and intended to marry a Mexican, had grown angry at the increasing ugliness of Ackley's remarks. Kevin himself felt squeamish but they both listened with poker faces as Ackley continue his tale.

"So, I stop them and, jist as polite as can be, I offer them a drink from my bottle. The brother, well, he jist wheels around and spits at me. At me, dang his brown hide, an American soljer! Well, by God, I ain't having no two bit greaser do that, so I pulls my knife and cut him good. I stab him twice. Hank's just a-standin there. I tell him, Hank, I sez, grab the girl. But he don't; he jist stands there a gawkin.

She won't stop screaming, till I fetched her a sharp rap on the jaw and knocked her plumb out. We pulled her behind a building, and shagged her, you know. At least she was quiet. Well, don't tell this. I shagged her, if ya want to know the truth. Hank, he just kind of stood there, he was too squeamish or else too scared to get it up. Heh, heh."

Murphy sat completely still. There was no change in his expression or his posture. Only Kevin could see the hard line of his jaw from the grinding of his teeth and the whiteness of his knuckles as he clenched his fists.

"On our way back to camp, I'm teasing him, and talking, not looking where I was going, and before you know it this Mexican colonel by the name of Moreno and four of his men surprise us. He says he lost one of his best soldiers in a knifing back in the village and that we're gonna replace him. Well, hell! We're still half-drunk, scared. There's five of them. What would you do? So, he takes us to his bivouac, has us strip and then put on these here Mexican uniforms. Three weeks later he gives us muskets and we're marched to this damn San Mateo Church. Mexicans in front, Mexicans behind. Hell, I never even shot my musket. I surrendered to the first American that stuck his head over the ramparts."

"Christ Almighty!" roared Sergeant Murphy.

"What's the matter? Don't you believe me?" Ackley whined. "It's the God's honest truth; I swear it. You've got to believe me! You've got to tell the brass that I ain't one of yez."

Sergeant Murphy's face had turned a beet red and he was flexing and unflexing his hands. His shoulders had bunched together as if he was getting ready to deliver a blow. Kevin put his hand on his arm to restrain him.

"That's not the problem, Ackley," Kevin said. "The problem is, we do believe you."

"Good, good. So you've got to tell Colonel Harney that I wasn't with you. Okay? 'Cause he's got it in for me anyway for some reason. Just tell him when they come that I wasn't with you fellers. I'm not a San Patricio at all, see? And that's the truth. It's all a mistake. I didn't do nothin wrong. I was all a mistake."

"It's a mistake, all right," Murphy said getting slowly to his feet. "And you'll be making another if you don't get your sorry yellow hide out of my sight. I'll kill you with my bare hands if you're not out of here in five seconds."

"Kevin," Ackley begged, holding out his hands in supplication. "Can't you at least..."

"Two... three..." Murphy counted.

"You'd better do like the sergeant says, Ackley, if you know what's good for you," Kevin said coldly.

Ackley scuttled backward and sideways, crablike, before the sergeant finished his count. He retreated to a corner where an American sentry was posted. His eyes were fearful but ingratiating as he approached the guard. He spoke quickly, gesticulating, nodding in the direction of Murphy and Kevin.

"Obviously explaining how he's not one of us," Murphy observed wryly as he watched Ackley talk to the guard.

Kevin looked over in time to see the guard turn contemptuously away. When Ackley slunk back to the compound, the Mexican soldiers in the vicinity gave him hard glances to show that he was not welcome among them either. Finally, Ackley squatted down next to a blond German boy who seemed dazed and indifferent to his surroundings.

"Christ Kevin! I'm sorry, lad," Murphy apologized. "He said he was a friend of yours from back in New England. That's the only reason I spoke to him at all."

"He was never a friend," Kevin replied. "He got me fired from the only decent job I ever had in America, turned a good man against me, and tried to ravish the girl I loved."

"Well," Murphy said consolingly. "I doubt if he needs to worry about a court-martial. If the Mexicans find out his story he'll be killed right here in the stockade. Him and his German mate."

Sunday, August 23, 1847.

By mid-day all the Mexican officers had been released and the wounded had been returned to their own forces. Some of the prisoners were transferred to other facilities, and fresh water and food was brought to the stockade by the women of the village. The armistice continued, however, and with it the rumor that the American high command was in fact planning a general court-martial of the seventy-two captured San Patricios.

That evening Major Riley called a meeting of the Irish prisoners. His demeanor was reserved and his clear blue eyes gave no inkling of the devastating news he had just received. He had been informed that General Scott would order that the San Patricios be tried under the Articles of War. Under its provisions, the penalty of death would me meted out to those found guilty of desertion during hostilities. Fortunately for Riley, he had deserted prior to the commencement of the actual war along with several others of the seventy-two charged. At least fifty of his men, however, would be facing the ultimate penalty.

Some of the soldiers Riley most admired in his checkered career as a military man were standing at attention waiting for his words. Private McDowell with his thin horseface, deformed by an ugly scar, carried the memory of Palo Alto and the long forced march from Matamoros. Sergeant Murphy, the almost-priest with his fluent Spanish, his Shakespearian quotes, his love of Latin that in another life would have made him a professor, carried the idealism of the battalion. Corporal Casey, loyal and dependable, knew more about the big guns than most U.S. artillery officers. It was his expertise which almost carried the day at Buena Vista and gave the San Patricios their reputation. Captain Patrick Dalton, his second in command, with his dream of settling in Mexico and becoming a gentleman rancher, symbolized the love of the Irish for this land and its people.

There were others who were not here, men he suspected of betrayal, who had been taken away this morning for reasons Riley assumed had to do with the trial. One was Tom O'Connor, a muleteer who joined the San Patricios reluctantly, a slacker and a malcontent, whom Riley had reprimanded several times. Never a true soldier for the Americans or the Mexicans, he was one of those who raised the white flag at the convento, only to have it torn from his grasp by Capt. Dalton.

Another missing from the ranks was Wilson. John Wilson, a British deserter who was promoted to artillery sergeant in the San Patricios. Riley had never trusted Wilson and not just because he was a Englishman. Wilson was aloof and superior; he never tried to fit in. He wanted to be an officer and when he was not commissioned after the defeat at Cerro Gordo, some men told Riley they had heard talk he might defect. Riley had never let him out of his sight. Since his capture, Riley had intercepted two letters from him to the British counsel.

Two others, Ackley and his German buddy, had also been removed from the campground. Probably for their own protection, Riley thought. Still, they could be informers and prosecution witnesses as well. Ackley had been loud in his claims that he was not a San Patricio, so the Irish hated him. And for another reason he was afraid of the Mexicans—guilty of an offense which, if discovered, would cost him his life at their hands.

"Men," Riley called them to attention. "I've been informed that tomorrow, the first of two court-martial proceedings will begin. Those of who go on trial Monday in Tacubaya will include Lieutenant Peel, Sgt. John Murphy, Patrick Casey, James Kelley, Alex McGee and, well, I won't read them all. There are forty-three names on this list. If you want to check your name, the list will be up here after this meeting. The list for the second general court martial includes me, Captain Patrick Dalton, James McDowell, Bill O'Connor, John Bowers, Kevin Dillon and others. There are twenty-nine on this list. Again, I won't read them all. Check the list for your name as well as the time and place so that you'll be mentally prepared.

"The first court martial will be held in the village of Tacubaya beginning tomorrow morning and continuing until all the men on the list have been tried. A second court will be held in San Angel beginning this Thursday. So, again, check the list after this meeting."

Riley rubbed his hands on his pants to dry the sweat. He had finished the easy part, an announcement of the general court martial. Now he had to tell the men he had led for two years that they were facing death and the only possible way to avoid that would be lie about why they made their decisions to fight for Mexican cause. He felt it was his responsibility, however, as an officer. These men were not spies or political revolutionaries. They were soldiers.

"I've brought you all together to discuss the charges, to tell you what you're facing in terms of penalties, and to ask for suggestions for defense strategy."

"As to the first, you'll be charged with desertion and bearing arms in the Mexican ranks.

"As to the second, the charges are punishable by firing squad if the desertion occurred after the official declaration of war, by whipping and imprisonment if not.

"As to your defenses, well, there are a few. Impressment and coercion are both legal defenses. I'll be glad to discuss these defenses with anybody who wants to use them. However, our brilliant guardhouse lawyer, Martin Lyndon of County Galway, has a more convincing defense which I think most of you will prefer after you've heard him explain it. Lieutenant?

Lieutenant Lyndon was a well-built man in his late twenties. He had a lively presence and clear, bold eyes. His life's ambition had been to be a barrister but economic conditions had forced him to emigrate and ultimately join the army. His desertion and joining of the San Patricios had less to do with Catholicism than it did with the prejudice, harsh treatment, contempt for the Irish, and impossibility of promotion which existed in the American army. Lyndon was a realist, not an idealist. But he knew the law and knew that, as soldiers, the San Patricios had certain rights and those he meant to insist upon. He had a photographic memory and, not only had he read the Articles or War and the "Procedures Governing General Courts-Martial", he had also glossed the commentaries on them. He spoke confidently and convincingly.

"I'm going to suggest that we plead the defense of drunkenness at our trials. Drunkenness as an excuse for desertion. Let me tell you why.

"Drunkenness is a proper defense in cases involving desertion because it goes directly to the issue of intent. It is not your burden but that of the Army to prove intent. Drunkenness is always admitted in military trials for desertion because it may result in a lesser included offense. In other words, if a soldier gets drunk and leaves his command, he is merely absent without leave. If the Army wants to convict him of something more they must show intent."

"How about the fact that we were on the other side of the walls at the San Mateo Convent?" asked Murphy.

"Well, let me ask you this? Were you carrying a Mexican *escopeta* or your own musket?"

"My own musket," Murphy replied.

"Then who is to say you fought against the Yanks? You're AWOL in the middle of a hostile country, recovering from a drunk. You've got your own musket, and you're prepared to defend yourself."

"With all due respect, Lieutenant, I hope you don't mind if I play the Devil's Advocate because these are likely questions we'll be asked by the prosecution."

"Not at all, Sergeant," the Lieutenant said comfortably. "Ask away."

"How about wearing the Mexican uniform?"

"Has any man ever got drunk and found himself stripped of his coat and boots?" the lieutenant asked the group.

Several responded in the affirmative.

"There you are, sergeant. And under such circumstances, when one recovers the next day, he steals whatever he can from a likely clothesline. Isn't that so?"

"I heard they got informers who will say which of us fired which cannon," Casey announced. "What do we do then?"

"If the informer is one of us, then his credibility is dubious. His value as a witness is negligible."

"Why don't we just tell the truth?" Kevin asked. "Say we preferred to serve God instead of the Yank. Say that we left the Saxon army as soon as we discovered that their plan was to invade a Catholic country."

"Ah, sure, there's the bold Irish bucko," Major Riley interjected. "And then give 'em the speech of Robert Emmet in the dock. 'Bury me not in Irish soil until my nation is free!'"

"Well, why not? It's the truth, isn't it. Why should we deny what we're fighting for? Why should we play off our role as a bunch of Irish drunks."

"Yeah," added McDowell. "What not just tell the truth?"

"Because," said Lt. Lyndon, "unlike what it says in scriptures, the truth shall not set ye free. The truth hanged Robert Emmet and it will hang each of us just as surely. You cannot stand up in a Yankee court in the middle of a war and make such a statement. They'd hang you for treason."

"Well, the boy's got a point," Sergeant Murphy noted. "They might kill us regardless of what we say. So, why not just tell them that we fought for the cause we believed in. If we're to die anyway, let's give them the truth and not a lie we'll choke on."

"They may indeed kill us regardless of what we say," Lt. Lyndon agreed reluctantly. "Some of us at least. Maybe no defense will get us all acquitted. But the drunkenness defense is our best chance. And even if we lose, we'll be shot like the soldiers that we are, and not hanged like dogs.

"Besides, they think that all us Irish are a bunch of drunks anyway. It falls right in with their prejudices and won't strain their credulity one bit. But you start your high and mighty speech about Catholics defending the Faith and we might find ourselves with 72 scourgings and crucifixions. As it is, they hate us and what we stand for. And don't you doubt for one minute that they know damn well what we stand for. They've seen our flag and they seen how many walked away from their army after they bombed the Cathedral in Monterrey. But the Yanks believe that we should have stuck to their side because they think they're the most evolved race. They're angry and astounded that we could leave their lovely army with its Stars and Stripes to fight besides the Mexican. You'll never convince them that their ideas are wrong, that the invasion was unjust. If you want a chance to live and maybe fight again, convince them that you were drunk, Sergeant, and didn't know any better. Otherwise their self-righteous fury will descend on these lads here with scourgings and brandings and hangings such as haven't been seen since the Middle Ages."

Captain Dalton, a tough leader but also a man with a love for the grog, stood up to give his opinion.

"Ah, sure, what's the big deal? Half the men in the U.S. Army have been drunk for most of the war. Remember Colonel Yell's Arkansas regiment that massacred the Mexican civilians before Buena Vista? 'Hell,' Taylor said. 'Just get these drunks out of my sight!' He just ordered them back across the Río Grande. No court martials, no punishments."

"Sure, ain't that the truth?" Sergeant Murphy added. "And remember the masscre by the Texas Rangers at Rancho Guadalupe? They killed twenty-four Mexican civilians, including women, and Taylor just gave them a reprimand."

"Yeah, but they were Texans and we're Irish," McDowell added doubtfully.

"Plus, they killed Mexicans," Casey observed. "We killed Yanks."

"'Drinking is the soldiers pleasure. Sweet the pleasure, rich the treasure. Sweet is pleasure after pain'," quoted Captain Dalton.

"And that's the point!" continued the lieutenant. "Drinking is always at the root of it. Taylor liked his nip now and again. So, does every officer in the army. They might hate it when a soldier goes off, does something stupid, even dangerous. But they don't hang him for a traitor, that's my point. They don't give him his just deserts. After all, they say, he was drunk."

"And if they all got their just deserts, none would 'scape hanging, to paraphrase the Bard."

"Well said, Sgt. Murphy," the lieutenant smiled. "Aptly put. Drink is the soldier's weakness and every officer who will be sitting on the panel has probably done something he regretted while under the influence of John Barleycorn."

"But if we claim ideological reasons, we make ourselves martyrs for a cause. And for what? We're soldiers not saints.

To speak for our faith means we lose our protection as soldiers and subject ourselves to hanging."

"What's to stop them from hanging us anyway?" McDowell asked.

"Honor," Lieutenant Lyndon replied. "The Americans' hands are already tainted by the invasion. No general would want to add to that the dishonor of hanging seventy or more Irish soldiers, especially since not a single U.S. deserter has been hanged so far, and thousands of them have left the service.

"Any more questions? Well, then I'll leave you to discuss this among yourselves. As Major Riley told you, the court martial lists are up here. Come up and check for your name. If anyone wants to consult with me they are free to do so. Dismissed."

Kevin withdrew from the others and went over to the wooden rail that fenced in the camp. He wanted to think. The absurdity of his situation struck him, as it did not seem to have yet stuck the others. They had deserted an invading army for the noblest of reasons. The had fought for a cause they believed in, under a banner which represented their faith and their ideals. They had shown courage and honor in battle and now they were about to negate it all by declaring that they were simply a bunch of drunks. Jesus, these Irish! Perhaps, the Americans were right in believing them to be unfit for self-government. Kevin shook his head in disgust.

The clouds moved in from the south and the air grew cool. Kevin shivered violently and, leaving off his reverie, approached the camp fire for warmth. Peripherally he heard the men discussing the various defenses they would use at the court martial. This one would say he was captured by the Mexicans. Another that he was drunk. Still, another that he was faced with a choice between the Mexican firing squad and fighting in their uniform. Kevin growled to himself and thought of caustic remarks but said nothing aloud. Gradually he turned inward again. This was not about the others; it was about him.

What am I to do? he thought. What am I alive for, if it is not to stand up for the things I believe in?

And even as he thought this he entered into the dark night of the soul; he surrendered to regrets of a life wasted, the hunger of Ireland, the days on the packed steamer, the fevers in Boston, the short idyllic months of kindness and love in Cambridge, the two years of comraderie and fighting in Mexico. What is the point? he thought. But somewhere in the channels of his mind flowed a true vein of something precious and significant. Something that had penetrated his thoughts when he first saw the green flag unfurled on the battlefield and, with the unleavened bread inside him, gave him the feeling that his strength was as the strength of ten because his heart was pure and because he was fighting for a truth he believed in.

He had suffered a profound disappointment today. The leaders he respected were willing to mask their idealism so that they could live to fight again. He knew that it was the sensible thing to do, perhaps even the soldierly thing to do. But he felt it was not the Irish thing to do. And as a man whose faith had fashioned his soul, he knew it was not a thing that he could do.

He withdrew from the camp fire and in doing so consciously withdrew from the efforts and purposes and ambitions of those who felt it was more important to live, even if living meant a lie. He would not spoil what he and his battalion had done by confirming that lie. Whatever happened he would say the truth.

Sergeant Murphy watched Kevin at the camp fire. He had observed him making gestures to himself, his breath hissing in and out of his clenched teeth, and then the single quick gesture of decisiveness as he withdrew from the fire and sat back against the wooden rail. The fire threw sombre gleams of red and yellow across the packed dirt and Sgt. Murphy watched as Kevin's pale face composed itself, the eyes reflecting a profundity of thought, and then the slow smile of acceptance.

CHAPTER 29

Charges and Specifications

Let us leave Kevin outside in the cold August night of the prisoners' compound as the storm clouds again gather. Leap forward in time for a moment and follow me to the National Archives in Washington, D.C. The clerk helps me insert the microfilm in the machine, and now scroll with me through the "Miscellaneous Papers, Office of the Adjutant General" and stop at the following. A letter from a Mr. Philip O'Brien of 329 Clay Street, San Francisco. In his letter dated October 25, 1895, Mr. O'Brien asks the Adjutant General if there is any truth to the story that a group of two hundred men who were Irish Catholics were captured at Churubusco and hanged.

The Adjutant General replies rather testily that there were 1,200 prisoners taken at Churubusco and that, while some were deserters and court-martialed, there is no mention in the reports of their race or religious affiliation.

For those of us who are familiar with modern courts of law and the meticulous attention to the rights of the defendant including counsel for the defense, transcripts of proceedings and right of appeal, the Adjutant General's remarks seem to be such that could easily be disproved by a careful scrutiny of the records.

So, instead of staying up with Kevin through his long nights of waiting for his day in court, follow your obtrusive narrator to Record Group #153, Department of War, Judge Advocate General's Office, Court-Martial Proceedings at San Angel, Mexico, and see what military justice consisted of back in 1847.

First, note that Kevin did not have a lawyer representing him in court. Capt. S.C. Ridgley was appointed by the Court as Judge Advocate. This position is a unique one which encompasses the duties of chief prosecutor and counsel for the defense, a conflict of interest which apparently did not trouble the Court, or Captain Ridgley for that matter.

There was no court reporter as such, so no actual transcript exists of the court martial. What does exist is a "minute entry" of each case which reflects the charges, the specifications, the composition of the panel, a synopsis of the prisoner's defense if he pleaded not guilty, and the sentence of the court. Let's look at the entry for Kevin's case:

> Private Kevin Dillon was brought into court, and the orders concerning it having been read to him, he was asked if he had any objections to the Members named therein, to which he replied in the negative; then the Judge Advocate having been duly sworn in his presence, the prisoner was arraigned on the following charges and specifications:
>
> CHARGE: Desertion to the Enemy
>
> SPECIFICATION: In that Private Kevin Dillon of Company "H," 5th Regiment of the U.S. Infantry, did absent himself without permission from proper authority, from his company and regiment while on picket duty north of Matamoros on the Rio Bravo on or about the 2nd day of May, 1846, until the 20th day of August 1847 when captured in arms in or about the city of San Antonio of the Republic of Mexico, clothed in the uniform of a Mexican soldier, the said republic and the United States being at war with each other.
>
> To which charge and specification the prisoner pleaded as follows:

To the specification—Guilty
To the charge—Guilty

SENTENCE
The Court having carefully weighed the evidence in this case finds the prisoner Private Kevin Dillon, Company "H", 5th Reg't Infantry, GUILTY of the specification and GUILTY of the charge exhibited against him and does therefore sentence him: TO BE HUNG BY THE NECK UNTIL HE BE DEAD, two thirds of the members concurring.

C.W. Ridgley, Bennet Riley,
Capt. 4th Art'y Brv't Col. 2nd Inf.
Judge Advocate President

So to be fair to the keepers of our national records, there is no evidence that Kevin Dillon ever was, or claimed to be, either Irish or Catholic, or that he was indeed a member of a group called the San Patricios, a group whose very existence would be denied well into the mid-20th Century by advocate generals and the keepers of the archives.

There was one minor alteration of the records, however. Under "Sentencing," the words "Hung by the neck" were amended to read "Hanged by the neck" by some conscientious army grammarian.

For those who pleaded not guilty the record is a bit more forthcoming. Thirty-two defendants took Lieutenant Lyndon's advice and argued that they had simply gone off on a drunken spree and ended up behind enemy lines. However, either the court did not wish to regard the lack of intent inherent in this defense or it simply refused to believe it.

Captain Patrick Dalton, confident and articulate at his trial as he had been with his comrades on the field, offered the court a more colorful story. After objecting to the presence of one officer on the panel because he had used harsh language toward Dalton in the past (a strategy certainly not designed to ingratiate himself with the court), he narrated a lengthy tale judging from the summary in the court record. His story of adventure included trips to the mayor's office in

Matamoros, a conversation with a German in Mexico who spoke English, descriptions of the flora of the countryside, an interview with Santa Anna himself, and finally his joining the Mexican Army. It may be that he felt a good story, while it might not set him free, could possibly spare him the noose. More likely, however, he had resigned himself to his fate and was simply taking advantage of the opportunity to tell one last good tale. Whichever his strategy, he was nevertheless sentenced to hang.

After receiving his sentence Dalton asked that he be permitted to receive the Sacrament of Confession from a priest and that he be buried in consecrated ground. This request was reluctantly granted. However, Dalton's death was to be neither quick nor easy. In the mass hanging at San Angel he was the last to die. Whether through malicious intent or carelessness, his noose had been improperly fixed and, according to one witness, he was "hanging for some period of time before... he was literally choked to death."

Two prisoners were found not guilty. One had never been on the payroll of the American Army. The other had never joined the Mexican Army and was also mentally retarded. When all was said and done seventy men had been convicted and fifty were sentenced to hang. Two boys, sixteen and thirteen years old, were pardoned by General Scott because of youth. Kelly, Sgt. Murphy and Major Riley, although originally sentenced to hang by the court, had their death penalties commuted by General Scott because they deserted before Congress declared war. Mitigating circumstances also saved Kevin's nemesis, Private Hezekiah Ackley, from the gallows but he, along with Riley and the others would be whipped, branded, and then sent to prison for hard labor for the duration of the war.

But let's leave the air-conditioned research rooms of the National Archives on 7th Street and Pennsylvania (back entrance) with their 3.2 billion documents, 1.6 million maps, 5.2 million photos and 110,000 reels of film, and return to a muggy September afternoon in San Angel where the thirteen members of the General Courts-Martial are about to file in to hear their next case.

Private Kevin Dillon has been sitting outside on a plank bench for two and a half hours waiting to be called. It is now 2:30 PM and the day's session began at noon. The court has just returned from a fifteen minute recess. We, of course, know Kevin's fate, just as we know that of Julius Caesar's when we sit down to watch a re-enactment of Shakespeare's play. But we continue watching anyway, just as I hope you will continue reading because we might just discover some insight which we missed before. For Kevin, of course, it is a singular event. There will be no curtain call.

He has been rehearsing what he would say for the past week. Some important points he's actually memorized but he is still anxious. Actually it is more than simple anxiety; he is truly scared. He has never done well speaking up for himself before authority figures. He has seldom had occasion to string together more than two or three sentences in any context. Now, he's on trial for his life and about to give a speech which will sum up the rightness of his cause and the honor of his race.

His mouth is dry. Although it is September, it is a warm and humid day, and he has had nothing to drink since early morning. He is still wearing the dirt and blood-encrusted Mexican uniform he was captured in. And, while he washed himself carefully this morning, his chest and legs are covered with sores and he can feel body lice crawling up his crotch. He is sweaty, itchy and miserable, but he is determined to speak up confidently and courageously. Inside the adobe building the court has re-adjourned.

"Ten-shun! These are the proceedings of a General Court-Martial, in which Colonel Bennet Riley, Second Infantry, is President, convened in San Angel, Mexico, by General Orders 263, Headquarters U.S. Army.

Colonel Riley (no relation to the maverick major of the San Patricios) is a medium sized man with a paunch. He has an easy-going manner and is generally considered to be fair. He is also of Irish descent and was raised a Catholic. He speaks slowly and deliberately.

"Be seated. The clerk will note for the record the detail of the court. (Write all their names, son, from the list of the panel there. That's it.) Today is September 8th, 1847, the time is 2:30 PM. The clerk will also note that Capt. S.C. Ridgley is appointed Judge Advocate of these proceedings and has been duly sworn as an officer of the court. Colonel Ridgely, call the next defendant."

"Sergeant at Arms, call the prisoner Private Kevin Dillon."

"Yessir!"

Captain Ridgely shows no expression as Kevin is brought into the room. Some of the other officers on the panel cannot conceal their contempt for the emaciated figure in the filthy Mexican uniform. However, Ridgely in his dual function as prosecutor and counsel, maintains a poker face.

"Private Dillon, this general court-martial is convened pursuant to General Orders No. 263, Headquarters U.S. Army by General Scott. Do you have any objection to any member who serves on this panel?"

"Nossir," Kevin croaked.

"Speak up, Private!"

"No, sir! I have no objection."

"Private Dillon you are hearby charged with Desertion to the Enemy. The specification of this charge is as follows: That Kevin Dillon, a Private in Company 'H', 5th Infantry Division, on or about the 2nd day of May 1846, being a member of an outlying picket detail north of Matamoros on the Rio Bravo, did then and there desert the service of the United States, taking with him his weapon, ammunition and other accoutrements, the property of the U.S. Government, and did continue absent from said service until captured in arms at the battle of the 20th day of August 1847 between San Antonio and the City of Mexico, clothed in the uniform of a Mexican soldier, the United States being at war with that Republic."

"How do you plead to the charge?"

"Guilty."

"How do you plead to the specification?

"The what, sir?" Kevin asked, confused by the terminology.

"The specification of the charge, Private. That you were in the Mexican uniform, et cetera. How do you plead to that?"

"Oh. Guilty, sir."

"Very well. Do you have any statement to make to the court at this time to show cause why the sentence prescribed in such cases should not be carried out?"

Kevin cleared his throat. He looked at the panel in the hope of finding a face that was not actively hostile. The Colonel presiding looked at least neutral so he spoke to him.

"Sir, I joined the American Army as an alternative to spending time in jail for the crime of defending myself against an assault. Since I immigrated to this country—with one notable exception—I have been a victim of racial hatred and contempt by its citizens.

"I joined the American Army and served at my post in a conscientious manner until I discovered that this army was invading a peaceful Catholic republic whose only offense was that its land bordered that of its Saxon neighbor. I witnessed the bombing of Catholic churches, the hatred of members of my faith by the American volunteers, and the contempt of my commanders for the Irish soldiers in the ranks. For reasons of faith, of justice and of loyalty to a higher power than that of the Anglo-Saxon eagle, I left my post and joined with the St. Patrick's Company."

"Son, don't waste your breath," Captain Ridgely said softly. He nodded at the clerk who had not written a word of Kevin's carefully prepared speech.

"If you pleaded 'not guilty' the clerk would write down any evidence you might have offered. As it is you've pleaded guilty. Nothing you say after that is relevant."

"Sir, I respectfully submit that I am a native of Ireland and a citizen of Great Britain. I am not and have never been a citizen of the United States. Therefore, this court does not have jurisdiction of my case."

"Your enlistment in the American Army, your oath of service signed in Boston, duly attest to our jurisdiction, Private. Do you have anything to add? Any reason why sentence should not be imposed."

Kevin appealed again to the President of the panel whom he had heard through scuttlebutt to be a fellow-Irishman and possibly sympathetic.

"Yes, sir. I contend that the cause of my separation from the American Army was its unlawful invasion of a Catholic republic which I, as a Catholic and an Irishman, could not in good conscience support."

Captain Ridgely shook his head sadly. Colonel Riley did not even blink. Ridgely closed his file, and said sympathetically:

"Private, even if I believed that your motives were as you state, they still do not exist as a basis for defense or mitigation. Colonel Riley?"

"The clerk is instructed to disregard the statement of the prisoner as not relevant nor responsive to the charges," the Colonel said crisply.

"You may be seated, Private," the Captain told Kevin.

Kevin, somewhat bewildered, sat down. He knew he had not accomplished what he intended. But he had said what he wanted to say. At least they were aware of his cause, his reasons for joining the San Patricios. Perhaps, one day a member of the panel might remember that in his memoirs. Maybe history would record some part of that.

Meanwhile the thirteen officers on the panel exchanged brief comments. Their careful deliberations lasted less than five minutes. They nodded to Colonel Bennet Riley who then rose to deliver the verdict.

"Ten-shun!"

All present, including the defendant, stood to hear the imposition of sentence. It contained no surprises and was concise for the genre of military prose.

"The Court, after due deliberation, confirms the plea of guilty by the prisoner Private Kevin Dillon of Company 'H', 5th Infantry to the charge and specification against him, and no legal reason appearing why sentence should not be imposed, does therefore sentence him to be hung by the neck until he is dead, two thirds of the members concurring herein. The defendant is remanded into the custody of the guard. Anything else? Yes, Captain."

"It's *hanged*, sir." Capt. Ridgley whispered to Riley.

"What's that?

"Hanged, sir. People are *hanged*, objects are *hung*."

"Quite right, Captain. I always get those confused." He turned to the clerk. "Change that will you, son? Put 'hanged by the neck until he is dead'."

"Yessir," said the clerk and he dutifully added an "ed" thus making the record correct.

"Damn nonsense, Ridgely."

"Sir?"

"This Catholic business, I mean."

"Yes, sir?"

"Hard enough to make rank in this army as it is without snot-nose punks like that trying to make out that Irish Catholics will use their religion as an excuse for disloyalty."

"Yessir."

"I don't want any of this nonsense in the record, and I don't want any of it to get back to the old man.

"Nossir."

But while Bennet Riley had some control of the record, he did not have control of Lieutenant Colonel Plympton who was also on the panel and would take note of Kevin's defense. Within a short time, at Plympton's suggestion, General Scott would issue General Order #296 which warned of a conspiracy of "false priests... to entice our gallant Roman Catholic soldiers who have done so much honor to our colors, to desert, under a promise of land in California, which our arms have already conquered, and which, forever will remain a part of the United States."

"Let all our soldiers," Scott's order continued, "protestant and catholic (sic), remember the fate of the Deserters taken at Churubusco. These deluded wretches were also promised money and land, but the Mexican government, by every sort of ill usage, drove them to take up arms against the country and flag they had voluntarily sworn to support, and next placed them in front of the battle—in positions from which they could not possibly escape the conquering valor of our glorious ranks."

Despite the fact that not a single San Patricio acknowledged or was even accused at the General Courts-Martial of being "enticed" by money or land in California, Scott's order indicated that was the primary motivation. Thus, while not acknowledging that Catholicism was an issue, he permanently disparaged the soldiers who were faithful to that cause as "deluded wretches" and gave a clear warning to any others so tempted to place God before country.

Ten others besides Kevin were also to plead guilty to both the charges and specifications. As in Kevin's case the official record did not take cognizance of any statements they made as to the cause of their desertion or their belief in a higher loyalty symbolized by the green flag of Saint Patrick. The victors had already begun to write their own history, deciding carefully what to put in and what to leave out.

Kevin was returned under escort to the prisoners' compound without much ceremony and put in leg irons. What he felt at that moment was a mixture of despair and relief. Despair because his words were unacknowledged and his death sentence sealed. Relief because the trial was over and he could return to the compound, wash himself, then settle down by the fire to pick the lice from his clothes and hair. We will leave him there performing this disgusting but necessary chore. To render the main character's every private act seems more a function of the photographic realist than that of a narrator of a history.

Besides, Kevin will not be a player in the next act. The scenes described in the following chapter are in reply to a letter from Daniel Malony dated March 1, 1896, directed to J.C. Gilmore, the Assistant Adjutant General of the U.S. Army. Mr. Malony asked for information on the hangings of the San Patricios. He wrote: "I think it was the biggest hanging affair that ever happened on this continent." Adjutant General Gilmore could supply little information at the time. We, however, are in a position to answer Mr. Malony's 100 year old letter with eyewitness accounts, Mexican and American newspaper reports, and church records.

CHAPTER 30

The Biggest Hanging Affair on This Continent

Although it had rained the night before, September 10, 1847 was a clear sunny day. On Tuesday, September 7th the armistice had ended and an intense fight had begun as American troops invaded the capital. But under orders of General Scott, some commanders, their staff, prisoners, guards, drummers and a detail from a rifle regiment, along with citizens and dignitaries of the surrounding communities were required to appear Friday morning in the tiny village of San Angel to witness the executions of a number of the San Patricios. Captain George Davis, who wrote an eyewitness account of the whipping and hangings, later said that "nothing on earth" could have induced him to come but a direct order from General Scott.

Shortly after 6:00 AM the condemned prisoners were marched to the plaza of San Jacinto, a pleasant tree-bordered square with a small Catholic church in the southwest corner. Sixteen of the San Patricios were brought to a halt beneath a large scaffold. Fourteen others were marched across the park and bound to trees in front of La Parrochia de San Jacinto, the parish church. All of the San Patricios were dressed in Mexican uniforms which were described as "ragged and dirty" This is not surprising since that had been languishing in leg irons on the dirt "floor" of a fenced corral for the twenty days previous.

Without further ado, their shirts were stripped from their backs and, under orders from General Twiggs, Mexican muleteers came forward to administer the first phase of their punishment: fifty lashes "well laid on" their naked backs with whips made of nine eighteen-inch knotted raw-hide strips. According to the American Star, the newspaper of the Army of Occupation, the reason for Twiggs choosing the Mexican muleteers to administer the punishment was that he felt it was too much of an honor for Riley and his men to be whipped by American soldiers. Other versions, however, hold that General Twiggs sarcastically stated that Riley, a major in the Mexican Army should not be whipped by a common soldier. His explanation for having the other Irish soldiers whipped by Mexican civilians is not recorded.

The muleteers were ordered to lay on the lashes with all the severity of which they were capable lest they suffer the same punishment. Twiggs conveniently forgot the count midway through the punishment so that, instead of the fifty lashes ordered by the court, fifty-nine had actually been laid on before the muleteers were ordered to stop. By that time each of the victims' backs, according to American eye witnesses, had the "appearance of a pounded piece of raw beef, the blood oozing from every stripe..."

Following this, branding irons were heated to a white heat and each of the prisoners were branded with the letter "D". Some were branded on the hip, but Riley and selected others were branded on the right cheek, just below the eye. In the case of Riley, the soldier with the branding iron applied the "D" upside down. He was therefore ordered to brand Riley properly a second time on the other cheek. The smell of burning flesh and the mangled and bloody backs of the San Patricios revolted General Davis, the aide-de-camp of General Scott, a reliable American witness.

For Mexican observers, the punishments were shocking. Not since Cortéz and the conquistadors invaded had such "savage outrages and barbaric tortures" been carried out in their country, wrote one commentator. Mexican newspapers that day did not fail to point out the irony of the situation. One editorialist, after recounting the executions in gory detail, concluded:

> "Mexicans: these are the men that call us barbarians and tell us that they have come to civilize us. These men who have sacked our homes, taken our daughters from their families, camped in our holy burial places, covered themselves in blasphemous uproar with the ornaments from our altars, kicking over the body of Jesus Christ and getting drunk from our sacred chalices. May all Christians be damned, if these are from God!"

There were five Catholic priests in front of the parish church who were forced to witness the whippings and tortures. They were now ordered to withdraw to the gallows to witness the next phase of this double header.

The scaffold was fourteen feet high and forty in length. There was a beam across the full length (also called a stringer because from it the nooses were suspended). The beam was supported by uprights at each end and in the middle. These were reinforced by wooden chocks. Sixteen nooses were hanging down from the crossbeam. There was no platform for the prisoners to stand on; no trap for them to fall through. Instead, eight mule-drawn wagons were brought up and two bound prisoners were placed on each one and the nooses secured around their necks.

The priests were the brought up to hear Confession and give the Last Rites of the Catholic Church. One priest held a large wooden cross; all were formally dressed in their canonicals. They gave absolution to seven of the prisoners who had confessed, and were reading the Last Rites for them when the drummers began their roll. The whips cracked and the wagons drove off leaving the sixteen victims suspended from their nooses.

There is some disagreement as to how quickly these men died. Since there was no trap, there was no great drop. Few would have died quickly from a broken neck as is common with traditional hangings. According to one Mexican eyewitness they swung there until they choked from their own weight. According to Captain Davis, the closest American witness, most appeared to have died without much of a struggle except for Capt. Patrick Dalton. Evidently his noose, as stated earlier, had been improperly affixed, and he was choked to death so slowly that it seemed to Davis interminable.

The priests were allowed to remove the bodies of Captain Dalton and the other confessed Roman Catholics who had asked to be buried in consecrated ground. They were taken to the *campo santo* located a half mile away in a village known today by the name of Tlacopac. The others were laid beneath the gallows while Riley and his fellow-sufferers from the lash and the brandings were forced to dig them rude graves. These men were interred in the same place they dropped when the ropes were cut, that is, directly underneath the gallows. Oral history suggests that citizens of San Angel later removed the bodies and interred them in a more decent place.

When the grave-digging job was finished, heavy iron collars were placed around the necks of Riley and his compatriots and they were led off to prison. For Scott's Army of Occupation it was a day's work. For others it would be a day remembered as one unparalleled in cruelty until Colonel William S. Harney was given his chance to be executioner the following Monday.

Necessary army maneuvers postponed the execution of the remaining San Patricios convicted at the first court-martial. However, they were unceremoniously hanged from a tree in Mixcoac, two miles north of San Angel on the road to Mexico City. Twenty of those sentenced to death had thus been accounted for. Thirty remained, and their fate, which Kevin shared, was to be the reason that the National Archives and American historians generally have been reluctant to go into the details of the last days of the San Patricios.

William Selby Harney, Colonel, Second Dragoons, United States Army, was appointed by General Winfield Scott to be in charge of the execution of the thirty San Patricios who had been sentenced to death at the second court-martial. The carefully-planned cruelty which Colonel Harney devised for this spectacle was in keeping with his long record of savagery, vengefulness, lack of restraint, and reckless disregard of human values.

Before returning to Kevin and presenting the inevitable graphic description of the unusual executions at Mixcoac, it might be useful to examine Col. Harney's military record and speculate on the reasons for Gen. Scott choosing him as the officer to head up the death squad. Harney, in the early days of the war (July, 1846) had taken badly needed wagons from General Wool's army at San Antonio and precipitously crossed the Río Grande on an unauthorized expedition. He had exhausted his supplies in a fruitless search for the enemy, delayed his return to the main army as he thrashed about on a private reprisal mission, and thus put Wool's forces in jeopardy. Wool issued an order for his arrest and sent a courier across the Río Grande with a recall order. Because Wool was short of men, however, and in a dangerous position, he subsequently released Harney with a reprimand after his return to San Antonio.

In January 1847, before General Scott could leave the Brazos to prepare for the invasion of Vera Cruz, he, too, was called upon to straighten out the affairs of the troublesome colonel. This time it seems that Harney refused to be separated from his command of the Second Dragoons in favor of Major Edwin Sumner whom Scott considered a "much safer and more efficient commander."

The matter proceeded to court-martial and also came to the attention of President Polk. The President elected to play party politics. Noting that Harney was a Democrat like himself and that Harney was also a personal appointee of former President Andrew Jackson, Polk decided to attribute the transfer order to Scott's pro-Whig feelings rather than to more solid causes.

General Scott, to insure that no such feelings would influence the outcome of the court-martial, took the unusual step of allowing Harney to choose the officers who would sit on his court-martial. Even with the hand-picked officers, Harney was found guilty on charges of insubordination and disobeying orders. He was sentenced to be formally reprimanded. Before the papers could be sent to Washington, however, the colonel was restored to command.

Nor was this the first time that Harney had been formally arraigned. As a matter of fact, the charges against him in the Mexican War were minor compared to those he had escaped from in his past. Harney had been soldiering for almost thirty years and had become notorious for his brutality, according to the War Department. He had served in both the Blackhawk and the Seminole Indian wars, and had been charged with hanging Indians indiscriminately without trial. He had been accused of ravishing Indian girls at night and then hanging them the next morning after he had taken his pleasure.

In St. Louis, Missouri, in 1834 he was indicted by a civilian court for the brutal beating of a female slave which resulted in her death. He avoided the likely conviction by jumping bond and escaping from the city. Legally, he was a fugitive from justice during the entire campaign in Mexico.

Scott was distrustful of Harney and at first refused to have him along on the Vera Cruz expedition. Likely he relented for political reasons, although he must have at subsequent times seriously regretted doing so.

After the invasion of Veracruz when Scott sent Harney and one hundred dragoons to reconnoiter Mexican skirmishers near his positions, Harney disobeyed his orders and attacked. That action cost two American lives and nine wounded. Later Harney would claim fifty Mexican casualties but they were not confirmed, and the number was considered highly exaggerated by the officers in the field and by his commander.

At the Battle of Cerro Gordo he again disobeyed orders and attacked in a blind rage, leading his dragoons beyond the support of their artillery and any hope of infantry reinforcement. This action resulted in his men being pinned down by the enemy until they could ultimately be rescued by mountain howitzer support. It was another close call.

Subsequent to the fall of Churubusco, as Santa Anna and the rest of the Mexican troops fled to the capital, Harney again exceeded his orders. This time General Worth had ordered a halt after a two mile chase down the highway to the capital. Harney and his dragoons, however, pursued the Mexicans nearly to the walls of the city, again without backup, and again resulting in American casualties and a narrow escape.

The record shows a reckless, insubordinate and arrogant officer who was also an indicted murderer, an alleged rapist, and a fugitive from justice. Protected by the highest office politically and subject to psychotic whims, this was the man General Scott would choose to execute the remaining San Patricios. The choice of Harney for the job seems calculated. A brutal man with a penchant for sadism, he was tailor-made for this detail. Nor would Harney disappoint the most vindictive elements of the army. Harney would do the job so well that the mark of his villainy would live a long time in the annals of Mexican history.

On September 12, 1847, Colonel Harney rode out with a group of his dragoons to a small hill near Mixcoac. Looking north he could see the ramparts of the Castle of Chapultepec, home of the Military College, and the last major stronghold. Tomorrow morning the major battle for the control of the capital would take place there. He ordered his men to get a carpenter and help him erect a scaffold there on the rise for the execution of the remaining thirty San Patricios.

Although similar to the one at San Angel, this scaffold was to be larger and more crude. It was to consist of two large beams as supports and a cross beam, or stringer, with thirty nooses dependent. It would be without spring traps;

indeed, without a platform for the victims to stand on. The men would be stood on wagons as at San Angel.

Colonel Harney and Lt. Broderick rode up to the hill on which the scaffold would be erected. They looked off to the north where a couple of kilometers away they could see the stately ramparts of the Castle of Chapultepec.

"That's where the last battle will be, Broderick. Tomorrow morning while we're stuck here getting rid of the trash. Our last chance to make any kind of rank in this war frittered away."

Lt. Broderick nodded. In these past months riding with Harney he had come close to death several times; twice because of the foolhardiness of his commander. Frankly, he was grateful to be assigned to this duty. Harney, he felt sure, would have managed to get all the dragoons killed in the last battle. "Yessir," he replied. "But this is important, too. General Scott certainly must think so if he assigned you to the detail."

Harney took off his Stetson and ran his fingers through his long red hair. He shook his head. Of course! Why hadn't he thought of that? He was chosen for this mission for a reason. Every door that closed meant a new one opening. What was it Emerson said? Something about there being a divine law of compensation. He put his hat back on and tilted it the cocky cavalry angle. He blue eyes twinkled.

"How many did they hang at San Angel, Lieutenant?

"Sixteen, I believe, sir."

"Sixteen. And Captain Davis, our resident historian said that it was the largest hanging in the history of the Americas. Tomorrow we'll hang thirty. That in itself will make history."

"Yessir," replied Broderick doubtfully, unsure of where Harney was heading.

"And one of them is the little bastard that attacked your wife, am I right?"

"Yessir. Dillon. The other managed to escape the noose."

"Well, Dillon won't, and neither will the other thirty. But hanging is too good for them, wouldn't you agree?"

"I'm not sure what you mean, Colonel."

"Tomorrow they'll be marched out here at sunrise. I'm ordered to carry out the sentence with all due dispatch. But that can be loosely interpreted in time of war. What if we place the nooses around their necks but then keep them there until our troops take the Chapultepec Castle?"

"But that might take hours, sir!"

"Exactly!" Harney exulted. "Hours of standing on a wagon in the sun, bitten by chiggers and flies, not knowing when the order will be given, waiting, waiting. Think of what will go through their minds! First they'll be defiant and cocky. Then their bodies will cramp and the pain will stagger them even as the ropes will hold them up. They will beg for death but it won't be forthcoming. As the battle rages on and the hemp tightens on their necks, they'll pray for American victory. They'll pray with all their Catholic hearts for an American victory and the sight of Old Glory so that they'll finally have the mercy of death."

"My God, sir!"

"You object, Lieutenant?"

"Well, sir. What can I say? It's, it's..."

"Beautiful! Right, Lieutenant? Fucking beautiful! History will remember tomorrow, not as the day the Americans took Chapultepec, but as the day the Irish cheered our victory just before they ended their feckless and wasted lives on the gallows."

He dug his spurs into his mount and rode down the hill leaving Lt. Broderick behind to think his own thoughts.

Beautiful was not exactly the adjective Broderick would have used to describe Harney's plan. Watching the muleteers whip the men at San Angel and the bloody paste of Ackley's back as he was herded off to prison had dulled the lieutenant's desire for revenge. The death of Dillon tomorrow would satiate it.

He understood Harney's frustration at being chosen for this detail. But he could not share his commander's lust for vengeance or the circuitous route he had mapped out for his own glory. The war had changed Broderick in a positive way. Having seen so much arbitrary and wasteful death, including that of women and children, he had become more of a life affirmer. He would fight to secure a position or to defend one; he was just as bold as a best of the dragoons. But he had no stomach for what Harney had proposed. Hang them, dammit, if that's what Scott had ordered. But this Tarquemoda torture was repugnant to him and to his New England upbringing. He did not wish to be a part of it, but he did not have the courage to refuse.

For a moment it occurred to him that the San Patricios had a special brand of courage to choose the dictates of their conscience over the compulsions of duty. He could not do it. He could face the enemy in battle, but not the contempt of his own commander. Like the rest of the dragoons, tomorrow he would carry out Harney's orders, however repugnant, and then stifle the taste of his self-contempt with whiskey in the officers' mess. He was an career soldier, for better or for worse, and he would not throw away his career for a handful of Irish rabble who would die anyway.

He remembered the quart of bourbon back in the tent. Way wait for tomorrow? Neither he nor Harney had to lead men into battle in the morning. And it didn't take a sober officer to lower his saber in the command for execution.

He rode down to his tent at the bottom of the hill and gave the private outside the reins of his horse. He went inside and sat down on his cot, drew out the bottle from his haversack, and proceeded deliberately and conscientiously to get drunk enough to pass out. As he nodded off he heard the carpenters nailing the gallows supports, and he dreamed of Roman soldiers on a hill of skulls.

One comes to count on the rains of September as the *temporada de lluvias* deepens in the Valley of Mexico. The afternoon *tormenta* is refreshing, cooling and purifying the air, relieving the oppressive heat. But there are days when the rains, through threatening, inexplicably do not come. The shadows lengthen interminably in the late afternoon, the clouds gather, the air grows heavy and close with moisture, but then the sun comes out from behind the clouds; the storm which seemed inevitable passes somewhere to the east, and night descends.

These are not nights for sleeping. Sweat clings to the skin, the flies and gnats find each orifice, ear, nose and mouth, maddeningly, persistently. The cicadas complain, persistent as a toothache. The atmospheric pressure builds and one feels as if one is in a vacuum, short of breath, suffocating, certain that one will not last until dawn.

Sunday, September 12, 1847 was just such a night. Kevin was tormented by the bugs, body lice, mosquitos, horseflies and gnats. The leg irons had chafed his ankles so badly that both legs had running sores the flies fed on. He shifted his limbs unable to find a comfortable position and listened to the grunts and snores of the men around him, the clink of the guard's keys, the clump of hooves on the mud and the jingle of the bridle as the officer on watch made his rounds. He scratched his crotch viciously between his legs bringing a temporary relief that was a hybrid of pain and pleasure. Then he shook a leg iron scattering a dozen voracious flies.

"Oh, God!" he prayed. "If it is your will, release me from this torment. And if it is not, give me the strength to bear it."

Around him others slept, but Kevin prayed on. His lungs seemed full of fluid, the air so pressurized and dank that it pressed down on his chest. He wondered how the others could bear it.

"Kev, are you still awake?"

"McDowell? Is that you?" he called over to a dark form to his left. "Yeah, I can't sleep. It's so damn humid. I feel like I can't draw a breath."

"Are you scared, Kev?"

"Yeah, a little. But to tell the truth, I'm more scared of shitting my pants than anything else. I heard most people do that when they hang. I don't want to do that in front of the troop."

"Or give that damn Harney the satisfaction."

"Yeah, that too."

"Did you pray, Kevin? You know they're not going to have a priest there. They only did that in San Angel for show. They're not going to bury us either from what I heard. There a big battle at Chapultepec in the morning. Harney's crew is going to hang us and then join the main army in the capital. No burial detail.

"Bastards!"

"Yeah."

"Kev?"

"Yeah, Jim."

"I can't remember the words to the Act of Contrition."

"Just say, 'Forgive me, Jesus, for all my sins.' It's an ejaculation, Sergeant Murphy taught me."

"It's a *what.*"

"A short prayer; an ejaculation, you know."

McDowell started laughing and couldn't stop. Finally, breathless, he sputtered.

"Ejaculation! Haw! That's what I was going to confess!"

Kevin smiled in the dark. "You asshole, McDowell!"

"Did you make that up or what. Ejaculation. Jesus, Mary and Joseph!"

"That's one!" Kevin said. "Jesus, Mary and Joseph is an ejaculation"

"My mother used to say that. Haw! Do you mean to imply that my sainted mother ejaculates? Ha!"

The both got a case of late night giggles like two kids at summer camp. They laughed until tears were streaming down their face and the guard had to come and tell them to hold it down or they'd get a rifle butt in the mouth.

They quieted down until the guard passed and then McDowell whispered to Kevin.

"And fuck him and the horse he rode in on."

"More likely the burro he rode in on," Kevin quipped.

"The *ejaculating* burro he rode in on!" chortled McDowell and they both fell to spluttering again.

Finally they settled down, feeling the pressure cooker heat of the night contract and expand with the occasional breeze. Kevin wriggled his body trying to find some comfort but he knew that he would be awake all night. He tried to pray again but he discovered only a vast emptiness where he expected God to be. He felt desolate and abandoned, denuded of hope. All the springs of his life had become quenched in him and he had no hope, not of life, nor of a peaceful death, nor even the hope of resurrection in the world to come.

He thought of his dog, Molly Malone, and hoped she was well. He heard her joyous bark in every yip of every coyote in the night. He saw the shine in her trusting eyes as he looked up at the stars. It was what he regretted most, losing the dog, and now dying before he could hug her, tell her how brave she was on the ramparts, how everyone in the battalion was proud of her. His heart constricted with the loss of it all, the failure, the final humiliation of his Molly out there, the Irish-Mexican dog begging for scraps—if she was still alive—from a Yankee army.

As dawn approached and the air cooled, Kevin fell into a fitful sleep. It lasted only minutes. Raucously the bugle sounded reveille, startling him awake. The guards rousted them quickly. All the prisoners who were to be hanged were taken to the rain barrel, given a scupper of water, and then marched out to Mixcoac under heavy escort. The other eight San Patricios who would be whipped and branded, were strung out on a rope behind the dragoons and marched (or rather pulled) double-time to the site.

At 6:00 AM they arrived at the hill where the massive wooden beams with their thirty nooses were silhouetted against the morning sky. Kevin took a deep breath and made the Sign of the Cross. At his side McDowell did the same. They were helped up on the wagons by the guards and their hands were bound behind their backs. There were fifteen wagons and two men on each except for the very last wagon in the line. Lieutenant Broderick inspected the guards, ordered the drummer forward, and then called the troop to attention.

Colonel Harney and his aide came out from the command tent which had been pitched on the near side of the hill. Harney's uniform was clean and freshly pressed, his boots shined to a high polish, his epaulets gleaming he were as if he were ready to go on parade. His left hand was at his scabbard to prevent it from striking his leg as he advanced quickly over the uneven terrain.

"Why in hell is there only one man in that goddamn end wagon, Lieutenant? What the hell is going on here? Do I have to see to every goddamn thing personally?" Harney was known for his cussing and seem to use it in the most ordinary speech whether angry or not. This time he merely seemed to be officious.

"Sir!" responded Broderick coming to attention. He offered no excuse or immediate response. There was no predicting Harney when he was in a martinet mood.

"Well, Lieutenant? I'm waiting."

"Sir. I've been informed by the surgeon that the prisoner O'Connor had both his legs amputated because of irreparable injuries, sir. I am further informed that the prisoner is dying and will probably not survive the day."

Harney glared at his underling and then spoke to him as if he were speaking to a retarded child.

"Of course he won't last the day, Lieutenant. And do you know why he won't last the day? Because the fucker will be hung this morning right up there with the rest of those sons of bitches!"

"But, sir. The surgeon said..."

"I don't give a damn what the surgeon said! Did you hear me? I said the fucker will hang. Now go get that prisoner. Bring that damn son of a bitch out. My order is to hang thirty men and by God I'll do it."

Lt. Broderick chose two of the guards to accompany him to the surgeon's tent. They returned shortly with what appeared at first to be a bundle of clothes. A closer look, however, revealed the emaciated trunk of a legless man, clothed in tattered remnants of a Mexican uniform. His bearded face was pale, what could be seen of it, and the eyes were deeply recessed and feverish. He cried out as they set him down on his bloody stumps, but he was too weak for more than a futile murmur of protest as they set the noose around his neck, fixing the knot under his chin so that he would stay propped up in the wagon until the order was given for the hanging.

"Jesus, Kev,. It's poor Frank O'Connor. Do you remember him? He used to give your dog Molly half his rations when the days were lean."

Kevin jerked upright, his bound hands chafing against the ropes. He remembered the kindly O'Conner well.

"Damn it, Harney!" he shouted out. "You'll rot in hell for this!"

Harney turned to see who had called out but by that time half the men were cursing and grumbling.

"You filthy bastard!"

"Harney, you're a sadistic pervert!"

Harney's face at first showed glowering rage and then in seconds shifted to a cold humor. It was just this kind of mood shift which often left his own men bewildered. It was to also catch the Irishmen by surprise.

"Now, now, boys," Harney smiled. "Quit your complaining. I don't see your friend kicking none!" Harney laughed at his own joke and some of the dragoons joined him. Others smiled and shook their heads as if to say, he's one crazy bastard. Thank God he's on our side. Harney turned to the lieutenant, his joking manner gone, the arrogant martinet returned.

"Let's got this hanging affair commenced. Call the men to attention, including the prisoners."

Harney then read General Order #283, Scott's official order for the execution of thirty men by hanging and the whippings and brandings of the remaining eight. Then, with a dramatic flair, he pointed to Chapultepec Castle which was clearly visible in the morning light despite the wisps of smoke from an advance artillery barrage.

"You see that castle a mile or so off there?" he addressed the prisoners bitterly. "Well, that's Chapultepec where the Mexicans will make their last stand. Since I have been ordered to deal with you sorry bunch of poltroons and am deprived of leading my troops to glory, I've decided to get full value from my orders.

"Therefore, you will remain as you are, at attention, until the Stars and Stripes are raised over the castle signalling the victory of American forces. At that time, and not until that time, will I give the final order for your execution."

The prisoners reacted with incredulity. The battle for Chapultepec had barely begin. Depending on the resistance they encountered from the Mexicans, it could be hours, even days, before the Americans took the fortified castle. Already the sun had come up from behind the hill. Sweat was pouring down their faces and with their hands tied behind their backs they could not even brush the voracious green bottle flies away.

"Damn your flag, you pusillanimous twit!"

"I'll see you in hell, Harney, you son of a bitch."

But McDowell and some of his quicker-witted compatriots tried a different tack. Aware of the fact that the colonel was unstable and given to quick mood changes, they made an effort to provoke him into giving an impulsive order which would speed them to their fate.

"A reprieve, a reprieve," called McDowell from the gallows. "They'll never take the castle. The ropes will rot in the rain and we'll all go free."

"Sure and how could they take the castle with Harney hiding out with his favorite Micks two miles away?" shouted another. Kevin caught on quickly.

"Oh, Colonel darlin', will ye be serving dinner this evenin'?" he asked in a melodious voice.

"Oh, now," replied McDowell. "We won't be needin' dinner tonight. A fast will do us good. Isn't that right, Colonel?

Harney smiled, "That's right you son of a bitch."

"Sure, if we won't be hung till yer dirty old rag flies from the Castle, we'll live to eat the goose that fattens on the grass of your own grave!"

Harney flushed a deep red and the veins stood out on his temples. Determined not to be provoked, he spun on his heel and looked off in the distance towards Chapultepec where the action had already begun.

"Give me that glass, Lieutenant."

Broderick handed him the telescope and Harney watched in impotent rage as the New York Regiment advanced onto the field far below. Instead of distracting him, the sight stroped his anger to a sharper edge. He lit a cheroot and puffed on it until the nicotine filled his blood and relaxed him. He returned the telescope to the lieutenant and headed for his tent for a well-deserved drink.

"Oh, Colonel, dear, would you grant a favor to a dying man?" called one of the Irishmen.

Harney turned around. The prisoner had an intelligent face and a dying request could be legitimate. Harney softened a bit and walked over to the man.

The colonel should have been put off by the "Colonel, dear" but the Irish were known for their diminutives and endearments, their "darlings" and "buckos" and "dears" which meant nothing beyond figures of speech. Plus, he was glad for this distraction. He had no desire to see any other troop but his own reap the honors of victory.

"Well?" he said approaching the prisoner. "What is it?"

"Would ye mind gettin' me pipe out of my pocket there, colonel? Ye wouldn't be denying a wee smoke to a dyin' man?"

Harney, a smoker himself, complied. His mood change to solicitous commander was as quick as the earlier one to angry martinet.

"And now, colonel, me darlin', would ye light it with that flamingly lovely red hair of yours. That way we won't be needin' a flint. Your hot little head will surely do the trick!"

"Araagh!" Enraged, Harney drew his saber to run the man through.

"Colonel!" Broderick yelled.

Quickly, Harney reversed the saber and struck the bound prisoner full in the face, breaking several of his teeth. He wiped the blood from the hilt on the prisoner's pants, then turned on his heel to walk away.

Unintimidated, the Irishman spit several teeth out, then raised his head. He called out to Harney.

"Bad luck to ye, Colonel. Ye've spoilt my smokin' entirely. I sha'nt be able to hold a pipe in my mouth as long as I live!"

Even Harney's dragoons laughed at this gibe until the Colonel glared them into silence.

"Lieutenant Broderick!" he snapped.

"Sir!"

"No one is to talk to the prisoners from this point on. They are to receive no water, no medical attention," this last with a meaningful glance at the legless Francis O'Connor whose noose had slipped dangerously close to his windpipe. "The prisoners are to remain at attention until the American flag is raised. Is that clear?"

"Yessir!"

"Be careful, Colonel," McDowell called. "Someone might return that favor in hell."

Harney did not answer. He retreated to the shade of his tent and the comfort of his Tennessee mash bourbon. He gave orders not to be disturbed until Chapultepec was taken. It was now 8:45 AM. The thirty San Patricios had been bound and standing in the nooses for over two hours.

With the absence of Harney, the grumbling and the gibes ceased. There was really no point. Each man retreated into his own shell of consciousness, as solitary as if each were on a desert island. The sun shone brilliantly and, despite the rasp of hemp around his neck, the stiffness of his bound arms, a part of Kevin felt free and strangely alive. He had been touched by the inexplicable but delicious feeling of newness and change that comes to any teenager on an Indian summer morning. His life was ending, he knew that in a corner of his mind, but that knowledge became more and more remote as the minutes passed. The familiar routine of washing up, of eating, or sharing stories and songs around a campfire, were over. And yet, viscerally he felt a stir of delight, a release from the chains of existence, the responsibility for the maintenance of his life, for upholding the rigors of soldierly discipline. He was going to another world and, with a secret wonder and excitement, began to lose himself as his mind composed his dreams of its delight.

He was carried on a deep tide out beyond the land; the sea breezes were cool upon his skin and the sun glinted off the blue-green waves. There were porpoises leaping in front of the bow, cavorting, their mammalian mouths closing in simulacra of smiles. His emaciated body had grown sleek again, his biceps were hard and polished as marble, his tanned stomach was flat and smooth.

Beside him was Samantha, naked except for a linen cloth around her loins. Her small nipples were puckered from the cool salt breeze, her smooth shoulders soft and brown beneath the sun. He embraced her, and beyond the headlands he heard the joyous laughter of children, the murmur of cool inland streams, the rush of the sea breezes in the rich foliage, and the songs of the laborers mowing the hay in the fields.

He sighed deeply and nuzzled against the naked shoulder of his bride. He who had lost all hope now found everything that gave his life ease and beauty. He looked into her eyes and saw his own reflection there. He held up her finger and kissed the Claddagh ring of red gold he had placed there on their wedding day, a symbol of their love and their undying faith.

"We must get back to the children," she smiled. "We've been too long away."

He trimmed the sail then and, with Samantha at the tiller, headed back to the village of Cahirsiveen. As they rounded the headland the gulls screeched and clamored around the small boat hoping for some of the day's catch. Kevin, cleaning the fish, tossed the heads and viscera to the hungry birds.

"Sure, there's enough for everybody," he called happily. "More than enough for all of you, no need to fight!"

He felt rich then, coming home to his cottage of stone with its clean thatch roof. The garden, richly fertilized with seaweed, had put forth a luxury of beans and lentils, cabbages and turnips, potatoes and leeks. And around the side of the cottage the grape vines hung heavy with their purple fruit.

He entered the hut and greeted his mother with a warm embrace. He wiped the tears from her eyes. Sure, hadn't she been worried half to death because they had been gone so long? And wasn't the sun, though shining as it declined in the west, trailing wisps of dark clouds as it went? A storm was coming. And, as he kissed away his mother's fears, he himself heard the sound of thunder like cannon in the distance and saw the wisps of storm clouds roil like smoke in the red skies of the west.

Little Kevin and tender Brigid clambered about his legs now asking for a story. Already washed and fed by their grandmother and ready for bed, they were restless and hungry for a tale and would not sleep till one or two were told. So he took them on his knees and told them, as his father told him, and as his own father, too, had been told, of the warrior Cuchulainn stripped naked for battle, circling his enemies three times (the magical number!), and then with his great sword attacking them in his righteous fury, until in the Great Carnage of Martheinne Plain, he slew all hundred and fifty of the kings (and countless rabble besides!), and not a man escaped without his thighbone smashed or his head, or without some blemish for the rest of his life.

And when his wife said that such a story would give tender Brigid bad dreams, he told them both of another Brigid, the saint of Kildare, who as a child gave away her own father's sword to feed a begger. And how she founded a monastery and became its abbess and fed all the poor for miles around, and gave shelter to the homeless and to any hapless traveller in the land. Then together he and his wife sang the "Dinner Grace" that Brigid had written. 'I should like a great lake of the finest ale/For the King of Kings/I should like a table of the choicest food/For the family of heaven.' And then the Brigid laughed and little Kevin shouted, "We are the family of heaven!"

They put the children to bed and went back to the kitchen to bank the fire. He embraced Samantha again there by the glowing turf coals, and he felt his desire for her arise in the warmth of his loins, and then the heavy door of the cottage slammed shut in the wind, and the wind extinguished the fire, and all was dark.

Kevin heard in the darkness outside the anxious yelp of a dog. The sound grew stronger and then he remembered. "Molly!" he cried out. "Molly!" He could not leave the dog out in the cold. He must bring her inside with him. He headed for the door but suddenly found that, though he could move his legs well enough, they seemed to be dancing on air. It was a foolish thought, he knew. And it was his last.

It was 9:30 AM. Minutes earlier the eagle and snake banner of Mexico was cut from its staff above Chapultepec by the saber of T.H. Seymour of the New England Regiment. The Stars and Stripes appeared above the castle and Colonel Harney, with as much sang froid as a man is capable of on a quart of sour mash, lowered his sword launching the San Patricios into eternity. They had been in the nooses for four and a half hours in 90 degree sun. Several were mercifully unconscious or delirious at the end. And the legless Francis O'Connor had been safely dead for over an hour.

Harney's work was not over yet, however. The eight remaining Irishmen were brought up and, as their compatriots swung back and kicked against each other in the involuntary spasms called "the dance of death," the others were tied beneath the gallows. There, they received fifty lashes from 18 inch whips of knotted rawhide and were branded with the "D" before they were unceremoniously marched off to prison. The hanged men were left swinging beneath the darkening September skies.

Molly was not far off when she heard her name called. She had followed Kevin and the others out to the hill and had kept watch silently beneath a eucalyptus tree nearby. Now that the soldiers had gone she approached cautiously. She sniffed around the gallows and then looked up into the vacant eyes of her former master. His boots had fallen off and his white feet dangled delicately just above her head. She licked them tentatively and then, detecting neither warmth nor life, she backed slowly away. She sat back on her haunches reflectively for a few minutes and then raised her head to the uncompromising sky. Then she howled, a piercing tremulous cry to the heavens which was repeated over and over again, now rhythmically like the keening of bereaved lover, now wild and hopeless like the call of a banshee on the wild hills of Kerry.

That night, the storm which had threatened for days finally burst forth in razor flashes of lightening that rebounded off the earth and lit the hill of Mixcoac in strobe flashes that illumined the twisting bodies of thirty men suspended beneath the gallows. There was a pounding hail which thumped against the dead bodies, high winds which tossed them this way and that, banging against each other like a chorus line of Punch and Judies run amuck. The thunder was terrible in its cracks and booms, more percussive than the sounds of the cannon during the day. Then the hail gave way to torrential rains which seemed destined to wash the earth away. All night the rains came down. But above the sound of the high winds and the rains and the cracks of thunder, the villagers could hear the piercing wail of the dog. No one could sleep for it.

The next morning when the rain had settled down to a gentle drizzle, some village men came to cut down the San Patricios and bury them. But they found that the dog, possessive and half mad in its grief, would not let them approach. It was not until three days later, when weakened by hunger and thirst, she finally allowed herself to be coaxed away long enough for them to dig the graves.

The dog, whose name local legend records as "Máli-maguí," was adopted by a family in Mixcoac. For years, she came each morning from her home in the village to the burial place and sat by Kevin's grave. Time passed and, eventually crippled by arthritis and no longer able to make the journey, she simply lay down in the graveyard and a kindly caretaker brought her food and water each day, until one day she was too weary to raise her head and drink. Her bones were interred by the villagers beside those of the San Patricios. She was, after all, one of their last recruits, and the most fiercely loyal.

MICHAEL HOGAN is the author of twelve books including *The Irish Soldiers of Mexico*, the definitive history of the San Patricio Battalion. He was historical advisor on the set of *One Man's Hero*, starring Tom Berenger and Daniela Romo —an MGM Pictures release— which recounts a fictional episode in the story of Riley and the San Patricios. Hogan lives in Mexico, where he is head of the English and Humanities Departments at the American School of Guadalajara.

Moly Malone and the San Patricios
was printed in January, 1999
in Guadalajara, Mexico
by Ediciones de la Noche.